ACHS Class of 1950
60th Reunion
August 21, 2010
Enjoy
Lyn

CONFIGURATIONS

A novel by
Marilyn Felkel Lingle

Published By Dunsford Books, Hillsboro, IL

First Hardcover Edition

Cover Art: Muffet Jones
Photography: Nancy Slepicka

Marilyn Lingle
930 Jefferson Street
Hillsboro, IL 62049

Library of Congress
Cataloging-in-Publication Data

ISBN Number: 0-9754688-0-4

Printed in Canada

FOR IVAN

At the touch of love
everyone becomes a poet.
—Plato

AUTHOR'S NOTES

Although CONFIGURATIONS is a novel, the setting is real—the former Felkel farm in South Central Illinois. The original house, destroyed by fire circa 1900, was replaced. Though the replacement still stands and is occupied, it was altered to meet both the story line and the needs of the Macklins. All characters are fictional.

The situation of the bums is real, as is the Moonlight Picnic; the Ku Klux Klan, the (only whispered about) counter-Klan Black Knights; and the local grass-roots political movement—the background for which was gleaned from interviews and historical columns in the Montgomery County News and the Springfield (IL) State Journal-Register.

The rampant prejudice of that period is, unfortunately, also real and written to illustrate how our society has progressed.

Some incidents are based on reality, but, with an author's poetic license, adapted and expanded to show life, love and death as it was for an average Illinois farm family coping with the early depression years and moving from a pioneer lifestyle into the emerging Twentieth Century.

The dogs? I just love 'em and have been fortunate to know many with the characteristics of Old Blue.

According to research, historical data are all accurate. Sources include the above-named along with THIS FABULOUS CENTURY, a Time-Life publication; the PBS AMERICAN EXPERIENCE series; newspaper excerpts from FOOTSTEPS FROM THE PAST BY Claude C. Pearson and Michael Rappe; FDR, THE NEW YORK YEARS (1928-1933), and FDR, THE NEW DEAL YEARS, both histories by Kenneth S. Davis; U.S. Department of Agriculture Economic Research Service; Encyclopedia at the Hillsboro Public Library; and my own memories, which, admittedly, are shaded by the passage of time.

The poem *Time, You Old Gypsy Man* by Ralph Hodgson—which, according to THE CONCISE TREASURY OF GREAT POEMS is "a contradiction in his own terms"—remains one of the most haunting of modern lyrics.

Special thanks go to my family and friends who share my dreams. In addition, I wish to thank Nancy Slepicka and Ed Kilpatrick for their photographic expertise; Ninzel Anoe for her inspiration and suggestions; Ben Donnell, Elizabeth Welge and Mike Puckett for computer wizardry; Mabel Chappelear, who gave me her inherited knowledge and early memories of the Moonlight Picnic before her death at the age of ninety six; Lloyd Kropp for early guidance; Andrea Stevenson and Sandra Moody for helpful editing suggestions; and last—but assuredly *not* least—my agent, Mark Sullivan, for his continual support.

Today

The bluff still stands like a bastion guarding what remains of a section of South Central Illinois bottomland. A road still snakes down its northern perimeter. At the base of the bluff an all-weather blacktop sweeps south and parallels the now-abandoned Chicago and Eastern Illinois Railroad tracks, veers west over a crossing a quarter mile down and cleaves verdant fields before bridging Shoal Creek beyond.

A decaying dowager of a farmhouse stumbles across the crest of the bluff; crumples inward, vacant window sashes tilting like multiple lopsided lorgnettes. Intruder weeds blanket the scattered-gravel drive that curves in from the road, circles the house and rejoins itself in a closed hook. At a respectful distance from the house, barns and outbuildings bow in shared decay. Three gnarled oaks—abandoned by their long-dead comrades—remain. Now posted with NO TRESPASSING signs, they shield the once-proud Macklin homestead from prying eyes.

* * *

Variant time: Constant when measured in days, years and centuries. Amorphous when today retreats to the infinity of yesterday.

Chapter 1

On a sultry, weather-breeder afternoon in August 1930 a farm wagon, silvery sideboards streaked with faint pink remnants of red, stood on a grassy strip between the south side of the circular driveway and the manure nourished, clay-base garden that nourished the vegetables that nourished the Macklins. In the wagon bed, a layer of straw cushioned cucumbers, ears of corn and several bushel baskets filled with tomatoes.

"Seth, pick another bucket of tomatoes. They can ride on the seat with me. No use letting 'em go to waste when there's folks in need."

Will's eyes crinkled in amusement.

Tomatoes….

First bad argument he and Soph had after the move to the farm was about the garden they planted. Soph said get tomato plants, he said they were poison, she said they weren't and he said Well, Ma said they were and she wouldn't have a tomato on the place. Soph said Ma didn't know what she was talking about. He'd been getting kind of hot under the collar by that time so he'd dropped it, but he *had* stopped by to borrow one of Doc's Encyclopedia books to read up on 'em. He'd known the Wops used tomatoes—probably why Ma hadn't—but he hadn't known some Spanish conqueror, Cortez if he remembered right, took 'em back to Europe from Mexico about—he scratched his head—1500 something? Anyway, people *did* think they were poison then, but a couple hundred years later they found out different.

Hell, folks been eating tomatoes for over two hundred years now and nobody's dead yet…well, at least from tomatoes. Some even called 'em love apples.

Love apples….

He never told Soph what he'd done, just bought the plants like she asked. Now he couldn't imagine a summer without tart, sweet tomatoes. Kids liked 'em, too. They'd raid the garden when they got hungry, pick and eat 'em right off the vine. Macklin Corner folks sure liked that red fruit, too. 'Course the country neighbors, if they even grew 'em, called 'em 'maters. But not the Macklins! Soph said *maters* were Latin mothers and besides the kids needed to learn to speak properly and their father had to set an example.

He was trying but, despite his wife's influence, Will Macklin's speech still carried more than a trace of his Irish and Lowland Scot ancestry. A few local descendants of those hardy Early Eighteenth Century immigrants—opportunists said to keep the Sabbath and everything else they could get their hands on—saw fit to forget their own foreign roots. His distant cousin, Harry Stone, was the worst. Will chose to remember.

Seems like Harry's got it in for just about everybody.

Will thought about the continuing resentment Harry nursed over Will's abandonment of Harry's sister, Clara.

Figured time'd take care of it. Always been squirrely, but he gets worse every year. He dismissed Harry with a shrug. *Water under the bridge.*

He shook his head to end his woolgathering. "Billy, you hitch up the team. I'm gonna move these baskets around and put a few watermelons in on top the straw." Shading his hazel eyes, Will scanned the sky and sniffed the heavy air.

No sign of storm. Yet.

He squinted at the sun. If he hurried, he should be able to make the four mile round trip to Macklin Corner and be home before the storm brewed up.

Too bad I can't take the Maxwell.

Trouble was he couldn't afford gas except for emergencies. Five gallons only cost eighty-five cents, but he didn't have an extra eighty-five cents.

Not enough room in the Maxwell anyhow. Sure could use a truck...

He stepped back to check the wagon's contents. He was glad he'd planted those extra rows of garden in the spring. Soph and Anne had canned until every jar was filled, and plenty still left over for the Macklin Corner folks.

And with that rain on the way, more coming on. Good thing, too.

The Depression had hit the townfolk hard. With the coal mine down, there was no work. No work meant no money. They needed all the food the Macklins could spare.

He ticked off his stops. Penskowicz, Koznik, Furello, Yankos, Lomaski, Turganyev. Names folks around here couldn't even pronounce, let alone spell, thirty or so years ago. Will shook his head. The furrows in his brow deepened. That mine had certainly changed their sleepy little village.

Will knew the miners, knew they were having one hell of a time in their Promised Land. Still, from what he'd read, he guessed they were better off in America than the Eastern and Southern European countries they'd abandoned in the early years of the Twentieth Century. He leaned against the wagon, pondering the Depression. No getting around it, 1930 so far had been a bad year for everyone and times didn't look to get better very soon.

Town folks aren't the only ones in trouble. Guess we're lucky, though. At least we've got food. But every month, it's a scramble to scrape the mortgage payment together. Wasn't for the gravel pit couldn't even make those. And now the county's cutting back on roadwork. We all pinch pennies till Abe squawks, even had to use Soph's butter and egg money to eke out last month's payment. Hell, the kids' blackberry picking money may have to go next. Banks foreclosing on more farms all the time. Don't think I imagined that gleam in Chester's eye when the July mortgage payment was late. Glad the hogs are about ready to ship.

Can't remember crop prices being so low. Not bottomed out yet, either. No extra money for anything, even school books for the kids. Good thing we got into saving ways when we took out the mortgage. Soph's made dresses for the girls and shirts for the boys on that old treadle sewing machine her ma gave her when she left for Oklahoma. Think I can scrape enough together for shoes and new overalls for the boys.

A wry smile twisted his face.

Guess the Depression did some good after all. Leastways, got rid of those knickers Soph's been making the boys wear to school. Now they can look like the other kids.

The smile faded with the thought.

Unless one of Soph's miracles comes along, her next butter and egg money'll have to take care of their books. Damn but I hate that. She only gets a quarter for two pounds of butter and about twenty cents for a dozen eggs. Better than nothing though.

The clip-clop of approaching hooves interrupted Will's glum thoughts. Work-hardened muscles rippled under his sweat-patched blue work shirt. He wedged the last watermelon in place and turned to watch his gangly older son back the team into the traces and secure the harness. The sun, shimmering on the sleek Percherons, drew russet highlights from the depths of their burnished, chestnut coats.

"Curried 'em down, did you Billy? Wondered what took you so long. Why Billy, those horses could lead the State Fair parade in Springfield!"

He tousled his son's coppery hair in thanks and climbed onto the wagon. The springboard seat squeaked under the weight of Will's solid, six foot frame.

Need to get that oiled. No time now. Do it later.

He tugged a faded red and white bandanna from his hip pocket to mop beads of sweat from his deeply tanned face and neck, hitched his overalls, settled the fraying straw hat firmly on his thatch of auburn hair, and turned to wave goodbye to his wife and children.

Twelve-year-old Billy and nine-year-old-Seth were already running past the orchard to the path winding down the bluff and across the tracks to the Shoal Creek swimming hole. "Mind the tracks!" he called after them.

His earlier gloom faded as he looked over the neat, well-kept farmhouse and outbuildings; returned when he noticed the scabby, peeling paint.

All need a good scraping and a coat of paint. Well, that'll just have to wait like everything else.

He turned to watch his wife at the backyard clothesline, keeping four-year-old Yahbut busy handing up clothespins. The new baby wasn't due until mid-January, but it was already hard for Soph to bend over. Will again marveled at the resemblance between mother and daughter. No wonder Soph spoiled the girl. Almost as much as her daddy, he reckoned. Yahbut already showed signs of her mother's beauty. Will's rugged features softened as he recalled the young Sophia.

Dark curls, pale skin, eyes blue as an October sky...

Wonder where Anne is? Probably got her nose in a book somewhere. That girl's got a lot of her Gramma Hattie in her. Enough grit in her craw to take on the world when she wants something. Skinny like Hattie, too. Sure hope she's not got high-falutin' ideas like Soph's ma, though. Hard to believe she'll graduate Eighth Grade this year. Almost through with her schooling.

Jingling harness interrupted his thoughts. The horses dipped their heads, snorted, and pranced in place. "Yep, guess we better get moving. Can't sit here all day or that storm'll catch us for sure." Will chuckled, first at the team's impatience, then at his habit of talking to animals. He slapped the reins on the muscled rumps of the gelded field team and clucked. "Giddup, Ned. C'mon Jed." Iron wheels crunched on gravel. The wagon circled past a freshly mowed alfalfa field and through a tunnel of oak leaf shade into the glaring heat of the yellow dust road.

* * *

Sophia fingered the rain wet towels and sheets still hanging on the line. There'd been no time to get them down before the cloudburst. She glanced at the lowering sun with practiced eyes. Yahbut looked up from her parade of damp, belle-skirted hollyhock ladies. "Can I catch clothespins, Mamma?"

"Not now, Honey. It's already five o'clock. We'll just have to leave these out overnight. They'll never dry in this steamy air."

Sophia winced as she lifted the heavy cistern cover to see if the storm had replenished their soft water supply for bathing, washing and cooking.

Still low.

Rubbing her rounded belly, she eyed the open-top filter sunk into the ground under the corner drainpipe. The barrel-sized, fired-clay cylinder—partially filled with large Shoal Creek rocks—caught, cleaned and channeled rainwater through a pipe leading to the underground cistern. She grimaced at the muddy residue coating the rocks.

Filthy thing needed scrubbing again. Well, if those boys can't remember to pipe the rainwater away till the roof dust's gone and it's clear, they'll just have to clean it themselves this time. Maybe they'll learn. I can't do it again. Not now.

She laid her hand protectively over her unborn child.

Her anxious eyes searched the road. Still no sign of Will. She knew he'd had enough time to make it to town before the storm. Her concern was the hospitality the townspeople offered Will.

The immigrants had brought their Old Country ways to Macklin Corner and, because they appreciated the virtues of beer, wine and whiskey, ignored the 1920 Volstead Act, hid their stills and brewed their own. All through Prohibition their cellars were stocked with white lightning, Dago red and home brew. Even though their present lack of money forestalled replacement, most had liquid remnants of prosperity laid away for an occasional festival or wedding. And to share with 'Farmer Macklin', who shared his vegetables with them. Their tastes suited Will's perfectly. Will, sober, was as fine a man as ever lived. But Will drunk… It was a good thing the horses knew their way home because sometimes Will didn't.

She remembered her mother's and the priest's warnings before she and Will were married. Yes, she'd known he drank but, flushed with first love, it hadn't mattered. The first really *bad* time had been after the Macklin Corner riots, when he'd still been Constable.

But then we bought the farm and things got better…

Sophia quickly buried unbidden thoughts behind a strained smile. "Come on, Yahbut. Let's go find your brothers."

* * *

Billy and Seth, still damp from the swimming hole and their dash home through the downpour, tussled in the front yard. A disapproving frown deepened the faint lines between Sophia's eyebrows as, hands on hips, she watched Billy pin his younger brother to the wet grass. She wished Will wouldn't encourage such rough and tumble play!

Anger at Will's absence sharpened her tongue. "Billy! Don't be such a bully. Let him up. NOW. Your dad's not home yet so you'll have to start the chores. And be sure to strip the cows. We can't have them going dry. We'll need the butter money for your school supplies."

Billy gave his younger brother a final push before helping him to his feet, brushed grass from his overalls and, Seth trailing behind chanting 'Bully-Billy Billy-Bully', grumbled off toward the barn. Sophia watched the Macklin sons trudge from the yard.

Strong like their father, yet far too young for the responsibility Will and the farm heaped on their shoulders. "Fresh peach cobbler for dessert," she called. Their pace quickened. "With cream," she added.

"Yes ma'am!" they shouted and broke into a trot.

* * *

Supper's atmosphere was fractious. Will's absence from the table heightened Billy's tendency to tease Seth and Yahbut. Anne, the oldest and most sympathetic to the strain on her mother's tired face, dried Yahbut's tears and took charge. Her soft voice echoed Sophia's mood.

"Billy, that's enough!" She poured hot water into the enamel dishpan and handed him the empty teakettle. "You can fill this at the well. I have to heat more to scald the dishes. And bring up a *full* bucket of water this time!" Her impish grin eased the stinging words. "Seth, you'll have to fill the foot tub at the well, too. Mamma says the cistern's still low so we'll have to wash our feet in hard water. Yahbut, you can help me with the dishes while Mamma rests. I'll wash, you dry." Sophia's grateful smile was Anne's reward.

By eight the children were in bed. Sophia lit the coal oil lamp, turned the wick high, and eased into her sewing chair to put the final stitches on an infant's flannel gown.

Almost done... But not yet...

She tightened her embroidery hoops over the gown's iron-on cherub transfer and searched through her diminishing supply of rainbow colored thread.

Pink or blue? Pink. I'll call her Lisa. No, Father Riley will never baptize a baby girl Lisa. It's not a Catholic name. Maybe she can be baptized Elizabeth, *though, and we can* call *her Lisa. But maybe she'll be a* boy*!*

She replaced pink with soft green and threaded her needle. Within minutes her busy fingers slowed. Exhausted by the day's work and her advancing pregnancy, her eyelids drooped. The cheap cotton housedress and denim apron sewn from Will's worn-out overalls faded, replaced by a luxurious black velvet cocoon of sleep. She dreamed of Little Lisa.

* * *

Old Blue led the heralding alarm sounded by the Macklins' adopted stray dogs. Abandoning her dreams, Sophia fought her way back to reality.

Will must be back.

She yawned, stretched, and glanced at the ancient Seth Thomas clock on the shelf. The filigreed hands pointed to a few minutes after nine.

And I didn't even hear it strike...

A sharp yap of pain erased the last traces of sleep. She knew that, even drunk, Will wouldn't mistreat one of the dogs. Fully alert, she leaned over, blew out the lamp's flame, felt her way to the kitchen window and froze.

Faint moonlight filtered through the dense leaves of the cottonwood sheltering the back yard and porch. Beneath the tree, a shadow jolted back and forth, up and down, inside a circle of snarling dogs. A foot darted out. The dogs dodged, backed off, moved in again. A kick. A yelp. Mesmerized, Sophia watched the primitive dance of survival until, with savage force, the figure followed a kick with a lunge past the snapping fangs and hurtled toward the back porch. Sophia raced to slam the kitchen door and slip the iron latch seconds before heavy work shoes thundered onto the porch. The screen door snapped open; the shadow retreated into two-sided safety, still kicking at the dogs attacking the triangle's open end. The solid-oak door shook under pounding fists.

Sophia had never known gut-wrenching terror. Now, the smell of it soaked her armpits. She bit her lower lip to silence the scream rising in her throat. Salty blood mingled with the metallic taste of panic as she drew on primal female instinct: the protection of her young. Behind her, the bare feet of four frightened children slapped down the back stairs into the kitchen. She spoke without turning.

"Load the shotgun, Billy. Anne, get Seth and Yahbut back upstairs. QUICK!"

Billy dashed for the gun while Anne herded owl-eyed Seth and sobbing Yahbut into the stairwell. Eyes riveted on the door, Sophia—praying that the hinges held—backed toward the wall rack of razor-edged knives, honed and ready for butchering day.

And through an open dining room window, above the din of the raging dogs, she heard gravel crunch under iron wagon wheels. Ned's and Jed's whinnies announced their return. Sophia's veneer of control crumbled. She raced to the screened window and released the suffocating scream into the night.

"Will! Oh God, Will!"

Her voice shrilled through Will's alcoholic haze. He shot off the wagon and roared onto the porch, scattered the dogs, sent the invader sprawling, then stooped, lifted the man by his shoulders and pitched him face-first into the muddy yard. Billy unbolted the door and ran out with the loaded gun. Will grabbed the gun, released the safety, cocked the trigger and shouted, "And don't come around here again, you son-of-a-bitch!"

Bloody rivulets flowing from his nose, the battered man snatched a damp towel from the clothesline and mopped his face as he sped toward the path to the railroad tracks.

* * *

The children had finally settled down. Will sipped his second cup of leftover black coffee and apprehensively watched Sophia heat the soup she'd saved from supper.

"I'm sorry, Soph. The storm caught me at Koznik's and…well…we just sat in the kitchen visiting, and one thing led to another. And I still had other stops to make…"

"…and drinking at every one of them!" She paced from stove to table, table to stove.

Will looked up at his wife's tearstained face, her swollen lip, and lowered his eyes. "Yes, and drinking. Right now that's the only way they got to say thanks for the food I take 'em. You know how proud they are. Time just got away from me. Then that Duke's mixture of wine and whiskey made me sick on the way home, and after I threw up I fell asleep under a tree. Good thing the horses…"

"But look what almost happened tonight because you weren't here!"

Will's voice raised in defensive anger. "Hell, Soph, never had any trouble before. How was I to know somebody'd try to break in? If I'd known I'd have been here! Now stop that pacing and sit down. We've got to talk."

She sat across from him and, hands on the table, leaned forward. "But who *was* that man?"

"I don't know. Never saw him before in my life. Probably one of those bums who get off the freight trains when they stop at Macklin Corner to take on water and coal. I heard today they're coming into town. Desperate. Looking for work. And hungry. Never thought of 'em coming here, though." He pulled a filthy, blood-spattered towel from his pocket and laid it on the table. "I found that at the top of the bluff where the path leads down to the tracks. He must've walked the rails south from town. There could be more, and they're hungry enough to steal. Maybe even kill. That's why we have to talk."

* * *

For the first time in almost a century, fear became an unwelcome guest in the old farmhouse. Will's daytime wagon trips to Macklin Corner continued, but were hurried. At night he slept with a loaded shotgun by the bed ready to protect family, home, smokehouse and livestock from any desperate man who might creep silently up the bluff.

Swimming in the creek across the tracks was forbidden. Danger lurked in shadows. Nighttime hikes to the outhouse were made under Will's supervision. Even during the oppressive heat of late August and early September, cows remained in their stanchions, locked in the barn from sundown to sunup. The acrid smell of ammonia, mingled with dung-rich air, stifled early morning milkers. Dogs guarded cattle, pigs, chickens and the family's sleep.

* * *

Four loaves of fresh-baked bread lay cooling on the battered wooden table. A warm, yeasty aroma wafted from the oven of the wood range where four more loaves nestled browning in their pans. Hands on ample hips, arms akimbo, Sophia surveyed her realm. A satisfied hum sounded deep in her throat. There'd been no trouble lately. Will was even squirrel hunting that morning.

Rays from a chill, late-October sunrise crept through the yellow muslin at the window. She opened the curtains, lowered the oil lamp's wick and blew out the flame. A rainbow ricocheted off a crack in the pane to brush her face. Irritated, she flicked at it as though it were a fly. Will had promised that, if he could sell the crops and any money was left after the mortgage payment and bills, he'd replace that window Billy had broken.

A rifle shot echoed from the distant hickory grove. She counted back. Three shots. Will seldom missed. He'd be home soon with three squirrel tails dangling from his hunting coat pockets. Sophia opened the pantry door and peered into the lard bucket. Not enough to make biscuits to go with fried squirrel and gravy for breakfast. She'd have one of the boys get another pail from the basement before they started chores. She glanced at the corncob box beside the stove. Plenty of cobs to hustle the fire along after the last loaves of bread came out. Biscuits needed a hot oven.

Sophia checked the clock. She'd have to wake the children soon, but…

Savoring the quiet, she poured a cup of boiled coffee from the blue granite ware pot on the back of the stove, added thick Jersey cream, and eased her bulk into a chair. Under her heart, Little Lisa stirred.

She must be waking up from a nap.

Content, Sophia drew the silence about her like a shawl.

* * *

Will's boots pounded on the back porch, shattering Sophia's serenity. Her hand flew to her mouth as her husband burst through the door.

"My God, Soph! They've butchered the heifer calf. Sneaked up the bluff, broke into the barn, killed and gutted it, and dragged it off. Didn't see the bloody trail when I headed out this morning…too dark…found it on my way home…ended at the tracks…must've hauled it onto a slow freight. A heifer. They killed a two-week-old prize Jersey heifer for *meat*."

Stunned, Sophia stared open-mouthed as Will's rage dissolved into slumping despair.

"I just don't know any more, Soph. Man does his best and still gets kicked in the balls. Lord knows I don't mind a few eggs, a chicken or so. When men are hungry they have to eat. But Belle's calf! What kind of men *are* they?"

The enormity of the loss hung between them. Sophia heaved her awkward body out of the chair and moved to cushion the outraged defeat of the man in the doorway. Will's work-roughened palms cupped her shoulders, slid down the soft flesh of Sophia's upper arms. Mirrored anguish drew them into an embrace of mutual comfort; held them together until the protesting child quickened between them. Wincing at the sharp kick in her belly, Sophia stepped back.

"But how did they get by the dogs?"

"No idea, " Will muttered. "Must be a bitch in heat somewhere. None of them were here this morning when I left…even Blue. What I can't figure out is how those damn bums knew exactly where to go. That calf was in the birthing pen, *behind* the cows. It's almost like they knew the barn layout." He squared his shoulders, settled his mouth into a grim slash, and pulled three squirrels from his hunting coat. "I'll clean these while the boys are getting dressed for chores."

* * *

The watch resumed. Brilliant October faded into gray November. On a wintry morning after Thanksgiving, Will sat at the breakfast table and watched his wife, heavy with child, move about the kitchen. She'd tossed and turned all night, and been up since five baking, fixing lunch sacks, and getting the older children off to school. She needed rest.

Yahbut dawdled over her oatmeal. "Mamma, you said you'd show me how to make curtains for Anne's old dollhouse today."

"I said maybe. Good heavens, child, I don't have time for dollhouse curtains. I don't even have time to think. Now finish your cereal before it gets cold."

Yahbut's face clouded with disappointment. "But Mamma, you promised…."

Will slid his chair back from the table. "Finish eating, Yahbut, then you can help me fix the chicken yard fence. Good girl! Soon as you're done grab your coat and hat and that box of staples. You can hand 'em to me as I need 'em." Yahbut's dimples deepened with her smile. She gulped her food and scampered to obey. "Mind your gloves. It's cold enough to freeze the hide off a bear."

* * *

Frost-stiff grass crunched beneath their feet as father and daughter moved along the fence. Will pulled the wire taut with a crowbar, steadied the crowbar with his knee, took the hammer from his jacket pocket and another staple from Yahbut's outstretched, gloved palm. Awkward going without the boys, he reflected, but Soph had her heart set on the kids not missing school. It didn't help *him* much to know she was right.

Will pounded the staple deeper into the post, then straightened to dig his fists into aching back muscles. His eyes roamed the Macklin acres. Saw the dogs working the hedgerow for quail and pheasant, the harvested fields, full hay barns and corn bins, the smokehouse where hams and bacons hung curing. Contentment welled within him. He glanced down at the solemn face of the watching child, smiled, tweaked her nose, and in a burst of exuberance scooped Yahbut up, swung her to his left shoulder and led her into *The Arkansas Traveler.* He quick-stepped as he sang, alternating lines with the laughing girl.

"…and he didn't have a bed…"

"…and he didn't have a bite…"

"…and if he hadn't fiddled…"

"…he'd of traveled all night…"

Frenzied barking interrupted laughter and giggles. Will tensed, eased Yahbut to the ground behind him, and through narrowed eyes watched the dogs race toward the edge of the bluff. A shabbily dressed man topped the path, hesitated, and warily eyed the dogs. At Will's sharp command, the hounds stopped inches from worn, scuffed shoes and knee-patched pants. Growls rumbled through bared teeth as Will approached the man.

The stranger's eyes darted from the dogs to Will and back to the dogs. Despite his obvious fear, his voice was steady. "Looks like you might could use some help with that there fence, Mister," he called. "Be glad to hammer some staples for a plate of food."

Sarcasm coated Will's words. "Reason I have to hammer staples is because you knights of the road keep trying to break into my chicken house!"

The dogs growled. The stranger stood his ground as Will moved closer. "Wouldn't argue that a bit. There's them as does such things but I ain't one of 'em. Never et no food I didn't earn. Now if you don't need no help, I'd surely appreciate it if you'd call off your dogs so's I can be on my way."

Will stared into the hobo's eyes, took his measure, noted the hatless head, threadbare jacket, frostbitten hands, and forthright manner. He hesitated, acknowledged to himself that this one at least had the decency to offer work for food instead of trying to raid the chicken coop or pry the hinges off the locked smokehouse door in the middle of the night.

The stranger accepted Will's scrutiny with quiet dignity. "Please, Mister," he said, "I don't mean you no harm. It's just that I ain't et nothin' for two days."

"Where you from?"

"Missouri."

"Ozark country?"

"Yessir. Lost my job in the steel fact'ry up to Gary. Tryin' to work my way home afore winter sets in solid."

"Well, you're going to have to hurry. Guess we better get at this fence." Will picked up his hammer and handed the crowbar to the man. "Yahbut, run and ask your mamma to fix this gentleman some breakfast."

"Yah, but Daddy…"

"Yah, but *nothing*. No buts. Scoot now."

As Yahbut raced to the house, Will again studied the man's face. *We'll see…*

Chapter 2

Overnight, a Gulf of Mexico warm front had worked it's way up the Mississippi Valley to penetrate South Central Illinois and temporarily banish winter. Will's foot broke through a melting ice puddle outside the barn door, spattering the legs of his clean bib overalls with mud and triggering a string of choice swearwords.

"What's wrong, Dad?" Seth called from the barn.

"Just slopped mud all over me. Guess I should have worn my barn clothes and boots, but never dreamed it'd thaw like this so close to Christmas."

Will lowered a full bucket of foamy milk to the ground, leaned on the barnyard gate, and looked west to the Macklin bottoms. His eyes swept over the intrusive silver railroad tracks to settle on the patchwork quilt of yellowed grass and rich, black earth seamed by melting snow fingers. A soft, southwesterly breeze caressed his face.

My land...never dreamed it'd ever be mine...mine and the bank's, I guess. Figured on the corn and hog money to make payments till the winter wheat's combined, but neither of 'em brought much. Well, guess we'll get by. Always have. This Depression can't go on forever, and no need to worry Soph about how serious things are with the bank right now when she's so wrapped up in the new baby coming.

He propped his foot on the lowest gate board and studied the fields spread out below.

Hell, Phineas could have stood right where I'm standing now...

* * *

Over the years Will, with the help of Uncle Ed, had pieced together a murky family history that, in time, reinforced his innate love of the land his grandfather had settled. While never openly acknowledged, it was whispered that Phineas, the first Macklin in the area, had been a gambler who followed his trade along the creeks and rivers northwest from his native South Carolina.

What was *known* was that in 1832 Phineas landed in St. Louis, Missouri on a riverboat and headed east across the Mississippi to scout Illinois, a non-slave state admitted to the Union in 1818 under skullduggerous conditions. The erstwhile gambler arrived just fourteen years after Congress accepted the required statehood population figure of 40,000 —'cooked' from 36,558 by counting some settlers two and three times, then adding transients.

Phineas found the bluff and bottomland below. With special lowland farming skills honed under his oldest brother's tutelage during periodic South Carolina floods, he understood the creek. Satisfied by further inspection, he headed for the Edwardsville land office and invested the majority of his riverboat winnings in a section of Kickapoo County land. Six hundred and forty acres at a dollar and a quarter an acre. Sweet, loamy bottomland soil, washed down from the upper county by the obliging creek each spring and fall, more than compensated for the barren clay uplands.

Lacking the slave labor of his abandoned state, Phineas hired a crew of rag-tag drifters, along with a few occasionally-friendly Kickapoo Indians—remainders of the main tribe sent west by the treaty of 1816—to build his cabin and help clear the land. While the felled trees seasoned, he farmed the rich land below, started a trading post on high ground two miles north, then set up a sawmill and, between crops, used his own oak and walnut to build his house, barns and outbuildings on the clay bluff. With his motley, ever-changing work crew, it took sixteen years.

By 1848 the clearing and building were complete. The prospering trading post became a store centering a small settlement. Forty-year-old Phineas, pockets jingling from the sale of land around the store, rode forty-five miles southwest to Edwardsville, site of the nearest post office, to mail a letter to his oldest brother in South Carolina. The message was brief: “I’ve cleared my land and built a house. Find me a strong, sturdy young woman of good breeding stock for a wife.”

While in Edwardsville, Phineas made arrangements for Macklin Corner’s general store to become an unofficial post office to serve the area’s increasing population. He assumed the role of postmaster, hired a rider for the weekly mail run to Edwardsville, and settled back to wait.

Some months later Phineas, after receiving his brother’s reply, resettled a Kickapoo woman and several half-breed children in a distant corner of the county near the few members of her family, remnants of the final 1836 tribal exodus. The woman, who had cooked, cleaned and cared for his personal needs, understood. It was time for them both to return to their own people. Besides, her generous settlement should attract a fine Kickapoo husband.

Having closed that chapter of his life, Phineas filled a sturdy, boat-shaped North Carolina wagon, built from Macklin lumber, with his own grain and hides, and furs bartered from local trappers. He hitched up the oxen, headed for St. Louis, sold his goods, refilled the wagon with supplies for the store and the farm, and drove to the levee to await and, perhaps, claim his bride.

From the deck of a riverboat nearing the landing, Ruth Edgecombe caught her first glimpse of the man she expected to become her husband. Standing far behind the happy, welcoming levee crowd was a tall, rawboned stranger with an identifiable mane of fiery Macklin hair.

When Phineas saw Ruth, the only unattached woman walking down the gangplank, he abandoned all thought of escape. His bride was not only good pioneer breeding stock but attractive, with strong features and almost as tall as Phineas himself. Her five-foot ten-inch stature, a detriment on the South Carolina marriage market, suited both the land and Phineas. Her governess background was a bonus. She could teach their children to read and write and cipher.

In turn, Ruth looked at the primitive but familiar transportation loaded with a wealth of merchandise, hitched her skirts, and climbed aboard. Phineas admired her shapely ankles and smiled. His brother had chosen well. The gambler's luck was holding.

They married in St. Louis that same day, and began their honeymoon perched atop the loaded wagon. It had taken Phineas three days to arrive at the river port. With secluded nights softened by the new featherbed Phineas placed under the wagon, the return trip took a week.

The house on the bluff, as much like a Carolina plantation house as Phineas could build with limited resources, was a pleasant surprise to Ruth, who expected a rough-hewn log cabin frontier home. In the privacy of their big southwest-corner downstairs bedroom, Phineas lustily sowed a crop of red-haired children to fill the four upstairs rooms, help plant and reap the bountiful harvests, and tend the livestock and Macklin Corner store.

His respect and love for Ruth deepened when Ruth took his youngest half-Kickapoo son under her wing. Just two years older than William Phineas, Ruth's first-born, the boy—too young to keep pace with the final migrants—was left with Phineas after his Indian mother died bearing a child by her Kickapoo husband. Renamed Ed Jameson, he was reared with the increasing Macklin brood.

In 1867, Phineas' sowing of both the land and Ruth ended abruptly. While fishing with companions, he stripped and dove into the creek to slip his fingers under the gills of the big, hookwise catfish and drag them from the watery safety of the creek's bordering willow tree roots. But his aging lungs betrayed him. It was his last gamble, his first big loss. Phineas William Macklin drowned at the age of sixty, hogging fish in the creek that had served him well. He was found with his hand wedged in a tangle of roots. From an underwater hollow, just beyond his reach, flat catfish eyes stared into the sightless eyes of the gambler.

Tall, strapping, seventeen-year-old William Phineas—called William P—sold the store and assumed the care of the farm, his aging mother, and the brood of fatherless children. Despite shifting markets, occasional crop losses, and the vagaries of South Central Illinois weather, the family continued to prosper.

In time, his five sisters' marriages wove the Macklins into the by-then-settled farm community to the south. If William P had disappointments, they were his younger brothers' lack of love for the land. However, Ruth had taught two of them well. One read law, one studied medicine. The youngest, a renegade overly fond of the bottle, was caught stealing a horse he didn't need.

With William P's blessing, the lawyer and the doctor migrated to St. Louis. Ruth's failure, tarred and feathered and ridden out of Kickapoo County on a rail, was never heard from again. The family was as relieved as the neighbors.

When William P was forty-one, his mother—defeated by twelve pregnancies, nine living children, and forty-two years of thankless labor—followed Phineas to the family plot in the church graveyard. William P, alone in the big house on the bluff, needed a wife.

Reluctantly abandoning his well-earned status as a ladies man, through lidded eyes he surveyed the local belles at church meetings and barn dances, weighed the value of maturity, and judiciously chose Clothilde Schneidekind, a spinsterish twenty-two-year-old Irish/German beauty whose sprightly ways matched her waspish tongue. William P was sure marriage, even a loveless marriage of convenience to both parties, would calm her disposition. It didn't. With each pregnancy, Clothilde became more bitter over her brood-sow role. Their five children grew up quickly and fled the farm.

Despite his love of the land, Will, the oldest, led the flight. In 1908, the summer before he turned fifteen, he rode west to join the Kansas and Eastern Colorado wheat field crews, moving north into Nebraska and the Dakotas with the harvest season. He reveled in the freedom of hard-working days and hard-drinking nights that spawned a thirst for alcohol that still, at times, swam like a devil-fish through his watered-down Presbyterian soul.

That fall, when the harvests were in and the work crew broke up, Will—unwilling to return to Clothilde's sheltering rage—headed for Denver, where his summer wages evaporated in the icy heat of liquor and willing women. Broke, he parlayed his work-hardened muscles and swaggering good looks into a job at his favorite brothel and spent the remainder of that winter—and succeeding winters—bouncing unwelcome rowdies out the back door while new customers entered the front. The ladies of the night were only too happy to quench the young fire in his cowboy jeans during their languid daytime hours.

In 1914, Will returned to Macklin Corner, took a room with a respectable widow, and spent three claustrophobic months working underground in the reopened coal mine before escaping to the less confining job of Macklin Corner Constable. Off and on he courted Clara Stone, a stolid country-school classmate and 'kissing cousin' on his mother's side of the family. Harry Stone, Clara's brother, assumed the two would marry.

So did Will. But on a fine, early-June evening he monitored the dispersing crowd attending graduation ceremonies at the Macklin Corner Catholic School. And tall, willowy Sophia Dubrovich waltzed down the steps in her white lace dress and into Will Macklin's heart.

To woo the sheltered girl, only child of a widow who supported herself and her daughter as a seamstress in a Macklin Corner dress shop, Will found it necessary to pay court to the mother. For almost a year of evenings he sat in the Dubrovich parlor on an uncomfortable, straight-back chair to watch Sophia while feigning interest in Hattie's endless tales of aristocratic English lineage, nullified by her marriage to a handsome—but by her current standards worthless—Russian immigrant. Privately, Will considered the dead Russian well out of it, but held his tongue and endured until Sophia returned his smiles.

Will's mother, outraged at her son's jilting of Clothilde's own cousin's daughter, and even more outraged by Sophia's Catholicism, threatened to call a meeting of the revived Ku Klux Klan to burn out the Dubrovich home and the church Sophia attended. The newly organized, anti-Klan Black Knights thwarted her plans. She proved no match for her young stallion, heir to his dam's fiery, independent nature.

William P, ebullient over Will's rebellion, sympathized openly with Clothilde but, behind her back, winked tacit approval at his son's victory.

Sophia's priest, unable to dissuade Sophia from marrying Will or persuade Will to join the Church, reluctantly consented to perform the ceremony on the condition that Will accept the Ne Temere dictum decreed by the Vatican in 1908—that any children born to their union be raised Catholic. Will, most of his early religious training negated by the boisterous companionship of his Denver years, signed the necessary document. Late in 1915 he and Sophia married in the living room of the manse. Will's parents did not attend the wedding.

The newlyweds moved into a small house in Macklin Corner, where Will continued to serve as Constable. Anne was born, then Billy.

The young Macklins' idyllic life ended when John L. Lewis, a former miner in nearby Panama where his many jobs included mule driver, was named national vice president of the United Mine Workers Union. An outspoken militant unionist, Lewis brought his message of safer working conditions, better pay, and fewer hours to the Macklin Corner miners. When the miners struck, owners in faraway New York contracted to bring in Mexican labor. In retaliation, Union fledglings hanged the owners in effigy. Management-generated dits and dashes summoning Pinkerton detectives hummed along track-side telegraph lines, supported by poles decorated with straw scarecrows dressed in moth-eaten business suits.

Outraged at the union activity and the affront to their dignity, coal tycoons authorized the hiring of Chicago goons—armed with shotguns and Gatlings and brass knuckles—to ride flatcars into Macklin Corner with the train from Mexico. Gunfire answered the catcalls, shouts of 'scab', and well-aimed rocks thrown at the immigrant-filled cars.

Will, a hunter from the age of six and no stranger to violent death, had always liked guns, but the sight of guns trained on human beings sickened him. Trapped in the crosshair sights of moral versus legal, he swallowed the bile in his throat and accepted his constabulary responsibilities. And called for reinforcements. But not soon enough.

By the time the sheriff and deputies answered his call, bodies littered the railroad right-of-way. Two dead, twenty injured, many of them Will's friends. The militia arrived to camp at the southeast edge of town and restore order. Having stirred his cup of discontent into the bubbling stew of the Macklin Corner miners' anger, John L. Lewis gathered his union organizers and returned to Springfield to lobby for miners rights, and move up as president of the national union.

Will's once-peaceful days were spent preventing bloodshed between disgruntled ex-miners and their dark-skinned replacements, the most recent wave of Macklin Corner immigrants. 'Little Mexico' took root on the southwest edge of town, isolated from its first generation and second generation American neighbors. And each night, grotesque dreams of violence haunted the Constable's alcohol-induced sleep.

While Will wrestled with bootleg whiskey and his conscience, William P's failing sight worsened to the point he could no longer work the land. In November 1920, during a Sunday afternoon visit while father and son inspected one of the barns, William P suggested that Will buy the farm. It seemed the answer to both Macklins' problems, but Will had no money.

"Can't just *give* it to you, Son. Wouldn't be fair to the other kids. Besides, your ma and me'll need to buy a place to move to and something to live on. Don't think Clottie and Soph'd take much to being in the same house together."

The two men hunkered down behind the barn, swigging barleycorn from one of William P's stashed jugs, trying to solve the problem. And finally William P gave a wrinkled wink and a whiskey chuckle.

"Indians!"

"*Indians*?"

"Yep. *INDIANS!* Indian *tools,* anyway."

Three generations of Macklins had accumulated prehistoric, Native American artifacts, unearthed each spring by sharp-bladed plows. Chert and heat-treated stone from Paleo hunters who followed vast herds of game near the ice corridors at the retreat of the last glacier were rare, as were the large-grooved axes, knives, stemmed arrow and spear points and pottery fragments left behind by hunter-gatherers at an Archaic Period seasonal campground. More common were intricate, polished-stone tools and, on occasion, necklace fragments from the Early and Late Woodland and Mississippian periods. Occasionally, spring plowing even turned up traded Ohio Hopewellian items.

The most numerous finds, however, were Kickapoo from a closed-end valley on the farm. Once a natural trap for deer and bison herded in, slaughtered, and butchered where they fell, the valley floor was a trove of abandoned or forgotten arrowheads, axes, flint knives and tools. Over the years, Macklins had stowed away box after box of findings under the attic eaves.

In the early years of the Twentieth Century, Edward W. Payne, a Springfield banker and real estate investor, began one of the largest prehistoric-relic collections in the United States. Payne, hearing of the Macklin trove, contacted William P several times about a possible sale but was always refused.

That day William P was emphatic. "Sell 'em!" He tipped the jug, took a deep swallow, and repeated, "Sell 'em! Why not if it'll keep the farm in the family?"

On a spring afternoon, with Clothilde at a quilting bee, Will borrowed a truck and father and son spirited the treasure boxes out of the house. Will drove to the state capitol and returned with five thousand dollars, enough for a down payment on the mostly-bottomland three hundred and twenty acres that remained of the original six hundred and forty acre section. Visits to the bank and the lawyer's office completed the mortgage arrangements before Clothilde knew what was happening.

Her fury was monumental. She raged even more when her husband used part of the down payment to buy a cottage ten miles away in Walnut Hills, far from her meddling relatives. In retaliation, Clothilde stripped the house of the best furniture, moved the massive pieces into the cottage where they dwarfed the small rooms, and scrubbed every inch of the farmhouse with Lysol.

When Will transplanted his growing family to the Lysol-reeking farmhouse in the spring of 1921, Sophia sniffed the air, opened the windows, filled the house with flowers, second-hand furniture and love and dismissed Clothilde from both her life and the house on the bluff.

And in 1921 the bottom dropped out of crop prices. Banks throughout the farm belt began to fail. 1921. The year the Macklins turned land poor.

* * *

Will shifted his foot from the fence gate to the ground, stomped to wake it up, and watched the creek meander through his fields.

Glad the Macklin Corner Bank's staying strong. Must be because of the mine. Good thing the Mexican problem's settled. Wonder how soon the mine will reopen, though? Guess it depends on how big the stockpile is and how much coal the trains need. Well, if we made it through the Twenties we can make it through this Depression. Good thing we've got the gravel pit money to help out with mortgage payments. Five more years...

He thought of his father. Sophia and the children loved William P and William P loved to visit. Because the farm had changed little, the old blind man had no trouble getting around. When he needed eyes, Seth led him from place to place. Will knew his father was ready for another visit but decided that, with Soph feeling poorly, it would have to wait until after the baby was born.

Hmph. Ma'll probably throw a fit about Little Lisa, too! Guess I shoulda told her...

Will shook his head in exasperation. When Ma's vinegar tongue got too much for Pa to handle, Pa had Will's youngest brother Jim, who lived and worked in Walnut Hills, write a letter. Will told Soph, they loaded the kids in the Maxwell, headed for Walnut Hills, and visited a bit. Pa talked about how he missed the home place, Soph said why not come for a visit, Pa said well now I just might, and Ma packed his clothes before he could change his mind. Nobody dared look at anybody else. They all knew it was a charade, like that game the kids played, but it was better than saying Ma and Pa couldn't stand each other a minute longer.

Will figured they'd drive over early March, show Ma and Pa the new Macklin, and bring Pa back for butchering day. Let him feel and smell spring coming on.

Billy popped his head through the barn door. "Anything

wrong, Dad? You've been standing there so long we're almost finished milking."

"Nothing wrong, son. Just woolgathering again. Be there in a minute..."

Chapter 3

Will hoisted his bucket of milk and picked his way down the slope to the milk house, set deep in the hillside to keep the temperature cool and constant.

He again considered letting the herd go dry. Dairy prices were the lowest he'd ever seen, and the price Soph got for butter seemed hardly worth the effort.

Helped out at least a little with the mortgage, though...something to think about with the county cutting back on road gravel.

Still, one cow like Belle would give all the milk the family needed. He poured warm milk into a battered pie pan for the barn cats even though, from the corner of his eye, he'd seen Billy and Seth squirting streams of milk from the cows' teats into the begging cats pink, open mouths.

Not worth scolding them for. Might as well give it to the cats as the hogs. Cats earn it with all the mice and rats they clean out around the barn. Hogs get more than their share anyway after Soph and Anne use the separator to salvage the cream for butter and clabber some of the milk for cottage cheese.

He checked the milk strainer, made sure the gauze was clean and tight before pouring the bucket of milk through the cheesecloth. Listening for the first dribbles to ping the bottom of the can, Will wondered when things would get better.

Christmas almost here and money scarce as hens' teeth...older kids already know it'll be slim, but there's still Yahbut...Soph made that doll out of scraps, stuffed it with socks past darning, guess that's all she'll care about, anyway...got enough set aside for oranges, bananas and nuts for the stockings...apples won't be much of a treat...root cellar stacked full of apples...

Will headed back to the barn, met Seth working his way down the slope with another bucket of fresh milk.

"Dad, are we still going to get the tree today?"

"Have to. Promised your mom I'd drive you all to church tomorrow. Got a dandy picked out. Had my eye on it since October, across the tracks on the squirrel hill. About nine feet high and close enough to the old logging road so we can take the wagon. Need to go early, though, before the ground thaws too much. Don't want to get mired in. Hurry and finish milking now."

He winked at Billy, on his way down the slope toting still another full bucket of milk. The boys excited voices followed him up the path. Will knew he'd have no trouble today getting them to shovel cow manure out of the drains after the herd was put to pasture. He whistled as he entered the barn and made his way to the last stanchion, where an impatient Belle stomped her feet and mooed a soft complaint. Settling himself on his milking stool, Will tucked his head into the warm hollow of the animal's flank and began the rhythmic, pumping strokes to ease the pressure of his prize cow's full udder. Belle, content, chewed her cud.

* * *

Sophia ladled circles of batter onto the heavy iron spider and added more sausage to the skillet. "You boys can't seem to get filled up this morning. I'll have more in a minute." She glanced a question at Will, just finishing his second helping of pancakes and sausage. He shook his head and rose to refill his coffee cup.

"Yah, but why *can't* I go with you, Daddy? Seth and Billy have all the fun!"

"Because Mamma says you're catching a cold. Besides, the tree's so big there won't be room for you in the wagon. And somebody has to help Anne unpack the ornaments."

"Yah, but..."

"Sarah!"

The child slumped in her chair and pushed bits of pancake around her plate. She knew it was useless to beg when her father called her Sarah. "May I please be excused? I don't want any more breakfast." Will nodded and watched Yahbut—lower lip protruding, jutting chin resting on her chest—slide off her chair.

Seth leaned to tweak a curl. "Careful, Brat. You don't want your pretty face to freeze like that." Yahbut fought back the smile that threatened her purposely-forlorn face and dramatically trailed out of the kitchen.

Will repressed his urge to chuckle. It would be easy to give in, but Yahbut was in a fair way of getting spoiled and it wasn't just Soph and him. The older kids did their share, too. Seth was the worst. Things would have to change when the new baby came. Will sipped his coffee and watched his wife move about the kitchen.

Doesn't look right. Tired, sure, but more than that. Wish she'd talk about her woman troubles, guess she thinks men aren't supposed to talk about things like that. Probably those nuns she went to school to. Maybe I can stop by on my way to town, ask Mary to drop in.

Mary Sullivan, born and bred in the farm community, had no trouble discussing earthy matters like birth and where babies came from. She was with Soph when both Seth and Yahbut were born. If there was a problem, Soph might confide in her and Mary could tell him.

Will scooted his chair back from the table. "Finish up, boys. Once the sun hits that hill there'll be no making it up the old road. I'll hitch up the team. And Soph, shouldn't be any trouble, haven't seen a bum around for awhile, but just in case I'll leave the dogs with you and the girls." He lifted his hat and jacket from a peg behind the kitchen door and headed for the stable.

* * *

"Wow! Look at that!"

"Yeah, Seth." Billy took the axe from the wagon bed. "It's a big one all right. Bushy, too. Not like that skinny thing we had last year." In a lofty, big brother voice he added, "But we'll have to trim it down some after we get it home. Mom will want those bottom branches for decorations and Dad'll have to saw the trunk smooth so we can nail it even on the stand. Or guess I could do that. C'mon, move it. We don't wanna be here all day."

Will's lips twitched. He bent, checked a scuff on his boot to hide a smile. Even though Billy wasn't quite thirteen, his voice was already changing and he was trying hard to be a man.

Good thing Seth's so agreeable. Good boys, both of 'em, even if Billy does get a trifle bossy.

The boys took turns chopping through the thick cedar. Together, they dragged the tree to the wagon where Will looped a rope around the trunk. The three hoisted it onto the bed and tied it in place.

"Can we go to the 'simmon tree, Dad?" Seth asked. "Maybe we can get enough so Mom'll make a pudding."

"If you want, but I'd almost bet the 'possums already got all the persimmons. That last hard freeze should have mellowed 'em out and nothing a 'possum likes better than sweet persimmons."

The boys raced down the hill toward the creek. Will pulled a can of Prince Albert tobacco and a packet of tissue-thin rumpled papers from his pocket, rolled a cigarette, lickspit-sealed the paper, struck a kitchen match on the nearest iron wagon wheel, and leaned against a sideboard to smoke.

* * *

"Dad! Dad!" Billy's voice cracked with distress. Will straightened to watch the anxious faces of the boys rushing toward him. "Dad, there are *people* down by the creek. They got a fire and they're sitting around it on old logs."

"Probably just hunters warming up."

"No, Dad," Billy insisted. His excited voice dropped from treble to baritone. "There's a man and woman and two kids. And they're just sitting there like there's something wrong. They look like they might've been there all night, too."

Will studied the wide-eyed, sober faces of his sons as he moved away from the wagon. "You boys watch the team. I'll head over that way, have a look." He ground his cigarette out with his heel and walked in the direction the boys pointed.

* * *

The commotion and shouting on the hill had alerted the family. Four frightened people stood in a semicircle around the fire watching Will's approach. The woman averted her face and wrapped a protective arm around each child's thin shoulders: a boy who looked a little younger than Seth, a girl about Yahbut's age. Will smiled at the children, nodded to the man, and tipped his hat to the woman.

The man bobbed his head and swallowed. "Guess this is your land. Didn't mean to trespass, Mister. My family and me, we're walkin' the tracks to my wife's sister's place in East St. Louis and we had to get off for the night. We didn't hurt nothin', just took some old downwood to build a fire with. See?"

Will saw. A kettle balanced on rocks over the fire. Four tin cups nearby. He guessed they'd boiled water from the creek to drink. There was no sign of food. Hooded eyes dominated the woman's gaunt features. The children's eyes rounded like saucers in their pinched faces.

Will turned back to meet the man's steady gaze. "How long since you've eaten?"

The man shuffled his feet and dropped his eyes, shamed by his inability to feed his family. His voice was low, his words halting.

"Well, guess it must've been yesterday morning. Our food gave out 'bout twenty miles up the tracks. We come through a little town just north of here but didn't have no money. I reckon it's only about fifty more miles, though. We oughta make it by day after tomorrow."

"Not without food you won't. You'd better all come with me. I've got a wagon over the hill there."

He saw the warning glance the woman darted at her husband, sensed her fear, and walked a short distance up the hill where he stopped to wait and watch the man lean close to the woman, talk persuasively, then gesture toward the children. The reluctant woman finally nodded, and the man approached Will. "Mighty kind of you Mister. Just give us a minute."

Hot rocks hissed and crackled as water from the kettle hit the glowing embers. While the man spread damp ashes over the ground with his boot, the woman collected the kettle and cups to pack in a satchel. Will watched with approval, then led the way to the wagon.

At least they've got warm coats and good shoes. And except for road grime they look clean enough. Good thing Soph's got the soup pot going this morning. Should be just about done.

* * *

"Mamma! Mamma!" Yahbut's excited voice shattered the quiet of the bedroom where Sophia lay resting. Yahbut had been glued to the window for the past hour, on watch for the tree-filled wagon. "Mamma, they're coming! And Mamma there are people with them." Dismayed tears rolled down her cheeks. "Mamma, there's a little girl sitting by Daddy and he said he didn't have room for me…"

Sophia rolled to her feet to join her daughter at the window. She stared at the wagon rattling across the tracks and rounding the corner south of the bluff; caught a glimpse of a woman and a little girl huddled on the wagon seat beside Will; saw a man and boy walking behind with Billy and Seth. None of them appeared to be talking or visiting as the subdued procession disappeared into the shadow of the bluff. "Call Anne, Honey. She's in her room studying. I'll have to get my shoes on." What now*?* Sophia wondered as she eased her swollen feet into too-tight slippers.

Yahbut ran up the stairs. "Anne! Anne!" she shouted. "Company's coming. Anne, hurry up. Daddy's got the Christmas tree."

* * *

Three Macklins slid the tree from the wagon and pulled it onto the back porch. "You boys put the wagon in the shed and turn the horses out to pasture. We won't need them again today." Will turned to the silent family. "Better wait here. I need to talk to my wife."

Sophia, a fresh Mother Hubbard over her housedress, stood by the stove stirring another quart of home-canned vegetables into the soup pot.

"Hope you've got plenty, Soph. Looks like we'll need it. That family out there hasn't eaten since yesterday morning."

Sophia's clipped words warned Will to tread softly. "Where did you find *them?"*

He explained while she tasted the soup and sprinkled a pinch of salt into the simmering broth, adding, "They sure don't look dangerous. The most important thing now is to get some food into them. We'll find out more after they eat."

"Well, since they're here you might as well take them to the basement, show them where to wash up. Give them a bar of that new batch of lye soap. It's cured enough." She turned to Anne, who had followed Yahbut into the kitchen. "It's a good thing I baked this morning. Set the table for four. The *kitchen* table. Soup bowls, big ones. And big glasses for milk, too. Yahbut, get the milk and butter from the cold box on the porch. I'll slice a loaf of bread."

Sophia glanced up as the road-worn family filed into her kitchen. She was glad she'd planned for leftovers and used the big soup pot that morning.

* * *

"Yahbut, get away from that kitchen door," Sophia snapped. "It's closed for a reason. Now go up the front stairs and help Anne get the last box of decorations from the attic. Then check and make sure none of the ornaments are broken."

Sophia and Will, a lagging Yahbut in tow, had moved to the dining room to talk while the family ate. With no playmates her age, Yahbut—despite her mother's stern look—had earlier exchanged shy smiles with the little girl in the kitchen. Sophia shook her head in exasperation as Yahbut skipped up the stairs.

"That child! She's almost *too* friendly," Sophia complained loudly. She lowered her voice. "Will, what on earth are we going to do with them? We can't let them go back on the tracks, not with those children. That little one's no older than Yahbut. They'd have to pass over the trestle where the Miller Branch runs through. Didn't you say the bums have a camp there?"

"Uh-huh. Bert was talking about it the other day. Well, I've been thinking on it. If they can get to East St. Louis to the woman's sister, they'll at least have a place to stay. I don't want them here." He glanced at Sophia's stony face. "Guess you don't either. Besides, we don't have room." He touched Sophia's hand and smiled. "And with our Lisa on the way you don't need extra people in the house right now. You could maybe use some help, but the woman doesn't look too work-brickle and you'd most likely wind up taking care of her. I think the St. Louis bus still stops in East St. Louis if we can get them on it."

"But if they don't have money for food, they don't have money for bus tickets. And heaven knows *we* don't have any extra money."

Will's eyes caught and held Sophia's. He kept his voice neutral. "There's the money I set aside to fill the Christmas stockings. That should be enough for two tickets. Those kids are skinny little things. I do believe Ken's still driving the St. Louis run. Maybe I can talk him into letting them sit on their folks' laps."

"Will! That's the only Christmas the children will have except for the things I've made them…"

"I know, Soph. But some things are more important than others. If we explain to the older ones they'll understand. And Yahbut will have that pretty little doll you made. That's all she'll care about anyway. We've sure got apples for the stockings and I found a hazelnut bush the other day when I was hunting. Kids all love hazelnuts, but I'll have to beat the squirrels to 'em."

With a dismissive nod Will rose from the table and turned toward the kitchen. "They should be about through eating. Let's go talk to them." A fuming Sophia followed.

* * *

"Sure you got enough to eat?" Will asked. Sophia glared at Will, but held her tongue as she noted the empty bowls and scattered crumbs.

While Will discussed possible solutions with the man, Sophia refilled the children's milk glasses, poured coffee for the parents, and cut four slabs of devil's food cake. She stole a tentative glance at the woman, thought her face looked a little less sallow, decided she'd be pretty if she weren't so thin. And if she were cleaned up. Sophia served the cake. The children, after a quick peek for permission, attacked the thick buttercream icing. The woman, intent on what the men were saying, ignored the cake.

"How much *is* bus fare to East St. Louis?" Will asked.

The woman spoke for the first time. "Two dollars one way when we left Decatur…half price for children. It should be about half that from here."

Sophia stared. "You walked all the way from Decatur? But that's over sixty miles!"

"Not down the tracks. And we were lucky. It didn't snow or rain and we had money for bread until yesterday. Clyde trapped a rabbit and cooked it one night. It hasn't been bad." Her voice was proud, authoritative like a teacher's.

Pity smothered Sophia's smoldering resentment. "We don't have much money but maybe we can scrape together enough for bus fare to your sister's. Can we, Will?"

Will's answering smile lit his face. "We can sure try." He turned to the family. "I'll get the Maxwell out while you finish eating and we'll be on our way to the bus."

The family sat in embarrassed silence while Sophia cleared the table and cut more cake for the children. "Eat slower, you don't want a tummy ache," she cautioned. The Maxwell pulled around the driveway as the last smears of icing disappeared from the plates.

"There's my husband." She smiled at the children. "Button up, it's turning cold again." She slipped a loaf of fresh-baked bread and four apples into Seth's creased, brown-paper lunch sack. "And take these in case the bus is late."

* * *

They left as quietly as they had come. The man followed his wife and children off the porch, hesitated at the bottom step to look back at Sophia's swollen body outlined in the open kitchen door.

"Thanks, ma'am. That was mighty good." His voice was thick with emotion.

The woman turned. Bruised eyes stared directly into Sophia's. Mouth open as though to speak, she blinked, blinked again. Suddenly her mouth clamped shut, rejecting Sophia's pity. Clutching the brown paper sack filled with food, still without speaking, she turned and led the way to the waiting car.

Sophia's heart softened even more at her brief glimpse of the mother's wounded pride. "Just a minute, Will," she called. She disappeared into the house and reappeared with a newspaper-swaddled bundle, tearing wrappings off as she approached the car. She smiled and tucked Yahbut's Christmas doll into the little girl's arms. "Here, Honey. This dolly needs someone to love."

Will's eyebrows arched. Sophia's arched in return. "Don't worry, I'll find time to make another."

Chapter 4

"Damn sock!"

Will swore as he jerked the hand-knit wool from his foot and turned the heel to the back before thrusting his foot into it again. On the bed behind him, Sophia—afraid the children would hear—stifled a moan. Bed springs creaked as Will stood to reach for the heavy shirt hanging over a nearby chair. Holding the cuff of his one-piece wool underwear with his fingertips, he worked first his right arm then his left into warm checked flannel and buttoned it to the neck. He stood storklike on one leg, then the other, to draw on his overalls. As he dressed, he struggled to keep his voice soothing, reassuring.

"Now you stay right there…I'll poke up the furnace before I ride Star into Macklin Corner for Doc…he'll have chains on his Ford, won't have any trouble getting out here through the snow...just be an hour at most…you know how fast that mare is…"

He padded to the closet to rummage for the seldom-worn, hand-tooled Western riding boots he'd splurged on so long ago in Denver. Supporting himself against the four-foot-high, coffin-length cedar chest that held Sophia's quilts and linens, he wriggled his feet into well-oiled leather.

"My old sheepskin coat still in the closet, Soph?"

Sophia's gritty words slid through clenched teeth. "Toward the back, under the shelf."

He retrieved the coat, returned to the bed and lifted Sophia's hand. "Sure you'll be all right? Don't think I ought to wake Anne?"

"She's too young to be in on a birth, Will." Sophia clung to Will's hand until the pain passed. "But stop by Sullivan's and pick up Mary on the way back. She's not above riding double." Sweat streaked her face as her body contracted again. She bit her lip. "Please," she gasped, "hurry…"

On the way to the barn, Will wondered if any of Uncle Ed's emergency moonshine was left in his hidden jar. Need a little snakebite, the old man would say with a wink, and Uncle Ed's emergencies were anything from a scratchy throat to an imagined cottonmouth bite.

Well damn, this is an emergency, but...

Swallowing hard he squelched his thirst with concern for Sophia.

Figured we were so lucky here in the country...isolated, that's what we are...no close neighbors, no telephone...guess if Sullivans don't think they need a phone, they don't, but makes us last on the road and the phone company won't run a line from the slab for just us...maybe they can't afford two dollars a month...well, we can't either, at least not now...glad I kept the mare for the kids to ride...Maxwell's tires almost bald, never make it up the long Macklin Corner hill in this snow...

Will swore again, this time at himself for not having tire chains, for not having money for new tires.

He jerked the stable door open. An earthy odor of fresh dung, normally perfume to a horse fancier like Will, drifted unnoticed into the chill winter air. He lifted the lantern from a hook inside the door and fumbled for a match. By the dim light he grabbed the saddle blanket, threw it on the mare's back, dropped the saddle in place, drew the cinch tight, and slipped the bit in Star's mouth and the bridle over her head. Ignoring the friendly whickers of the big Percheron workhorses, he extinguished the lantern, led Star from the barn, mounted, and headed up the road to Macklin Corner.

The snow had finally stopped. Scudding clouds across the full moon cast moving shadows on deep drifts. Blue's mournful howl sounded over the frozen fields. Will looked back to be sure the dogs were still on the porch. Glancing at the sky, he wondered if there could be something to that old wives tale about a full moon bringing on a birth. He'd read somewhere, maybe in one of Doc's books, how people were mostly water, how they reacted to the pull of the moon like ocean tides.

Wonder if animals are like that, too? If that's why dogs and wolves howl at the moon? Is it pulling on 'em?

Will was sure the dogs would guard the house with their lives, equally sure no bums would be out on a snowy January night.

Probably gone south for the winter anyway...any around, they're holed up in that hobo jungle under the trestle arch down the tracks.

He flicked the reins. Star responded like her racehorse sire.

Snow muffled the galloping thuds of Star's hoof beats pounding out unwelcome memories of his last snowy winter night in Denver. What triggered those tonight of all nights, when Soph needed him most? The boots? The snow? He'd been doing so well, staying away from whiskey, but he'd not only wanted Uncle Ed's moonshine tonight, he'd needed it. He forcibly shifted his mind from whiskey to the woman he loved.

Best thing that ever happened to me was Soph. Lots of hard work and no money but we've got a good life, even if I do fall off the wagon once in awhile and raise hell. No wonder she gets mad. Soph can't understand about the drink and I can't tell her.

Ahead, a lamp burned in Sullivan's kitchen. He reined his mind back to the present. Mary was still up. He'd stop on his way to town so she'd be ready when he came back by. He worried about Mary riding straddle behind him even if, at almost sixty, she was a game old thing.

Stringy as a bean, but tough as toenails.

Mary peered through the window, recognized Will, and opened the door. "Thought I heard someone out there," she called. "I was just getting ready to wake Les. Good thing the moon's out or you might have tasted buckshot." She searched Will's face as he dismounted and ran to the porch. "Sophia?"

"The baby's early. Couldn't take the Maxwell in this snow, not enough tread on the tires. On my way now to get Doc. Think you can ride double with me on the way back?"

"Better than that. Les put chains on tonight. I'll wake him and he can drive me now. She'll need someone with her. You'd best get going. Les would drive you in, but with all this snow you'll probably make better time on that racehorse of yours."

Will's chest heaved with relief. "Thanks, Mary. I'm much obliged. Oh, say…the dogs are out…you think…"

"Don't worry about the dogs, Will. Blue's top dog and he and I are old friends. What he says goes. The other dogs won't bother me if Blue's around."

Will offered a silent prayer of gratitude for people like Mary and Les Sullivan, remounted, settled his boots firmly in the stirrups, and guided Star back to the road.

* * *

"What do you mean Doc's not here?" Will roared. "Where the hell *is* he?"

Ellen Campbell's voice was crisp. "Settle down, Will, you'll wake the neighbors. That temper of yours will get you nowhere here. This isn't Sophia's first child, you know. She's had four others. She'll be fine."

"But Soph's not been well with this one. It's been troublesome! Now where is he?"

"Over at Kozniks' house. Their youngest has whooping cough and was taken bad tonight and he…"

"They got a phone?"

"No, you'll have to ride over. It's two blocks east and three…"

Will cut her off again. "I know where it is." He started off the porch, turned back. "He have chains on the Ford?"

"Look in the shed where Tom keeps the car. If they're not on the nail by the door he put them on. But Will…"

He ignored her and headed for the shed. The door was open. Cobwebs covered the rusting tire chains. Will snatched them off the nail, remounted and flicked the reins. Ellen's shout followed him down the street. "But don't go in, Will. The family's quarantined."

He dismissed her warning with a flick of his hand and raced toward the Koznic house.

* * *

Soft light from a shaded oil lamp outlined the bulky form in the doorway. Will looked past the doctor, saw Mrs. Koznic's anxious face hovering over the cot where her son lay, his small body wracked by continuous coughs. Steam from a kettle, perched atop the iron potbelly stove, floated past Will and fluffed into soft wisps in the cold night air. The doctor's voice was hushed as he stepped outside and closed the door.

"Have to keep that steam inside. Helps control the coughing. You shouldn't be around here anyway, might take it home to your kids. Listen Will, I'm sorry. I just can't come right now. The boy's having a hard time breathing, and the medicine doesn't seem to be taking hold. I'll come as soon as I possibly can."

"But dammit, Doc, Soph needs you *now*."

"Get hold of yourself, Will. I can't come now. That boy in there might die."

Will's shoulders slumped. "Well, if you can't you can't but get there as soon as you can, hear? Oh, I brought the chains over from your house. You'll need 'em on the long hill coming out of town. I'll put 'em on now so the car will be ready when you are. You got your bag?"

"Never go anywhere without it, Will." His eyebrows quirked. "Don't you remember? That's where I keep the babies! Appreciate you doing those chains. This belly of mine gets in the way when *I* try to put 'em on. Only difference between Soph and me is she'll get rid of hers. You get on home now. I'll be there soon as I can. You say Mary's with her? That's good." The door opened and clicked shut behind him.

* * *

Star trotted into the yard. The cottonwood stood stark against the lunar sky, it's naked branches casting a web of shadows over the back yard and porch. A sudden wedge of light from the kitchen door tangled new shadows on the fresh snow. Billy, dressed in boots and barn clothes, lantern in hand, stepped into the wedge. His shadow smudged the tracery of bare branches limned by the moon, overrode his father's.

"Took you long enough." He moved close, surreptitiously sniffed his father's breath and stepped back in relief. "Mr. Sullivan went back home. Mrs. Sullivan's with Mamma. Anne's made coffee, there's plenty left. I'll put Star up for the night." He examined the mare. "She's pretty sweaty. You rode hard!" Respect replaced his resentment over his mother's pregnancy and the impending birth. "I'll rub Star down, you go on in. Mamma needs you."

Will scrutinized the sturdy figure before him. A young man stood in a boy's boots. He started to tousle Billy's hair, but instead clasped his shoulder, man to man. "I know you're worried about your mamma but she'll be fine. She's just having a baby. It's natural."

Billy's fear-fueled resentment blazed again. He glared at his father with hostile eyes, turned on his heel, and led Star toward the stable.

* * *

Mary closed the bedroom door and bustled through the parlor

and dining room to the kitchen. Billy and Anne, hands clasped, sat at the dining room table. Will kept watch at the window, staring up the empty road.

"Daddy," Anne asked, "is there anything else we can do?"

"Don't think so, Honey. Billy's chopped enough firewood to last until Easter." Will deliberately twinkled his eyes. "No one wants to move too fast around the cook stove or on the porch. We're liable to get buried under all that wood he's got stacked up. You get those old sheets off the top closet shelf for Mary?" Anne nodded. "And I've got just about every bucket we own filled with water and boiling on the stove. Doc's going to need lots of disinfecting after Koznics' whooping cough. No, I can't think of another thing. And Lord knows when Doc will get here. Best thing you can do is get on to bed. You know Mamma will want you both in school tomorrow."

Billy and Anne exchanged startled looks. Billy spoke first. "But we wanted to be here when…"

"No. You both get on upstairs. Best if you're there anyway in case Seth or Yahbut wake up. Your mamma didn't want you kids in on this, but you've sure been a help." He moved to the table, patted Billy's shoulder and bent to kiss Anne's forehead. "Go along now."

"Oh, Daddy," Anne sobbed. "It's so awful!"

"I know, Honey, but it's how we all get here." He turned to Billy. "Seth and I'll do the milking tomorrow morning…*this* morning, I guess…so you can get another hour's sleep. When you wake up you'll have a new brother or sister."

Arms around each other's shoulders, Billy and Anne tiptoed through the kitchen to the back stairs. Will watched them comfort each other, envied their closeness.

Doesn't seem all that long ago they were babies, but they're almost grown. Anne, just turned fourteen and with budding breasts. Billy a year younger with peach-fuzz whiskers beginning to darken.

Will felt excluded.

Must be how Seth feels. Left out.

He wandered back to the window to resume his watch.

* * *

Mary moved briskly into the room. "She's resting now. Sorry the kids woke up when I came. The dogs barking, I guess. Oh, I brought coffee, Will. Want some? Almost have to spoon it out of the pot, but that's my fault. I told Anne to make it strong. Figured Doc might need it. Don't suppose the Koznics have any money to buy coffee." She saw Will stiffen, touched his arm. "I know, sometimes you don't either but this is different. Just bring us some fresh liver next time you butcher. You always do, anyhow. Come sit down now. You won't bring Doc any sooner by staring out that window." She handed him a steaming mug.

"Thanks, Mary. Soph sleeping?"

Mary spoke sharply. "Why don't you call her Soph-EE-ah?" Will looked up in surprise at Mary's unexpected outburst. "Sorry, Will, but you know she hates when you call her 'Soph'." Her voice softened. "It's just that Sophia's such a pretty name and 'Soph'…well, she says it sounds like one of your cows. Guess I'm on edge. What on earth happened?"

"Figured you might tell me. She's been short with everybody the last few months, not like herself at all. Remember, before Christmas, when I asked you to stop by and visit with her? She had me worried then. 'Course, I knew she was tired, but… She say anything when you were here New Year's Day?"

"Only that the baby had finally quit trying to kick its way out. It had dropped. They usually quiet down when they drop. She's as excited about this baby as she was the others, maybe more. She's so sure it's a girl she's even named it."

"I know...Little Lisa. That's about all she talks about these days."

The clock struck two. "Where on earth *is* that doctor!" Mary hesitated. "Will, you might as well know this looks serious. I was with her when Seth and Yahbut were born and they were both easy for her. I didn't want to say anything while Billy and Anne were here, but it's a good thing you sent them to bed."

She glanced into the parlor at the shedding Christmas tree flanked by stiff, leather-sheathed horsehair furniture. "That tree's stayed too long at the ball. Time someone took it down. It's dangerous. All dried out, could cause a fire."

"We were going to take it down yesterday, but..."

"I know. Too much else going on. Well, it's only the third. Not Epiphany yet." She stared at the bedraggled tree. "Sophia's father was Russian, wasn't he?" she asked absently. "Wonder if he celebrated Orthodox Christmas?" She shook her head. "Lordy, listen to me run on. Must be Anne's coffee. Guess I've got those caffeine nerves the Postum people talk about all the time on the radio."

A sharp bark jerked Will to his feet. "That's Blue. He's got the best ears of the pack." He hurried to the window and pulled the curtain aside. "It's Doc, just rounding the corner. I'll go quiet the dogs."

* * *

Will paced from kitchen to dining room, around the table and back again, waiting for the doctor to finish his examination. When the bedroom door finally squeaked open, his fists clenched with controlled tension. He watched the doctor ease the door shut, cross the front parlor into the dining room, set the kerosene lamp on the table, and blow out the flame.

"Need to oil those hinges, Will."

"The hell with the hinges, Doc! What about Soph?"

"We've got trouble." The doctor moved to the table, where he tested each chair and lowered himself onto the sturdiest. Elbows propped on the table, he cupped his head in slim, supple hands. "Better sit down. Mary, get us another cup of coffee, will you?" He straightened abruptly. "Will, I can't find a heartbeat. I'm sure the baby's dead. And I think it may have been dead for several days. Soph hasn't felt it move since New Year's Day. From what she says, it probably happened when it dropped. They usually quiet down then, but still there's *some* movement. What I think happened is it got the umbilical cord wrapped around its neck and strangled. It was always active, and that happens sometimes with the extra-active ones. They…"

"WHAT ABOUT SOPH?"

"She's still all right, or at least she will be if she can deliver. The thing is, I don't know how long this can go on. Her labor's stopped. She's just plain worn out. What I want to do is take the baby. It's dangerous, but I'll have to use high forceps. Mary's disinfecting them now, but Soph's a good Catholic and she won't let me touch her as long as she thinks the baby might still be alive." His voice dropped. "She's asking for Father Riley. Will, if I were you I'd keep her away from that priest right now. I've given her something to relax her, help her rest so she can get some strength back. They don't call it labor for nothing, you know. It's up to you to talk to her."

* * *

Will eased his way into the darkened bedroom. The full moon, lowering toward the west, reflected off the new snow and cast a luminous glow through the south window. He stopped just inside the door. Watched Sophia's head turned toward the window, her thick dark curls fanned out across the pillow. In the subdued light, it was easy to drop back in time…to erase fifteen years. He swallowed, swallowed again. Thought of how he loved the silky feel of her hair brushing his face.

"Come in, Will. I'm not asleep." Her weakened voice was almost a whisper.

He moved to her side, dropped to his knees, and took her hand between his callused palms. "Soph…Sophia…Love…I can't make it without you."

She moved her head to find his face. In the dim light, his eyes glistened. Tears? From Will? A tired smile curved her lips. "You smell like horse, Will. Thank you for riding to get Doc." They held each other silently. Finally she whispered, "We can't just think of ourselves, Will. We have to think of Lisa. We have to put our faith in God."

"Right now, we have to put our faith in Doc. Sophia, he can't find a heartbeat. He's sure the baby's dead. We have to think of the living, *that's* who we have to think about. Anne, Billy, Seth, Yahbut. They need you. *I* need you! We *all* love you and need you." He searched her face, willed her to look at him. "Soph, we're not old yet. We can have other babies. But Soph, there's only one you."

Their eyes met, held for a long moment. The movement of her head on the pillow was reluctant, almost imperceptible. Up. Down. Will's body sagged with relief. He passed his hand over his wife's damp forehead, leaned to kiss her cheek, and rose to call the doctor.

"Will, if she *is* dead see that Father Riley baptizes her as Elizabeth before she's buried."

He nodded mutely and moved to the door. "You can come in, Doc. She's ready."

* * *

The mingled smell of carbolic acid and alcohol permeated the kitchen. The doctor, shirtsleeves rolled above his elbows, stood at the sink scrubbing his hands and arms in a basin of hot water. "Soph should be all right, Will. We got to her in time. Always a danger of gangrene, infection you know, in a case like this."

"The baby?"

"A boy. Pity. He had a strong little body. Mary said she'll stay until Soph gets back on her feet. Ought to be at least a week, but I suspect she'll be up in two or three days. You know Soph." He turned, looked Will squarely in the eyes. "She says you promised her another baby, Will."

"I had to, Doc, to get her to agree."

"Well, that's between the two of you, but I'd make it a lot later than sooner. There was some tearing and forceps damage. I sewed her up as best I could, still…" He packed his instruments into his bag. "I've got to go. Promised Koznics I'd stop back by after I was through here. You bring her in to the office soon as this snow's gone."

Will's voice was husky. "Thanks doesn't sound like much, Doc, but it comes from the heart. And you know you'll get paid soon as we can scratch up the ten dollars."

"Don't worry about it, Will. Just bring some of that corn-fed beef by next time you butcher."

"It'll be there, but it'll be the interest. We'll pay you the principal when we can." He hesitated. "Uh, Doc, she'll want the baby baptized before he's buried."

"I'll stop by Father Riley's on my way home."

Chapter 5

Sophia's voice echoed up the stairwell to the room Yahbut shared with Anne. "Yahbut, time to get up if you're going with Daddy."

Yahbut stirred awake. Familiar early morning sounds and smells floated through the floor register from the kitchen below. Anne saying Mamma let me do that for you. Billy's funny new voice teasing Seth and Seth's familiar boy-laugh answering and Anne saying now you boys shush. Water splashing in the enameled wash basin.

She sniffed the tantalizing aroma of pancakes and sizzling sausage. Her mouth watered in sympathy with demanding growls from her stomach.

The little girl burrowed deeper into the featherbed, luxuriating in the double pleasure of waking up dry and the fresh, cool April breeze that played across her forehead. She risked a squint. Anne had left the window open and the shades up. Yahbut drew the quilt over her head to protect sleep-dilated pupils from bright sunlight. She cradled her body, holding tight to thoughts of the wonderful day ahead.

"Yahbut! Daddy will be back from the hog lot soon. If you've not finished breakfast by the time he's ready to go you'll stay home."

Eyes squeezed shut, Yahbut popped her head out of the covers. "Coming, Mamma." She ducked back into the darkness then slowly lowered the quilt, letting the pupils of her black-lashed, October-blue eyes adjust to brightness. Counting to ten, she took a deep breath and leapt into the morning chill. Her teeth chattered as she skinned out of her flannel gown and into the clothes Anne had laid out for her the night before.

Overalls! Today she got to wear a pair of Seth's old overalls. And one of his outgrown shirts, too. Mamma said it was okay just this once since she'd be walking with Daddy down the weedy wagon track to Uncle Bert's and Aunt Molly's. The seldom-used lane ran right by the schoolhouse Daddy went to when he and Uncle Bert were little boys but not brothers…just cousins, so they could study with the same class in the big room where everyone else studied no matter how young or old they were. She hoped he'd tell her about it again today. Yahbut never tired of Daddy's stories.

She was glad Daddy was walking Belle to visit Uncle Bert's big bull on a school day. Usually Billy or Seth went along to prod whatever balky cow Daddy was walking, but today *she* got to be Daddy's helper. Daddy said Belle was so gentle he wouldn't need much help, but when she pouted he smiled and said well of course even the best cow balks once in awhile so you'll have to watch your Ps and Qs.

And maybe they'd see the kids that still went to the old country school having recess. She couldn't wait to start school in Macklin Corner so she'd have someone to play with.

Yahbut wondered why people walked cows. Uncle Bert and Joe used to walk cows over to see them, but that was when the bull still lived in his pen behind Daddy's barn, before it went to live with Uncle Bert. She remembered the excitement the day Uncle Bert came to take the bull away. She'd stood on the veranda with Mamma and Aunt Molly watching Daddy and Uncle Bert and Joe and Billy and Seth, all armed with pitchforks, load the big animal into Uncle Bert's truck. When she asked why the bull wore a big earring in its nose Mamma said so Daddy could make it behave. She'd giggled when Mamma tweaked *her* nose and said maybe she'd try that with her adventurous little *girl*.

Mamma was happy then. Yahbut wished she'd be happy again like the way she acted when Aunt Molly laughed and said she didn't see how one little girl could look so much like her mamma but be just as contrary as her daddy. Then Aunt Molly told Mamma how much they appreciated getting the bull. And Mamma said it was good for both families because Will was afraid one of the children would wander out around the barn and get hurt.

Yahbut's thumb crept into her mouth. She knew Mamma had been talking about her. She'd not *meant* to get so close to the pen last spring when she went with Mamma to the barn looking for one of the setting hens that sneaked off to lay eggs and hatch baby chicks. She just wanted to say hello like Daddy did to all the different animals, but the bull almost knocked the fence down while Mamma screamed and Daddy came running with the pitchfork and Mamma grabbed the big bow on the back of her pinafore and jerked her away. Now, instead of Uncle Bert walking cows to their house, Daddy walked cows to Uncle Bert's.

Yahbut remembered that Daddy said big girls didn't suck their thumbs and thrust both hands deep into overall pockets. She practiced swaggering around the bedroom like Billy, watching her reflection in the mirror.

"Yahbut! I'm not going to call you again!"

Yahbut recognized the finality in her mother's voice, grabbed the hairbrush, drew it across the top of her tangled curls, and smiled at herself in the mirror. Today she and Daddy would be the only people in the world—at least for a little while. She skipped down the stairs and raced to the outhouse, where she fitted her small bottom over the low children's hole just in time.

* * *

"Hate to leave you, Soph, but a cow's only fertile for twelve hours each month. If we want a late-winter calf it's got to be today. Sure you'll be all right while we're gone?"

"I told you, Will, I'll be fine. But I do wonder if that walk will be too much for Yahbut."

"She'll be okay. It's only a little over a mile through the country and she can rest at the house with Molly while Belle's with the bull. Don't worry so about her! Honey, you've got to loosen the apron strings a little. Yahbut's getting smothered under all that mother love of yours."

Sophia's head bowed, accepting the rebuke. "I know. But I can't seem to help it. She's my baby now…" Her words trailed off in sorrow.

He took her hands in his, gently squeezed them to soften his firm tone. "Soph, it's time to put all that behind us. Past time. You can't keep on grieving this way."

"Our son would be laughing and cooing and turning over now…"

"If he'd lived, but Soph he didn't and you can't put Yahbut in his place. You trying to keep her a baby…well, it's not good for any of us." He drew his wife into the protective circle of his arms. His voice broke. "He was my son, too. I know how you feel."

Will's shoulder dampened under a shower of tears. Sophia's voice was muffled. "How *could* you know, Will? Did you carry him inside you? Feel him grow, kick, move? Then feel him die?" Uncontrollable sobs shook her body.

Awkwardly, Will patted Sophia's shoulder, stroked and soothed, wondering what else he could do or say. "I miss him, too. Funny how you can miss someone you never really got to know, but I've still got you and I'll settle for that any time."

Doc had said she'd be like this for awhile, but it was over three months now and she didn't seem any better. He couldn't count the times he'd come in the house to find her fingering the baby clothes she'd made but never used. "When do you see Doc again?"

"I don't know, maybe next week." She sniffled, pulled away, drew a handkerchief from her apron pocket and wiped her eyes. "It's on the calendar. I'm sorry, Will. I know it's not easy for you, either. It's just that I've got this awful hole inside." She forced a watery smile. "You'd better round up Yahbut and get going before she tires herself out."

"Sure you wouldn't like to walk along with us? Might do you good. We'll walk slow and you can visit with Molly while Belle's getting serviced."

"Not today, Will. I'm not fit company for anyone…even myself."

Will hesitated, considered insisting, then remembered Doc's advice to let her work out her grief by herself. "Whatever you say, Soph. But don't answer the door if any bums show up." He laughed at her consternation. "Forget I said that. I'm leaving Blue and the other dogs here so nobody will even get near the door. Try to get some rest. We'll be back by noon for dinner."

"Please don't worry. I'll be all right." Her eyes lowered before the perplexity and concern in Will's. She raised her head, touched his cheek in apology. "And Will, thank you for asking me to go along."

* * *

Sophia watched at the kitchen window as Will led Belle past the garden and across the field to the once well-traveled, now little-used wagon track shortcut that linked the Macklin homestead to the farming community farther south. Yahbut proudly marched behind, the stick in her hand raised and ready to prod Belle should she need it.

A smile dimpled Sophia's somber face. She'd never seen Yahbut act so responsibly. And Belle was taking no chances. The Jersey cow kept her head level with Will's shoulder, one big brown eye on the scrap of a girl bringing up the rear. When the little procession moved out of sight, Sophia attacked the pile of breakfast dishes. Then she'd make the beds and dust and…

…and go to the cedar chest…

No! She wouldn't! She spent too many hours mourning the lost baby. The older children almost tiptoed around her, as though they were afraid she'd break. And Yahbut chafed under her mother's constant attention. Will was right, she *was* overprotective. Maybe even a little crazy sometimes. Maybe they'd be better off without her. Maybe she belonged in the asylum over in Jacksonville.

I've got to stop brooding, but how?

If only they were into the busy season on the farm and she could recover her strength, she'd have something to do with her spare time. She dried the last dish, stored it in the cupboard, and sat down to rest before completing morning chores.

It seemed to make little difference how hard she fought to contain her grief or how much she tried to be a good wife and mother. The tiny clothes bundled inside the lace-trimmed shawl in the cedar chest still drew her like a magnet. She closed her eyes, remembered each stitch on every shirt and gown; the fine embroidery lavished on the white silk christening gown she'd made from an old dress found in an attic trunk. A gown never worn by a nameless dead baby hastily christened before burial in the snow-covered, frozen ground of Bridgeton's Catholic Cemetery.

Not even a name...just Baby Macklin on the death certificate...

The ghost of that perfectly formed body, a body seen for a brief moment through a curtain of pain before he was taken away forever, haunted her every waking moment. Lost dream-baby cries disturbed her sleep. Tiny spirit fingers closed around her thumb. Long, slender fingers. Her eyes widened in recognition.

Like Papa's. And that fine-boned face, that cap of dark curls...

She still remembered her father's funeral, her intuitive little-girl knowledge that she'd never see him again. Maybe if she'd seen the baby buried, she'd be more able to accept the reality of *his* death.

The day after Dr. Campbell took the baby, Mary tended her while the rest of the family attended graveside services. Even her determination hadn't been enough to overcome her weakness and

Dr. Tom's orders to stay in bed. Will's and Mary's concern became relief when she collapsed on the pillow, unable to sit up, let alone dress and leave the house.

If only he'd been buried in his christening gown... But in the hectic aftermath of the delivery and her subsequent illness, hurried arrangements were necessary. Her conscious mind accepted, but her heart still ached.

Was it too late to give him a name?

When Billy was born, she insisted he be named after Will and Will's father, old William P. When Seth came along, they discussed naming him after *her* father. Will thought it a wonderful idea, but Sophia remembered the prejudice she'd encountered as a child against anything foreign. Boy babies were named Chris or Jess or Joe or Sam. Sergei Macklin? They'd laughed together and compromised on Seth. And she'd been so sure the last baby was a girl, she'd not even thought of boys' names.

...little Sergei...maybe Papa will find his soul, take care of him for me...

A thin veil of transcendent peace settled over Sophia's troubled mind. As though guided by her father's metaphysical Russian presence, she knew what she must do. Dr. Tom could put the name on the death certificate. The other thing she must do herself.

Sophia's steps to the cedar chest were firm. Salty drops spotted the shawl-wrapped bundle she carried outside. A light breeze brought the perfume of peach blossoms across the veranda.

...the orchard...

Blue joined her to pad silently by her side as Sophia found the spade, made her way to the orchard, and laid the bundle on a low branch of the largest peach tree. At the base of the tree, she dug a deep hole in the spring-soft earth. Kneeling, she lined it with new grass, placed the bundle on top of the grass, and shrouded it with peach blossoms. Tears dampened each handful of soil that covered the petals. When she finished, Sophia scattered more petals over the raw earth. Still kneeling, she touched her forehead, heart and each shoulder with muddy fingers, clasped her hands, and intoned the prayer for the dead.

As she prayed, the black mass of frozen pain, nurtured since January, thawed. Appreciation for her healthy, living children slowly replaced the overwhelming loss of one.

"Thank you, God", she whispered, concluding her prayers. "And thank you, Papa."

She rose, patted Blue's head and looked around. The cloudless April sky and greening world wrapped her in a celebration of life.

Sophia started to leave the orchard, then returned to the tree to break off a sprig of blossoms. Guarded by the hound, she made her way back to the house. She wondered about what she had done. And why. It didn't make sense. Had anyone seen her they'd have thought her crazy. And she had to admit that, had she seen anyone else do such an outlandish thing, she'd certainly think the same. But instinct had overcome conscious thought, bringing a mystic cleansing of crippling hurt, dynamic in its intensity.

Still puzzling over her unusual experience, Sophia checked the pantry to find something for Will's and Yahbut's dinner. When Blue's deep voice signaled the news of their return, Sophia finished setting the table, touched the sprig of peach blossoms in its centered vase, and stepped out onto the back porch to watch their approach. And laughed her first genuine laugh in months.

Will's left hand clutched the lead rope attached to Belle's halter. His right arm supported a sleeping girl snuggled against his chest.

"Let me take her, Will," Sophia called as she ran to meet them.

"Too heavy for you to handle. Almost too much for me. My right arm's about to drop off. We barely left Bert's when she conked out on me. Here…you take Belle."

The little group strolled slowly, savoring the promise of spring.

"It's a beautiful day, Will."

"Hmph! Be better when my arm wakes up. Hang on to that cow. I'll pasture her soon as I put this lump of lead down for her nap."

"But her dinner…"

"She doesn't need dinner after all the cookies and milk Molly fed her." He grinned. "Guess you were right after all. That walk *was* too much for her."

"No, Will. *YOU* were right." She smiled at the familiar quizzical lift of his right eyebrow, the rough tenderness of the fingers that wiped away the dirt smudge on her forehead. "No…not now…I'll tell you about it while we eat, but it's a secret. And you have to promise *never* to tell *ANYONE!"*

Chapter 6

Anne brushed brownish-blond, flyaway bangs away from her forehead and turned for a disgusted peek in the dresser mirror across the room. Frowning at her reflection, she touched the cropped, straight hair skimming her earlobes and nape in an ear-to-ear crescent. Another Dutch bob. She *hated* the Dutch bob Eddie gave her twice a year.

Mamma said a traveling barber in the neighborhood was so convenient and besides Eddie needed the money. Lately Eddie was cutting Daddy's hair, too, because Daddy said he didn't have an extra quarter for the barbershop so she guessed Eddie was cheap. But he could only cut girls' hair in a Dutch bob.

Eddie stopped by with his scissors and clippers each spring and fall, lined the unlucky children up on the back porch to take their turns on the stool, and when he was through Anne's, Billy's and Seth's hair all looked alike. Well, *almost* alike. Hers looked like he'd set a bowl on her head and cut around it, but he shingled the back of Billy's and Seth's hair like Daddy's. Theirs didn't look too bad, but … A week ago yesterday was spring haircut day. And then…Monday…

Anne's face burned as she remembered walking into the schoolyard with Billy and Seth, and seeing Jimmy Yankos waiting by the old elm tree. Big Jimmy Yankos with high water, patched overalls and ragged shirt and dirty hands, so dumb he'd been in first grade three years because he couldn't even speak English.

Billy snickered. "Hey, 'Annie', there's your boyfriend waiting for you."

Seth came to her defense. "He's not her boyfriend, Billy. He just wants to be. Anne doesn't even like him."

Jimmy sashayed over. "Hey, Annie. Whatcha doin'? Dem brudders uh yours takin' good care a youse?"

Anne marched straight ahead, ignoring Jimmy's advances,

Billy's grin and Seth's sympathetic scowl.

Jimmy covered his embarrassment at Anne's rejection with derision. "Hey, looks like Miss Stuck-up Farmer got herself a haircut. Jesus, youse looks just like yer brudders. Looks like somebody trew a hatchet atcha!"

Anne's face flamed. She turned her head so Jimmy wouldn't see her hurt tears. Jimmy didn't, but Seth did. He dropped his books, lowered his head, rammed the off-guard older boy in the stomach, and knocked Jimmy flat. Jimmy grabbed Seth's leg and pulled him down. Billy jumped on Jimmy.

"Fight! Fight!" The cry spread through the schoolyard like wildfire. Students raced from all directions to form a ring around the scuffling boys.

Mr. Peterson sprinted outside. "No fighting in the schoolyard!" the principal bellowed. He broke through the excited circle, separated the boys, collared Billy and Jimmy, and marched them toward the school. "Anne and Seth in my office, too," he called over his shoulder.

Two penitential Macklins trailed up the stairs after Mr. Peterson and his unrepentant charges. The principal was very nice when he found out what happened. She must have imagined the quirk at the corner of his mouth, because she knew he'd never laugh at something so serious. And he didn't punish her or Billy or Seth at all and just kept Jimmy in his office for awhile to talk to him. She'd thought it was all over, but now at recess and noon Jimmy Yankos and his friends taunted her with "Who trew da hatchet at youse, Farmer?" "Hey, Farmer! Who trew da hatchet at youse?"

Anne mourned. She made the boys promise not to fight Jimmy again or tell Mamma, but she wondered what Mamma would do if Eddie gave *her* a Dutch bob. Mrs. Sullivan cut Mamma's and Yahbut's hair because Eddie said he didn't know what to do with curls.

Why do I have to have hair like Gramma Hattie? I guess it's because I kind of look like Gramma Hattie...small and thin. SKINNY. Mamma tries to be nice. She says fine-boned. My eyes are beautiful like Mamma's, though, and I guess like Grampa Sergei's.

She felt her nose. People said she had her mother's delicate English nose, too. She wondered if she'd ever get any taller.

Careful not to wake Yahbut, Anne scooted her chair closer to Phineas' old library table. She shoved her stack of schoolbooks back toward the window, opened her notebook, picked up a pen and checked the nib. Splayed! Yahbut must've been trying to write with it again. She glanced at the bed where her sister lay napping and wished she could have a room of her own. She knew her mother needed a sewing room and that her grandfather had to have his own room when he came to visit, but Yahbut was always using her things and asking questions. It *was* better since their mother taught Yahbut to read. Her eyes narrowed.

Now she'll probably be into my books!

She'd be glad when Yahbut stopped wetting the bed for good. Anne hated waking up at night to the nasty smell and clammy sheets. And she hated the sticky rubber pad they put under the bottom sheet to keep the featherbed dry. Even when she woke Yahbut in the middle of the night and made her use the chamber pot, Yahbut still wet sometimes. Anne was glad it wasn't watermelon season! Yahbut loved watermelon, but...

Anne worked the damaged nib out of the pen shaft, opened the drawer, searched for a new one, slipped it in place, and dipped the nib into the inkwell. She stared at the blank page. Anne Macklin decided she hated Sunday afternoons. Maybe she just hated everything. She looked around the room.

The furniture was all so old it was like living with dry, dusty history. She made a face at the walnut bedroom set, so heavy that when Aunt Clarilla died it took her father, Uncle Bert, Billy and the hired man to carry it up the stairs when it came on the train from Altamont. So it didn't get scratched on the way home, Mamma sent thick quilts to wrap it in and Daddy covered the biggest farm wagon's bed with straw before he drove the horses to the Macklin Corner station to pick up all the stuff Aunt Clarilla's lawyer sent. The dining room set and hers and Yahbut's bedroom furniture. That big barrel filled with the good English dishes Mamma kept in the china cabinet and wouldn't let anyone use. The cedar chest in Mamma's and Daddy's bedroom stuffed with stacks and stacks of linens. All of it *old.*

Who cared if Great-Great Aunt Clarilla brought the cedar chest from Massachusetts in a covered wagon pulled by oxen? Thinking about all it held, Anne decided that was why it was so big…the old woman put everything she owned in it. Of course, she probably hadn't been old then or she'd never have been able to stand the two-month trip to Illinois.

Anne barely remembered the ancient, wrinkled lady Mamma had taken her to visit when she was four. It was hard to imagine Aunt Clarilla ever being young. She remembered the train ride to Altamont, though. That was fun.

She studied the Victorian carvings on the headboard, foot-board, dresser and washstand. Her mother was proud of the bed-room set and was always telling her and Yahbut to be careful with it, but as far as Anne was concerned it was *ugly.* The rag rug was nice, though. Mamma made it out of all their worn-out clothes. It was like picking out a puzzle, remembering what everything was before it was a rug.

Demanding cheeps from a nest in the cottonwood drifted through the open window. Anne glanced out at the orange and black male oriole flashing through the new lime-green leaves to perch on the edge of the swaying cradle. She felt a stab of pity for the desperately wriggling worm dangling from his beak and flinched as he dropped the worm into a waiting open mouth. The male flew away for another just as his yellow and brown mate soared in with a fat caterpillar. Those baby birds ate all day long.

She didn't see how the parents built a nest like that. Daddy said they wove the top to the branch and made it deep to keep the babies from falling out, but strong to support them as they grew, then lined it with downy cottonwood seeds. That spring the nesting pair found one of Yahbut's narrow pink hair ribbons and wove *it* into the cradle. Anne studied the ribbon. She hoped the baby birds were girls.

The nest just hung from the cottonwood branch, swaying back and forth all day long.

Did the babies sleep at night? Yahbut hadn't!

She guessed birds were the same as people. If you had babies you had to take care of them.

She fingered an erupting pimple on her chin, a reminder that 'Aunt Rosy' was due for her monthly visit. Anne thought it was awful being a girl and would be even worse being a woman. She guessed she'd get married and have babies someday. Everyone did, but she didn't have to *like* the idea.

Daddy coming home late drunk, Mamma tired and worn out since her little brother was born dead last winter but still cooking and cleaning and washing for us all. And the house always a mess and people just keep getting hungry. And those dirty boys never wipe their barn boots when they come in and I hate scrubbing up that manure mess. Wish Yahbut was old enough to help.

She propped her chin in her hands and watched the busy birds.

Anne really wanted to be a teacher. She was a straight-A student in the Macklin Corner eighth grade, but was afraid her schooling would end there. All the Macklin children walked two miles to grade school and two miles home. Bridgeton High, however, was *five* miles away. Mamma and Daddy would never allow her to walk ten miles every day, nor let her ride Star, nor walk to the slab and hitchhike like the boys would do. Boys were expected to go to high school. Girls weren't, at least the girls she knew.

She sighed, tore her eyes away from the birds and stared at the blank paper. She probably wouldn't like high school anyway. All the Bridgeton girls had pretty hair and store-bought clothes. Mamma sewed all her dresses. It made no difference in Macklin Corner, but in high school…

Anne took a deep breath, spat on the nib to moisten the dried ink, wiped it with an old piece of felt, dipped the clean nib into the inkwell, and wrote the title of her theme on a fresh sheet of paper: MY ASPIRATIONS.

* * *

The house was quiet, the children asleep. Will was rereading RAINBOW BRIDGE, a Zane Gray novel about Mormons. Sophia, checking the mending basket in her lap, wished they could afford a new battery for the silent Philco console radio in the corner. It would be nice to have music in the house again. She missed her programs, too, the ones that came on while she fixed Will's noon dinner—'Helen Trent', 'Ma Perkins', and her favorite, 'Our Gal Sunday'.

The opening lines of the fifteen-minute weekday serial ran through her head. "Can a girl from a little mining town in the West find happiness as the wife of a wealthy and titled Englishman?" She guessed she'd never know.

She missed the news programs as well, missed starting her morning with the early KMOX news from St. Louis "…brought to you by Uncle Dick Slack". She hoped Uncle Dick Slack had a *few* furniture customers left.

When they could still afford a newspaper, she'd read it front to back, even the advertisements. Now she never knew what was going on in the world unless Will brought home discarded magazines and papers from the feed store or the doctor's office. And the news was old by then.

The wick of the coal oil lamp on the table between them, turned high so Will could see to read, began to smoke. Sophia lowered the wick, reminded herself to trim the charred edges the next day and check the coal oil can. Even though lamp fuel only cost eighteen cents a gallon, she wasn't sure they could afford it. Will was so distant when she mentioned money these days, and the worry lines between his eyebrows seemed to grow deeper every day. But when she asked why, he'd tell her not to fret, that he'd take care of things. Well, worry wouldn't solve anything and he worried enough for both of them.

She rummaged through her sewing basket. "Will, I've got something to show you."

"Just a minute, Soph. I'm almost through with this chapter."

"Are you sure you don't mean through with this chapter again?" she chided. "You've already read that book at least twice. I hope you're not planning to turn Mormon and add another wife to *this* household." She handed Will the crumpled paper retrieved from under her darning thread. "You need to read this. I found it wadded up on Anne's study table this morning. It's blotted, smeary, hard to read. I think the blots are from tears. She must have cried while she wrote that and copied it over for school."

Will grudgingly took the paper, smoothed it and spread it on the table under the lamplight. His scowl deepened as he read. "Hmph! Didn't know she was so set on it. Heard her rattling on about being a teacher but figured it was just...you know...kid's talk."

"Kid's *dreams*, Will and she's not a 'kid' any more. She's almost grown, she's serious and she's got a good mind. What's even more important is that she knows how to use it. Don't you think we should help her if we can figure out a way?"

"I don't know. Had a lot on my mind lately and guess I never thought past her eighth grade graduation. I just figured she'd stay home like the other country girls. Help you with the house and kids till she gets married."

"But she doesn't *want* that kind of life. Besides, there are more chances for women these days. At least educated women. Did you know that last January there were twelve women in the Sangamon County jury pool and *six* of them were on the first panel? The first women jurors ever allowed in a jury box in Springfield! And they showed they were capable. Times are changing, Will. Anne *needs* an education. Surely we can think of some way to get her to school in Bridgeton. Is your Cousin Bert's son still going to high school? Maybe if we paid for his gas with some of my butter and egg money he'd pick her up on his way."

"Yeeaah…but I hate to see you throw money into that wreck of a Model T Joe drives. Not safe. Held together with baling wire. Besides, he couldn't get over the short-cut road through the bottom and across the creek most of the school year. He'd have to drive the long way round, come in from the slab. What about when it rains? You know what that road from here to the slab's like then—nothing slicker or deeper than wet, yellow clay. He'd get stuck for sure. And when it's dry, there's ruts. That jalopy'd fly apart."

"Well, when you see Bert maybe you could ask him, anyway." She sorted through her basket, searching for the right yarn. "Why do you call the new hard road the slab?"

"Why do *you* call the new slab the hard road? Oh, because it's paved I guess. Not muddy or dusty." He grinned sheepishly. "Well, guess it's because we always called the old *National* the slab. That was the first transcontinental highway—a big slab of concrete that cut close by here across the middle of the United States. Then after the Great War, they routed that new 66 west of Walnut Hills where the land was flatter and tore out the National. Remember the ruckus on this side of the county when Walnut Hills got the benefit and started to grow? Getting bigger all the time, too...

"Since his place was close to the slab, Les Sullivan boarded some of the horses they used in those three-horse-team dirt wagons when they put in our Route 127. They used mules, too, for the heavier loads but Les wouldn't board them…too stubborn.

"Still a part of the old National where it headed off east to Vandalia, just north of Greenville. Dead ends in a field, but it's still there. We ever get where we can afford joy-ride gas again I'll drive you and the kids down, show it to you." He picked up his book. "About Anne. I'll think about it." He dismissed the problem and resumed reading.

Sophia tucked her marble darning egg into the worn heel of another sock, threaded her needle and reinforced the heel with neat, woven stitches. She rewarded herself with an inner smile. The seed of Anne's hopes was planted.

* * *

"Hold still, Yahbut. I swear you grow tangles." Sophia worked the heavy comb through dark curls. Will should be in soon and she wanted to be ready to go when he got home. She thought again about learning to drive. It would be a lot easier than dragging Will from the field every time she had to see the doctor. She felt better lately, but the last time she saw Dr. Tom he said he'd still need to check her again.

"There, all done." She brushed a final curl into place. "I think I hear the harness jingling. Run out and see while I get dressed. And try to stay clean. Yahbut! Don't hold that screen door open, you're letting in flies." The door slammed. Yahbut was gone.

While she waited for Will to put the horses in the barn and get the car out, Sophia put away the dishes Yahbut had dried and moved the bums' pie pan and fork to the back of the stove. Silly thing to do, she thought, I always wash them last and scald them, but still…

This year's warm southern breezes had brought both spring weather and hungry bums. So far, the Macklins had a caller almost every day but Sunday. She puzzled over their pattern of arrival. Never more than one a day and always after the Macklins' big noon meal.

Do they watch from somewhere to see Will come up from the field? Because if they do they must wait till we finish eating. But how do they know?

Rain or shine, after dinner they'd hear the dogs' warning barks. When Will stepped out on the porch, there'd be a bum standing hesitantly at the top of the bluff. Most of them offered to help in some way and Will, respecting their pride, always tried to find something for them to do. The boys hadn't chopped kindling or wood for weeks.

Each bum followed the same routine. After he finished whatever chore Will could find, he washed his hands with Sophia's homemade lye soap in the pan now permanently kept next to the bums' tin cup that hung by the well. That was Sophia's signal to heap the pie pan with food for Will to take out to the man perched on the edge of the back porch. When he finished eating, he'd draw a fresh bucket of water from the well, fill his bottle, tip his hat, and be on his way. They all acted the same. Even though Will said they were always polite, she and Yahbut stayed in the house till the men were gone.

Food was certainly no problem because they raised almost everything they ate. And lately she cooked extra just for leftovers, but she did fret about them perhaps coming when Will was away. Will said not to worry, the dogs would handle it. Recalling the savage shadow dance under the cottonwood tree, Sophia shuddered. She remembered Uncle Ed shuddering and saying, "Somebody just walked over my grave." She shuddered again.

* * *

Sophia watched carefully as Will shifted gears going up the

long hill into Macklin Corner. First he pushed that pedal in with his left foot, then moved the metal rod that stood in the middle of the car floor. But how did he know which way to move it? She concentrated, saw a pattern emerging.

His voice broke her concentration. "Planning to learn to drive, Soph?"

"You're reading my mind again, Will. To tell the truth, I have been thinking about it but I'm not sure I can. I just hate to take you out of the field all the time."

"Don't worry about it. I don't. Oh, didn't have a chance to tell you yet but I saw Bert this morning working his field that backs up to one of ours in the bottom. Asked him about that school thing. He doesn't think Joe's going back in the fall. Said he'd let us know, though." He pulled up in front of the doctor's office. "I'll be back in a half-hour or so. Yahbut, you come to the feed store with me."

* * *

Sophia lay on the examining table, her feet elevated in cold, steel stirrups. A sheet draped tentlike over her knees and the stirrup bars, covering her bare stomach and outer thighs. Self-conscious, she shielded her eyes with her right forearm and breathed deeply to relax while the doctor inserted the speculum. She could almost hear Mary muttering, "False modesty, Sophia. You don't have anything that doctor hasn't seen before." And she knew Mary was right. Yet, despite the fact that Dr. Tom had taken care of her since she was a child and attended the birth of each of her children, she still found pelvic examinations humiliating.

"Looking pretty good, Soph." The doctor's head bobbed up over the draped sheet. "You're healing well. You'd heal quicker, of course, if you could stay off your feet more. There's some scar tissue from the tearing, and the uterus wall is weakened. Sorry about that, but I had to work fast that night. You should have been in a hospital. Be nice if they ever get enough money together to finish the one in Bridgeton. Over your crying yet?"

"Almost. I think I settled things with myself but once in awhile I… Did you change the birth certificate?"

The doctor nodded. "What about physically? Are you feeling okay?"

"Well, I get tired, but with all the work on the farm that's to be expected. Anne's a big help."

"Anne's a fine girl. Smart, too, just like her mother." He removed the speculum, slipped her feet out of the stirrups, moved around the table and helped her sit up. "She graduates Eighth Grade this spring, doesn't she? Guess she'll be going on to high school in the fall?"

Sophia drew the sheet over her legs; picked a lint ball from the flannel fabric and rolled it between her thumb and forefinger. "Well, we're not sure. We don't have family in Bridgeton she can stay with, you know. And Will's so concerned about money these days and meeting the mortgage payments, we can't afford to board her. She says she'll walk, but five miles each way is too far, especially in bad weather. Since the hired man left, Will does all of the farm work so *he* can't take her. Besides, gas costs money we don't have right now. And we can't let her hitchhike like the boys will do. We hoped she might ride in with Bert's son, you remember Joe?, but Will's worried about that old car Joe drives. Anyway, Bert isn't sure Joe's going back this fall. Anne *wants* to go. We're trying to find a way."

The doctor listened attentively while he removed and stored the stirrups and sterilized the speculum. "She good with kids? No, never mind. With that brood of yours, I know she is. Listen, there's a new doctor in Bridgeton, nice young fella. Talked to him the other day. He was asking about someone to help his wife part-time with the kids. Think Anne would be interested?"

"Dr. Tom, the only thing Anne's *really* interested in now is going to high school. She wants to go to college, too, and be a teacher, but first things first."

"Well, what I was wondering, if they've got room and would like to try it maybe she could live with them while she goes to high school. They've got two boys, three and five. Anne could help with them mornings and after school, then once they're in bed she'd have her evenings free to study, just like at home. She cook?"

Carried away by the possibilities, her busy mind already planning ahead, Sophia didn't hear the doctor's question. A thoughtful smile erased the tension from her face.

"Soph?" The doctor snapped his fingers. "Soph? She cook?"

"Oh! I'm sorry, I was thinking. Yes, simple meals, enough for the children certainly. What's the doctor's name?"

"Greenberg. Joshua Greenberg." Sophia's face clouded.

"Something wrong, Soph?"

"Is…is it a Jewish family?"

An exasperated frown creased his normally good-natured face. "With a name like Greenberg? Of course they're Jewish, but I don't think they're Orthodox. Dr. Greenberg certainly doesn't wear side curls." His exasperation mounted. "And I've never seen him with his shoes off, but I don't expect he's got cloven feet either! Besides, if a sensible Jew could put up with a Catholic I expect if a Catholic's got a lick of sense she ought to be able to put up with a Jew. Or at least try."

"Father Riley…"

"Father Riley be hanged."

"And Will…"

"Now that could be a problem. With that mother of his and her Klan ideas about foreigners and negroes, guess some of what she said probably rubbed off on him. Look, I don't even know if they'd be interested or if they're still looking for someone, but if they are it would certainly solve the problem of Anne's schooling. Shouldn't wonder they'd give her some spending money, too, if she does a good job. She'll need books, clothes, all those other things girls always seem to need. Soph, would you really let prejudice stand in the way of Anne's education?"

"I'm not prejudiced, Dr. Tom!" The doctor snorted. "I'm *not*. How *could* I be? You know what a name like Dubrovich meant here thirty years ago. It's just…"

"It's just you're afraid of what your Irish priest will say! Bet the Greenbergs wouldn't mind if Anne went to Mass every Sunday. That's certainly more than she's able to do now. I don't know about Mrs. Greenberg, never met her, but the little I've talked to him he seems broadminded, able to take things in stride. Good doctor, too." He turned on his heel and strode toward the door. "Well, it was just a thought. Get dressed now."

"Dr. Tom!" He turned, making no effort to hide his irritation. "Dr. Tom, will you talk to the Greenbergs? And if they're interested, Will and I would want to meet them. Anne, too, of course. And…well…maybe I am a little prejudiced after all, but I won't let it show."

The gruff voice gentled. "Guess we're all prejudiced about something or other. Just can't let it get in the way of living, that's all." He patted her shoulder. "Of course I'll talk to the Greenbergs. Now you'd better get dressed, Will and Yahbut are waiting for you out front. See me again in a month or so. And don't get any ideas about more babies yet, hear?"

After the doctor left the examining room, Sophia sat, head bowed, considering the convoluted power of prayer. She dressed, let herself out and moved down the corridor toward the reception room where Will and Yahbut waited. She paused at the open door of the doctor's private office. Her eyes were bright with grateful but unshed tears, her parting smile tremulous.

Dr. Campbell watched her leave, then leaned back in his chair and mused. Sophia had been a pretty girl, but she was a beautiful woman. A little on the heavy side maybe, but still… Lucky man, that Will.

Sophia. Meant 'wisdom' if he remembered his college Greek correctly. But she had an earthy quality, too. Must come from that Russian father.

Had a college roommate that did research on early religions. Said Sophia was supposed to be the female part of God who decided to kick the traces, make the world by herself. Kind of an Earth Mother. Sophia. A wise Earth Mother? Well, not sure how wise she is, but she does *seem to be making progress.*

He rose, turned the crank once on the wall phone to ring for Central. "Josie? You got the number for that new doctor in Bridgeton? Greenberg. Joshua Greenberg."

Chapter 7

Slanting August sunlight beamed through Will's and Sophia's southwest bedroom window. Will tipped back the dresser mirror, adjusted it for his height, and leaned close to examine his short sideburns. He scowled at the traces of glinting silver and ducked to check the hair on top his head.

Still thick. No bald spot yet. No gray up there, either.

Well, he guessed it was time to start checking. He'd turned thirty-eight last March.

Damn that sounds old. Guess I just thought I'd never get *old. Guess like Bert always says, consider the alternative.*

His palm caressed his fresh-shaved face and strong neck, still pinkish from the finely honed straight edge razor. He lowered his head to study the thick, dark-reddish brows and lashes that framed his hazel eyes. A deprecating grin crinkled his face.

Soph was always riding him about his vanity. "Handsome is as handsome does, Will." If he'd heard it once he'd heard it a thousand times.

Hell, she just might be right, but whoever said it was a sin to appreciate what the good Lord gave?

His inspection moved to heavily muscled white shoulders and hairy chest, set off by the 'farmer's tan' vee at his neck where his work shirts opened to the sun. Turning sideways, he pulled in his slight paunch and flexed his arms in a Charles Atlas pose. He moved close to the mirror, stretched sensuous lips in an exaggerated smile to inspect his teeth. Satisfied with his perfection, he reached for the T-strap undershirt and freshly- ironed starched shirt Sophia had laid out for him.

Hmph. Couldn't even tell where Soph turned the collar.

He admired the way the white cotton dress shirt set off his summer-tanned face. Be nice if he had Old Phineas' gold watch and chain to wear, but he'd pawned the heirloom to buy seed corn that spring and didn't know when or if he'd ever be able to redeem it.

Pa'd have a fit if he knew.

* * *

Milking and chores were done early that evening so everyone could bathe and dress for the Moonlight Picnic. Sophia's chicken, fried before the day turned hot, hung in a large bucket deep in the cool well along with potato salad and sliced tomatoes. The three-layer devil's food cake, baked the previous night and topped with swirls of seven-minute icing, centered the kitchen table. The children were warned not to even *think* of running a finger around the base for a taste of frosting.

An air of anticipation filled the house. Upstairs, Anne had spent the previous hour taming Yahbut's wild curls and waving her own hair with a curling iron, suspended over the lighted coal oil lamp's chimney until its rod and clamp reached just the right heat. Still wearing only her cool white cotton slip, she helped Yahbut into a frilly blue pinafore, then admired her new peach-colored dress lying on the bed.

Her mother said peach was a good color for her. That it brought out the honey in her hair and set off her eyes. Anne wondered how her mother knew so much and could do almost anything. Despite all the garden work and canning, she'd found time to make both daughters new dresses from remnants salvaged at the Bridgeton Dress Factory.

A lump rose in Anne's throat. In less than two weeks she'd go to live with the Greenbergs in Bridgeton, where she would attend high school. She should be happy, but…

How will Mamma get along without me?

There was so much work to do and Yahbut was still too little to help. Anne would have six weeks off every summer when Mrs.

Greenberg took the boys to visit her parents in New York, so she'd at least be able to help with some of the canning. And Mamma *was* feeling better.

Now that it would never really be hers again, Anne couldn't believe she ever hated this room. Of course she'd be home at least part of each summer. And the one weekend a month she had off. Easter and Christmas, too. The Greenbergs had insisted on that. But from now on it would be Yahbut's room and she'd just be a visitor. It would never feel the same again.

But the Greenbergs had been really nice when Mamma and Daddy took her to meet them, even though the June heat wave was at its worst and Daddy was cross and not very friendly. And the little boys were sweet. Later, when Daddy said she could go if she wanted to, she'd started crying because she did but knew he didn't. Then Mamma started crying and even Daddy's eyes got wet. They'd all been half sad, half happy. And Daddy had called her Kitten again. He'd not done that since she started first grade. If she weren't careful she'd cry again.

She studied each picture and every piece of furniture in the room, lingering on the rag rug and imprinting it on her mind. The baby orioles must have felt scared, too, when it was time to leave their hanging cradle and learn to fly. Gosh, it was hard to grow up!

She swallowed, patted Yahbut's bottom, and reached for her little sister's hand-me-down polished white slippers. "Here, Yahbut. You can buckle your own shoes. I have to get ready, too."

* * *

In the boys' room down the hall, Billy talked his brother into taming his carroty cowlick. "See, Seth," he explained in his newly permanent baritone, "you got to part it just so, then comb the hair *around* that place. Here, put some of this Vaseline on it. Well, more than a dab. That's it. Rub it around now. Yeah, that's the way. Rub it in good then comb it the way I showed you. See?"

* * *

Sophia, on her way up from the basement where she'd been the last to bathe in the big tin tub, shook her damp curls and paused to listen to the excited voices floating down the back stairs.

The Moonlight Picnic, always held on the Thursday in August closest to the full moon, was the highlight of the farm community's summer. Crops had their final lay-by, most of the canning was done, and the neighbors were ready to socialize at the old clapboard church.

Phineas had been one of the church organizers in 1843. For almost eighty years the family, when they worshipped, worshipped there. Though no Macklins attended now, Will and the children were always warmly welcomed to the annual celebration. And the women, while not exactly friendly, were invariably polite to Sophia.

At least we'll have Bert and Molly to sit with...

Sophia worried, not for the first time, about her children caught between two different ways of life. Their Macklin forebears had been staunch Scotch Presbyterians yet, because of her, they attended the Catholic Church.

Instead of going to the small one-room schoolhouse with the country children, only a mile away, they were being educated twice as far from home in Macklin Corner. And she had to admit she'd been guiltily pleased in 1922 when the Catholic School closed and the school district boundary was redrawn at the southern edge of their property. Due to the large number of immigrant families, more teaching skills were required, and it was an open secret that the town school offered better educational opportunities. But because she had accepted her husband's rural roots, her children's ways were country, alien to those of their classmates.

They didn't really fit in anywhere. She worried again about how Anne would adapt to the Greenberg household, still another alien culture.

Remembering Dr. Tom's concern, she'd waited to talk to Will until, on a school day while Yahbut was napping and they were working alone in the garden, she'd taken the bull by the horns.

"Anne? Living with *Jews*? My God, Soph, you must be crazy!"

Clothilde's Lysol bigotry, subliminated in Will's brain since childhood, spewed from his mouth like poison. She'd stood horrified while he ranted on and on about Kikes and necromancers and worse names she'd never heard before.

Dr. Tom had been right...Will, of all people, roaring the hate he hated in his mother...

She'd waited while he purged his mind, then managed to keep her voice calm enough to ask if he had another way. He said he'd think about it.

She'd thought about it for weeks, from the first conversation with Dr. Tom through the beginning of the June heat wave. Through days darkened by clouds of topsoil from Kansas and Oklahoma. Through drought-fueled heat that climbed to over a hundred degrees, frazzling nerves, killing both people and horses. Through suffocating nights that sent Macklins outside to seek cool, restful sleep on palettes on the veranda. And as the drought worsened, tempers soared with the temperature.

The second week in June, the doctor had braved the dusty yellow clay ruts to drive out with the news that the family would like to meet them before Mrs. Greenberg left for New York. Despite Dr. Tom's enthusiasm, Will remained noncommittal. Then early the following Saturday, after the children left to pick blackberries before mid-day heat descended, they'd talked for over an hour at the kitchen table trying to find another solution.

"Look, Soph, I know I blew my stack in the garden that day and I'm sorry. Guess what I heard from Ma when I was little got stuck in my head, but right now I'm trying to be sensible about this. You know how people talk. And it's not just what they'll say about Anne, it's what they'll say about *all* of us. That family's probably a fine one or Doc wouldn't have gone out on a limb about this, but they're Jews and they don't fit in with people like us. And we don't fit in with them, either. Do you want people talking behind our backs? Making cracks about us? You just don't realize what a can of worms this will open."

"If you're talking about the farm people…"

"It's not just the farm people. It's the Macklin Corner people. The Bridgeton people. Your Catholic friends. I'd bet even your priest. Everyone we know. I'm telling you, it'll stick in their craws and they'll take it out on us. And I've not even mentioned Ma."

Sophia flared. "Well, *I'll* mention Ma. She acts like she hates everyone, but *especially* Catholics. Do you think I've forgotten what she did before we were married? And the Lysol after we bought the farm? She swore she'd never set foot on this place again and I guess she meant it. She's not been back here, even for a short visit, since we moved in. Will, she even acts like our *children* are pariahs. Did *you* think the way she does when you met me? You certainly didn't act like it, and if you did you got over it in a hurry!"

She paused to collect herself. "This isn't about us, Will. It's about Anne's education. It would be nice if we had the money to board her in Bridgeton, but we don't. Almost every cent we make goes for mortgage payments. And we're too poor to be proud. You stood up to your mother before, more than once. Surely you can do it again for Anne's sake. And together we can stand up to all the others, too."

Will slid his mug back and forth over a spilled-coffee ring on the battered table, mulling over Sophia's words. Finally…

"All right, Soph. If you and Anne are so set on her schooling, doesn't seem to be any other way. Since Doc thinks it's okay, I guess it won't hurt to see 'em, but *no* promises. Do you want me to talk to Anne?"

"Let's do it together, Will, when she gets back from the berry patch."

And now her first baby was leaving home and it was her fault. She brushed away the sudden tears that flooded her eyes and hurried to the bedroom to dress.

Will, still preening, adjusted the mirror to study her reflection. Curly tendrils of dark hair framed her flushed face. Her soft body strained against the clinging, damp robe. His reaction was immediate. The restriction Doc had put on their loving was getting harder and harder to live with.

Dammit! If Soph just wasn't such a good Catholic...

He averted his eyes and sidled out of the bedroom. "I'll pack up the food basket and get the kids together while you dress, Soph."

* * *

"You three older ones get in the back seat with the picnic basket...I know it's crowded but hold it on your laps...no, we can't put it in the trunk, too dirty back there...Yahbut will sit up front in the middle...no, Yahbut, you can't sit on your mother's lap, she has to hold the cake...there's no room in the back for you...you don't need to look out the window..." He thought longingly about the just-announced 1931 nine-passenger Peerless he'd seen pictured in one of the feed store magazines, so far the biggest luxury car ever built.

Will tipped his old straw boater forward to shield his eyes from the lowering sun, straightened his tie, and surveyed the carload of children. Anne pretty as a picture with her softly waved hair, wearing the new dress Soph made her. Copper-haired Billy, dark red peach fuzz shading his upper lip. Solemn, carrot-top Seth who looked so much like Pa he even had Pa's cowlick. Will's puzzled eyes rested on Seth. The boy looked different, hair slicked down, greasy, only a few strands of the cowlick standing.

Well, too late to do anything about it now.

His gaze moved to Yahbut with her dark hair rolled into fat banana curls.

Bet Anne did that. Good looking kids, all of 'em. But then why shouldn't they be? Look at their mother and father...

He turned away to hide his too-obvious pride, cleared his throat, spit and turned back. "Well, now, I'd say you all clean up pretty good."

Sophia, cool and beautiful in a white cotton dress sprigged with gentian blossoms, stepped off the back porch carrying the cake. Will moved to her side and with a courtly bow took the cake plate from her hands, escorted her to the front seat of the car, settled her in place, and handed the cake in. The children poked each other and giggled as Will went around the front of the car to get behind the wheel.

"We can take the road through the bottom tonight, ford the creek. That's the way we used to go. Creek's low again after that early July cloudburst that ended the drought. Road's good and dry, too, and the county grader's just been through so ruts won't be bad." Will grinned. "Now if I was Billy's age I'd ride Star over, spark the girls." He circled the driveway, shifted into low, and eased the Maxwell down the steep hill.

Yahbut wriggled between her parents, kicking the floor-mount gearshift rod with her feet. "Daddy, tell us about the Moonlight Picnic when *you* were little."

"I will if you'll stop being such a wiggle worm." Will glanced over his shoulder, saw the resigned backseat faces. "You kids think you can stand to hear it over? Remember, this is Yahbut's first Moonlight Picnic. Your mom was sick last year and she stayed home with Yahbut the year before." He bobbed his head to signify their forced agreement.

"Well, Honey, people used to go in buggies. Or wagons. That's how we'd have had to go then because we wouldn't all fit in a buggy.

"And your Great-Grampa Macklin's family went to the Picnic when there wasn't even a church there. One of your kissing-kin ancestors donated the land, and the ice cream social part was how they raised money to build the church. The whole neighborhood worked to get the grounds ready. Then early Thursday morning some of the men filled their wagons with straw and got the heaviest old quilts they could find. They drove to the Macklin Corner ice house, filled the wagons, and covered up the ice blocks with those quilts to try to keep it from melting."

Billy snickered and leaned forward to tug one of his little sister's curls. "And when it was hot the wagons did what *you* do when you wet the bed, Brat. All the way to the church."

Yahbut's expectant joy vanished. Her head drooped. Shame flooded her face.

"Billy!" Sophia reprimanded her son, balanced the cake with her right hand and slipped her left arm around her mortified daughter.

"Sooooory." A most unsorry Billy slumped in the seat and pointedly stared out the window.

"Well, Billy, that's about what happened except your little sister's *working* on *her* problem." Will cast a stern look over his shoulder at his recalcitrant son, then smiled at the little girl wedged between her parents. "Anyway, Honey, the men always managed to get enough ice to the grounds. 'Course, they all had to take their own ice cream freezers to use.

"By the time the men got there with the ice, the women had their cream, milk, eggs, vanilla and sugar ready. They'd pour that rich mix in the freezer cans while the men put the ice in gunny sacks and broke it up with sledge hammers. Then the men packed ice and salt around the cans and took turns at the handles till the ice cream froze."

"Just like we make it at home, Brat." Billy's loud whisper was ignored.

"But don't they still make it that way, Daddy?" Anne asked. "I mean, there's no electricity at the church, either."

"Pretty much, Anne, except they pick up the ice in Jim Willbourne's old farm truck now. It's a lot quicker. Easier, too."

Sophia chimed in. "And the night before or in the morning before they went to the church, each woman baked her best cake. Second-rate wouldn't do. They all tried to outshine the others." She glanced with pride at the cake balanced on her lap.

Seth licked his lips. "Bet none of 'em were ever as good as Mom's!"

"That's right. Never tasted a better cake than your mom makes." Will shifted into low, steered the car down the sloping roadbed, across the shallow creek, and up to the road on the other side.

Yahbut's face was thoughtful. "Who took care of the little kids while their mammas and daddies were making ice cream?"

"They locked 'em in a shed to keep 'em quiet, Brat!"

"That's *enough* Billy. If you didn't want to come you should have stayed home and let the rest of us enjoy ourselves." Will patted Yahbut's knee and continued. "Well, the children had to go along because everybody was at the church grounds getting ready and there wasn't anyone at home to take care of 'em, but they got to lick the ice cream paddles and play under the trees. The older kids helped the grownups or watched the little ones. In later years, after there'd been some burials, they'd walk around the graveyard and look at the tombstones and remember who was buried where.

"There's even a slave, a nigg…"

"Will!"

"Sorry, Soph. A *negro* nanny buried way off by herself in the northwest corner. Nobody *had* slaves in Illinois, you know…she belonged to a family passing through to Missouri when it was a slave state, back before the Civil War. Anyway, they camped by the stream in the grove across from the church to rest and water the oxen and she got sick with smallpox while they were there. When she died, they figured they were that close to a graveyard they'd just bury her there, but Harry Stone's grampa, one of the elders that lived close by, got wind of it.

"Caused quite a stir. The church folks didn't like slavery, but they didn't like nig…negroes much either. They called a big meeting, the preacher finally suggested maybe they could put her there if she wasn't close to the whites, and the elders agreed because they wanted the family gone. They figured if the nanny had the pox, the kids could get it next and pass it around the county and they'd have an epidemic on their hands."

"What happened to the family, Will?"

"Nobody knows, Soph. They headed on west and no one ever saw 'em again. They maybe all died with the pox, I guess. But they thought enough of that slave to plant a cedar tree to mark her grave. Tree's gone now so nobody's sure just where she is but you can bet no church member's ever been buried in that corner.

"You kids got a lot of ancestors in that old graveyard. Ought to look 'em up before it gets dark tonight."

Anne, seeing Billy's mouth open, jabbed her elbow in his ribs. Billy's mouth clamped shut.

Yahbut tugged at her father's sleeve. "The picnic, Daddy…"

"Well, after the work was done and the ice cream cans were packed in briny, ice-filled horse troughs to season, the troughs were covered with blankets to keep the cold in and the heat out. Then everybody went home to do their chores and get cleaned up before they went back for the evening.

"If they lived nearby they walked back, but some folks used to drive fifteen miles or more just to come to the Moonlight Picnic.

That was a long way to go in a buggy, but the moon was always bright so there wasn't any trouble getting home with the horses. They made it an all night party. Folks drove out from Bridgeton and Macklin Corner and even Walnut Hills. They'd all unpack and eat their picnic suppers and then buy ice cream and cake from the church ladies for dessert. The best cakes weren't cut. They saved *them* for the cakewalk. Pretty sure that's where your mom's cake will wind up tonight."

Yahbut gave a disappointed cry. "You mean we can't have any?"

Sophia stroked her hand. "That's all right, Honey. I'll bake one for us. One tree of peaches is almost ripe, too. If your dad and brothers will make peach ice cream, we'll have a special party at home before Anne starts to school."

A miasmic cloud settled over the passengers as the car turned into the churchyard. Seth's greasy cowlick spiked to full attention.

* * *

Will wiped cake crumbs from his mouth with a napkin and turned to Sophia. "Think I'll walk across the road to the grove, Soph. Have a smoke, visit with the men awhile. You kids help your mom get things packed away."

"Is Uncle Ben playing his fiddle tonight, Dad?" Seth asked.

"You know Uncle Ben always plays for the cakewalks. I'll be back by then, though. Just want to find out what's happening in the neighborhood." Will considered inviting Billy along, but decided against it. Besides, he'd noticed Billy eyeing the little Alexander girl earlier. He rose, straightened his tie, and sauntered off.

"Be careful, Will", Sophia called after him. She knew from experience that some of the men occasionally had a bottle in the bushes off the church grounds. Will flicked an irritated gesture over his shoulder and crossed the road to the grove.

* * *

Light from the full moon penetrated the oak leaves, highlighting the shadowed animosity on Harry Stone's face and the whiskey bottle in his hand.

"Trouble with you is you ain't satisfied if you're not runnin' the show, Will. Dammit, I don't care *what* you say. We need to get a vigilante committee together and burn out that hobo jungle under the trestle arch. You've had as much trouble with 'em as the rest of us. Prob'ly more since you're so close to the tracks. Only way we can keep 'em from bothering proper folks is to get rid of 'em. Let 'em know they're not welcome."

"Look, Harry, I already told you most of those bums are out-of-work men riding the rails out of the cities, trying to get back to the hills. They're from Kentucky and Tennessee and the Missouri Ozarks, been up north working the factories. Besides, we never had any bums or stealing trouble until the country got in this Depression. Yeah, we did have several ruckuses last fall. Lost a calf and a few chickens. But none of them have bothered us since."

Harry snorted in contempt. "Well, hell, that's because you and yer wife feed 'em. Guess you're still trying to feed them furriners in your grampa's town, too. Don't see how you can sleep nights with that rabble so close. Look's like you'd a'learned after that calf got rustled."

"I'm telling you, Harry, the bums don't bother us anymore. What they do is come up right after dinner and ask if we've got leftovers. And Soph always does. Matter of fact, lately she cooks enough so she'll *have* leftovers. She feels sorry for 'em. So do I. And yes, when we've got extra garden truck you *bet* I take it into Macklin Corner. Those folks are hungry and they don't have any money."

"Who *has* got money these days?"

"Nobody. But we've got food. Lots of it. And there's no market for it. Hell, Harry, I'd almost rather *give* it away than sell it for the prices we're getting now. They're decent people, most of 'em. So are the bums."

Harry passed the bottle to Bert. "That why you sleep with a loaded gun by the bed? Because you got decent bums?"

Will's eyes narrowed. "Didn't say I trusted 'em. With hunger gnawing their guts, humans get like animals. Wouldn't have a bum on the place longer than it takes 'em to eat. And when Billy and I are in the field, I make the dogs stay at the house with Soph and the kids. The bums all seem to know about the dogs. They must have some sort of communication system figured out. Anyway, they're scared of those dogs of mine."

Will's cousin Bert, seated on a stump, wiped the rim of the bottle with his hand, tilted it, swallowed, and passed the bottle up to Will, slouched against a tree. "So am I. When Molly and I come to visit we just don't get out of the car till somebody calls off the dogs. Where'd you get that big bluetick hound, Will? He looks like he'd tackle a tiger."

"Just wandered in one day a couple years ago. Hungry. Soph fed him. She's got a way with dogs. They all seem to like her and she can't stand to see anything go hungry. The dogs know it, too. They're loyal." Will grinned at Bert. "Soph calls Old Blue 'True Blue' when she doesn't think I can hear her." He tipped the bottle to his mouth, took a long pull and passed it on to Harry.

Harry Stone tilted the bottle back and forth and studied the pale liquid glinting in the moonlight. "Well, I guess when those thievin' bums steal all our livestock and rob our gardens we'll know where to eat, then."

Will's voice rose in anger. "Come on, Harry. You throw more good food into the slop bucket for your hogs than any of us. Here you are, one of the church elders. What about that Good Book of yours? Doesn't it say something about the brotherhood of man?"

"Why don't you darken the church doors some day and find out? Why, Will, your Ma'd be ashamed of you if she knew. You ain't been to church since you married that Catholic."

Will straightened. His eyes flashed. "Just what are you getting at?"

Harry backed away, ducked his head. "Nothin', Will. Forget I said that. Your wife's a fine-lookin' woman. She's just not like us."

"And a damn good thing I'd say, too! Harry, you best watch your tongue. And maybe if you'd spread some of that milk of human kindness you preach about all the time, you might not have so much trouble. You're a hypocrite, that's what you are!"

Bert stood to drape his arm around Will's tense shoulders and avert the escalating hostility between the distant cousins. "Think I hear Uncle Ben tuning up, Will. We better get back to the women. They'll be wondering about us. Come on, let's go now."

* * *

Sophia's eyes were apprehensive as Will and Bert entered the churchyard, talking in low tones. Molly, seated next to her, touched Sophia's hand. "He's all right, Soph."

Sophia acknowledged Molly's gesture with a grateful nod before turning to the approaching men. She forced a nervous smile. "Good, you two got back just in time for the cakewalk. Jenny's selling chances now. I'd better find Yahbut. I promised she could try to win our cake." Sophia hurried away.

* * *

Five of the finest cakes were displayed on a table by the church steps. Sophia watched Yahbut, right forefinger in her mouth, stand first on one foot then the other while she studied the cakes.

"Do you still want to take a chance on ours?"

"I don't know, Mamma. That one with the chocolate icing and walnuts on top looks awful good. If I win it will you still make yours for Anne's party?"

"Of course, Honey. But you have to decide which one you want to try for because the cakewalk's about to start and the chocolate one is first in line."

"Okay, the chocolate one, then. What do I do?"

"Well…see those big squares of cardboard over there in a circle, under that tree where the lanterns are hung? Each square has a number on it. You go pick out the number you want to start on and stand by it and I'll buy your ticket. While Uncle Ben warms up his fiddle, Mr. Stone will collect the tickets and then, when Uncle Ben plays, you all walk in a circle around the numbers. Be careful not to step on the squares because they have to last for all five cakewalks. When Uncle Ben stops playing, you stop walking behind the nearest square. That's when Mr. Stone will draw the winning number from that cigar box. If he draws yours, you'll win the cake." Yahbut's face glowed with anticipation. "You know, Honey, you probably won't win. There are twenty tickets sold for each cakewalk."

"I know, Mamma. But I guess I prob'ly will."

* * *

'O, Susanna', the first of the Stephen Foster medley favorites, leapt from the violin. Sophia joined Will, Bert and Molly at their table. Yahbut's siblings watched her curls bounce around and around the circle: Billy from a blanket spread on the grass, where he sat next to Geraldine Alexander; Seth with his friends at the entrance to the cemetery; Anne standing with a group of girls on the far side of the circle. Keeping perfect time with the music, Yahbut skipped and hopped from one number to the next.

"Look's like she's got your rhythm, Will," Molly whispered.

"With her looks you'll have to watch that one."

Will beamed. "I do believe you may be right, Molly."

The music stopped. Yahbut waited expectantly behind number fourteen. Harry Stone's voice rose over the hubbub. "Number seven. Number seven wins the chocolate cake with walnuts." Yahbut peered down to recheck the number in front of her. Her face puckered, her eyes searched for her mother. Sophia beckoned her daughter back to their table.

Will watched the despondent child join the adults and lean into the circle of her mother's comforting arms, then searched through his pockets. "Here's another dime, Yahbut. Let's try again." Father and daughter headed for the ticket table.

Yahbut pranced around the numbers three more times. Three winners, none of them Yahbut, claimed their prizes. Sophia's cake reigned in solitary splendor over the depleted table. Harry Stone picked it up, held it high in the air and stepped to the center of the cakewalk ring. "Come on, folks. This is the beauty you've waited for. Take a gander at *this* humdinger! Jenny, who baked it? Sophia Macklin!!!" His face froze. "Well…well…well, come on, get your tickets. Don't want Uncle Ben's fiddle to cool off."

Will stared at Harry for a long moment, then made his way to the ticket table, bought four tickets, and signaled all four Macklin children to take places for the final cakewalk. He gave Harry a dismissive nod, strolled back to the table, tapped Bert on the shoulder, sat next to Sophia, and rested his arm possessively across the back of her chair.

"Will, what on earth is going on?" Sophia hissed. "That's eighty cents on those cakewalks. We can't afford that. Our cake only cost about a nickel to make and that was for the flour and cocoa and sugar."

Will touched her lips with the tip of his forefinger. "Hush, Soph. Uncle Ben's getting ready to play." The fiddler broke into 'Camptown Races'. The final cakewalk began.

With each chorus, Uncle Ben's bow picked up speed, moving the tempo from sedate to lively. The bow raced from string to string, faster and faster, pushing the walkers into dizzying momentum. Led by the music the watchers clapped, sang and swayed. In mid-chorus, Uncle Ben thrust the bow high in the air, releasing the exhausted participants. The final note soared into the moonlight, free from the happy, panting churchyard celebrants and the cheering onlookers.

Harry Stone stepped to the center of the circle and drew a number from the cigar box. "And the winner of Sophia Macklin's cake is...........nuuumber twelve. Number twelve? Who's got number twelve? Looks like *Seth* Macklin."

Startled, Seth stared at the number by his feet. He whooped as, with a tight smile, Harry Stone moved to present Seth's mother's cake. "Can't get your ma to *bake* one for you, got to *win* it, eh, laddie?"

A bemused Seth stepped forward to shake hands and accept the cake while the exuberant crowd applauded. "Th...Thanks, Mr. Stone..." His face alight with a lopsided grin, he moved to where his father was collecting the other children at the edge of the breaking circle. Harry, hand out in a conciliatory gesture, approached Will. Will stared coldly at Harry, briefly accepted the proffered hand, and abruptly turned to his family. "Let's go."

Sophia, picnic basket on her arm, pulled her husband aside to whisper, "What on earth was that all about?"

Will tucked Sophia's hand into the crook of his right arm, appropriated the basket with his left hand, and grinned devilishly. "Just a comeuppance for Harry. Needed taken down a peg or two again. And Seth's winning was the icing on the cake...in more ways than one. Nothing to worry about." He winked triumphantly at Bert. "Let's go home and eat cake."

Chapter 8

Overwhelming quiet permeated the house on the bluff. A mid-morning thunder-and-lightning deluge racing in from the north-west had broken the month-long drought, laid the September dust that shrouded the land, drove the dogs to the protective veranda, and kept Sophia and her Monday wash from the clothesline.

A gentle shower lingered, soaking the thirsty land. Only the raindrops' patter and an occasional groan from the old house stirred the silence. Intermittently, Blue's left hind leg thumped rhythmically on the wooden veranda floor, drumming cadence as he scratched at an elusive flea.

Sophia hung her laundry in the basement, hoped it wouldn't mildew, and climbed the stairs to her spotless kitchen where she collected a rag to wipe flecks of yellow dust from the dining room and parlor furniture.

She paused at the mute radio, piled high with well-thumbed papers and dog-eared magazines from the feed store and the doctor's office. Everyone had been through them at least twice and they were ready for Yahbut to cut into squares for the outhouse. While not necessary, it gave Yahbut something to do, kept her quiet, and improved her manual skills. Besides, Sophia appreciated the nicety. She found the Sears and Roebuck catalogs that met the needs of their country neighbors—and many of the Macklin Corner families lacking indoor plumbing—offensive.

Still, better than the leaves Old Phineas used on his trips into the woods. Sophia's nose wrinkled in disgust.

Maybe I'd better count my blessings.

She longed for the rolls of paper they'd had in town. 'Waldorf Tissue, soft as old linen.' That nickel a roll seemed a fortune now.

When Seth invited his little sister to be his school guest for the day, he made her promise not to talk during class. Sophia was skeptical. Stemming Yahbut's prattle was akin to damming

Niagara Falls, but the silent house seemed to miss her chatter as much as her mother.

What on earth will I do next year when she starts to school?

"Yahbut's still too young for that two-mile walk," Will had said. "Maybe I'll drive the kids in, spend the day fishing at the lake, pick 'em up on the way home." He'd grinned at Sophia's sharp glance and dubious expression. "I said *fishing*, Soph. Besides, no point wasting gas, is there? You boys think you can rustle up some bait so I can catch a mess of fish for supper?"

While Will brushed cobwebs from his summer-idled fishing pole and tied it to the Maxwell, Billy dug red worms from the cured-manure pile and Seth searched for crickets under boards behind the barn. Sophia fixed the children's lunches, sliced extra home-cured ham for Will's sandwiches, waved goodbye to her family, cleaned up the kitchen, hung her laundry, dusted, and prepared to revel in solitude. Instead, she wandered through the empty rooms wondering what to do.

Pausing by the twin parlor doors that led to the veranda, she traced a finger over one of the etched-glass peacocks, wondering why Clothilde hadn't taken *those* treasures as well. She grimaced at the sudden imagined whiff of Lysol, then giggled at the conjured vision of Clothilde dragging the heavy doors down the shaded drive and up the muddy road.

Still laughing, she opened the screen door, stepped onto the veranda, sniffed the scrubbed air, and delighted in the rain-dappled trees and bushes. Her face tightened momentarily as her eyes shifted to the whorls of yellow mud smeared with chicken droppings that mottled the sidewalk. Leghorns were good layers but better flyers, impossible to keep in the chicken yard.

The porch swing swayed invitingly with the breeze. She dried a spot with her apron and settled back to enjoy the welcome rain. And from the heavy, moist air the shadow of a young Sophia, no older than Yahbut, moved into her mind.

Dewy evening walks to the lake with Papa...

Sophia's mother, by then disenchanted with Sergei Dubrovich's striking good looks and rolling Russian 'r', hadn't bothered to mask her growing disapproval of his struggling English. Sergei's retaliatory refusal to talk at home created an impasse. Sergei stopped trying to speak English, Mattie refused to learn Russian or allow their daughter to learn the foreign tongue. A pall hung over their kitchen, where meals were eaten in silence. But each evening when Hattie rose to clear the table, Sergei wrapped a fine-boned, callused hand around his daughter's and led her from the somber house.

And Papa becomes Papa...a tall, handsome man with dark curls, high Slavic cheekbones, eyes the color of an October sky, a deep voice and a booming laugh that makes me happy.

"Good evening," neighbors call.

"Good emis," Papa answers, his smile proud beneath the crisp mustache that tickles my nose when he kisses me goodnight.

At the lakeshore, Papa always spread his jacket for 'my Sophia, my liddle Rrrussian prrrincess'. Sophia had no need to understand the poorly translated Ukrainian fairy tales and folklore, the bits of family history he tried to give his daughter. She heard love in each mispronounced word and misconstructed sentence. Proper English wasn't necessary to describe the wildflowers she and Papa gathered in woodland dells.

Spring bluebells are best...soft, lavender buds blending into delicate shaded blue flowers...

Nor was translation needed for the Russian prayer he murmured over folded hands when he tucked her in each night. Elegant hands, out of place in the faraway mine that killed him.

Sophia was left with a cold, straitlaced English mother and memories of a father who, as a child, had ridden in *his* father's arms over vast Russian acres. Her father's words had been bitter. "Papa say, 'I marry wrong. Lose all this for you.'" The child was never to know what he meant or why her father fled his beloved Mother Russia.

Sophia's tears mingled with the sudden spate of windblown rain that dampened her face and shelved her memories. Old Blue, sensing his mistress's lingering sadness, dismissed the other dogs and moved to rest his sympathetic muzzle on her knee. As she scratched his ears, showers softened to drizzles, drizzles gave way to blue patches behind gray clouds. The emerging sun brought a cloak of steamy air.

The noon St. Louis Special whistled for the crossing a quarter-mile down and brought Sophia to her feet. Even if she did rehang the sheets and pillowcases outside, they'd never dry in time to make the beds. She gave Blue a final pat and went inside to raid the cedar chest.

A heady fragrance of dried lavender and cool cedar forests, a blend of beauty and strength, floated from the open chest. Will had laughed, but indulged her fancy when she planted the row of lavender at the edge of the vegetable garden. And in succeeding Aprils, he had been careful not to disturb it with the plow. Sophia suspected, though she knew he'd never admit it, that Will enjoyed the perfumed linens as much as she.

She rummaged through the chest.

Where are *those sheets?*

Her fingers brushed silk, uncovered a demure, aged-ivory nightgown buried beneath a stack of blankets. She drew it out, draped it against her body, and waltzed around the bedroom trilling a quavering Billie Burke imitation of 'She Was Only A Bird In A Gilded Cage'. As she twirled, she inspected her own cage. Comfortable, but more shabby than gilded.

Suddenly, in mid-note, she stopped. Remembered. The gown had been part of what her mother insisted on calling her trousseau.

It had fit then.

She drew it close, luxuriated in the sensuous fabric, then let it flow through her fingers to the floor in a shimmering stream of moonlit remembrance. Her eyes darkened, saw

Will's eyes...mirrors of wonder...

She heard his love-rough voice.

My God, Soph, I thought you'd be...cool...thought those nuns and priests tied you down so much it'd take forever to thaw you out but you...you're like...fireworks...

Remembered her murmured response.

Will...my stalwart hero...

For fifteen years, until her last pregnancy, passionate nights had more than compensated for drudgery days. Despite their present lack of money they ate well, lived comfortably, and looked forward to the time the land would be Will's, free and clear. They worked together, their children were healthy and, except for the endless ache left by the baby's death and Will's occasional bouts with the bottle, their marriage had been happy.

Then why was Will distant? Unresponsive?

She stared at her mirrored reflection. A rounded face stared back. High cheekbones, once chiseled, were blurring. A double chin threatened her firm jaw line. Contentment and rich food had added pounds to the lithe body of the girl who won Will's heart. And five pregnancies hadn't helped.

Does Will still love my body?

She studied padded shoulders and hips, sagging breasts, thickened waist. The years had been cruel.

Will, on the other hand, seemed to grow more handsome. Women's veiled appraisals followed wherever he went. Will noticed and knew she did, too. Delighted at her jealousy he laughed, swore his only interest lay in his 'pleasingly-plump Madonna'.

But it was over a month since Dr. Tom pronounced her healed. That same evening she'd waited until the children were asleep to bathe, wash her hair, dust her body with scented powder, and slip into the robe she'd sewn from another remnant. October blue, Will's favorite color. When she swayed enticingly through the parlor, Will raised and lowered his head in one fluid motion and glued his eyes to his book. In the bedroom, she brushed tight, damp curls into loose waves and returned to sit near Will. He yawned, said he was tired and went to bed. When she joined him to curve her body against his, he snored.

The stirring dogs on the veranda brought Sophia back to the present. Blue barked a welcome, but remained stationed just outside the parlor doors. The others raced toward the Maxwell.

Will must have been at the lake when the storm broke. He'll be soaked.

Sophia replaced the gown in the chest, found sheets, made the bed and laid out dry clothes for her husband.

* * *

Sophia kissed Will's cheek and touched his shirt. "You're dry! I thought you'd been caught in the storm."

"Never got to the lake. Dropped the kids off and ran into John Hall at the feed store. Did you know he's Democrat committeeman for Precinct Seven now?"

Sophia shrugged. "How would *I* know, Will? I depend on you for news and you've not been to town this summer except to deliver butter and eggs and take food in."

"Guess so. Seems like the only thing we do any more is get up, work, eat, and go to sleep. And nothing to show for it! That's what John and I were talking about."

"But aren't the Halls Republicans? They were when *we* lived in Macklin Corner."

"Seems like there's a lot of leopards trying to change their spots. Everybody seems pretty fed up with Hoover. He's sure not doing much of anything to help the country right now. Says the economy will come back by itself but it's getting worse every day.

"You see that Will Rogers column in one of those last papers from Doc's office? The one that said we can't worry about a balanced budget when we've got seven million hungry people out of work? Why Soph, some of those people in Macklin Corner are near starving to death, at least the ones who don't have a cow and a garden and some chickens. They're *trying* to help each other, but if push comes to shove they have to take care of their own first. The little bit I do is just a drop in the bucket to what they need. I doubt if most of 'em have had meat in the past year or so.

"Thing is, it's not just Macklin Corner or Kickapoo County. It's all over. Nobody knows what'll happen next. And I *voted* for Hoover, too."

"Well, it does look like you'd learn, Will, but you're the one who says you can't teach an old dog new tricks."

"Voted Republican since I could vote, but I'm beginning to think it may *be* time for a change. Anyway, I never did get to the lake. I'll just have to go back later and pick up the kids. Storm came up, so we sat around the feed store and talked. Surprised me. The other farmers hanging around there seemed to feel pretty much the same as John. Why Soph, Illinois country folk have voted Republican since Lincoln. Be interesting to see what next year's election brings. There's a new man the Democrats are talking about, New York's governor now. Guy named Roosevelt. Teddy's cousin."

Sophia raised an inquisitive eyebrow. "New?"

"Well, not new I guess. *You* seem to know about him. Anyway, he's been in politics a long time. Even ran for vice-president in 1920."

"I just know the name, Will. I was so busy with babies then all I can remember are diapers. But I do know the Roosevelts are Republicans—at least Teddy was—and they're all rich East Coast people."

"Yeah, but this one's different. Name's Franklin. He's a *Democrat,* and a cripple. John says he had infantile paralysis. Legs aren't much good. Uses a wheelchair. According to John, most folks don't know he's crippled because he sits behind a desk or supports himself on one of those speaker things when he gets his picture taken for the papers. Anyway, he says there's nothing wrong with Roosevelt's brain. See if you can find that Will Rogers paper before Yahbut cuts it up. I'd like to read it again. Like you to read it, too. If the Cherokee Kid can support Roosevelt, maybe I can, too. You eat yet?"

"No, I was going through the cedar chest for sheets. I had to hang the ones I washed in the basement and they won't be dry before bedtime. I was thinking about moving them outside just before you got home. Why? Weren't the sandwiches enough?"

"Well, I brought 'em back home. Thought we might share 'em, have a picnic in the orchard if it's not too wet, or sit in the swing, eat there. Can't remember the last time we had a day alone. Any of that last batch of root beer left?"

"I think so, but I've not checked lately. Look in the basement, north side shelves. Watch those sheets."

While Will felt his way down the dark stairs, Sophia hurried to the bedroom, stripped off her apron and brushed her hair. She exchanged a conspiratorial smile with the face in the mirror, opened her box of hoarded bath powder and puffed scent between her breasts.

* * *

The swing glided as lazily as the lethargic bees that buzzed around the orange trumpet vine flowers trailing up the nearby trellis. Will and Sophia sipped root beer, brushed away bothersome flies, and tossed crusts and bits of ham fat to the begging dogs. Hazy skeins of mist, fathered by the sunlight that flooded their world, drifted above the creek and bottomland below the bluff.

Sophia banished thoughts of mildew-threatened sheets and stroked Will's hand. "Will, do you still love me?"

"Of course I love you, Soph. I know I don't say it often enough, but I do. More than anything in the world." He raised his eyebrows in surprise. "I thought you *knew* that."

Blue eyes caught and held hazel eyes. "Then why don't you want to make love to me? Is it because I've gotten fat?"

"Fat! You're not fat, Soph, just pleasin…"

"…gly plump, I know, Will. But if it isn't that, what *is* it? I told you over a month ago that Dr. Tom released me."

Will turned away to hide a rush of emotion.

"Will?"

"Dammit, Soph! Just *looking* at you makes me want you. Almost went crazy the night you put that blue thing on. Thought I was going to loose control right there in the parlor." He swung to face her. "It's not because I don't want to. You know me better than that!"

"I thought I did, but now I'm not sure. What is it, then?"

Will's jaw tightened. "Look, Soph, do you think I already forgot about last January? I can't get that picture out of my mind. You lying there all tired and worn out. I was afraid you were going to die and you damn near did. Every time I think of you and me making love, that night comes back." He leaned forward, elbows on thighs, and buried his face in his hands. "Soph, I can't risk losing you. And you're hell-bent on me not using protection, so if we make love we may make a baby." He sat up straight, determined. "You can't go through that again. Neither can I. Doc said…"

"I know what Doc said. He said it to me, too. But he's old. We're *young*. Besides, I don't want some other woman thinking she can take you away from me." She stopped the swing with her foot, rose, and walked into the parlor. Will watched her hips sway across the veranda, heard her rummage through her mending basket. She returned, stood behind the swing, tapped his arm and handed him a clipping.

"*Birth control*, Soph? What'll your priest say about *that*?"

"I found it in one of Dr. Tom's old magazines. No, don't read it all, just skip down to here, where it talks about rhythm." She leaned across his shoulder to engulf him in fragrance as she led his eyes down the page with her finger. Startled and wary, Will glanced at the clipping. "I've been watching the calendar, too, and today's alrigh…"

"Why hell, Soph, that's been around forever."

Sophia's inviting mood vanished abruptly. She straightened, her face flushed with indignation. "Then why didn't you tell *me?* All this time…"

"Because you and your priest said *no* birth control. Besides you never want to talk to me about woman things. Hell, Soph, you don't even like me to talk about breeding the animals. Every time I'd think maybe we could talk about something like that you'd turn shy and shut me out. Anyway, it was never a problem before now. The kids came along about right and we've always been able to take care of 'em."

Blazing, Sophia snatched the paper from Will's hand. "Then you won't need *this.*" She wadded it into a ball and threw it across the veranda, further startling the already huddled dogs. "Will, I never wanted you to use those…those…*things,* but that article says the rhythm method is approved by the Church. And now you tell me you've known about fertile periods all these years we've been married?"

"Known about 'em all my life. Soph, I'm a farmer. How the hell do you think I breed the cows? Just send 'em off on a honeymoon when they look like they're bored? Anyway, I figured you knew *something* about it. Your mother…"

Sophia spoke through embarrassment. "Mamma never did talk to me much and certainly never about things like that. She was so…so controlled, so *English.* And when Papa was killed and we moved to Macklin Corner so she could work in the dress shop, she said she was too tired to talk at night, that I shouldn't bother her. She didn't tell me *anything,* Will. You know Mamma and I were never close. I think she resented me because I'm so much like Papa."

She raised her chin. "Anyway, after Papa was killed she said he'd meant me to be raised a strict Catholic, so she put me in the parochial school and turned me over to the nuns. And all the nuns told us was to remain chaste until marriage. Will I was *seventeen* before I knew the difference between chaste with a *t* and chased with a *d.*"

Will was incredulous. "But didn't you talk to the other girls?"

"The nuns said it was a sin to talk about…that. And when we got older one of the girls had to leave school because she was going to have a baby and the nuns got even stricter. They watched us *all* the time. We couldn't talk to each other! Will, how could you *expect* me to know anything about rhythm?"

"Hell, Soph, I knew you were innocent, but I didn't think you were dumb. Didn't you ever ask Doc?"

"Ask Doc? Are you crazy, Will? That would be like asking Father Riley! Oh, damn, I don't know who I'm more mad at, you or my mother or the nuns!" Her hands tightened on the back of the swing. Her fury concentrated in a violent forward push.

Will scrambled to his feet to avoid being pitched headlong from the swing and off the veranda. Eyes blazing to match Sophia's, he steadied himself against the nearest column, regained his balance, stalked toward his wife, grasped her shoulders, and shook her.

Sophia's anger evaporated in the shock of what she'd done. Her face paled. "I'm sorry…I didn't mean to…"

"Just hold on Soph-*ee*-ah." Will punctuated each syllable of her name with an additional jolt. "You've got no call to be mad at me. All these years I've tried to respect your wishes and *now* you blame *me*, try to dump me off the veranda and break my neck!"

"Will, you're hurting me!"

"Well, you damn near *killed* me." And then he saw the fear burgeoning in her eyes. Anger became consternation. "Oh God, Soph, I'm sorry." His hands relaxed, began to massage her bruised shoulders. Slowed. Caressed.

Passion, heightened by earlier anger, shimmered between them. Sophia moved slowly into the embrace of the man she loved, watched his pupils dilate into black pools of wanting. Soft gasps fluttered her lips. Mutual desire led the reunited pair inside. The blended fragrance of lavender and cedar, intensified by the heat of love, drifted through the silence of the house on the bluff.

Chapter 9

"While Yahb…Sarah's taking her nap, I'll get the Greenbergs some apples from the root cellar. And remember, I'm *first* in the tub this time."

Sophia lifted a peck basket from a pantry shelf. "Seth, be sure to put Skippy back in his cage when you're through playing with him. Put a piece of wood in the cage so he can sharpen his teeth, too. He's been trying to gnaw the window sills again." She paused to watch the feisty young squirrel scale Seth's right arm and wriggle inside his shirt. Skittery paws tickled bare ribs and sent Seth hopping and chortling around the kitchen table. From the safety of its improvised nest, the animal thrust its head above the vee of Seth's shirt and scolded Sophia, who in turn clapped her hands and laughed as the squirrel ducked out of sight.

Will had found the kit at the foot of a hickory tree in late August, dehydrated and near death.

Fell from the nest. Second litter, I guess. Just a baby…never make it on it's own.

Will bent to end it's suffering, but weak chatter from the tiny mouth stilled his hand. Shoe-button eyes defied the human's touch. "Spunky little devil, aren't you?" he muttered and lifted the furry bundle for closer inspection, then nestled it against his body to carry home to Seth.

Guided by Sophia, Seth had coaxed the kit to accept warm milk from an eyedropper. The baby moved into a long-dead canary's cage fetched from the attic, scrubbed with lye soap, and lined with an old flannel shirt past patching. A walnut meat became his pacifier and Seth his surrogate parent.

Sophia watched her younger son fish a cracked nut from his pocket and cradle his pet then, humming to herself, hurried out the door.

* * *

Saturday night was shopping night in Bridgeton. While the economic climate of 1931 was even worse than 1930, the last of the wheat money had paid the taxes and made the October mortgage payment. After the November payment money was set aside, enough was left to replenish staples like salt, flour, sugar and kerosene.

Sophia's shopping list included thread from the Dime Store. She hoped to find matching colors for the three almost-new wool skirts and the jacket Mrs. Greenberg had given Anne, gifts from her mother that Ruth Greenberg's added Midwest pounds made unwearable.

When Sophia had first inspected Anne's hand-me-downs, she'd marveled at the New York labels, the beautifully cut fine fabric, and envied the doctor's in-laws for still having money. Her envy quashed, she was preparing to alter them for her slender daughter. Still thinking about the clothes, she stopped on the back porch to watch Billy mope down the toilet path toward the house.

She frowned at the open Chick Sale door swinging on its hinges, started to scold, saw the boy's troubled face, and softened her voice. "Billy, you know I hate field mice," she called. Billy looked up, puzzled. "You left the door open." The boy grinned at his mother and retraced his steps to close the toilet door.

* * *

Sophia sorted through the apples, choosing the firmest and best for the Greenberg household, and thinking.

How different the children are. Seth and Anne both sensitive and tender...Yahbut straining for everything life offers...Billy so like his father, boisterous but hard for him to say what he thinks.

Poor Billy. With Anne gone he has no one to share his adolescent confusion.

"Need any help, Mom?" Billy stooped to enter the low-ceilinged root cellar.

"Bless you, Billy…you can help me fill this basket for the Greenbergs and then put it in the trunk of the Maxwell. We'll stop by to see Anne before we shop. If she's not too busy maybe she can come with us, or at least visit a bit. Oh, not those Winesaps, they're still too tart. No, the Ben Davis need to mellow. Use these Jonathans, they're best right now. And if you find any with spots or wormholes put them in that pan. I'll cut the bad places out and make pies tomorrow."

"You miss Anne, Mom?"

"Of course, Billy." Sophia's hand covered her son's. "You miss her, too, I know. And she misses us. But it's a wonderful opportunity and the Greenbergs have gone out of their way to be kind."

"Yeah. Anne told me she likes 'em. 'Specially the kids."

Mother and son worked side by side. A companionable silence filled the root cellar until…

"Mom, are Kikes the same as Jews?"

Sophia's lighthearted mood vanished in an unguarded explosion of anger. "*WHERE! DID! YOU! HEAR! THAT! WORD!"*

Shocked, Billy jumped back. "At…at school," he stammered. "But even Joe was talkin' about it in the field last Saturday."

"*Uncle Bert's* Joe?"

"Y…yes." Billy watched his mother warily.

Sophia's voice was icy. "And just what 'it' was he '*talkin'* about?*"*

"…I…well…what he said was some of his friends at Bridgeton High were laughin'…laugh*ing*…about Anne being a Catholic and living with Kikes." He examined his mother's face, dropped his eyes and added, "And the guys at school say Kikes are different from us. That they cut little boys tails off and kill babies."

So Will was right after all. And Joe had *gone back to school. All this could have been avoided…*

Sophia pounded clenched fists on the packed-clay storage shelf. "Damn! *Damn! DAMN!"*

Billy had never heard his mother swear. His eyes darkened with apprehension. "But Mom…but the Greenbergs sound real nice. What's different about 'em?"

Sophia's voice dropped to a ragged whisper. "They *are* nice, Billy. Just give me a minute." She gulped air into her lungs, exhaled slowly to still her roiling mind.

…shadows hiding behind trees...pelting rocks…run Russian run…dirty Catholic…Papist…the smell of Lysol…prejudice…

"I guess we should have expected it." She forced deep, even breaths. "I'm sorry, Billy. I shouldn't have exploded like that, but those people make me so angry. What those boys said is called prejudice. I suppose the Macklin Corner boys' parents brought it from the Old Country and passed it along. The farm boys? I don't know *where* that comes from. Ignorance, I suspect, and ignorance is hard to fight."

The frown lines between her eyebrows deepened. "I felt funny about Jews, too, but I think I'm getting over it. You know my father came from Russia and I guess his prejudice came with him. He talked about the Czar's pogroms when Cossacks killed whole villages of Jews. When he was little, he was told Jews drank Christian blood to make them look like Christians. And that the Jews caused the Black Plague in the Middle Ages by poisoning wells. But I found out *none* of that was true and what a terrible thing prejudice is. Still, I guess some of his feeling rubbed off on me. And I feel so *guilty* about it. That's probably why I blew up like I did. The Greenbergs have been wonderful to Anne.

"The difference? I guess it's because Jews think Jesus was just a prophet instead of the Son of God. That makes a lot of Christians angry. And some priests *still* say the Jews killed Christ. I've never understood that because Jesus *was* a Jew."

"The guys say the Jews caused the Depression, too. That they took all the money for themselves and don't care about folks like us who have to work for a living."

"Use your head, Billy. You read the old papers and magazines your dad brings home, don't you? Well, who owns most of the big stores and businesses and factories? People like the Vanderbilts and Astors and Carnegie. And the men who own the Macklin Corner mine certainly aren't Jews. From what I've read, there were far more greedy Gentiles involved in the Wall Street Crash than Jews."

"What're Gentiles?"

"Christians like us, who think Jesus *is* the Son of God. People who aren't Jewish."

"But I thought we were Catholics?"

"We are, but all Catholics are Gentiles."

"Presbyterians, too?"

"Yes, Presbyterians, too, and Lutherans and Methodists and Baptists and Episcopalians—all the Christian religions. Anyway, except for the Kahns who own the shoe store in Bridgeton and now the Greenbergs, there aren't any Jews around here. Those boys don't have any idea what they're talking about."

"But it makes me mad when they tease me and when they talk about Anne, Mom. And it's not just a few of 'em. Almost everybody says it."

"Not everybody, Billy. Only stupid numbskulls who don't know any better." Her eyes widened. She clasped her hand over her mouth. "Good heavens, I sound just like them. Maybe now I'm getting prejudiced against prejudice..."

She picked up an apple, turned it over and over in her hands. "Billy, I wish I could help you understand. What I *do* know is hate is terrible, that it poisons peoples' minds. And prejudice is hate. Maybe people can't hate what they can't see, what they can't do anything about, like this Depression, so they hate what's different." She hesitated. "You know, Billy, there are people your father grew up with who are prejudiced against me because I'm Catholic. They call me a mackerel-snapper because I won't eat meat on Fridays or Holy Days and say I worship the Pope and the Virgin Mary instead of God."

"You mean like Gramma Clothilde and Mr. Stone?"

Sophia wondered what Billy had overheard, but plunged ahead. "Yes, like them. But they aren't the only ones. Lots of people call other people names."

"Yeah. The kids in Macklin Corner call the country folks hicks and clodhoppers and…" he lowered his eyes "…and shit-kickers. And the kids in the country call the Macklin Corner people that used to work in the mine Wops and Dagos and Hunkies."

"What do they call *you*?"

"They don't know *what* to call me 'cause they don't know what I am. Sometimes I don't know what I am, either. They just call me Billy. And sometimes Bill. I kinda like that." He hoisted the filled basket to his shoulder.

"That's who you are. My wonderful Billy, my growing-up Bill." She reached deep in the apple bin, selected a crisp Northern Spy, polished it with her apron, and slipped it into his pocket. "That basket's pretty full, don't let any roll off. Thank you, Billy. Bill." She stood on tiptoe to kiss her gangly son's cheek.

* * *

"Your mom says you boys are splurging tonight, going to the picture show." Will's voice vibrated with the Maxwell over the corrugated road leading to Route 127.

"Yeah, Dad." Seth sat forward on the back seat. "There's a new Tom Mix movie." He folded his hand into a fist, extended his forefinger and pointed it at Billy. "Reach for the sky! Remember,

Straight Shooters always win!"

Billy ignored his brother. "Show starts at seven, Dad. It was six when we left home and we still have to stop by to see Anne."

"Hold your horses, Billy. I'm going as fast as I can over these washboard ruts. Just be glad it's not raining or we'd be axle-deep in mud. Be nice when the county gets some money so the crews can spread more gravel and buy it from us. We could sure use the cash. Breaks my heart to think of that pit just sitting there durn near idle. We'll be at the slab soon. What's the matter with you, Yahb…Sarah? Cat got your tongue?" Will was having a hard time using his younger daughter's given name, but Sophia said that since she was starting to school next year Yahbut shouldn't tag along.

Sarah, alias Yahbut, sulked in the front seat between Will and Sophia. "Mamma says I can't go to the show with Billy and Seth."

Her mother stroked the girl's hand. "I told you, Sarah, you're too little. Besides, the show costs a dime. Billy…Bill and Seth sold blackberries last summer for spending money. When you're older you can pick blackberries and sell them, too. Tonight you go shopping with me." Sophia teased her voice and smiled. "I have to go to the Dime Store."

Sarah's pout vanished. She loved the Dime Store with aisle after aisle of interesting things to inspect, the candy cases just inside the door, the basement where beautiful dolls and funny toys filled the counters. "Can we go look at the toys, Mamma?"

"If we have time, Honey."

Will stopped the car at the main road junction, turned off the headlights, checked south over the hill for the beams of oncoming cars, switched the lights back on, shifted into low, and drove onto the paved highway leading to Bridgeton.

* * *

Will rang the doorbell of the unpretentious two-story frame home. Hands in his pockets, he whistled tunelessly and surveyed the house while he waited. He rubbed his chin speculatively.

Not much of a place for a doctor, but guess he's just getting started. Anyway, Anne's finally got a room of her own, but ours is twice the size of...

"Daddy! I didn't know you were coming to town tonight."

Will scooped his daughter into his arms, gave her a bear hug, and held her at arms length. "You get prettier every time I see you, Kitten."

Anne blushed. "You always say that, Daddy. Wish it was…were…true. Is Mamma with you?"

"She's in the car with the kids. We need some things from town, but the weather's been so good I've been shucking corn all week, so we decided to come in Saturday night and stop to see you. Brought a basket of apples…Jonathans, I think, plenty for everyone. Maybe you can come along with us tonight if it's all right with the Greenbergs?"

Anne's delight faded. "Ohhhh, Daddy, I'd like to. It would be such fun to be with you all again, but the Greenbergs aren't here. I have to stay with the boys. Oh, heck. Well, come in for a minute, anyway. Little Josh and Levi are just finishing their supper in the kitchen." Apology tinged her voice. "I'm afraid they're sort of dirty because they've been playing in the leaves, but I'll bathe them before I put them to bed." She stepped around her father, waved, and ran down the sidewalk to her family.

* * *

Cars lined the county seat's Main Street. Sophia glanced up and down the business district. There seemed to be more people in town than usual, even for Saturday night.

Will had loaded groceries in the car and driven to the new feed store for a block of salt while Sophia and Sarah walked to the Dime Store. They found the right thread, inspected all the displays and toys, then window-shopped along Main Street searching for the Maxwell. She eyed the rowdy loiterers in front of the pool hall, steered Sarah across the street to avoid the men's rude stares, and held the little girl's hand tightly as they wound through the crowd to the movie house. Everyone was to meet there at nine when the first show let out. The clock in the ticket window showed half past eight.

"I'm tired, Mamma. I want to sit in the car to wait. Where's Daddy?"

"He'll be here soon, Sarah, just be patie..."

Drums thumped in the distance.

"A parade, Mamma!" Sarah pulled away from her mother's hand and dashed between parked cars to the street. "Look, Mamma, Halloween ghosts. And they're carrying fire."

Sophia rushed to her daughter's side and stared south. Thump-thump-BOOM. The noise reverberated from building to building. White-robed figures with red KKK letters over their hearts filled the street, marching in measured cadence behind the bass drums. Sandwiched between rows of torch bearers, sheeted men clutched bouquets of small American flags.

Conversation died as the marchers approached. Sarah's voice rang out in the quiet. "Mamma, they're wearing dunce caps."

"Hush, Sarah." Sophia's restraining hand clamped Sarah's shoulder.

"And hankies over their faces. And there's red around their eye and mouth holes..."

Flag carriers broke rank, distributing red, white and blue banners to watchers along the way. Sarah started forward. Sophia's grip tightened. A Klansman veered to place a flag in Sarah's outstretched hand.

"Mamma, you're hurting my shoulder!"

"Don't touch that flag, Sarah. They've dirtied it."

"Yah, but..."

The pressure increased. Sarah's enthusiasm ebbed. Baleful eyes glittered through slits in the cloth covering the face raised to Sophia's.

The eyes...angry...familiar...

The figure shrugged contemptuously and rejoined the marchers.

Thump-thump-BOOM. The procession reached the Kickapoo County Courthouse lawn. The drums stopped. A few people straggled north to join the rally.

Sophia started as a strong hand grasped her elbow. A deep, gruff voice cut through the crowd noise. "What're you doing in town tonight, Soph? You've got no business here."

"Hi, Dr. Tom," Sarah piped. "Did you see the parade?" The doctor smiled. "Sure did, Yahbut." His face became stern as it swung back to Sophia. "Now what are you doing here? And where's Will?"

"We didn't know anything about a Klan rally. We just needed supplies and came to town. We took some apples by Greenbergs, saw Anne for a minute and Billy...I guess he's Bill now, he's growing up, too...anyway *Bill* and Seth went to the show while we shopped. Thank heavens they weren't here for that demonstration."

"Stop blathering, Soph. I asked you, where's Will?"

"At the new feed store, getting a salt block. He should be here any minute. We were all to meet near the ticket window at nine. Sarah and I looked for the car, but I don't suppose Will could find a Main Street parking place with all these people in town. He's probably parked on one of the back streets."

Furrows creased the doctor's forehead. He fingered the chain draped across his vest, tugged on the ring of a large gold watch and pulled it from his fob pocket. "It's five till now. If he gets here soon there'll still be time."

"Time? Time for what?"

The doctor scrutinized the crowd, lowered his voice and leaned close. "Listen, Soph. That was more than a Klan parade. That bunch is up to no good. I just found out they're planning to burn a cross on the Greenberg lawn tonight. Soon as that rally's over, they'll march back down Main Street and head there. Don't have a cross with 'em, so they must've stashed it somewhere along the way."

Sophia blanched and drew Sarah close. "Dr. Tom, Greenbergs aren't home. Anne's there alone with the boys…"

"Easy, Soph. Will should be here soon. We'll take care of it. No harm will come to Anne." He raised his right hand shoulder-high, palm outward. "Solemn promise." The doctor stretched to his full height, craned his neck to peer over the heads of the people crowding the sidewalk waiting for the second show. He scanned the street, saw a tall figure break through the group of men in front of the pool hall and bolt toward the theater. "Will! Will Macklin! Over here, quick!"

Will elbowed his way to the small group by the ticket window. "Just heard, Doc. You okay, Soph?"

"I'm fine, Will, but Anne…"

"I know. I'm headed there now. You wait here for the boys then take all the kids to the car and lock the doors. It's down that side street. I'll be back for you when this is over. Coming, Doc?"

"Of course I'm coming. Looks like a big part of this might be my fault."

Sophia's voice broke. "I want to go to Anne, Will."

"Someone has to be with the boys and Sarah. Besides, it'll be safer for you all uptown. Their devilment's planned away from any crowd." His voice hardened to forestall her protests. "Soph, you'd just be in the way."

The doctor interrupted. "He's right, Soph. You and the kids

will be safer here. Come on, Will. My car's parked behind the show. We can get out quick. I've already called the police. Let's get going before that rabble comes back down the street."

* * *

The doctor turned off the lights, glided his Ford into the alley behind the Greenberg home and parked in a secluded area at the far end. "According to Chief Crawford, this was just supposed to be a Main Street parade. Looks like your old nemesis Harry Stone's behind it, too. Since the Black Knights went after the Klan again, Harry could only get five or six locals so he called Springfield to send men down. And that Springfield Klavern is always ready to pack up their drums and march. The head of the Klan up there knew Crawford used to be a member so he called him, checked Stone out, assured the chief there wouldn't be any trouble, and asked him to lay off.

"Crawford gave me a song and dance about a raid on a blind pig tonight, probably Lizzie's, and the law's known all along she was running a bootleg bar in her house. Guess Crawford set the raid up to be in the clear with the City Council. At least that's what I *think* he did. What he *said* was Springfield assured him it would be peaceful so he's going ahead with the raid. Seemed surprised about the cross burning, though. Promised to stop by here after the raid. We'll see if he shows up or not.

"Since the Supreme Court declared the Klan 'undesirable' in 1928, the imports'll have their orders not to cause a disturbance. Up there they call it a lodge now, trying to sound respectable, and *they* won't want any part of a cross burning so I think we can bluff 'em out. They shouldn't be a problem, and if we handle it right we can take care of Harry and his cronies. I'd sure hate to be in Harry's shoes, though, when Springfield finds out about *this*.

"As far as that cross is concerned, seems to me the best thing to do is keep it as quiet as possible, not let Stone and his stragglers get the publicity they want to stir things up around here again. Both papers *will* have to report the rally, but Amos and Ezra hate the Klan and what it stands for as much as just about everyone else. I'll have a word with the editors about keeping the Greenbergs' name out of it. Word will probably leak out about the cross, bound to be a few rumors, but rumors aren't news.

"Probably be better for all concerned if we don't say anything about what I just told you. Could cause a tempest in a teapot, play right into Harry Stone's hands, bring some leaners his way. Better to ignore 'em like the no-accounts they are. Wouldn't even tell Soph what she doesn't already know if I were you, especially about Stone. Just give her something else to stew about and she doesn't need that. Wasn't time to get the Knights together, but with the Klansmen parading they probably won't be armed so here's what I think we better do…"

* * *

The men eased the closing-door thuds and walked the remaining half block in silence. Will slipped the latched alley gate quietly open and shut and the two moved along the path to the front of the house. Only the faint rustle of dead leaves disturbed the moonless night.

Dim light from a hall sconce lit the downstairs windows. Will looked up. All but one of the second story panes were dark. In a back bedroom, a halo of light surrounded a figure studying at a desk.

The neighborhood was late-night still. Lights shown from surrounding houses. Several doors down, a lone street lamp cast a pool of light on the boulevard. Will stepped onto the porch, rang the doorbell and waited impatiently. Through narrow, lace-covered windows on either side of the door he watched Anne, cautious but not frightened, tiptoe down the stairs.

Good head on her shoulders.

The porch light snapped on. Anne pulled a window curtain aside, peeked out, unlocked and opened the door. "Daddy!" she bubbled. "You came ba…"

"Turn the porch light off, Anne. NOW!"

Her fingers fumbled for the switch. Darkness reclaimed the porch.

"Daddy, what is it? Did something happen to Mamma? What's wrong?"

"Come out on the porch, Kitten, close the door. Doc's here, too. We have to talk to you." Will led the way to a deeply shadowed corner, away from the street lamp and prying eyes. "Everyone's okay, Anne. Now what time are the Greenbergs due home?"

"I don't know for sure. They took the train to St. Louis yesterday afternoon so they could celebrate Friday Seder with friends, then stayed over. Saturday's the Jewish Sabbath, you know. They should be back on the eleven…"

The doctor interrupted. "They drive their car to the station?"

"Of course, Dr. Tom. They couldn't *walk* there. It's almost a mile and they had suitcases and Mrs. Greenberg was wearing high heels."

The doctor leaned from the porch to peer down the driveway toward the garage. "It's all right, Will. The door's closed. They'll think Joshua's home and the car's put away for the night. That's good."

"Daddy, what's *happening*?"

Will put his arm around the bewildered girl, drew her close. "Kitten, do you know what the Ku Klux Klan is?"

"We studied about it. But that was after the Civil War, during Reconstruction. People dressed up in sheets and tried to scare the freed Negroes and the ones who helped them. But the book said the Klan disbanded..."

The doctor snorted. "Outdated history books again. Well, guess some folks might think that, Anne, but there are still a few members around. And they use the same scare tactics on whoever they please, usually people with a different way of life than theirs. Now Anne, the Greenbergs are different. They're Jewish."

Anne shivered. "Do you mean the Klan's coming *here?"*

Will held his daughter. "Looks like it, Kitten. They'll probably be here soon, too. Doc and I'll stay out here and wait for them. There's no time to get you and the boys out of the house, so you best go on back upstairs. Don't wake the boys, no point in that, but lock all the doors, leave the hall lamp on like it is, turn off your study lamp, and stay away from the windows."

Torches flickered in the distant darkness. "Go on, Anne. Upstairs. When this is over you can get your things together while I head back uptown, get your mom and the other kids, and we'll take you home as quick as the Greenbergs are back." He guided her into the house and closed the door behind her.

* * *

Raised torches highlighted conical hats, streaked snowy robes with angry splotches of orange and yellow. As the marchers advanced, extinguishing house lights created an ongoing tunnel of curious darkness. Only the street lamp's feeble glow rivaled the rows of fire. A figure disengaged from the throng to arc a stone toward the boulevard lamp. The sound of breaking glass shattered the eerie quiet. Torches took over the night and flared in triumph as thirty marchers formed a crescent in front of the Greenberg house. Two men, carrying a kerosene-soaked pine cross, emerged from the darkness and stepped into the crescent's center. At the sight of the cross, unrest rippled along the outer wings of the semi-circle.

A tall, heavy figure with a prominent paunch moved from the shadowed porch into the flickering torchlight.

"Jesus, it's Doc." "Doc Campbell." "What the hell's he doing here?" Agitated whispers rippled through the core of the ghostly phalanx.

"You boys celebrating Halloween? Little early, aren't you? Believe my calendar says it's still a week or so off."

A tall, paunchless figure stepped to the doctor's side. One hand was thrust deep in his jacket pocket.

"Howdy, boys. Out playing trick or treat?"

The same cloaked men buzzed like angry bees. "...and Will Macklin!" "...got wind of this?" "...do now?"

The doctor's voice boomed. "Why, we're gonna talk, unless you boys are paying a social call to welcome the new doctor to town. Mighty glad he's here, aren't you? Always good to have a doctor on hand in case someone gets hurt...or shot." He nodded toward Will, whose extended finger moved in his pocket. "Too bad Dr. Greenberg's not here right now to welcome you. He and the missus are out of town. Kinda spoils your little surprise party, doesn't it? Say, you boys really plan to burn that cross? Terrible waste of coal oil!"

A voice twanged from the center of the faceless mob. "Not burn it, Doc, we're fixin' to *light* it. You best think about the difference. And you could be in for a heap uh hurt if you don't stay out of it. You know this ain't none uh your bizness. It don't concern you."

"Whatever happens here concerns me. Concerns us all. Now you boys may think we don't know you because we can't see your faces behind those silly masks, but I know some of you by your voices. Tell you what, if I'd not been on hand when your mamma birthed *you*, Robert Maxwell, you wouldn't be traipsing around here tonight. See, we all kind of depend on each other.

"Thing is, I'm getting a little long in the tooth. Been thinking of closing my office, so we need another doctor to help take care of folks. Ever think what might happen to you without doctors? And your kids! Little Jamie McPherson would've died with pneumonia if it hadn't been for Doc Brown. Harry Stone's boy'd have a crooked leg if Doc Graham hadn't been on hand to set that multiple fracture he got when he fell out of the sugar pear tree."

He named other cases, each chosen for impact. One coned head after another bowed. Feet shuffled. The doctor continued, "And I probably helped a few of you into this world. But all us doctors are getting older, and younger men won't take kindly to a community that's not hospitable to newcomers. Why don't you go on home now before Chief Crawford gets here? Yeah, I called him…told him about the cross, too. Should be here any minute now." Hooded men at the periphery began to extinguish their torches, remove their robes and fade into the night. He watched speculatively, waiting until only the center klansmen remained in an undecided huddle. "Now you five better get on home, think about things. Oh, and don't forget that cross. Make mighty good kindling. Don't think you want it around anyway when Crawford gets here or you *could* be doing time in the Kickapoo County Jail."

The doctor returned to the porch, sat on the top step, motioned Will to join him, and pulled two cigars from his breast pocket. He searched for and retrieved a silver pen knife, leisurely clipped the cigars' ends, handed one to Will, lit both with a kitchen match, and looked up in surprise. "You boys still here? Best get on home now…looks like rain."

The remaining torches were extinguished. The final robed figures, carrying the kerosene-soaked cross, retreated into darkness. One by one, neighborhood lights blinked on. Will and the doctor sat on the quiet porch watching the silent street. Will coughed and stubbed out his cigar. "Dammit, Doc, I don't even *like* cigars."

"I know that, Will. Takes practice."

* * *

Doc had been adamant. "Listen Will, I *won't* drive that bucket of bolts of yours. You take my Ford back up, leave it there and bring Soph and the other kids back here in your car. I'll stay with Anne and wait for the Greenbergs, then you can drive me back for mine. Uh…unless you expect me to walk up after it?" Will studied the doctor's considerable girth and held out his hand for the keys to the Ford.

* * *

No further disturbance marred the night. Sarah and Seth slept in the Greenbergs' living room, Sarah stretched out on the sofa and Seth curled in an easy chair. Bill drowsed over a magazine. Dr. and Mrs. Greenberg, Dr. Campbell, Anne and her parents sat around the kitchen table. The Greenbergs had returned a little after eleven.

Dr. Campbell's voice rumbled softly. "Probably never heard much about the Klan in New York, Joshua. Started up in Tennessee right after the Civil War to keep negroes from voting and drive out the carpetbaggers. Disbanded, at least officially, in 1869. Then that 1915 D. W. Griffith movie BIRTH OF A NATION glorified it, got the people worried about immigrants stirred up and the Klan started all over again. Griffith made some good movies, but he sure started a ruckus with that one.

"About 1924, Columbus Day I think it was, they had a big rally up in Springfield to stop immigration. Even had the National Imperial Wizard there from Atlanta, Georgia—Dr. H. W. Evans. Made me ashamed. A *doctor* preaching white, protestant, Native American supremacy, too dumb to know Indians are the only *real* Native Americans."

Will interrupted. "Get off the soap box, Doc. We don't need a history lesson."

"Well, now, after tonight maybe we do. They make me so damn mad. Most Klan members are uneducated, narrow-minded bigots who think violence is the answer to everything, but the *big* problem is those smart manipulators who exploit the ignorant. *They* know better. They just want *power*!

"Only about five members left around here now. According to Chief Crawford, the rest of those men were out-of-towners. He stopped by just before you got back with Soph and the kids, said *they* won't here again. I can't think there'll be any more trouble."

He turned to the young doctor. "Don't make any decision now. At least sleep on it. I'll be mighty surprised if the town itself doesn't see that's the end of Klan demonstrations. Fine folks live here and I believe they'd like you to stay. I know I would, but it's up to you."

"It's not just me, Tom. Personally, I'd like to face them down, but I have to think of Ruth and the boys. Her parents were upset enough when I brought them to Illinois. They were sure we'd all be scalped by Indians or eaten by wolves. When they hear about this, I don't know *what* they'll say. Ruth?"

"I don't know either, Josh. And after tonight I don't know what to think about Bridgeton myself. The women I've met so far have been pleasant, not really friendly, but that could be my fault. Until Anne came I was busy with the boys and didn't socialize much." She turned to Sophia and Will. "Do you *really* have to take her home now? She's become part of our family and the boys adore her."

"Well now, Mrs. Greenberg, we're as concerned about our daughter as your husband is about you and his sons. It's just luck I happened in town tonight." A rueful grin stole over Will's face. "Glad those good ole boys never called my bluff. They ever find out all I had in my pocket was my hand don't know *what* they might do. And you know, Mrs. Greenberg, Anne could be a big part of your problem. Good ole boys aren't all that crazy about

Catholics, either." Will saw Sophia's startled glance. His eyes apologized.

While talk continued, Sophia studied her daughter's dejected face. Finally… "Don't you think we should ask Anne what *she* wants to do, Will? After all, she's almost fifteen."

"Why, she's coming home with us tonight. She knows that."

Anne's eyelids clenched to hold back tears of disappointment. She rejected images of bed-warm early morning toes recoiling from freezing floors, racing trips to the outhouse, cold water splashing from bucket to wash basin, the pig-slop pail hidden behind the stove, the endless battle against the yellow dust or mud that each season rode boots and field shoes into the kitchen, the hundreds of drudgeries that made her mother's life so hard. Determined to escape that life, she opened her eyes, knuckled away her tears and faced her father.

"Daddy, I know you're worried about me. And I know you and Mamma love me. I love you, too. *All* of you. But I like it here. I like the Greenbergs and I want to go to school. Dr. Tom says there shouldn't be any more trouble. Daddy, I want to stay, at least until the Greenbergs decide what they're going to do."

Will stared at Anne. "You're sure, Kitten? Sure you won't be afraid?"

Anne knuckled back fresh tears. "Daddy, do you *really* want us to give in to those awful men? I may be scared, Daddy, but I'm not a coward. I'm sure!"

Unwittingly, Anne had played her trump card against her father. Chagrined, Will studied his daughter's face, pondered the situation. Macklin determination stamped her still-childish features. He nodded slowly.

No, she's not a coward. Sure braver than me when I was that age. Hell, when I was even older *than she is now.*

He slid his chair back from the table and stood. "Well, Soph, looks like our brave little girl's planning to stay." His eyes misted as he swallowed the lump in his throat. "Guess we better bundle up the other kids and take 'em home. That squirrel of Seth's will be missing him."

* * *

The Macklins, accommodating their passenger's bulk, drove toward town to retrieve the doctor's stranded Ford. Near the business district, Will glided the old Maxwell to a stop, turned off the headlamps, touched his forefinger to his lips, motioned everyone out, and pointed to the sky above Main Street.

A skein of snow geese arrowed south directly above the peaceful, deserted street. Pale down undersides reflected the lights of the hushed town; became sleek, opalescent ovals of silent, moving beauty.

Earthbound watchers gazed in wonder.

Chapter 10

"Shouldn't be long now, Will. That iron's getting pretty hot."

"I do believe you're right, Uncle Ed. You boys got that barrel half-filled like I asked you? Don't want too much water in there or it'll slop over and scald us when we dip the hogs." Will peered into the barrel. "Just right. We'll make butchers out of you two yet."

The first cold Saturday in November was always butchering day at the Macklins. Will inspected the preparations. A block-and-tackle, its rope attached to a singletree salvaged from an old one-horse buggy hitch, hung from the sturdy branches of the oak behind the house, directly over the water barrel. Old buggy and wagon springs and sundry scrap iron buried in the outdoor fire would, when red hot, be retrieved with tongs and dropped into the barrel until the water was near boiling. Tubs and dishpans stood in prim rows beneath a nearby trestle table. Finely honed butcher knives lay on top. Will ran his thumb lightly along a blade. "Don't see how you do it, Pa. You put an edge like a razor on these knives."

The old man shrugged away his son's compliment. "Hell, Will. Don't have to see to sharpen a knife. All's I need do after I hone it is run it over my thumb to make sure it's sharp enough to cut up those hogs. Been doing it all my life. Just *you* see that water's hot enough to loosen the bristles so's they scrape clean."

Crisp late-autumn air embraced the amiable group basking in the capsule of warmth around the fire. Will had driven to Walnut Hills Wednesday, visited his mother and returned with his father. Tall, knobby Ed Jameson—half Kickapoo with Macklin features—hiked in the day before with his usual greeting: "Figured you might need some help. Besides, nothin' more larapin than fried pork liver and fresh, crisp-cooked sidemeat!"

Ashes flew and flames leapt as Bill dropped another log on half-burned wood. "How's your knee this morning, Uncle Ed?" he asked. The night before, he and Seth had stopped by the room Ed shared with their grandfather and found Ed stretched out in bed with the right leg of his long underwear pulled up to his lower thigh and a giant leech plastered on his swollen knee.

"Lots better, Bill. That leech just sucks all the rheumatiz pizin out, takes the swelling down. Why, I'm a new man today." Ed danced a jig to demonstrate the leech's restorative powers.

"How much does that thing weigh, Uncle Ed?" asked Seth.

Ed tucked his tongue in his cheek and winked. "Oh, maybe somewhere around a half pound, depending on when it ate last. Stretches out close to a foot, but when it's not stretched it fits a pint jar pretty snug."

"Just be sure you keep that thing in the jar when it's not having supper, Uncle Ed." Will was emphatic. "Don't know how Soph would take to something like that loose in the house."

"Shoot, Will, she don't even know I got it. Brought its jar in my satchel and put it back in every time after it's done its duty."

"Well, don't get your jars mixed up. Don't think that critter would take to getting dumped in moonshine."

Uncle Ed ducked his head and chuckled. "I'll be careful, Will. No point ruining good 'shine. Besides, that leech wouldn't know good 'shine from bad. Anyway, I've got air holes punched in its jar lid so's I can tell the difference if I reach for it in the dark. Say, time's awastin', we gonna stand here jawing all day or you gonna shoot them hogs so we can get at it?"

"Guess we better. Come on Billy…sorry, Bill. Say, that's taking some getting used to. *Bill*, you hitch up the team while I get my rifle. It's a long haul from the hog lot to here."

William P sniffed the smoky autumn air. "Always wondered, Son, why you moved the hogs so far from the house. Why, I can't even smell 'em."

"The smell's why, Pa. It bothered Soph when Seth was on the way. And we got used to not having that stink around all the time.

It's kind of nice. Besides, the hogs are safer up there…not so close to the tracks. Some farmers are having trouble with the bums stealing livestock."

"Seems awful far to carry slop."

"No trouble, Pa. Seth, you and Grampa stay here and watch that fire. Coming Uncle Ed?"

"Your dad means watch *me*, Seth," the old man grumbled. He tucked his tobacco chaw in his cheek with his tongue and spat. Seth dodged. Everyone knew better than to stand too close to Grampa when he chewed. "Let me tell you, Will, maybe I can't see but I can feel if I get close enough to that fire to burn. I can *hear* good, too, and don't you forget it. And don't you forget to slit those hogs' throats after you shoot 'em so the blood drains out good, neither. Will? You hear me Will?"

"They're gone, Grampa."

* * *

The loaded wagon moved along the bluff toward the oak tree. Will kept a tight rein on the horses, wild-eyed from the fresh-blood smell behind them. Two red trails, draining from gaping slits across each hog's throat dangling out the rear, marked the wagon's route.

Bill perched next to his father. "Boy, this wagon seat sure squeaks, Dad. Want me to oil it tomorrow?"

"Why I'd appreciate that, Bill. Been meaning to do it myself, just never got around to it."

The dogs barked at a short, thin ragamuffin of a man climbing the path up the bluff. "Dad. There's a bum coming."

"Damn. Early for them, not much past nine is it? Hmph. Thought they'd all gone south by now. We sure don't need one around today of all days." Will squinted at the hesitant figure. "Bill? Is that who I think it is?"

"Mike!" Bill whooped. He hopped off the wagon, ran toward the bluff, scattered the dogs, lifted the man off his feet and swung him in a circle.

"Billy? That really you? Put me down, you scalawag," he gasped. "My, you've growed some since I saw you last, boy. To think I used to do that to you."

Bill grinned, set the little man on his feet and draped a companionable arm around his shoulder. "It's me all right, Mike, but I'm *Bill* now." An affectionate squeeze accompanied the name-change announcement.

"What's all the ruckus, Will?" Ed called from his seat atop the dead hogs.

"It's Mike Reed, our old hired hand. How about you get up here and hold these horses, Uncle Ed?"

Bill gave the newcomer a final pat and ran to tell his grandfather the news. Will transferred the reins, jumped down, clasped the former hired hand's bony shoulder and extended his hand.

Mike pumped the proffered hand. "Howdy, Will. Figured you might be butchering today. Need any help?"

Will studied the hand in his.

No grip…skin and bone…

He masked his concern with a chuckle. "Mike, you old son-of-a-gun, thought you were in Detroit where the big money is. Leastways that's where you were headed last time I saw you…spring of 1926, I think?"

"Tell you, Will, Detroit wasn't what I thought it'd be. Just didn't *like* city living. Couldn't get a drink anywhere. And if somebody was lucky enough to find a good bootlegger and old Henry Ford found out about it that man wasn't lucky any more, he was *fired*. But I kept my nose clean and made my five bucks a day till this Depression come along. Sure got thirsty, though!

"Now there's nothing in Detroit but soup kitchens and bread

lines. I got laid off early 1930. Used up my savings, started bumming around, tried to find a job, heard they was hiring out west at that big Hoover Dam project. Paying eighty-five cents an hour for powder monkeys, but everybody was headed there and I figured the jobs would be gone by the time I rode the rails out. Anyway, got down this way and wondered if you ever found someone to take my place here…" His voice trailed off. He stood for a moment, then raised his eyes to Will's. "No, sir. That ain't true. I come on purpose. Been hanging around the trestle camp down the tracks till the weather got cold enough for butchering. I got no place else to go."

"You hungry, Mike?"

"I'm starving, Will, and that's gospel." He turned to stare at the boy leading the old man toward the group. "Don't tell me…is that little Seth with old William P? Why, he was just a tyke when I left."

"Who you calling old, you old goat? I may be blind, but I'd know that voice anywhere. Heard it enough calling cows in the morning, trying to keep from having to go to the pasture after 'em. Get over here and shake my hand."

"Damn, William P, didn't think you'd still be around."

"*Me*? Hell, I plan to be around forever. The Lord don't want me and the devil won't have me."

While the two old cronies bantered, Will sent Seth in for Mike's food.

* * *

The butchering team worked smoothly. Will and Bill, the strongest, transferred heat-red iron to the barrel. When the water was hot, they hooked the hind legs of one hog to the singletree, swung it into place above the barrel, and lowered the carcass. Grampa called advice. "Don't douse it too long. Just want to loosen them bristles, not cook the whole hog." Ed and Will pulled up the singletree to lift the hog and swing it away from the barrel. They secured the rope and, careful not to break the skin, began to scrape with the backsides of the sharpened blades. Bill fished scrap iron from the barrel to dry, then buried it in the fire to reheat for the second hog's scalding. Seth ran errands. Mike sat with his back against the tree, absorbing strength from his meal.

"We're ready to slit this one, Seth. Get the tub for the innards," Will called. "Then run and get the rendering kettles and lard press for your mom. And make sure there's plenty of stove wood in the house."

The first hog transferred to the trestle table, Will and Bill scalded, scraped and slit the second. Ed and Mike, after washing up in the basement, separated the organs from the entrails, threw kidneys and lungs to the waiting dogs, then ran dull knives the length of each intestine, forcing the contents into a bucket below and saving the cleaned intestines for sausage casings.

"Be sure you get that gut clean," William P called. "Don't like surprises in my sausage."

"What the hell, William P? How come you always know what's goin' on?" asked Mike.

"My nose knows hog shit, inside or outside a hog. And don't nick 'em, neither, or the sausage'll pop out. I've not forgot the way you work, Mike. Always been clumsy as a bear cub playin' with his prick."

A guilty flush suffused Bill's face. Will's voice was sharp. "Watch your tongue, Pa! Good thing Seth and Sarah are in the house. You got to be more careful."

The old man was chagrined, "Sorry, Will. Damned eyes. Can't tell who's around any more."

"He still like that, Ed?"

"Hell yes, Mike. William P's William P. He'll never change. With that white hair and beard and mustache he may *look* like

Santa Claus but don't let that fool you none. He's just as ornery as ever. And getting fatter every day. He gets any rounder, we're gonna butcher *him*."

The old men's jocular familiarity continued while Seth piled livers, hearts, brains, tongues and heads in dishpans to carry to the kitchen. There, Sophia removed brain membrane, threw it in the slop bucket, saved the brains to scramble with eggs and put aside enough fresh liver for the family and to share with Sullivans. She simmered the remaining liver, heads, other organs, onions and spices in a giant kettle. When cooked, the hearts and tongues would be pickled; the remainder ground into headcheese.

* * *

Sarah ran from the house, open coat flying behind her. "Mamma says you'd better all come in and eat now so she can clear the kitchen to start the lard."

Mike studied the child. "This one wasn't here when I left, Will. She's a beauty. Looks just like her mother. What's your name, Honey?"

Sarah, uncharacteristically shy, hid behind her father. "Button your coat, Sarah, and say hello to Mr. Reed."

"Mamma says you're our hired man."

"Used to be. Sure would like to be again," he said, looking sidewise for Will's reaction.

Will glanced away. "Tell your mamma we'll be there in a minute, Sarah. You others go ahead and wash up. Mike and I'll be along. Seth, watch Grampa on the basement stairs."

* * *

Will squatted on his haunches and threw his pocketknife in an aimless game of mumblety-peg. Mike, features strained with uncertainty, leaned against the oak and watched.

"The thing is, Mike, we're just like the rest of the country. We don't have any money and no prospects right now. I'm beginning to think we might not even have the farm. Every month it's a struggle to get the mortgage payment together. Milk's not worth selling. We've been giving it to the hogs and hogs are only bringing about a nickel a pound."

"I understand, Will. I truly do. And those strapping boys of yours look like they're real good help, but I been just about everywhere since I got laid off. It's the same wherever you go. And like I told you, I got no place else. You wouldn't have to pay me nothing till things get better. I'd sure enough earn my keep, you know that…leastways I will soon as I get some strength back. And I see my old house there across the field is still empty…" He watched Will retrieve the knife. "Well, guess not mine but I always did my best to take care of that cabin Phineas lived in till the big house was built. Must be about a hundred years old now."

"Not till next year. Anyway the roof leaks some. We've been using it to store odds and ends. And Mike, we don't have room in the house." The hobo's face fell. "I know it sounds like we don't want you, but I really don't know where we'd put you."

"Hell, Will, I can fix the roof. Besides, anything would be better than the Hoovervilles I been sleeping in. Under bridges, paper boxes in alleys, sometimes doorways. Why there's places a man don't even dare *go* to sleep. Some of them city sons-a-bitches will kill you for your shoes! I damn near froze to death in Chicago last winter, and the only reason I didn't starve to death up there was because of Al Capone's soup kitchens. He had 'em set up all over. Had the police and the politicians in his pocket, too. Heard he's serving time for tax evasion now. Poor Al. Huh! Crooked cops all over the place and people talk about Chicago gangsters." Will thought of the Denver jail, took careful aim and threw the knife again. Mike, misunderstanding, said "Guess you don't want to hear about all that.

"Anyway, I got out of Chicago, but hopping freights is risky business, too. I seen men get their hands and feet and even their legs cut off trying to jump a freight. They just lay there and bleed to death. More than a few fellas I knew took the westbound. Hell, even if you make it on, the lines all hired railroad dicks to try to chase us off. Will, I just don't think I can go on much longer. I used to be able to work anyone under the table, now I'm so weak that Seth of yours is stronger than me."

Will retrieved his knife without speaking and turned to study Mike's face.

"Dammit, Will. Don't make me beg! I know I shouldn't have gone off like I did with no notice. I told you then I was sorry and I'll say it again." Desperation cloaked each word. "I could sleep in the hay barn till I get the cabin fixed up. Sure wouldn't be the first barn I slept in, if I got lucky. I wouldn't cause you no trouble, honest. All's I need's some grub and a place to sleep."

Will chose his words carefully. "I've got to say this, Mike. We've had a run of bums here since the factories started closing. They were probably all good men once, but the life they've been living changed 'em, made some of 'em mean. Hard to tell the good ones from the bad. And now *you* stand there talking about Al Capone like he's some kind of savior. Truth is, I worry every time I go to the field and leave Soph and the kids here alone. The dogs are good protection, but still… Had one fella try to break into the house last August…"

"Heard about that."

"And one…maybe two…got into the barn and butchered and hauled off Belle's heifer calf a couple of months later."

"Now I *didn't* hear about that. Surprises me. Word gets up and down the tracks pretty quick."

Will examined the knife, cocked and threw it again. Mike's face was bleak. "Guess you're wondering if maybe I changed, too." Will's silence was his answer. "Well, looks like maybe I better mosey on, but Will you gotta know your family's not in danger any more, at least from 'bos. Not many people as kind to us as you and the Missus been. The word's out that nobody touches this place. It's marked for protection. Most of those men *are* still good. There's rules of the road I been traveling. We all know we're goners if we don't abide by 'em, too. No, Will, no harm better come to any of you. The 'bos would sure enough take care of whoever did it."

"Kind of like shutting the barn door after the horses are out, isn't it?"

"They got their ways." Will's mouth opened, but Mike held up his hand. "No, I can't tell you and you don't want to know. Besides, we got a code and I won't break it. I am telling you, though, your place and family are safe." He pulled himself up to his full five-foot-four-inch height and spoke with dignity. "Will, I want you to know they…we…appreciate your food and kindness." He bent to retrieve his knotted kerchief and stick and forced a grin. "And just for good measure, they're scared to death of those dogs." He turned to go.

Will watched the hunched figure move toward the path. Mike was only five years older than Will, but moved like a man twice Will's age. Compassion overcame good judgement. "Mike!" The little man turned slowly to face Will. "Believe you better stick around awhile, at least until things get better out there."

Mike's voice trembled with emotion. "Thank you, Will. You won't regret it."

"Sure hope not! Well, if you can stand to eat again we better wash up. And don't talk about Capone around Soph and the kids. Watch that damn cussing, too, or Soph'll wash your mouth out with lye soap."

* * *

The curtains were down, the windows open, the battered table stripped of its cloth. All doors leading from the kitchen were closed and sealed to prevent the heavy, hot-lard smell and film from penetrating the rest of the house. Rendering kettles bubbled and spattered on the big wood stove. Empty five-gallon lard pails waited on old newspapers strewn across the floor.

"This one's ready, Bill. Roll your sleeves down. There's nothing worse than a grease burn and these cracklings pop."

"Where're the potholders, Mom?"

"Right where they always are, on the hook by the stove. I'll hold the cheesecloth while you pour. Be careful."

While Bill and Sophia worked in the kitchen, the men cubed more fat outside. Sarah sulked in her room. Her mother had told her to stay out of the way, like she was a baby!

"That's all that'll drain through the cloth, Bill. Get the press."

Sophia knotted the cheesecloth. Bill hoisted two short, wooden paddles, fastened together at the wide end by a leather strap, and laid them on edge across a half-filled lard can. His mother held the bag between the paddles while Bill squeezed the remaining fat from the cooked cubes.

"My, those muscles of yours do come in handy, Bill. It would take me forever to press this lard."

A nonchalant grin spread across Bill's maturing features. "Aw, Dad'd help you. He's almost as strong as me." He squeezed the last drops of lard into the pail. "Want me to take these cracklings out to the crew?"

"Yes, please. They'll be hungry. Throw some to the dogs, too."

Seth delivered another dishpan of cubed fat. "How many more, Seth?"

"Maybe one or two. Where's the meat saw? They want to cut a few chops before they smoke the loins. Do you want shoulder steaks?"

"Maybe enough for a meal. They should keep several days in the cold box. Here's the meat saw. Draw a bucket of fresh water from the well, too. Those cracklings will make the men thirsty. And don't forget the dipper."

The pans of bubbling fat not quite ready, Sophia sat on the top kitchen step leading to the landing and leaned against the sealed stairway door to rest. Butchering day started early and ended late. She'd baked and started a big pot of stew before she fixed breakfast and sealed the kitchen. The remainder of her afternoon would be spent cleaning up the lard mess. Then she'd fry Uncle Ed's favorite liver and uncured bacon for supper while the boys did chores. That night, shoulder meat and pork scraps would be fed into the outsized sausage grinder Phineas had imported, along with his bride, from South Carolina.

Sophia was already exhausted. She rubbed her cheek and drew her hand away in disgust. Her skin was coated with grease, her hair sticky.

Thank heaven we only butcher hogs in November and March!

The bull calf would be ready by January, but beef wasn't as messy as pork. She studied the greasy walls.

Maybe Bill and Seth can help wash them down tomorrow. Sunday? Well, we won't be going to Church. We might as well wash walls.

What was she going to do with Mike? He'd never bothered anyone when he was with them before, just stayed to himself in the old cabin, but with that leaky roof he couldn't stay there now. And she didn't want him sleeping in the house, not even in the basement. He was dirty, he smelled, and he might have body lice although she hadn't seen him scratching. But his clothes were filthy. Will said Mike could sleep in the barn tonight. She'd have to find an old blanket for him. She frowned.

I'll worry about Mike later.

She wiped her hands on her apron, rose, checked the rendering kettles, opened the door and called, "Bill, I need you. Two more kettles are ready."

* * *

Stretched lengthwise in bed, careful not to disturb his sleeping brother beside him, Bill couldn't sleep. He decided he had insomnia, like the man in one of Dr. Tom's medical magazines.

He thought about the day. A *good* day. Grampa and Uncle Ed here and then Mike showing up after five years. He'd missed Mike. When he was a kid he'd trotted behind Mike, helped mend fences and cut brush and do all the things that needed doing on the farm.

Butchering day had been fun. Almost like a big party, with everybody helping everbody else. And they all called him Bill and treated him like a man.

Even Uncle Ed, telling me about the bee tree and offering to help me smoke the bees out while it's cold so we can harvest the honey.

Bill licked his lips in anticipation.

Mom's hot biscuits, sweet cream butter and wild honey...

He moved his hand across his belly, remembered his grandfather's remark about the bear cub and jerked it back. No, he wouldn't do that any more. That was kid stuff. He wished he had someone to talk to besides those galoots at school. He couldn't talk to Dad and no *way* could he talk to Mom. He read every medical magazine from Dr. Tom's office, but couldn't understand most of what he read or what was happening to his body. He wondered about talking to Mike but decided against it. Maybe Joe? Joe was older, but not grownup yet.

He groaned, rolled over, sniffed the pungent hickory odor that floated from the smokehouse through the slightly opened window and listened to the voices drifting up the stairs from the kitchen.

He relaxed. Slept.

* * *

"Soph, we've ground the headcheese, it's in that crock in the cold box and the sausage is ready for its second grinding, but we can't find the feeding tube for the end of the grinder so we can stuff the casings. I know the boys brought it up from the basement."

"It's here, Will. I had to wash it again. Sarah was pretending it was a horn, parading through the house with it, then singing through the big end like it was a microphone. You know Sarah."

The huge grinder, mounted on a heavy board that bridged the seats of two sturdy, facing straight chairs, centered the kitchen. Ed anchored the board on one chair, ready to slip casings over the end of the newly-installed feeding tube as needed, then twist and coil the links into the waiting tub. William P anchored the other end to turn the handle while Will fed seasoned sausage into the grinder's open top. To Sophia's relief Mike, worn out from the day's unaccustomed work, was asleep in the barn. Sophia scalded the dishes, scrubbed tabletop and cabinets, and sneezed at the mingled pepper and sage smells.

Will glanced up. "We'll get this sausage finished, Soph. Won't take long. And we'll wash everything up after we get the links to smoking. You look like you're dead on your feet. It's almost eleven. Better go on to bed."

"I think I will, but I'll bathe first. When you're ready to wash up, there's hot water on the stove and the last of the lye soap to cut the grease. I'll make more as soon as I save enough drippings. If you're hungry there's cake in the pantry and coffee in the pot. Don't put all the sausage in casings. I'll fry patties for breakfast and make gravy."

William P perked up. "Biscuits, too? You make the best biscuits I ever ate, Ma'am."

Sophia's answering smile was tired. "Yes, Pa, biscuits too. Will, can I see you for a minute?"

Will followed his wife into the dining room and closed the door. "Make it snappy, Soph. Don't want Pa trying to feed the grinder. There's enough meat in that sausage already."

Sophia bridled at Will's brusque tone. "All right! You have to tell Mike to clean up if he's going to take meals with us until the cabin's ready. He's dirty! And it's not just his clothes, it's *him.*"

"Shoot, Soph. Didn't think it was *that* bad. Nobody but you seems to have noticed."

Will's offhand manner irritated Sophia even more. "Nobody but me *needs* to notice. I put some of Bill's outgrown clothes in the basement for Mike, by the tub. He'll have to keep his shoes—we don't have any to fit him—but tell him to put the clothes he's wearing in the paper sack I left there, then burn them. When he's clean, he can sleep in the basement by the furnace till the cabin's ready…it's too cold in the barn. I'll look in the attic for a coat and hat in the morning. And if *you* don't ask him to bathe and wash his hair *before* breakfast tomorrow, *I* will."

"Well, don't get your feathers ruffled! You want me to wake him up and tell him now?"

"That's not necessary and you know it. You know what I'm talking about, too."

"All right, Soph. Have it your way. Look, we're both tired, and I've got to get back out there before Pa…"

Sophia left.

* * *

Strings of sausage joined hams, loins and bacon curing in the smokehouse. The grinder and tub were washed and returned to basement storage. Will, William P and Ed sat around the kitchen table. Will poured coffee for his father. It was well past midnight.

William P touched the mug handle and exploded. “You know better’n to give me one of those damned mugs, Will. Get that big cup and deep saucer Soph keeps for me. *She* knows I like my coffee saucered and blowed.”

“Sorry, Pa. Just forgot.”

“Hmph. Forgot! Been drinking my coffee that way all your life. All *my* life, too, just like your grampa and his grampa and all the way back to the first Phineas. It’s a damned tradition, that’s what it is. One you’ve gone and broke.”

Ed, relieved to see someone else the butt of William P’s wrath, came to Will’s defense. “Ain’t many folks as does that any more, but I ‘member old Phineas telling about the first Phineas going down to London and stopping in at one of them fancy coffee houses. First time he ever tasted coffee.”

“My God, Uncle Ed, what year *was* that?”

“Well, probably middle sixteen hundreds I’d say. Certain before he come to the Carolinas. Anyway, he took coffee back to Scotland and taught everybody how to drink it saucered and blowed. Folks think it’s too countrified to drink it that way now, but it sure enough got started in them London gentlemen’s clubs.”

Mollified, William P listened as Will transferred the thick, dark brew from the mug to his father’s cup, then placed the cup on the saucer.

“Coffee, Uncle Ed?”

“Want something stronger than coffee, Will. How about you, William P? Like a little snort?”

“Just might!” William P rolled his chaw into his cheek, felt for his spit can, and aimed a stream of brown liquid. “Been a long time since I had good Irish coffee. You got some moonshine left, Ed?”

“Enough for a dab apiece, but I’ll have to go up to our room and get it.”

“Dammit, Will, what’d you do with that mug? You’re just like a fart in a skillet, always doing something even if it's wrong. If I'm gonna have whiskey in my coffee, damned if I'll have it in a saucer. I want those fumes to tickle my nose."

Will pulled a wry grin, winked at Ed and transferred William P's coffee back to the original mug. "Don't make any noise going upstairs, Uncle Ed. That third step from the top squeaks something fierce. Wouldn't want to disturb anyone's sleep *now*, would we?"

While Ed quietly made his way up the stairs and back, stepping over the telltale third step each time, Will checked on Sophia. "Sound asleep," he reported. Ed poured generous helpings of whiskey into each coffee mug. The three tired men sipped, rehashing the day's events before turning in.

* * *

Plop!

Sophia buried her head in the pillow, ignoring the strange sound.

Plop!

A second thud echoed through the quiet house. Sophia fought awake, lay rigid, counted. About a minute between each Plop! She touched Will's shoulder. He rolled over and belched. She evaded the whiskey stench. "Will," she whispered, "there's someone in the house."

"Probably one of the kids using the thunder mug."

"Shhh… That's not it. I know every sound and I've never heard this before. Listen."

Plop!

"It's coming from the back stairs, Will."

Will fumbled for his gun, slid the safety off, eased out of bed and felt his way to the kitchen. Sophia, barefoot but with a shawl over her heavy flannel nightgown, followed close behind. The sound was louder, closer. Will stationed himself by the back stairway door, leveled the gun, motioned for Sophia to open the door and step back. The stairwell was empty.

Plop!

Will's sudden laughter boomed through the house, bringing sleepy children to the head of the stairs, and rousting the two old men from their bed. "Light the lamp, Soph, and bring it over here," he gasped between guffaws.

Sophia approached cautiously. The lamp's flame flickered over Uncle Ed's leech inching its way downstairs, already sliding to the edge of another step.

"Will, what *is* that thing?"

In the upstairs hall, Uncle Ed cautiously peered around the door of his and William P's room. Bill and Seth, together at the head of the stairs, joined their father's guffaws, slapped their knees, pounded each other and pointed to their now-clowning father—long underwear drooping, gun aimed leech-ward—at the foot of the stairs. Sarah, rubbing sleep from her eyes, peered around them trying to see. Ed sheepishly turned back for the creature's jar. William P felt his way along the wall to the stairwell. "What the hell's going on?" he roared.

Will snapped the gun safety in place before he laid it down, took the lamp from Sophia's hand, set it on the steps, and gathered his wife in his arms. His body shook with silent laughter.

Sophia clung to Will. "It's awful! What *is* it?"

"You weren't supposed to know it was here, Soph. It won't hurt you, it's just ugly. It's a medicinal leech, probably an old Kickapoo remedy. Uncle Ed uses it to draw the swelling out of his knee." He tried unsuccessfully to control his mirth.

Sophia stepped away from Will and surveyed the scene. Fear gave way to relief, relief became indignation. Ed, overalls hurriedly drawn over his underwear, edged his way downstairs. His eyes darted from Sophia to the leech and back to Sophia. She waited while he held the jar in its path. A final Plop! Ed fastened the lid and returned his critter to his valise while the laughing children returned to bed and William P joined the adults gathered in the kitchen.

When Ed limped back down the stairs, Will was still chortling. “Good thing today’s Sunday. It’s already four and nobody’d feel like school with the smidgen of sleep we all got. How’d that thing get loose, Uncle Ed? Couldn’t have crawled through the air holes in the lid.”

“Must of put it on my knee and fell asleep. All that climbing around yesterday riled up my rheumatism, swelled my knee something fierce. I was so tired and…tired, I must’ve dropped off. I’m sure sorry, Ma’am. Didn’t mean to upset everyone.”

“You don’t suppose that leech had some Saturday-night moonshine, *too,* do you? Decided to go out on the town?” Sophia snapped. She scrutinized Ed’s dejected face.

Her voice softened. “It’s all right this time, Uncle Ed, but I’d certainly appreciate it never happening again.” She turned to leave, paused, and turned back. “By the way, you’ll be getting your own breakfast this morning. I’m going to sleep in.” She nodded an emphatic dismissal and left.

William P grasped Ed’s arm and punched it hard. Ed rubbed his bruised muscle. “Why for did you do that, William P? That hurt!”

“You and that damned leech, Ed. There goes our biscuits and gravy. Why don’t you just git on back to your end of the county where the hoot owls screw the chickens?”

Chapter 11

A worried frown creased Seth's forehead. "Mom, is Dad sick?"

"Oh, Seth. I didn't hear you come in." Sophia dropped another peeled potato into the pot. "Mashed potatoes, green beans, ham and gravy for Sunday dinner. Hungry?"

"You know I'm always hungry, but *Dad* never seems to be lately. That's not like him, either. What I want to know is if something's wrong with him..." His voice trailed off when he saw the 'I-don't-want-to-talk-about-it' look on his mother's face.

Sophia busied herself peeling another potato. "What makes you ask that?"

"Because he's not acting like Dad. He stops in the middle of doing something and just stares off at nothing. Or walks away from what he's doing and looks across the tracks at the fields. And sometimes he just disappears out in the pasture with the cows."

"But he's always stopped to look around at the farm. You know how he loves it." Sophia dropped a final potato in the pot, carried it to the stove and dumped the peelings into the slop bucket.

"Yeah, but this is different. It's been going on for over a week now. He doesn't *talk* any more. He's really acting funny. And just now I passed the stable and he was in there sort of mumbling to Star, all sad-like. It's been a long time since he has, but I wondered if maybe he was...uh...well...maybe drinking again?"

Sophia shook her head. "He's not drinking, Seth. I can always tell. And he doesn't have money for whiskey, anyway."

"Well, I walked up close so I could smell his breath and he wasn't, but he looked...gee, Mom...he looked like he wanted to cry and couldn't."

"Have you talked to Bill?"

"Aw, Bill doesn't see stuff like that, not if it doesn't hit him between the eyes. He says I'm just imagining things again. But I'm not!"

Sophia sighed, thought a moment and, faced with Seth's probing concern, considered her cautious reply. "I'm not around him outside, but I've noticed things in the house, too. He doesn't act sick, though. I suspect something's worrying him and you know how hard it is for him to talk about problems." She hugged her son. "I'm sure if he wants us to know he'll tell us. Now would you mind getting a quart of tomatoes from the basement? They'll taste good with this salty ham."

"But Mom..."

"Don't *you* start worrying, too, Seth. You know your father. He'll tell us when he's good and ready and not before. Now get the tomatoes, please, then go see what Sarah's up to."

* * *

By 1920, European farmers were recovering from the devastation of the Great War. Europe's need for American agricultural products diminished accordingly. American farmers, who continued to grow for export, glutted the domestic market. Commodity prices collapsed. Lower incomes left farmers who had borrowed to finance additional land purchases between 1910 and 1914—the Golden Age of Agriculture—unable to repay their loans. Loan losses caused the failure of many farm belt banks. The first Kickapoo County bank failed in the early 1920s. Others followed. Problems worsened with the general economic collapse in 1929...the beginning of the Great Depression. Farmland prices fell from a 1919 high of sixty nine dollars an acre to a Depression low of thirty three dollars an acre. From 1930 to 1935, farmer bankruptcies topped out at 28,280.

* * *

Sunday night, Will sat at the dining room table, head buried in his hands, the oil lamp casting dim light over piles of papers and a well-thumbed ledger.

Sophia finished a basket of ironing and moved to put an arm around Will's shoulders. "It's ten o'clock. You've been at those figures since the children went to bed. You'll ruin your eyes."

"Ruining my eyes is the *least* of my worries right now."

"Do you feel like talking about whatever's bothering you yet?"

"Looks like I'd better. Never wanted to burden you with finance problems, but guess I'll have to tell you sometime. Now's as good a time as any." He combed his fingers through his hair. "You know I've talked about the bank and me owning this land? Even laughed about it? Well, it's beginning to look like it'll wind up belonging to the bank instead of me. Everything we've worked and scrimped for, along with the ten thousand I already paid. Never thought it could happen. It's been Macklin land for a hundred years." He shook his head in despair.

"Oh, Will, are you sure? Things are really that bad?"

"Afraid so. I've gone over the accounts again and again, looking for a way out. What I got for the winter wheat last summer that usually takes us to spring barely pulled us through November. Thought maybe I'd make enough on the corn to do us till the hogs are ready to ship next fall, but that only brought us up to March. I feel like I'm trying to pull myself out of quicksand by my bootstraps…the harder I pull, the deeper I sink."

"How much is still due on the mortgage?"

"A little over two thousand, almost four years to go."

"Have you considered selling some of the land? Bert's always wanted that field next to his in the bottom…"

"I can't, not with a mortgage on it. The bank still holds the deed. One missed payment, Soph, o*ne* and this place is the bank's in forty-five days—*ninety* days to final foreclosure and that's to give us time to have an auction, pack up and get out. Damn! If I could just figure a way to hang on till times get better."

"Could you take out a second mortgage?"

"When I can't figure a way to make payments on the *first* one? Not sure Chester would let me do that, anyway."

"But what about your gravel pit? You always said..."

"Saw the road commissioner last week in Macklin Corner. Rufus tells me the County Board's cutting back on gravel. Again. Looks like farmers are gonna get stuck in more ways than one."

"Didn't the sawmill want the walnut trees from that stand of timber in the north pasture several years ago?"

"Already talked to George about it. He says not now, that there's no market for fine wood. No market for *anything*."

"The bull over at Bert's? It's still yours, maybe Bert would buy it."

"I can't ask him to do that, Soph. He took it as a favor to us and besides we need it to breed *our* cows if we can keep 'em. That was our agreement and we shook hands on it. A man's only as good as his word.

"I did think about selling the cows but nobody's buying dairy stock now. Even if we do manage to pull through this, we'll never put as fine a herd together again and they're too good to be slaughterhouse hamburger cows when we've got summer pasture for grazing and corn and hay to feed 'em through the winter. Hogs get that skimmed milk, too, and at least bring in a *little* something when I ship 'em. Hogs and cows and chickens and garden are what keep us from going hungry like the folks in town.

"Thing is, we've got damn near everything we need right here except fifty dollars a month. Seems like a fortune.

"Soph, I've thought of everything you suggested and more. Even setting up a still in the Indian valley. It's far enough back so nobody'd ever smell the mash cooking. Bet that's what Old Phineas would do." He studied Sophia's horrified face. "Yeah, figured that's how you'd take it, but it's a sure way to make some money off that corn. Hell, they're *burning* corn in Iowa. It's cheaper than coal. Seems like whiskey's about the only thing there's a market for any more."

"There's my butter and egg money."

"I even figured that in. Five dollars a month tops and that's if the hens are laying, which they won't be again until March. Might keep us in flour and sugar and coal oil, but… How much you got in your baking powder can?"

Sophia left the room and returned wiping a flour-coated Clabber Girl tin with her apron. A sorry smile crossed Will's strained face. "See you're still burying it in the flour bin."

"It's the safest place I could think of. I don't know how much is there, but I've not spent any lately. With money so tight I thought I might use it for just small Christmas gifts for the children, but you're welcome to it."

Will's shoulders slumped. "Christmas again. Last year's was slim. This one will be worse. Hell, we may spend *next* Christmas in the Poor House on the County Farm." He shook his head in despair, emptied the small pile of coins on the table and stacked them in neat rows. "Fourteen quarters, twenty-seven dimes, thirty-four nickels. Hmph."

"You forgot my lucky Indian Head penny."

"Nothing to joke about, Soph. Less than eight dollars here. And I've got about two dollars in change in my pocket. Can't believe this is all the money we can scrape up between us."

"I usually have a little more, but I bought coffee from the McNess salesman when he came by last month. And when you were short last fall I gave you all I had. Oh, Will, I knew we didn't have much money, but you've always handled what we had and I just didn't realize things were this bad. Why didn't you tell me?"

"Didn't see any need for you to worry about it, too. Besides, what good would it have done? You already make every penny do the work of a dime. Patch everything twice, sometimes three times. Dress factory remnants to make clothes, old flour sacks for towels. You'd make overalls and shoes on that rackety treadle machine if you could. And I don't think anyone else has made soap since covered wagon days."

"When we both save where we can, I don't mind. Remember how sore the boys' and your hands got when you shelled all those bushels of corn last fall for spring planting?"

"Yeah, grew good corn, too. Until it got washed away. I'd known then what prices would be now, I'd never have pawned Phineas' watch to buy more seed."

"I don't know how much they're worth, but if it will help I can sell Aunt Clarilla's antique Spode dishes and silver."

"No! Those are your heirlooms. I know how much they mean to you." He coughed to cover the catch in his voice. "Fella down towards Greenville wanted to buy Star some time back."

"Will! You and the children *love* that horse."

"I know, but none of 'em ride her much any more and *I've* not had time to keep her exercised. She's half racehorse and wants to run. *Needs* to run. He's got a stallion cousin of hers and wants to breed the two of 'em, see if he can get both speed and endurance in a colt. A year or so ago he offered me three hundred dollars, about half what she's worth. Don't know if he's still interested, or even if he's still got money, but three hundred dollars is six payments, take us through August."

"But the boys would be heartbroken. And you, too."

"Well, I'm still thinking. We've got till March. Comes to it, I'll write and see. If there's a choice between selling Star and losing the farm there *isn't* a choice. You know that. And the kids will just have to understand."

"Maybe you should talk to them. At least about how hard times are getting. Seth was after me this morning, worried about you. He even wondered if you might be drinking again."

"Seth said *that?"*

"He wasn't prying or being a smart-aleck, Will. He was concerned. Besides, you should know by now there are no secrets in this house. Well, I guess there's *one* you managed to keep. They don't seem to know you might lose the farm. *I* certainly had no idea. What I told Seth was that you didn't have money for whiskey and that if you wanted us to know something was wrong you'd tell us. Now he thinks you're sick. He's worried and you know how tender hearted he is. Talk to them, Will."

Smarting over Seth's conjecture, Will muttered, "I'll think about it. And I guess I need to stop by the bank, see if I can work something out with Chester. Maybe I'll ride Star in tomorrow, save gas. She needs to get back in shape if I have to sell her."

"Would you mind taking some money from the can to pick up a sack of flour? We're almost out."

* * *

Monday evening the boys, expecting their father to start chores, dawdled on their way home from school. Sophia's face was tense when they scuffed into the kitchen.

"Where's Dad?"

"I've no idea. He rode Star into town about ten this morning to pick up a sack of flour and said he'd be back by noon. I've been waiting to bake pies. And I'm *still* waiting… You'd better change and start the milking. Take care of the hogs and horses, too. Get Mike to help, he's strong enough now."

By eight, supper over and dishes done, Sarah was asleep and the boys upstairs studying. At half-past eight Star trotted into the yard. Sophia looked out the window to see Will slide from the saddle and collapse. Sure he was hurt, she threw an old coat over her shoulders and ran out to him. When stale whiskey fumes erupted from his slack, gaping mouth her concern twisted to anger.

I should have known…

Bill and Seth, huddled at their upstairs window, watched in

alarm, then hurried to help their tight-lipped mother.

Disgust overrode Sophia's anger. "He's limp as a wet noodle. See if you can get him inside to bed before you stable Star for the night."

One on either side of the man sprawled on the ground, the boys hooked their hands under their father's arms to hoist and half-drag, half-carry him onto the back porch. Sophia held the door while they maneuvered him into the kitchen, then followed them through the house, where they dropped him on the bed.

"I'll take care of him now. See to Star then get to sleep. Mike can handle the hogs in the morning, but you boys have to be up early to take care of all the other chores before school. Your father won't be able." Her sons dismissed, she bent to remove Will's shoes.

* * *

Sophia spent the night on the parlor divan. She waited to wake Will until after the boys left for school, an arguing Sarah in tow.

"Yah, but I don't *want* to go to Mrs. Sullivan's alone. Can't we take her pan back together?"

"Don't argue, Sarah! Just go with the boys. Tell Mrs. Sullivan I'll walk up later to bring you home."

Seth took the pan from his sister's hand. "Come on, 'Yahbut'. I'll carry it for you." The boys picked up their books and lunch sacks and, with final searching looks at their mother's grim face, pulled their sister out the door and headed up the road. Sophia watched until the trio turned the corner, then went to the bedroom.

Will stirred as the door squeaked opened and made an effort to sit up, but fell back on the pillow. He glanced down at the clothes he'd slept in, up at Sophia's controlled-anger face, groaned, and closed his eyes. "My God, Soph. What happened…"

"That's what *I'd* like to know! You left at ten yesterday morning. Star brought you home last night so drunk you fell off and passed out in the yard. The boys had to half-carry you in to bed. Maybe that was a blessing. At least you weren't raising Cain with all of us!

"I hope you're proud of yourself, Will. *Now* do you see why Seth said what he did? Change your clothes and clean up while I fix something to eat. I don't suppose you've had food since yesterday morning."

The slamming bedroom door escalated the sledgehammer pounding in Will's skull.

* * *

Sophia, her back rigid, cleared the table and poured coffee for the still-suffering man. She broke the silence that had smothered the kitchen since Will sat down to eat. "That's the last of the coffee and I can't buy more, but you look like you need it."

"I'm sorry, Soph…"

"You're *always* sorry. And I know you always mean it. What I'd like to know is why you did this after all that talk about losing the farm. I know how worried you are, too, but when are you going to learn you can't drown problems in a bottle?"

"Soph, you don't understand, don't know what it is to have to deal with these things. You and the kids to worry about. No money. The mortgage. All the hard work I put into the crops and nothing coming back…"

Sophia slapped the table with her open hand. "What do you *mean* I don't know? I worry, too, and work as hard as you and sometimes harder and don't see any money either. I never get enough sleep! I'm tired all the time! But it seemed worth it because I loved you and I thought you loved me…"

Will's chair toppled with a crash as he shoved back from the table and grabbed Sophia by the shoulders. "I *do* love you Soph!"

She shook off his hands and backed away. "Then *why*…"

Will's dangling, empty hands clenched. "Makes me feel good, I guess. At least for awhile. Helps me forget."

"Forget what? Us? And it *doesn't* make you feel good, it makes you feel sorry for yourself and mad at me and the children!"

"Maybe so, but that's later. While I was drinking yesterday I forgot this money mess I'm in and…well…for sure not you and the kids. What I think happens is afterwards I get mad at myself and that makes me so mad I get mad at everybody else, but I'm trying to handle that. And I've never passed out before. Been so long since I had a drink, guess I wasn't used to it."

"Excuses, Will. Tell me *why*."

"Why? Maybe I got a taste for it while I was little. All the men I knew drank. Ma wouldn't let Pa drink in the house so he hid a bottle outside, somewhere around the corncrib. All us kids knew it. And Uncle Ed kept his own jug in a hayloft corner for when he came to visit."

"But neither of them ever acted like you do. You just don't seem to know when to *stop.*"

His voice rose. "Let me finish!" He took a deep breath. "Look, I never talked about this before. Trying to think my way along. Anyway one day, I was maybe ten, I sneaked away to the barn when Ma was having one of her fits and I caught Uncle Ed with his jug. When I spotted him I tried to hide, ashamed because I was crying. He gave me a nip of white mule, maybe to settle me down… Smelled like kerosene and tasted worse, but it *did* make me feel better. At least once I got it past my nose. Uncle Ed made me promise I'd never touch his jug when he wasn't there and didn't, but every time he came he'd give me a taste. I got so I liked it. And then, out west…"

Suddenly his voice turned defensive, angry. "Hell, Soph. I don't *know* why. Besides, you know how worried I was…no money…thinking of losing the farm…you knew that!"

"But where did you get money for whiskey? Night before last you were telling me how *poor* you are." She stopped, stared. "Where's the flour?"

Will avoided her eyes. "Didn't get it. Ran into some old friends from the mine and spent the money on white mule."

"You spent *my* butter and egg money on *booze?* How could you!"

"Don't worry, you'll get your money back if I have to steal it."

"I don't care about the money and you don't have to steal to put it back. I care about what you *spent* it for. You know how I hate when you drink. I hope you didn't go into the bank drunk!"

"Didn't go to the bank at all. That's what started things off. The miners heard a rumor about the bank going under and some of 'em still have a little money there, talking about pulling it out. Surprised me. I thought they were all flat broke. We stood around talking and someone finally said if their money was gonna be gone anyway he'd just as soon have a drink to remember it by." He glanced up at Sophia's incredulous face. "I know, didn't make any sense, but with the troubles we've all got the bank maybe folding seemed like the last straw so it sounded like a good idea to me, too. We pooled what cash we had, found a bootlegger, bought a couple of quarts of white mule and headed for the lake."

"Too bad you didn't all fall in. *That* might have brought you to your senses."

Will raised remorseful eyes to Sophia's. "Guess you wish we had. Anyway, didn't go there in December to swim, went there to drink, but I sure in hell didn't mean to tie one on like I did. Oh God, Soph, I truly am sorry about the flour money. I just didn't think and it had been so long since I'd had a drink. Can you forgive me?"

"Again? I don't know. Maybe you should ask if you can forgive yourself. It makes me sick to think of your sons putting you to bed and I don't imagine they feel any better about it. After last night they deserve some kind of explanation, though."

She turned away. "Sarah's up at Sullivans. I sent her up with the boys this morning because I didn't know what would be happening here. Maybe you could 'exercise' Star some more and go pick her up. The cold air might clear your head…"

Chapter 12

On a January Monday in 1932, Will rode Star to town to deliver butter to the few customers who could still afford the luxury, then stopped by the feed store. John Hall followed him in. "Will, come look at this car of mine. Don't know what's wrong with it."

"Hell, John, I only know horses. You know more about machines than I could ever hope to learn."

John grasped Will's elbow and steered him outside. "Dammit, Will, I want to talk to you in private and you stand and argue with me in front of half the farmers in the county. Now lift that side of the hood and act like you know something about engines. You and Soph be home Thursday?"

"We're home *every* Thursday. And Friday and Saturday and…"

"Someone I want you to meet. Senator Fairwell's coming through from Springfield on his way to Southern Illinois."

"Fairwell?" Will was dubious. "Now hold your horses, John, Fairwell's a Democrat. I'm a registered Republican. What's he want with me?"

"Rather not say just yet, but if it's okay with you we'll drive out Thursday morning around ten."

* * *

Thursday arrived crisp, clear and cold.

"Sarah, don't touch those doughnuts, you've already had two. Besides, the ones on the blue and white Chinese plate are for company." Sophia carefully lifted four cups, four saucers and four dessert plates from the glass-front china cabinet and set them on the dining room table.

Will stepped in, admired the creamy linen cloth and napkins and whistled. "Clarilla's Spode? Didn't think you'd *ever* let anyone eat off that. How old is that set?"

"Early 1800s, I think. It's written down some place. Josiah Spode started making it in the late 1700s, but this isn't one of the first sets…it was Aunt Clarilla's mother's…or maybe grandmother's…anyway, whoever it was bought it at the Stoke-on-Trent factory just before they left England…Will, what *difference* does it make? I always liked the oriental pattern so Clarilla left it to me!"

"Well don't get all upset, I was only curious. I just hope they don't think we're putting on the dog."

Sophia bridled. "John Hall knows us, he'll know better. What's the use of having nice things if we don't use them once in awhile? Besides, it's not china, only earthenware. It's the glaze that makes it pretty. And it's not *every* day a state senator drops by."

"Doubt if either of 'em knows Spode from crockery. I wouldn't if you hadn't told me, but it sure does dress up the table."

"We'll use Clarilla's silver spoons, too. Those old pewter ones look terrible next to the good dishes. Sarah, don't wipe your fingers on your dress. I asked you to try to stay clean." She rummaged through a buffet drawer, polished four teaspoons and a sugar shell; examined the table and returned to the china cabinet for a crystal creamer and sugar bowl.

Will fingered his starch-stiff, turned collar, hitched his pants and wished he were wearing overalls. "Took the last of the butter money, but it'll sure be a treat to have coffee again. Hope they *appreciate* it. Wonder what they want?"

"We'll find out in about fifteen minutes. It's a good thing the ground's frozen. I'd hate to have the senator's car mired in."

"Might be a good thing. Maybe the county would spread some gravel on those roads."

"And maybe *you'd* better put the dogs up before they get here."

* * *

"These doughnuts remind me of my grandma's kitchen, Mrs. Macklin. Can't remember the last time I had homemade doughnuts. It's the fresh lard frying that does it. I'll just bet you folks render your own lard?" Will nodded. "My, that does bring back memories. Butchering day…hot cornpone with cracklings crumbled through. Umm-*um*!" His voice dropped to a confidential level. "I come from a farm family myself, you know." Sophia passed the doughnuts. "Well, now, don't mind if I do. That's only three, but who's counting? Heh, heh, heh." The senator undid his bottom vest button and patted his belly.

Sophia carried Senator Fairwell's coffee cup into the kitchen for a refill. She paused and turned in the doorway behind their guest. Her eyes sought Will's; her brows raised a question. Will's eyes flickered uncertainly.

So far the four had discussed children, farm prices, bank failures, the weather, livestock and crops. The Senator admired Seth's caged squirrel and offered a scrap of doughnut between the wires. Skippy ignored both the stranger and the sugary treat, preferring to search his old flannel shirt for a walnut. Sarah was chucked under the chin, invited to call the senator Uncle Jim, announced that she already *had* an Uncle Jim, and retreated to the parlor. John Hall said little, preferring to let the politician carry the conversation.

Sophia replaced the senator's filled cup. "John? More coffee?"

"No thanks, Soph. Why don't you sit down? I believe the Senator wants to talk to you both."

"Well, yes, I did, but I'm beginning to think we came to the wrong house, John."

He traced a finger over the intricate Spode pattern, lifted the heavy sterling, hefted the cut-glass lead crystal creamer, and inspected the dining room furniture. "I'm looking for folks in need and seems these Macklins were born with silver spoons in their mouths."

"More like pewter, Senator." Will shared a tight smile with

Sophia. "But we are luckier than most, at least for now. We've got a roof over our heads, raise enough to eat with some left over to share, and our kids are healthy. We do have just about everything, everything but money. The silver and Spode and crystal, even the tablecloth and napkins and furniture, are heirlooms from my wife's family. Soph's offered, but I just can't see her things sold."

The politician studied Will's face, seemed satisfied with his open honesty. "Would you like to see something done about the way things are now?"

Will studied the Senator's face in turn. "Maybe. Depends."

"Can we assume what's said in this room stays here? At least for the time being?" Will looked at Sophia. Both nodded. "The Democrat Party needs rebuilding. We're looking for good men to take over local leadership." When Will's mouth opened to protest, the senator raised a restraining palm. "I know you're a Republican. John told me. John was a Republican, too. He also told me that you and hundreds like you are damned…excuse me, ma'am…dissatisfied with the way the country's going. Or *not* going as the case may be."

"That's true enough, but I don't see where I fit in."

"Maybe I'm being presumptuous, but I thought I might be able to lure you over to the other side, get you to call for a different ballot in the March primary. I've got a sneaking suspicion there's a Democrat lurking inside that Republican pelt." He turned to Sophia. "I understand you've always been a Democrat, Mrs. Macklin, at least since women won the vote. Look, do you mind if I call you Soph? Seems like everyone else does."

Sophia smiled, glanced at Will. "Make it Sophia and I won't mind a bit, Senator."

"That's a deal! Well, Sophia and Will, here's the situation. You know John's been a convert for some time now." He leaned to pat John on the shoulder. "We've been so pleased with what he's done as Precinct Committeeman we've got even bigger plans for him.

But we need someone who's well known, respected and liked to replace John. Someone we can trust. Now we've got a good presidential candidate in Roosevelt. I tell you, I can almost smell the meat a'cookin', but in order to get it off the spit and into hungry stomachs we've got to reorganize from the grass roots up. Macklin Corner needs someone to get Roosevelt's message to the people. We think you're that man. And we think Sophia's the woman to back you up."

"Never thought of myself as a politician, Senator. Don't believe I'm qualified."

"Nobody *is* qualified when they start, except maybe John here, but with one foot in the farm community and one foot in town you've already got a head start. Kills two birds with one stone right there. Plus you're a good man. I heard about the food you hauled into town the past two summers. You worked in the mine, so you've got an in with the miners. And from what I understand, even though you were Constable when the Mexicans were brought in, you didn't turn on the locals.

"John tells me you get along with the farmers, too, at least most of them. They've always gone Republican, cancelled out the town vote, but with someone they know and respect in the Democrat corner, we think we can bring them around, too, carry all of Precinct Seven. And Seven's one of Kickapoo County's key precincts. With you and Sophia on our side, we should be able to count on most of those votes, start getting this economy turned around.

"That's what you could do for America, your neighbors, your friends. And your only pay would be satisfaction. But let's talk about what we might be able to do for you."

"Senator, I'll tell you straight out, we're not much for pork barrel politics. Soph and I may vote different tickets but we always vote our conscience. I just don't think I'd like myself much if I sold out for personal gain."

"This isn't pork barrel. That's a little like getting something for nothing. What I'm saying is that *both* parties show gratitude to supporters and workers." He noted Will's quirked eyebrow, his skeptical frown. "You think the Republicans don't do that? Ask John sometime. Look...if the Democrats win this next election, there'll be a lot of jobs changing hands, but there are only so many to go around and we need the best people available *for* those jobs. Politics is like life, Son. You scratch my back, I'll scratch yours, same as you farmers when you help each other with harvest.

"More to the point, the job John has in mind for you is one you can handle better than anyone we know around here. That's the *big* reason he brought you to my attention, but if you're not interested..."

Will pondered, balanced pride and growing dislike for the senator against mortgage payments, and searched Sophia's hopeful face. "Didn't say I wasn't interested, Senator, just that I don't like to feel obliged to anyone. I'd sure have to think about it." His eyes focused on John. "What job were you thinking of, John?"

"Kickapoo County Road Commissioner. Rufus is about ready to throw in the towel. His term doesn't end until 1934, but he's got some serious health problems. You'd go to work for him, learn the ropes, then when he resigns we see that you get appointed. That way, with the backing of the party and Senator Fairwell campaigning for everyone on the ticket, you'll be a shoo-in on the'34 ballot."

Will stared. "*Me*? Run for office on the *Democrat* ticket?"

"That's what we're thinking, Will." John cleared his throat. "You ought to know the senator's not talking personal to everyone like he is to you two. What I'd like you and Soph to do is come to our monthly Democrat get-togethers, acquaint yourselves with the folks you might not know yet, find out how things work. You're a natural leader, Will. The others will recognize that and when I resign next January you should be able to get elected as precinct committeeman and take my place. That's the first step."

"John, that's a lot of finagling. Besides, how could I be Precinct Committeeman and Road Commissioner at the same time? Even if that's acceptable and I did happen to win the 1934 election, how could I do both jobs?"

The senator sat forward, elbows on the table. "You can't. That's where Sophia comes in. We need to get the women's vote. Did you know some wives still don't vote because their husbands don't think they should? And it's not just the women! A lot of naturalized citizens don't vote because they're afraid to, a carry-over from the Old Country. We need to see all eligible non-voters registered, *then* see that they cast their ballots. Remember, Will, it's the wheel that squeaks that gets the grease and people have to be heard to get results!

"Now, Sophia, after John gets everyone registered for the March primary and the big November election, we need someone to go door-to-door with sample ballots, show folks how to vote and, if they can't read English, even go into the booth with them." The senator overrode Will's beginning protest. "That *is* allowed. Every citizen, natural or naturalized, has the right to vote. We'll have cars to drive 'em to the polls, too, if they can't make it on their own." He coughed delicately. "Uh…most of the candidates show their appreciation with a monetary gift to the campaigner, Ma'am." He winked. "Shouldn't wonder you could use a little extra pin-money?"

His eyes returned to Will. "We need the women, but we have to be careful how we encourage them. What we don't want to do is antagonize the men. The first woman we support has to be above reproach in every way, like Sophia here. If the Democrats sweep November like we think, Will, you'll have smooth sailing ahead. And when it's time for you to resign as Precinct Committeeman *Sophia* takes over. For someone who can handle a family and home like this and has the townspeople's trust, it'll be easy as pie.

And since Macklin Corner's mostly Catholic now, she's a natural." Admiring eyes again shifted to Sophia. "I can tell just by looking you'd be a perfect Precinct Committeeman."

Will's eyes scanned Sophia's startled face. "Jesus, Senator. I don't know. She's never done anything like that before."

"All the more reason she should. Doesn't take that much time, and John tells me Sarah starts to school in September. You two talk it over, call John tomorrow, let him know what you decide. Short notice I know, but with the primary less than two months off we have to move fast." Fairwell checked his watch. "Say, Will, can I use your phone?"

"Sorry, don't have one Senator. We're last on the road and the telephone company won't run a line for one family."

"Well now, anyone that's going to be Road Commissioner needs a telephone!" The senator's fierce little eyes skewered John. "What say? Think you can use some influence with your friends in the office? Get this family a phone?"

"Shouldn't wonder, Sir." He stirred in his seat and rose. "We'd best get going. Still a few more stops to make."

"Yes, yes, I know, hope the others are as pleasant as this one. One of my few remaining pleasures is to meet new constituents." He shook Will's hand, bowed over Sophia's and brought it to his lips. "It isn't often, Ma'am, that a man encounters true beauty, both inner and outer. It's been an honor." He turned to Will. "Remember, let John know tomorrow what you decide." Sarah stood in the parlor doorway, waiting for the senator to leave. "Got a goodbye hug for your new Uncle Jim, Sarah?"

Appreciating Sarah's discomfort, Will grinned at his daughter and grabbed his coat to hurry the departing guests. "Think I'll catch a ride up to the mailbox with John, Soph, see if there's an answer about Star from Greenville yet. That mile walk back'll do me good."

* * *

"Mamma, I don't think I like that man." Sarah nibbled another doughnut. After the offensive chin chucking, she'd spent the morning playing in the parlor as far from the senator as she could get. Senator Fairwell's goodbye hug was not returned.

Sophia carried the dishes to the kitchen. "I'm not sure I do either, Honey, but he's a politician and politicians always act like they're everyone's special friend. It's just their way." Sophia, her head spinning, checked the linens for spots, shook crumbs from the tablecloth and returned it to the cedar chest, dropped the napkins in the dirty clothes basket, washed and put away her treasures, and poured fresh coffee into a thick mug. And once again considered the convoluted power of prayer.

* * *

Will stomped into the kitchen, hung his coat, poured coffee, and helped himself to a doughnut. "Nothing about Star yet. I wrote over a month ago. Looks like I'd get the letter back if they couldn't deliver it."

"After this morning, I should think you wouldn't *want* it delivered."

Will pointedly ignored Sophia's remark. "Getting colder out. Say, these *are* good. Thought that windbag was just putting you on." He licked sugar from his fingers.

Sophia stiffened. "He may be a windbag, Will, but it's still nice to hear a compliment. Besides, he made a lot of sense. And that job would be an answer to a prayer. What are you going to do?"

"Don't know yet. Not sure I trust the senator. Pa always said 'Never trust a saint when his charity generates his paycheck.'"

"Will Macklin! You know William P never said anything like that."

"Well, no. I read it somewhere, but I never forgot it. Politicians, priests…" He backed off at Sophia's withering look. "I'll sleep on it. By morning I can maybe separate the wheat from the chaff, drive in tomorrow afternoon, talk to John, pick the boys up after school. Sure would be nice to have a phone. Say, time for the noon news! Let's find out what's going on today." He scooted his chair back from the table. "Reckon Ma'd say Anne has the gift of second sight, and if I didn't know better I'd think she *was* the seventh daughter of a seventh daughter, else how'd she know to fix up that radio just when we might need it most?" They smiled at the shared memory of Christmas morning.

Sophia had wakened early to the sound of carols and laughter and nudged her husband. "Will, wake up. Where's that music coming from?"

"Kids singing," he mumbled, burying his head in the pillow.

"If our children can sing like that, we'd better put them on the stage. Wake up!"

Will sat up and ran his hand over his disheveled hair. His eyes widened. "Sounds like the radio, Soph."

The puzzled pair slipped quietly out of bed. A floorboard creaked. Silence replaced the joyous sounds from the parlor. Will cracked the door and peeked into the room to see all four children sprawled on the floor in front of the radio. He blinked to clear traces of sleep from his eyes and squeaked the door open.

"Merry Christmas!" Anne scrambled up to kiss her parents. Bill extended a long arm and turned the newly responsive volume knob as high as it would go. Carolers burst forth. 'Glad tidings to you…'

Sarah and Seth hopped up and ran to Will and Sophia. "Anne did it," Sarah shouted over the carolers. "Now the radio talks and sings again."

Anne covered her ears. "Turn it down, *Billy-Boy*, we're not deaf." She ignored her brother's glare and turned to her sister. "We *all* did it, Sarah. I only bought the battery." Relenting, she smiled at her brother. "*Bill* and Seth had to take out the old one so I'd know what kind to buy, then put in the new one. And you had the hardest job of all. You had to keep the secret." She tweaked one of Sarah's curls.

"But where did you get the money, Anne?"

"From the Greenbergs, Daddy." Anne's impish grin lit her face. "Dr. Greenberg said they couldn't give Christmas presents, so he gave me a dollar for every day of Hanukah. Eight dollars, Daddy!"

Sophia's eyes were moist. "And you spent some of it on us? Oh, Honey, what a thoughtful thing to do. It's a gift we'll *all* enjoy. Isn't this wonderful, Will?"

Will forced a smile. "Makes what we've got for you look pretty puny, Anne."

"Daddy, give me ham for breakfast and we'll call it even. I'm so hungry for pork I could die." Laughter blended with music. Will relaxed and joined the rest of the family and the radio singers in the final chorus of 'We Wish You A Merry Christmas'.

The old Philco caroled all Christmas day. The following morning, a family conference was called to work out a listening schedule. To conserve the battery, the radio would be used one hour daily for the morning, noon and evening fifteen-minute newscasts, with the remaining fifteen minutes allotted to the children. Bill opted for 'Jack Armstrong, the All-American Boy'. Seth chose music. Sarah wavered between love of adventure and loyalty to Seth. Sophia forestalled the impending argument. "Seth, you like Jack Armstrong, don't you? And I know Sarah likes music. Why not listen to Jack Armstrong during the week and music on Saturday and Sunday?"

The schedule had held for the past two weeks. Now, Will wiped his lips and rose from the table. "Yep, I do believe Anne has the gift." He chucked Sarah under the chin, laughed at her indignation, and led the way to the parlor. "Sure good to know what's happening when it happens instead of a month later." He and Sophia settled down to listen to the noon news. Gusting January wind rattled the shutters and whistled through the closed-off fireplace chimneys of the house on the bluff.

* * *

Above the kitchen porch, cottonwood branches creaked in subzero cold. During the night, Arctic air had blasted in over the Great Plains and sent temperatures plummeting. Will drove the boys to school, returned to break the ice in the pond with an axe, led the horses and cows out to drink, scooped the drains, and herded the livestock back into the barn. Except for Blue, curled in a ball outside the back door, the dogs huddled in the stable near the warm horses.

Will pulled his gloves off and massaged numbed fingers. "Hope I got enough gas to get to town and back again this afternoon. May have to raid the baking powder can." Sophia stiffened. "For *gas*, Soph. You know I put that flour money back. But I don't have any cash on me. Hadn't planned on taking the boys in this morning."

"Well, they couldn't *walk* in this weather. They'd have frozen before they got to Sullivans."

"They could have stayed home. Bet that's what most of the town kids did today. Only reason I got our car started was because it was parked in the hay barn between the cows and the horses. Animal heat."

"Will, you know…"

"Yeah, yeah. Don't tell me again." Will's voice raised in falsetto mimicry. "'They can't miss school unless they're sick'. At least it's Friday. Don't have to worry about school tomorrow. Any coffee left?"

Sophia poured a steaming mug, refilled her own, put a plate of leftover doughnuts on the table, and sat across from Will, who uncurled thawing fingers from his mug's warmth to reach for a doughnut. "Not as good as they were yesterday, but they'll do."

"I can put them in the oven a minute or so..."

"No, they're fine. Oh, I checked on Mike. Sure glad he got the cabin weatherproofed. Still a few chinks need filling, though. Hope he doesn't start a fire. He's got that pot-belly monster going full blast, says he's never going to be cold again."

"He cleaned the soot out of the pipes and chimney, didn't he?"

"Well I sure in hell *told* him to. Where's Sarah?"

"In her room, reading."

"Warm enough up there for her?"

"Will! You *know* the heat from the kitchen stove goes right through the floor register into that room. What's the matter with you?"

"I don't know. Yes, I guess I do. Truth is, Soph, I don't know what to do about that political thing. Couldn't even sleep last night. I know the country's in trouble. Maybe the right thing to do *is* support Roosevelt and it's not just the job, though Lord knows we need the money right now. What we're looking at is a whole different way of life. I want to farm, walk the same acres old Phineas walked, get the same dirt on my boots, and there's no way in hell I can take on a job and run this place the way it should be run."

"But the mortgage payments! And you talked about letting some of the land lie fallow, at least until the Depression's over. And Mike looks stronger every time I see him. If you only farmed half the ground, enough to feed the livestock, couldn't he handle that? I know Bill and Seth could take care of the stock. They already do most of it anyway."

"Guess I'm spoiled. I like being my own boss. Don't want other people telling me what to do."

"And you'll never change. Pa says you've always been independent as a hog on ice. I never really understood that till now. But if you were Road Commissioner you'd be your own boss and have people working for *you*. It's not like you'd be working for someone else."

"Never your own boss in politics, Soph. Anybody takes a public office, *everybody's* his boss. And there's you. The way Fairwell talked, you'd get dragged into it right along with me. Politics can get awful dirty. Don't know if I want you in on that."

Sophia was exasperated. "Will, is *that* what all this is about? You don't want me involved?"

"Big part of it. I just don't want you to bite off more than you can chew. Besides, no Macklin woman's ever had to go to work yet."

"And what do you call what I do here from five in the morning till ten or eleven at night? Play? Campaigning in Macklin Corner would be a holiday!"

"It's not the same. A man's got his pride, Soph. If you turn into a precinct committeeman and I get elected, folks will say I'm riding on your coat tails. Or hanging onto your apron strings and that would be even worse."

"Bosh. There's not a person we know who wouldn't jump at the chance being offered to you on a silver platter. I'm not crazy about the thought of politics either, but we *need* the money. And I would like to see Roosevelt elected. Every newscast has something about another bank failure. That's almost five thousand banks now. And if the Macklin Corner bank goes down… *You* were the one who told me about Roosevelt in the first place and since then I've been reading everything I can find about him. I really think he *is* America's salvation. From what you've said, you think so, too."

"Don't throw my own words back at me, Soph. It's one thing to think and talk, another thing to do. Roosevelt's talking about a new form of government. Sometimes he sounds more like a Socialist than a Democrat."

"He's talking about ideas to put people back to work, Will. That's not Socialism, it's common sense."

"Well, it's sure not Republican."

"Do you *want* to see Hoover reelected?"

"No. I just want to farm my land and take care of my family."

"And I'd like to sit on a silk cushion and be waited on hand and foot, but I know I can't."

Will's head snapped up. "Really, Soph? You'd really want that?"

Sophia laughed. "About as much as you'd want a manservant following you around all the time. But it would be nice not to have to work so hard."

The tension broke. Will chuckled. "Guess you wouldn't look bad on a silk cushion at that. Maybe wearing some of those see-through balloon pants." He sobered. "What are we going to do? I'm supposed to meet John at three."

"Think about it. You already know how I feel, but you're the one who has to decide. And while you're thinking, you might make sure there's plenty of wood for the furnace and cook stove. I'm going to collect eggs before they freeze, then bake pies. It's a shame to waste that hot oven."

* * *

Sophia stirred the big pot of stew on the stove, thought about Mike, peeled two more potatoes and carrots and dropped them in the pot. She jumped back from a splash of hot broth, heard Sarah giggle and looked up at the face peeking through the register. "You look all checkered through here, Mamma."

"I know, Honey. Your face looks checkered, too. Did you wake up from your nap dry?"

"Uh-huh. No wet beds for a month now. I told you I could do it."

"I knew you could, and I'm so proud of you."

...another prayer answered...

Sarah's nose twitched. "Goody, stew. Are you making dumplings, too?"

"Would you like dumplings?"

"Ummmm...maybe. But Seth and Daddy would. Where's Daddy?"

"Picking up the boys at school. Come on down and have your milk now so you don't spoil your supper."

Sophia moved the stew to the back of the stove to simmer and retrieved a pitcher of milk from the cold box. Frozen. The steadily dropping mercury had finally settled at ten below zero. She chipped icy milk and put slivers in a bowl just as Sarah ran down the back stairs into the kitchen.

"Get a spoon, Sarah. You'll have to eat your milk." Sarah's face brightened at the unexpected treat. Sophia put the milk in the pantry to thaw, brought rock-hard butter inside to soften and looked at the clock. Almost four.

No decision had been reached before Will left for Macklin Corner. She wasn't sure what upset her most, the unexpected blizzard or Will's mulishness. Retracing her steps to the kitchen window, she looked up the empty road then checked the cabin across the field. A plume of smoke drifted lazily from the cabin chimney.

At least the wind's died down.

She hoped the Arctic front passed through by Monday so the boys could walk to school. Will was right, they didn't have money for gas. She wished she knew what Will had decided.

"What's the matter, Mamma? Are you mad?"

"Oh, no, Honey. Do I look mad? I'm just thinking."

Outside the kitchen door, Blue barked. Muffled barks answered from the stable. She returned to the window to see hatless Bill, open coat flying, leap from the car and slide the hay barn's double door open. The Maxwell turned into the animal-warmed shelter.

* * *

"You boys get on to the house, change your clothes. Better wear your rubber boots, too. Those cows have been in all day so that barn's a mess. You can scoop the drains again while I take the stock to the pond and break the ice." Will pulled his hat over his ears and turned his sheepskin collar up. "Put plenty of fresh straw down, too. Get Mike to help you. Better milk early. And put a couple buckets of water on the stove. The hogs need hot slop tonight."

"Gee, Dad, are you sure that's *all?"*

"Well, Bill, it'll do for starters. Get going now."

Bill and Seth raced for the house. Sophia held the door open and closed it quickly behind them. "Bill, are you *trying* to catch pneumonia? How many times have I told you…" Bill blank-stared his mother. Irritated, Sophia turned to Seth. "Where's your dad?"

"Chopping ice so the cows and horses can drink. Stew for supper? Did you make dumplings?"

"See, Mamma? I told you Seth wanted dumplings."

"So does Bill, Brat." He tugged one of Sarah's curls for emphasis.

Sophia stepped between the two before Sarah retaliated with a kick. "No, I didn't make dumplings yet, Seth. Yes, I will make dumplings for supper. For *everyone.* Do you boys want something now? I baked apple pies."

"No time. Dad says do the chores early. Gotta change." Bill retrieved the lid lifter from its hook, moved one of the front stove lids to the back, and hoisted the slop bucket into position directly over the fire. "There's your stew, Seth."

"Bill, what are you doing?" Sophia demanded.

"Dad says heat water for the pigs. Just thought I'd heat the slop, too. We got room for two more buckets on the stove?"

"I'll make room. You'll have to draw water from the well. The cistern pump's frozen. Get changed first, though. And bring your rocks down. I'll put them in the oven. Hot Shoal Creek rocks for cold feet tonight! Bring their flannel wrappers, too. Seth, see if you can coax Blue to the barn with you. He can't stay on the porch all night." Sophia lifted the other front stove lid, added several sticks of wood, replaced the lid and adjusted the damper. "Did your dad say anything?"

"About what?"

"Oh…nothing." Her face was grim.

Sarah giggled. "Mamma's thinking again."

* * *

Sophia examined the worn tablecloth. A few spots but it would do. She lifted plates and glasses from the cupboard. "Here, set the table, Sarah. Put spoons out for the stew gravy. Set a place for Mike, too. He'll eat with us tonight."

When Mike had picked up the hot slop, Sophia checked for dirt before inviting him to join the family meal. "Where's Will?" she'd asked. "He didn't even come in to warm up."

"Aw, he's got that heavy sheepskin coat, Missus. He's not cold. Anyway, he wants to make sure all the stock will be okay through the night. Says it's gonna get colder than Billy He…uh…cold tonight. Those scraps for the dogs? I'll drop 'em by the barn on my way to the hog lot. Bill should be in for the water buckets in a minute. What you want to do about Blue, Missus? He won't stay out there with the other dogs, keeps slipping back here to the porch."

"Put him in the basement. Will won't allow a dog in the house and I'm afraid he'll freeze on the porch."

"I'll take care of him for you, Missus. You want some of this food left here for him?"

"No, there'll be scraps from supper."

Now, Blue safely in the basement, Sophia watched Sarah set the table. Her agitation increased moment by moment. She scraped a circle of frost from an east window to watch Mike fight the rising wind on the way to the barn. Moved to a west window to see the winter sun, pale as the yolk of a wheat-fed chicken's egg, creep below the horizon. At a north parlor window, she pulled the curtain aside and shivered in the cold seeping through the glass.

Where was Will?

She returned to the warmth of the kitchen, made the dumplings, dropped spoons of batter on top of the bubbling stew, and quickly replaced the lid.

Will's heavy boots finally stomped onto the porch. Sophia, body arched with tension, gripped the table and waited. The door opened. "Well? Well?"

Will's face, almost blue with cold, was teasingly inscrutable. "Well, sure is cold out."

"Don't be a dunce, Will, I know it's cold. And you know I'm not asking about the weather. Did you get that mugwump mind of yours off the fence?"

"Sure did, Soph. We'll have a phone as soon as this weather breaks enough to dig postholes."

"And?"

Will's grin almost masked the apprehension in his eyes. "And the first meeting's next Tuesday night. Think you can make it?"

A seed of fear sprouted beneath the elation that flashed across Sophia's face.

Chapter 13

Sophia admired her new kitchen windowpane, but found she missed the occasional rainbow the cracked one had sent her way over the past two years.

Too late now...the rainbows are gone...

Mike had installed the replacement the previous day. June morning light through the flawless pane highlighted a glass churn, half-filled with clotted cream, waiting on the bare, scarred table. She wiped away a splash of cream and stepped outside to call her daughter.

"Sarah, you've been in that black raspberry patch for half-an-hour. Haven't you picked enough for your breakfast yet?"

"Almost, Mamma. I keep forgetting and eating them."

"Well, *stop* forgetting and stop *eating*. If you're going to turn this cream into butter, you'd better hurry. Heavens, child, you look like you washed your mouth with purple ink! Bring in what you picked. I'll wash *them* while you wash your face. I saved enough cream for your oatmeal and berries." Sarah popped another raspberry into her mouth. "Sarah, now!"

As he had for the past five months while learning the job, following an early breakfast Will left for the Road Commissioner's office a little after six. Bill, Seth and Mike did the milking and other chores and ate before hitching up the horses to head for the fields. Sarah had wandered down the back stairs a little after eight, still half-asleep. Now, as she straggled onto the porch with her meager bowl of fruit, Sophia wondered how she would ever get the child up and moving when school started in September.

Sarah turned for a final look at the sparkling morning. "Oh, Mamma, it's so pretty and new outside."

Sophia's exasperation melted. "I know, Honey. Next to October, June's my favorite month. Wash your hands and face. I'll start churning while you eat."

Sophia settled in a chair opposite her daughter. Her right hand and arm circled rhythmically, turning the handle that moved the gears that drove the wooden paddles through the heavy cream. Pale-gold froth spattered the inside glass. "You know, Sarah, you need to stop dawdling. This fall you'll have to be ready for school when the others are. You'd better start getting up with Bill and Seth."

"But that's too early!"

"Not the way you move and not as early as you'd get up if you had to *walk* to school. You're lucky. This year you'll all ride in with Daddy, but you must be ready by half-past seven."

"Will Daddy bring us home, too?"

"No, he works till five. You and Seth will walk home together. It's only two miles and you can stop and rest on the way."

"Billy, too? He goes to high school this fall."

"Sarah, remember, it's Bill now. I told you, I'll make arrangements with the principal so you and Seth can be there early and wait outside till the school opens. Daddy will drop you both off, then go on to the office or the shed or wherever he's working that day. Billy…oops…" Sophia covered her mouth and raised her brows in mock consternation.

Sarah giggled. "You mean Bill, Mamma…"

"…*Bill* can walk to high school from there. He'll hitch-hike home."

"Why can't Anne come back home? She could ride to school with Daddy, too. I miss her a lot."

"We all miss her, Honey, but Mrs. Greenburg needs her."

Sophia wondered how much the Greenberg's decision to remain in Bridgeton was influenced by Mrs. Greenberg's difficult pregnancy. She must be feeling better, though, because she was taking the boys to New York again. Someplace called the Catskills.

"Anne will be home soon for a whole six weeks. Now eat your

breakfast and don't dawdle. We still have to pick potato bugs after you churn."

"Me? I have to pick potato bugs? Ugh. I thought Daddy sprayed them all away."

"He sprayed earlier, but once the plants start blooming he can't use Paris Green. The arsenic could go into the potatoes and make them poison. Eat! I can't start the cottage cheese until you take over this churn and I promised Daddy cheese pie tonight." Sarah swallowed a final bite and took her mother's place. "Remember, the faster you churn the quicker the butter comes."

While Sarah churned as fast as her small arm could go, Sophia poured a pan of clabbered milk through a cheesecloth-lined colander, tightened and knotted the cloth, let the whey drip into the pan beneath and emptied the pan into the slop bucket.

"It's hard to turn the handle, Mamma. I think the butter's here."

Sophia inspected the floating golden chunks. "Almost. It still has to come together though, so churn more slowly…never mind, I'll finish while you get the kerosene cans. Then we'll have a glass of buttermilk before we go to the potato patch."

* * *

Sarah's eyes widened with revulsion. "I can't do it, Mamma."

"Yes, you can. Just pick them off one at a time and drop them in the kerosene. And be sure you get all the bugs. Look. This little wormy thing with spots is a young potato bug, a larva. The grownups are shaped like ladybugs but they're yellow and a lot bigger. And they've got black stripes. See?" Sarah cringed. "Honey, I told you they won't eat *you*, they just eat potato plants. Check under the leaves for eggs, too. See these little orange patches? When you find *them*, break that whole leaf off and drop *it* in the can. Remember, if we don't get rid of bugs now we won't eat potatoes this winter. Watch me."

Sophia methodically picked each voracious beetle and larva off the first plant, then checked for eggs. "Now you do it." She watched Sarah apprehensively approach the plant. She sympathized, but there was no help for it. Potato bugs were thick this year. "That's fine, Honey. You start here and I'll work that side of the patch." Sophia bent to her task, working rapidly down the row, and thought about the strange spring. She looked up to watch high, dark clouds filled with Dust Bowl soil shadow the perfect sky and wondered what else might go wrong.

Will had started work in January, eager to learn as much as possible about the Road Commissioner job before Rufus resigned. He found the office poorly run and Rufus' records non-existent. To make matters worse, as his health declined Rufus spent less and less time at the office. Will, lucky to see his boss an hour each morning, worked ten and twelve hour days, set up a record system, learned by doing, and by the first of June had all the responsibility without the commensurate salary. The men that ran the graders and spread gravel made more than Will.

After he bought his own gas to get to and from job sites and check needed road improvements, Will's salary barely met the monthly mortgage payment. And because he was Assistant Road Commissioner, they'd lost the meager gravel pit income. Will said in his position he couldn't buy gravel from himself. Sophia swallowed her frustration, packed a well-filled lunch bucket for him each morning, and used some of her campaign money for a thermos bottle. He needed hot coffee during early morning and lunch hours spent trying to make sense of Rufus' office mess.

At least we can afford coffee again.

When Sophia questioned the long hours and low pay and suggested he talk to John Hall, Will shook his head. "I can't do that, Soph. Rufus is dying of cancer. He's got doctor bills and is trying to put money aside so Martha can get by when he's gone." Sophia appreciated and shared Will's compassion, but the Macklins' financial situation went steadily downhill.

Then, for the second year in a row, spring rains were delayed and Will finally told Mike to plant the fields farthest from the creek. Young, green shoots appeared with the first deluge. The creek overflowed, spread wider and wider until it engulfed the tender corn. The rest of Sophia's dwindling hoard of primary election money went for second-planting seed. The drought came, then the bugs. And now Bill's craze for football, a rough-and-tumble game Sophia both despised and feared.

Sophia dropped potato beetles into kerosene and thought of Senator Fairwell.

Pin money, indeed. Except for my new dishes, the window and Will's thermos, we've used every red cent of that money to survive. I won't *feel guilty about my dishes, though. I've put up with cracked and chipped everyday dishes for years...*

She stood, rubbed her aching back, and luxuriated in the memory of opening the box of ivory china edged with delicate blue flowers. Removing each piece from the excelsior. Washing and placing it in the kitchen cabinet.

And some things *were* getting better. They had a phone. Someday, maybe electricity? The Rural Electric Association was beginning to run lines in their area…

She checked the sun. "Time to stop, Sarah. The boys and Mike will be up from the field soon. We'll finish after we eat."

"But I have to take my nap."

Sophia lightly touched her daughter's nose and smiled at the forlorn face lifted to hers. "Since when have you *wanted* to take a nap? Besides, first-graders don't have time for naps."

On the way to the house she stopped to untie the bulging cheesecloth, securely knotted to the clothesline to finish draining, then squeezed and kneaded to break the firm contents into nuggets. Fresh cottage cheese mixed with cream would be a welcome addition to the leftovers she'd heat for their noon meal…and for their daily bum.

* * *

Bill's voice filtered through the screen from the well where he, Mike and Seth were washing up. "Mom, did Coach Munson call?"

"I don't think so. Sarah and I were in the potato patch for several hours, though, so we couldn't hear the phone."

In his constant search for team prospects, the Bridgeton High coach attended eighth grade graduations at all unit schools. When big Bill Macklin lumbered across the stage to accept his diploma, Coach Munson first made a notation in the book he carried in his breast pocket, then an appointment to talk to the boy and his parents. He'd driven out to the Macklin farm late in the evening a week after graduation. Will, delayed at a road job on the far side of the county, wasn't home.

And probably a good thing, too.

She knew Will would be pleased should Bill be accepted for the football sports program. She also knew Will would like Mr. Munson, a huge man with a loose engaging grin, sad eyes, a lumpy face, thinning gray hair, and trousers belted below his paunch. Through middle-age fat invading his athlete's muscles, he radiated understanding. Bill had responded to him immediately and swelled with pride when the coach checked his size and strength.

"Good potential there, son. Still going through the awkward stage, but you'll catch up with your feet before long. Football improves coordination, too. Think you could manage to make it to practice after school?"

Bill's eyes sought his mother's. Longing warred with responsibility.

"I'm sorry, Coach Munson. Bill will have to talk to his father about that. Since my husband's been appointed Assistant Road Commissioner, Bill's taken over the lion's share of work here on the farm."

The coach watched the boy's disappointed face. "Well, practice doesn't start until mid-August. I'm just scouting now. Tell you what, talk to your dad, see if maybe you can work something out. We try to schedule classes so the football boys have their last period free. That way we get in two solid hours of practice every evening and we're generally through by half-past four."

"But he'd still have to be home in time for chores. That five-mile walk is at least another forty-five minutes, maybe an hour. And what about games? And homework? I don't want *anything* interfering with school."

"Varsity games are mostly Saturday afternoons, Ma'am, with weekly Junior Varsity games after school, but those are over by five. Except for out-of-town games, the most he'd give up here would be for Jayvee games and an hour or so practice weekday evenings." He grinned at Bill. "Grades? That's pretty much up to him. However, in order to be eligible for football, students have to maintain at least a C average. As for getting home…"

Bill's desperate longing peaked. "I could *run* home, Mom. I do that most of the time now, anyway. Heck, I make it from Macklin Corner in fifteen minutes easy. Wouldn't take more than half an hour from Bridgeton even if I can't hitch a ride to our turnoff."

The coach's eyebrows raised. "So *that's* where those leg muscles come from. That's good practice, Bill. Like I said, talk it over with your dad. I'll be out of town a few days, call you when I get back. That all right with you, Mrs. Macklin?"

Torn between sympathy for Bill's longing and concern for his safety, Sophia's nod was noncommittal.

Will had been late each evening since, arriving home to eat and stumble wearily to bed. Bill was waiting for the right time to talk to his father. Now he finished scrubbing his hands, arms and face and stepped into the kitchen. "Maybe I can talk to Dad this Saturday if he's not too busy."

* * *

Bill maneuvered the harrow through the turn and lined up the tines to scour out weeds between the rows of new corn. Satisfied, he flicked the reins on the Percheron's rumps and followed the harrow through the field. Damn! he thought. He'd never wanted anything in his life as much as he wanted a chance to play football. And Mom didn't want him to play. It wasn't *what* she said, more how she didn't *say* it. He knew he couldn't count on her when he talked to his dad. But boy, would he like to show those galoots who made fun of Anne and the Greenbergs. He'd teach 'em not to mess with the Macklins!

He closed his eyes and imagined stands filled with people. People cheering for *him* as he dodged down the field with the ball, barreled around the interference and charged into the end zone for a touchdown.

Guys slapping me on the back, pretty girls in little short skirts yelling Bill, Bill he's our man, if he can't do it no one can.

"Bill! BILL!! You got wax in your ears? Straighten out that harrow, you just dug up ten feet of corn!" Mike's shout imploded Bill's daydream. "Damn, boy, you can't get jimsonweed out of corn with your eyes closed. How in hell we gonna explain that bare patch to your dad?"

Bill examined the damage and turned a rueful face to Mike. "I'll tell Dad I did it. Don't want him chewing on you." He guided the harrow back in line, slapped the reins and started down the field.

Maybe if I promise to buckle down on the books Mom'll back me up...

* * *

Friday evening Will rested in his chair by the radio, waiting for the news. In the kitchen, Sophia put the finishing touches on dinner and Sarah argued while she set the table. Will still wasn't used to a big evening meal, but Soph said with him gone in the middle of the day it didn't make sense to fix dinner at noon any more.

Hard on Soph, though. Not out of the kitchen much before eight now. Well, guess it doesn't make much difference. I'm usually asleep by then anyway. Too tired to talk, let alone make love, even if she wanted to. Taking her a long time to get over her snit about the flour money.

Feels funny to sit here doing nothing while Mike and the boys finish the milking. Nice to be home early for a change, though.

While voices drifted in from the kitchen, Will's mind drifted into the day's conversation with John Hall and Senator Fairwell.

He'd not seen Fairwell since January and was just finishing a sandwich and going over some papers when the senator showed up.

"Decided to drop by while I was in the county, Will. See how things are going."

"Come on in, Senator. There's a little coffee left in the thermos if you'll wait till I wash this cup out."

"No, thanks. John and I just finished lunch. With it getting harder for me to get around he's driving me these days. He'll be in as soon as he parks. What I really want is to thank you and Sophia for the primary turnout you two got in Precinct Seven."

"Don't thank me, Senator. I was up to my ears trying to figure out everything in this office. Soph's the one who shanks mared it door-to-door. Don't know yet how she got some of those people to go to the polls. She took sample ballots to every house, showed 'em where to put their x's. They all voted, too. Hell, the election judges counted till five a.m.! Good thing both John and the Republican Precinct Committeeman were watching, else the

Republicans would have sworn the ballot boxes were stuffed."

"Well, you tell her for me it was worth it. Roosevelt's primed to go." He turned to John Hall, just coming in the door. "Say, John, I left my cigars in the car. Get 'em for me, will you?"

Will half-listened to the senator expound on Roosevelt's drive, qualifications, political prowess, and the upcoming convention while John played errand boy. Will's eyes narrowed, his face hardened when John returned and Fairwell offhandedly accepted the cigars and John obsequiously stepped aside. The senator, noting Will's reaction, belatedly patted John on the shoulder and said, "Thanks, Buddy."

Will's shoulders tightened. He turned away to hide his irritation, dusted off two chairs and waved the senator and John to sit. Side by side. "You go to all the political shindigs, Senator?"

"Well, not all of 'em. I've got duties in Springfield, you know. But you can bet your bottom dollar I'll be in Chicago in July for the Democrat Convention. Might just take John here along with me, too. He's sure handy to have around. Well, we didn't come to talk politics. How are you getting along, Will?"

"Pretty good, I think. I guess John told you about Rufus?"

"Said he was on his feet and not much more, that you're running this whole shebang by yourself now."

"Yessir, and going broke doing it." He turned to John. "Been meaning to ask you, any way I can get some gas money? I don't mind driving all over Kickapoo County as long as the Maxwell holds out, but buying gas sure makes a hole in what I get paid."

John and the Senator exchanged startled glances. "You've been buying your *own* gas for *county* business, Will? And driving your own car?"

"Don't know any other way to check on the jobs. Rufus is so sick *he* can't go. And he needs the county truck to get around in."

"But I thought he set up an expense account for you last January. I sure *told* him to and…hmmm. Looks like I'll have to talk to him. Senator?"

Fairwell lit a cigar, puffed and deliberated about the non-existent expense account. Will ducked away from the cloud of offensive smoke hovering over his desk. "Guess it's about time for him to resign, John. *Past* time if what we're thinking is true. But don't mention my name, hear?"

Rethinking the senator's visit and wondering about the expense account, Will rubbed tense neck muscles. He again decided he didn't care much for Fairwell.

Maybe Rufus just forgot. Glad I didn't mention the gravel *account... Just have to put up with Fairwell, I guess. He comes with the job. In for an inch, in for a mile. But poor John, seems like he sold his soul...*

"Will?" Sophia gently touched her husband's shoulder. "Honey? Are you asleep? It's almost time for the news."

"Just thinking with my eyes closed." He patted her hand and sat up. "Boys in from the barn yet?"

"No, they were a little late coming up from the fields. Their hair was damp so I think they stopped to skinny dip. Mike pretty much lets them do what they want."

"Don't blame 'em a bit. Fieldwork's hot and dirty. Used to skinny dip myself. Still do when I have a chance. Nice way to get cool and wash the dirt off. Didn't hurt those cows to wait some. It's kind of nice sitting here by ourselves, anyway." Sarah popped through the door. "Well, *almost* by ourselves. Feed any bums today?"

"Just one. As usual, right after we finished eating and he was gone by the time Mike and the boys went back to the bottom." She turned the radio on, dialed the news, and sat down to rest and wait for the boys.

* * *

On Saturday morning, Sarah tripped into the kitchen. "Goody, egg bread for breakfast."

Bill glowered. "It's not egg bread, Brat, it's French Toast. At least that's what Anne says the Greenbergs call it."

"Mamma slices old bread and dips it in eggs and fries it. It's *egg bread*. Ooof, you smell."

Sophia glanced down. "You seem to have stepped in a cow pie, Bill. Please clean your feet. And then wipe that mess off the floor before you wash up. Hurry. Breakfast will be ready in a minute."

"What's Dad doing today?"

"I don't know. He was sleeping so well I didn't want to disturb him. Thanks for getting Seth up and doing the chores. Your dad needs all the rest he can get."

Will yawned his way into the kitchen. "Thanks to you boys, I *got* all the rest I needed, too. Can't remember when I slept so well. Did you and Mike finish getting the corn laid by yesterday, Bill?"

"Sure did. Want to go down to the bottom today and look over the fields?"

"Sounds like a good idea, but maybe I've got a better one. Why not everybody go down? I'll hitch up the wagon and if your mom's got something for a picnic we'll spend the day at the creek. We're all about due for a little fun."

Sarah hopped with excitement. "Can we take our swimming suits, Daddy?"

"Sure, Honey, if the moths haven't eaten 'em up. Last time I had mine on it had a few holes in it."

Sophia turned from the stove. "Yours is darned, Will. I found some wool thread in my basket that almost matched, but I'm not sure mine still fits."

"Wool stretches, Soph. You'll get into it. Think you can rustle up some picnic fixins?"

"Yes, if Bill can clean his feet and get that mess off the floor. Sarah, call Seth for breakfast."

* * *

Sophia's cool print housedress brightened the bank where she sat watching Seth and Sarah splash in the shallow, sand-bottom pool leading into the deep swimming hole. "Don't go too far, Sarah, you can't swim yet and there's a drop-off there."

Will and Bill ambled toward the fields, enjoying the clear, late-morning air. "Best time of the year, Son. Nice and warm, not too many mosquitoes yet. Say, for a late second planting the fields look good."

"Yeah, that last rain helped. Broke the drought. Uh, there's kind of a hole over there. I wasn't watching careful enough and I took out some corn with the weeds."

"How much?"

"About ten feet. Guess I was woolgathering."

"Well, won't make us more broke than we already are, but make sure it doesn't happen again."

"It won't. Dad can I talk to you about something?"

"Sounds important."

"It is. I've got a chance to try out for football practice this fall at Bridgeton High. That's what Coach Munson came out to talk about last Tuesday. You know, that evening you were so late?"

"Hmph. Figured that was what he wanted. Coaches see big strong farm boys like you and start thinking about touchdowns."

"I probably won't get to play, I'll just be a freshman, but I'd sure like to try. Training doesn't start until the middle of August. That'll give me time to get all the summer fieldwork done and there won't be any more till harvest."

"What about evening chores? Seth's still too young to handle everything alone, and I'd hate to ask Mike to do anything else around the place since I'm not able to pay him yet."

"Umm…well…I already kind of talked to Mike." Will stopped

short and turned to search his son's face. Bill's eyes dropped. "Gee, Dad, since you weren't here I had to talk to *someone* and Mom doesn't like football so *she* won't talk about it. Anyway, I'd be here for all the morning work and Mike says he wouldn't mind at all helping in the evenings. Did you know he always wanted to play football? He was just too small. He even wants to come to the games if I make the team. Besides, practice is over by half-past four. If I run home, I can be here to help finish up."

"Run home? Five miles every night after football practice? And then chores? Who do you think you are, Bill? Charles Atlas?"

"I can do it, Dad. I know I can. And I want this more than I've ever wanted anything in my whole life!"

Will's eyes probed the pleading eyes almost level with his own. His son was growing into an intense young man. "I don't know, Bill. With me working, you know I depend on you to take charge of things around the farm. There's your mom and the kids to think about, too. With Mike here I don't think we'll have any more trouble with the bums, but we can't be sure."

"Gosh, Dad, the only time we ever *had* trouble was at night and you're always home at night now. Well, almost always. I'd be here night times anyhow and if you're worried about Mom, she'll *have* to be by herself during the day when Sarah starts school. Mike will still come up from the field at noon to eat, just like you did, and the dogs will be with her. Blue would *kill* anyone that tried to hurt Mom."

"I know that. It's just that there's so much to think about. We're not like town families that don't have to work all the time. When's football season over?"

"End of November."

"End of harvest, too."

"Dad, I'll work *twice* as hard, and I'll harvest the fields on Sunday. I'll even start studying so Mom won't be mad about my grades."

"Hmph. You must want to play football pretty bad if you're willing to study. Ma always said the Lord works in mysterious ways. Hmmm. When do you have to let him know?"

"He said to talk to you and he'd call me when he got back in town, so I guess right away, as soon as he calls."

Will thrust his hands in his pockets, deep in thought. Bill, on tenterhooks, watched his father.

Finally, "Guess we might try it, see if it works out. If it doesn't you can always drop it. And if it does, I've been thinking about resting a few of the fields next year, anyway. They're about due. Good time to do it with grain prices down. And Bill, I should have the office under control by September and be able to finish up by five. You can stop by, ride home with me, and we'll both pitch in on chores."

Bill's wild whoop silenced the twittering birds in the trees shading the swimming hole, where Sophia still guarded her two youngest children.

Chapter 14

Sunday's noon dinner was over, dishes washed and put away. Bill and Seth, after making Sarah promise not to pester, had allowed her to tag along on their search for arrowheads, still occasionally found in the Indian valley. Armed with three bottles of homemade root beer to cool in the valley's stream, the three waved goodbye to Anne and hiked southeast across the alfalfa field.

Anne's suitcase, packed with new skirts, blouses and dresses sewn by Sophia during July, stood just inside the kitchen door.

"Oh, Mamma, it feels like I just got here and six weeks are gone already."

"But *good* weeks that we spent *together*, Anne. Besides, after all the canning and garden work you did, you'll feel like you're on Easy Street when you get back to Greenbergs. *I* would if I were in your shoes. There's a sack of green beans and new potatoes, a basket of tomatoes and a few onions to take. Mrs. Greenberg won't have shopped since her train got in so late last night and the stores are closed on Sunday."

"They'll love them. Dr. Greenberg says he's never tasted vegetables like ours. I guess they're not always as fresh in the New York City markets. Daddy's loading the car. I have to go." She hugged her mother, ducked her head to hide her tears, picked up the suitcase and ran out the door.

Sophia's eyes misted as she watched her daughter tuck her skirt beneath rounded hips and slide into the front seat of the Maxwell beside Will. She still couldn't believe how Anne had blossomed. Patterns had been cut back here, added to there to accommodate the curves that seemed to appear overnight. Standing on the back porch to wave a final goodbye, Sophia pondered Anne's new maturity.

I'm losing her.

The realization that she was instrumental in that loss made the ache in her heart more painful. Had it been wrong to put Anne's dreams within reach?

No, Anne must *have her chance. And whatever life brings she's got both feet on the ground, not like that flighty Alexander girl who tried to wrap herself around Bill at last year's Moonlight Picnic. Football might be good for Bill after all. With school and practice and farm work, he'll be too tired to think about girls. Everything's changing so fast! I'm not ready...*

Accepting the inevitability of her ripening children, she turned her thoughts to July's Democrat National Convention. Only bits and pieces were audible between the radio's crackling, thunder-storm-generated static. Will gave up trying to understand what news made it through and went to bed, but Sophia stayed by the old Philco until she knew Roosevelt won the nomination on the fourth ballot. She'd been too busy since to get details from the newspapers. She found the ones she'd saved and settled down for a quiet Sunday afternoon. Maybe there'd be something about Huey Long. She brooded over Roosevelt's ties to the crooked Louisiana governor.

Will's right. Politics does *make strange bedfellows.*

* * *

Sophia wakened to a light tap on her shoulder.

"Soph, it's almost five."

She stirred, sat up in a daze as newspapers rustled from her lap to the floor. "Oh, my. I must have dozed off. Are the children home yet? I didn't hear them come in."

"Bill and Seth are starting chores. Sarah's asleep upstairs. From what the boys said, she was a trouper. Managed to keep up with them, but it wore her out and she went right to bed when they got home about an hour ago."

"She's taking a nap this late in the day? Oh, Will, you shouldn't have let her. She'll be up all night."

"I just got home myself a few minutes ago. Stopped by the office to catch up on some paper work while it was quiet. I'll wake her if you want. What were you reading that was so interesting you fell asleep?"

"Just trying to catch up on the Chicago Convention."

"Soph, that was a month ago!"

"I know, but I was canning and sewing and…you know how summer goes. Anyway, I saved the papers. Did you know Roosevelt was the first candidate ever to go to the convention and make his acceptance speech? Look at this headline, all in capital letters. 'ROOSEVELT FLYS TO CHICAGO TO DELIVER ACCEPTANCE SPEECH IN PERSON'. He flew, Will. He got on an airplane and *flew*." She picked up another paper. "And listen to this. 'I pledge you, I pledge myself, to a new deal for the American people.' A *new deal*, Will, isn't that stirring?"

"Hmph! I'd feel better if Garner had taken the Vice Presidential slot to back him up. I still wonder about Roosevelt."

"According to the papers, Garner didn't want to give up his power as Speaker of the House. But you're right, it would have been a strong ticket. Roosevelt from New York and Garner from Texas, both corners of the country tied together. Are you hungry? I guess we'll have leftovers tonight."

"Plenty left over. You fried enough chicken at noon to feed Coxie's army. Why'd you fix so much?"

"I thought your brother Jim and his family were due. They always seem to know when the garden's at its peak. It's been several weeks since they've driven over and since they never tell us when they're coming I thought this time I'd be ready for them. They're always hungry. I don't see how they manage to feed that family of theirs in town, do you?"

"Sure don't. I tried to tell Jim he could put a garden in his back yard, but guess it's easier just to come over here and load the car from ours. He's always nice about taking things back for Ma and Pa, though. Jim still thinks of the farm as home, you know. They all do, even Ma."

Sophia's relaxed expression turned stony. Will studied her closed face.

Guess she'll never forgive Ma for the Lysol...can't say I blame her, either, but it would make my life a lot easier if they'd settle things between them. Good thing she doesn't know about the Klan threats!

"Doesn't hurt to share, does it? We've got plenty. And we can't very well send things to Pa and not Ma." The silence continued. Will moved to a safer topic of conversation. "Anne had a little surprise today when I dropped her off at Greenbergs."

"Good? Or bad? Is Mrs. Greenberg all right?"

"Seems to be. But in her condition, her family was worried about her traveling with those two little boys. Her brother came back on the train with her to help out."

Sophia was puzzled. "So? That sounds like a wise decision to me. What's he like?"

"Tall, dark curly hair, good looking. And eighteen years old. Says that since he's never been out of New York before, he wants to see as much of Illinois as he can while he's here. Seems he'd like to look around our farm, too. He'll be going to college in September, though, so he'll only be here about three weeks."

"*Three weeks!* In the same house with *Anne*? Is he... Does he... Did he look like a gentleman, Will?"

"Hard to tell a gentleman from a caveman when the sap's rising. He's a snappy dresser, though. Anne seemed sort of dazzled. Of course, she's used to country boys and small-town fellas. Never showed any interest in boys before, at least that *I* know of." Will cleared his throat. "He seemed kind of taken with her, too."

"Do you think we should bring Anne home while he's there? We could say we know how crowded they are. Or I could say I need her at home for something."

"You know we can't do that. She's not a little girl any longer and she'd know exactly what we were up to. Besides, Ruth Greenberg's got eyes in her head. Reckon her family would be as upset as us if those kids got together. You can bet she'll keep an eye on them both.

"Boys will be in soon. Chicken hanging in the well bucket? I'll pull it up if you'll slice some tomatoes and wake Sarah. Mind adding some corn to the rest of those green beans for succotash?"

* * *

Sophia's hands were deep in bread dough when two short rings jangled through the house. "Sarah, please answer the phone. I can't."

She rounded the dough, thumped it over, and continued kneading. Sarah pulled a chair close to the box on the parlor wall, climbed up, and lifted the receiver.

"Mamma, it's Anne. She wants to talk to you. Shall I tell her you can't?"

"No. Tell her I'll be there as soon as I get the lard off my hands."

During the three days since Anne's return to Bridgeton, Sophia had half-expected, half-dreaded Anne's call. She wiped her hands, buried her anxiety under a cheerful tone, and picked up the phone. Sarah eavesdropped nearby.

"Anne, Honey. Is anything wrong?…No, it's just that you don't usually call during the week…Yes, your father told me about him, he sounds nice…What's his name?…I'm sure you did, but you know how Daddy forgets names…Well of course you can…Oh, I'm sorry, didn't I tell you? We're not going to the Moonlight Picnic this year…Well, with Bill at football practice and your dad never knowing what time he'll get home it just didn't seem to work out…Fine, Honey, we'll see you Sunday."

* * *

"Sarah, check the hen house for eggs while Daddy's washing up for dinner."

"But Mamma, I gathered the eggs this morning."

"Check again. Some of the hens have been laying in the afternoon and we don't want the eggs to spoil in this heat. And be sure to look everywhere, they don't always lay in the nests."

Will watched Sarah walk out the door, swinging the egg basket. "What was that all about, Soph?"

"I wanted to talk to you alone while the boys are still at the barn with Mike. Anne called today."

"And?"

"And she wants to bring Abraham Eisenfeld out this Sunday for dinner. She said he's never been on a farm before and wants to see what it's like."

"Same thing he told me. Abraham Eisenfeld. Hmph. So *that's* who he is. All I could remember was it was a mouthful. Well, sounds like a good Irish name."

"It's not funny, Will. I told her it would be all right because I didn't want her to think we wouldn't approve. That's the surest way to start a spark even if there's not one there already. But I think there may be. She sounded so…so grownup."

"She is. Almost sixteen." Will mulled over the situation. "I don't like it either, but I think you're right. He'll be gone in a little while though. And you know she's got a good head on her shoulders. Let's just act easy on it. He wants to see an Illinois farm, we'll show him one."

"She asked if we could take him to the Moonlight Picnic with us, too. I told her we weren't going this year."

A familiar devilish grin split Will's face. "Why not? They

could do the cakewalk together. That would *really* light Harry Stone's fire…give him and his cronies something else to crow about."

"Don't even think that, Will. I won't have Anne's name bandied about by those yahoos any more. You know what they said when Anne went to stay with the Greenbergs."

Will's face sobered. "Well, Soph, that wasn't any of my doing. It was your idea, and it's got us in several pretty kettles of fish already."

Tears seeped from Sophia's eyes. "I know. It's all my fault. And there's more. We always have fried chicken on Sunday? Well, this time I'm going to have to *bake* it."

"Baked chicken? In August? My God, Soph, you'll turn the whole house into an oven."

"Well, I can't fry it in *lard*, can I?" Sophia laid her head on the table and sobbed.

* * *

Sunday arrived beautiful and cool. Except for patches of flaking paint, the farm had never looked better. On Saturday, Seth scrubbed the back porch, veranda, sidewalks and rambling-rose-covered privy while Bill cut grass and weeds with a long-handled, wide-blade scythe. Sophia's zinnia beds overflowed with riotous blooms. Then, as though on cue, an overnight shower cooled the air and rinsed away the yellow dust, leaving the Macklins' corner of the world sparkling and clear. An air of expectancy hovered over the house on the bluff.

Will, wearing dress pants and shirt, stood on the veranda admiring his bottomland fields and thinking about the day ahead. In the kitchen, Sophia fussed over Sarah's breakfast. "Soph," he called through the screened parlor doors, "leave that kitchen and come out here a minute. Talk about beautiful!"

Sophia stepped onto the veranda with a bucket of fresh-picked green beans and a huge pot. "If you're going to admire your land, you might as well do something useful while you're at it."

Will took the beans, settled into the swing, snapped and dropped bite-size pieces into the pot. "Guess since the ham's all gone, you're going to flavor these with bacon drippings?"

"Don't be nasty, Will. I didn't realize how much we depend on the pigs for food. You'll have your beans flavored with onion today. I'm cooking new potatoes with them, too. I'll just have to tell him the rolls are made with lard. I made plenty of noodles, though, so he won't miss them. And those two old hens made rich broth."

"Good thing you thought of chicken and noodles. Be a shame to heat up the house on a day like this."

Still despondent, Sophia joined Will in the swing and started snapping beans. "I just wish today was over."

"It will be. What time are they coming?"

"About ten. They have to use Dr. Greenberg's car and he needs it to make rounds first. I asked Bill to show him around the farm while Anne and I get dinner on the table. Then there'll be the afternoon to get through."

"How'd you like some *good* news for a change? I've got an expense account set up for work gas money. And Rufus finally resigned last week."

"Oh Will, that *is* good news. I didn't see how we could keep going the way things were. So now you're officially Road Commissioner?"

"Not cut-and-dried yet but the County Board meets next week, then I will be. All the Board members know the situation. I've been pretty sure something was cooking, just didn't want to say anything until it was settled. And here's more good news. John says I can use the pickup to go back and forth to work. That way, if I have to, I can check on jobs in the south end of the county before I go to the office. The Maxwell's just about worn out, but if you still think you'd like to learn to drive..."

Sophia threw her arms around Will, upsetting the bucket of beans. Her delighted squeal brought a curious Sarah to the veranda.

"Oh, Mamma, now we have to pick beans *twice.*"

* * *

With a deadpan face, Will studied the dining room table. "No Spode today, Soph?"

"Now that's mean. I've eaten about all the humble pie I can stand. Do you want me to choke on it? The new everyday Sears and Roebuck china is fine. It's enough that I had to polish the silver. It gets tarnished if it's not used and we never use it. As soon as we get caught up on the bills I'm going to order some of those new stainless steel knives and forks, too, and get rid of that old pewter."

"No spoons? Guess we can forget the soup? Well, he can always admire the Spode in the china cabinet. You've really spiffed things up." Will nodded at Sophia's family treasures glistening behind spotless glass. He sniffed the bowl of roses on the table. "Pretty. Don't *smell* like they came from the privy."

"It's all that natural fertilizer, Will. Besides, he doesn't need to know where they came from."

"Only rambling roses on the place. If he's got eyes in his head and has to use the privy while he's here he'll figure it out. By the way, what do we call him? Abraham? Abe? Honest Abe? Can't just keep saying 'he' and 'him'."

"Let's see how Anne introduces him." Blue's bark set off the other dogs. Sophia looked out the window. "Well, here they come." She stripped off her apron, hung it behind the kitchen door, stepped out on the veranda and settled a welcoming smile on her face.

* * *

"Mamma, this is Abe Eisenfeld." Will stepped forward. "And you remember Daddy. You two met last Sunday." Sarah ran down the front stairs and skipped onto the veranda as Abe and Will shook hands. "And this is my little sister, Sarah."

Will's eyes crinkled in amusement as Sarah bobbed a curtsy.

Little mimic! Wonder where she learned that*?*

Abe smiled, bowed in response to her old-fashioned greeting and lifted the little girl's hand to kiss. "Sarah! What a lovely Old Testament name. It means 'Princess' in Hebrew, you know." Will and Sophia exchanged dismayed glances. "It fits you. A pretty name for a pretty little girl." Sarah blushed through the smile that dimpled her face.

Anne tousled Sarah's curls. "It used to be Yahbut because she argues all the time, but she's *almost* a Sarah now."

During the introductions, Sophia surreptitiously studied Anne. Her maturing daughter's hair had warmed to a rich honey that framed her face in deep waves. Her eyes, duplicates of her mother's, sparkled between darkened lashes. Faint touches of color highlighted her cheekbones. Her lips were suspiciously pink. Surprised, Sophia realized Anne was wearing makeup. She wondered what Will would think of *that*…

"Where are the boys, Mamma?"

"Collecting bait. They thought your friend might like to go fishing at the creek this afternoon if you don't have to leave right after dinner." She neglected to mention that she had suggested the fishing expedition.

Anne was surprised. "Fishing? In the afternoon?"

Will, a party to the conspiracy, joined the conversation. "Doubt if they catch anything, but it'll give Bill and Seth a chance to show

Abe the creek and fields across the tracks while you're helping your mom wash up the dishes. Like to sit in the porch swing a bit, Abe? Nice view from there."

"Everything's beautiful, Mr. Macklin. Anne told me it was but I never imagined anything like this. The closest I've ever been to the country is a hotel in the Catskill Mountains."

A droll expression crept across Will's face. "Ever run into old Rip?"

"Old Rip?"

"Rip Van Winkle. Thought you might have read about him in school. He's the Dutchman who had a mite too much to drink up in the Catskills?"

Abe laughed uncertainly. "I may have heard about him. You seem to know more about Upstate New York than I."

"Never mind. Rip was just one of Washington Irving's creations. Old fella who went to sleep before the Revolutionary War, a little over a hundred years after the first Macklin landed in America. Rip slept for twenty years and woke up to find his world all changed. Sort of a parable. I just thought you might feel a little like Rip in reverse out here in Illinois, away from all that big city progress, kinda like you stepped back in time instead of forward. Guess it wasn't much of a joke after all. Now, what about the Catskills?"

"Nothing, really. Just that our family goes to a hotel there every summer to escape the city heat." A breeze whispered across the veranda. "This is much nicer. You really appreciate quiet beauty like this after living with city noise most of the year."

Bill and Seth rounded the corner of the barn and headed for the house. "Hey, Annie," Bill called as Seth ran to hug his sister.

Laughing, Anne stepped back to protect her dress from Seth's manure-streaked hands. "I'll hug you as soon as you wash your hands, Seth. This is Abe Eisenfeld, but don't you *dare* shake hands until you wash up. And that's my brother Bill."

Bill acknowledged the introduction with a wave from the yard. "Come on, Runt. We'll see the company as soon as we scrub off this worm juice."

"Do you need any help, Mamma?" Anne asked.

"Not right now. We can sit and visit a bit, then Bill can show Abe around the upper part of the farm while you and I get dinner on the table."

"What do New Yorkers think of Roosevelt?" Will asked. The conversation drifted into politics. Bill and Seth, freshly scrubbed, joined the group. Seth, fidgeting, finally set off for the orchard with the dogs. Sarah, despite her instant infatuation with their guest, became bored with grownup talk and trailed after Seth. Bill, deep in a football fantasy, leaned against a column.

Pollinating bees drifted from flower to flower. The smell of ripening peaches in the orchard, the lush green of the fields, and an aura of drowsy warmth all came together in a saturation of fertility. To Sophia, the Garden of Eden seemed very near.

"Excuse me, Will, but I'm sure Abe is anxious to see the farm. Bill, would you do the honors?"

"Sure, Mom." Bill eyed Abe's highly polished brown loafers. "Say, Abe, what size shoes do you wear?"

"Eleven. Why?"

"You don't want to wear those in the barns or fields. I wear twelves, but I've got some old boots that might fit you."

"Anne told me what it would be like. I have old shoes in the car, but thanks anyway."

"How about some overalls? Be a shame to get those ice cream pants dirty."

"Fine, if you have an extra pair."

Anne watched dubiously as Bill and Abe went through the parlor doors and up the open front staircase.

* * *

"This isn't the first barn. The old one was a two-story built almost a hundred years ago, but it fell in about ten years back. When Dad built the new one he made the middle part—the hay barn—tall, then sloped the roof down to the cow barn on one side and the stable on the other. Like wings. That big double sliding door lets us drive the horses right into the barn so we can unload the hayrick there instead of having to pitch it up high. That way we can store all the hay in one place. See? We just feed the cows and horses through those connecting windows. When the hay starts to get low around January, we move it to one side and park the Maxwell in here instead of the garage. The heat from the animals makes it easier to start. Gets pretty cold winter times in Illinois."

He pointed toward a lean-to on the north end of the barn. "That's the birthing area where the cows have their calves if we can catch 'em in time. What they *like* to do is find a quiet corner in the pasture back there, but…well…sometimes that's not safe for the new calves."

"Are wolves a problem?"

"Just two-legged ones. That's about it, unless you want to see the hogs. We keep them up there, on the other side of the alfalfa field, because of the smell. And the gelding. Mom can't stand to hear 'em squeal when they're gelded."

"Gelded?"

"Yeah. When pigs are weaned we call the females gilts and the males shoats. We geld the shoats, that is unless Dad wants to let one of them grow up to be a boar and use him for breeding." He noticed Abe's confusion. "You know, nip off their ba…uh…testicles so they're its instead of hims."

Abe winced. "No, I didn't know. Gelding. That's interesting. What do you do with the nipped-off ba…uh…testicles?"

"Most folks around here eat 'em. They're considered a real delicacy, sort of like mushrooms. Call 'em Rocky Mountain oysters. You slice ‘em, dip ‘em in batter and fry ‘em. But Mom won’t fix ‘em so Dad gives ‘em to the neighbors or takes ‘em to Grampa and Gramma.” He looked at Abe speculatively. “Ummm…you want to see the hogs?”

“I’d like that. Do we have time?”

“Plenty of time. We won’t eat till noon, and it’s only half-past eleven now.”

Abe checked his wristwatch. “Right on the button. How did you know that, Bill?”

“Well, farmers mostly tell time by the sun. It’s just something you learn. Those are the storage cribs over there. Almost empty now, but by the time we get through shucking corn they’ll be all filled up for winter. You should *see* this place at harvest time!”

“That would be nice, but I doubt if we come to Bridgeton when Ruth’s baby is born. If it’s another boy, we’ll probably just meet them in St. Louis for the bris since there’s no rabbi here.”

Bill, beneath a polite veneer, was still immersed in football. “What’s a bris?” he asked absently.

“It’s a Jewish religious ceremony. Actually, it’s a circumcision.” It was Bill’s turn to look confused. “The rabbi cuts the foreskin away with a very sharp knife.”

Bill’s mouth dropped open. The blood drained from his face. “You mean you’ll cut his…his…uh…”

“Penis. That’s the nice word for it, anyway. Most of the guys in New York use slang words like cock. Or dick.”

Bill’s face went from white to red. “Most of the guys I know say tallywhacker. Guess you got to call it something. Did…did they do that to you?”

“Yes. It’s a ritual for all Jewish boy babies, kind of like your baptism. It’s really for cleanliness. A lot of Christians are beginning to have it done, too, but for Jews it’s an important part of our religion.”

Bill’s stomach churned. It *was* true! The trust he’d always placed in his mother evaporated, leaving a gaping, painful hole. He didn't want to believe it, but a Jew had just admitted it himself.

"Bill? Are you all right? I'm sorry, I didn't mean to offend you. You're so big I forgot you're still fourteen."

"Well…uh…that's okay. Say, are you sure you want to see the hogs? It smells something fierce up there and I feel kind of sick to my stomach. Besides, we oughta wash up and get these overalls off before dinner." He turned back toward the house.

Abe followed, puzzled by the sudden change in Bill.

* * *

"This is a delicious meal, Mrs. Macklin. Would you mind terribly if I had another roll? I've never tasted better."

Shortly after everyone sat down to eat, Sophia had left the table to get another serving spoon. By the time she returned, Abe was eating a roll and the damage was done. She ignored Will's ironic smile. "I'm glad you like them. I made them this morning when it was still cool. If we can help it, we don't heat the oven during the day in summer. Would you like more noodles? Chicken? Green beans?"

"No, thank you, but perhaps another roll and more of those tomatoes? They're wonderful. We don't have tomatoes like these in New York City."

"Bill, you've hardly eaten anything. Are you sure you feel all right?"

Bill glared accusingly at his mother, then looked away. "I'm fine, Mom. Just not hungry." Bill's face was still pale and strained.

"Be sure to save room for some of Soph's devils food cake, Abe. She made it with butter. Baked *it* early this morning, too. Her devils food cake is famous in these parts. Don't know how she does it in that old wood stove oven, no heat regulation at all."

Sophia smiled. "All you have to do is learn to gauge the heat and check to see if the cake's done. Some women never learn that, I guess. That's why their cakes fall. I just stick a new broom straw in the middle. If it comes out clean, it's through baking."

"Well, however she does it, Abe, you never tasted anything like it."

"Oh, Will, not everyone has a sweet tooth like yours."

"I do, Mom," Seth said. "What's it like in New York, Abe?"

"Well, lots of tall buildings and crowds of people all the time. And traffic. Sometimes I think that city is just one big automobile horn."

"But what about the museums and the theater, Abe?"

"Of course we have those, too, Mrs. Macklin, but one can always come into the city for culture. It's not necessary to *live* there. It's just that my father's law office is downtown and he hates to commute. A lot of people do commute from the suburbs, though. The city has an excellent public transportation system and they're expanding it all the time."

Seth helped himself to more noodles. "Do you live in a tall house?"

"No, in an apartment building, on the eighth floor. A house like yours would be too expensive in New York. But we live near Central Park and have a nice view from our living room window."

Seth goggled. "Eight floors? Don't you get awful tired climbing all those stairs?"

Abe's laugh was friendly. "Well, unless there's a power failure we don't have to climb stairs. We use an elevator."

"Gee, I've never *been* in an elevator."

Sophia smiled. "Neither have I, Seth." She turned to Abe. "What else are you planning to see while you're in Illinois?"

"My father wants me to see Temple B'rith Sholom in Springfield. It's a conservative reform temple that one of his friends, Julius Rosenwald, helped found. His father, Samuel, was born in Springfield in 1862 in a house across the street from

Lincoln's home. And I'd like to see the Lincoln home and Memorial, too. Ruth tells me there's bus service to Springfield."

Will heaped more green beans on his new china plate. "Did you say Rosenwald? Isn't he the head of Sears and Roebuck?"

"Yes, but you'd never know it. He's very modest about all he's accomplished. He and my father roomed together in college and he's almost a member of our family. In fact, we call him Uncle Julius. Do you think I might have more of those tomatoes, Mrs. Macklin?"

* * *

Seth was still asking questions when they reached the creek. He turned to call to his brother, lagging behind. "Come on, Slowpoke. You've got the fishing poles."

"Well, you've got the bait, Runt."

"I know, but we can't put worms on our fingers to catch fish."

Abe walked back toward Bill. "Here, let me help with those poles. I've never fished before, you know. You'll have to show me what to do."

The three fished for half an hour with no more than a nibble while Seth's questions continued.

Bill pulled his line back to the bank. "No point in fishing if you're going to scare 'em away with all that talk, Seth. Wrong time of day to fish anyway. Why don't we just head home?"

"Hey, let's show Abe our swimming hole! Bet he's never been skinny dipping."

"You're right, Seth, I haven't and I've always wanted to. Okay with you, Bill?"

Seth already had his line out of the water and was wrapping it around the pole. "Come on. It's not far, just around that bend in the creek. We can leave our poles here and pick 'em up on the way back."

Seth raced ahead, unbuttoning his shirt as he ran. By the time Abe and Bill reached the sand spit that bordered the swimming hole, Seth had tossed his clothes over a limb and was diving into the deep water.

"Be careful, Runt," Bill shouted over the noise of splashing water. "Remember what happened to Great Grampa." He lowered his voice. "Here, Abe. You can use this limb. I'll put my things over there."

Bill dropped his clothes and ran for the water. "Be careful where you dive. The deep end's down..." He turned to point, froze, and gaped. Abe's phallic glory drooped from a nest of dark pubic curls. "Why, they didn't cut it off! It's still there! I thought you said..."

Abe blinked in bafflement, then roared with laughter. "Is *that* what upset you so? Good God, Bill, you've been hearing those horror stories about Jews, even here in the Midwest! Yes, it's still there. All that gets cut off is that loose skin. I *told* you it's easier to keep clean that way."

"Guess I wasn't paying much attention. We were talking about gelding the pigs and all and it kind of ran together. And I was sort of thinking about football..."

Abe's shoulders shook with laughter. "I'm sorry, Bill, but you should see your face. It almost matches your hair."

Bill swallowed his embarrassment and squared his shoulders. "Guess I'm just a dumb country hick."

Abe sobered immediately. "No, you're not. You're bright as a new penny. But you *were* misinformed." He slapped Bill on the back. "Come on, let's go skinny dipping. Then I want to know what happened to Great Grampa."

* * *

Bill, Seth and Abe trooped up the path to the top of the bluff and cut through the orchard, laughing and talking all the way. Seth carried the poles to the garage while Abe and Bill joined the rest of the family on the veranda.

Will eyed their damp hair. "Should have known you boys couldn't get near that creek without skinny dipping. I was just getting ready to come after you."

Anne was already on her feet. "Dr. Greenberg called, Abe. He has to see a patient and needs the car. We should leave immediately."

"Just as soon as I say goodbye to Seth and Sarah. Where *is* Sarah, Mrs. Macklin?"

"She's napping, but I'll tell her for you. Oh, Will put a basket of tomatoes in your car. Don't hit any bumps going back, some of them are pretty ripe but those are on top so you can use them first." Her smile was genuine. "It's been a pleasure to have you with us today, Abe."

"The pleasure was mine, believe me. And we'll relish every tomato. Tell Seth goodbye for me, too. Thank you all so much." He shook hands with Will and Sophia, winked at Bill, and punched him on the shoulder. "Honestly, I haven't had as much fun in a coon's age. So long Sport. Show 'em who's boss on the football field!"

* * *

Sophia and Will rocked gently back and forth in the swing. Will's wicked grin was back. "Well, Abe still *looks* healthy. Guess those lard rolls didn't hurt him any. I think he only ate four. And did you notice I didn't tell him he was eating off Sears and Roebuck plates? Say, hope we didn't have a Sears and Roebuck *catalog* in the privy." Will's snicker was his own, and the only, reply. "Anne say anything while you two were busy in the kitchen?"

"Not really. After all, she just brought Abe out to show him what life was like on an Illinois farm, remember?"

"I thought her color was a little high."

"It was rouge, Will," Sophia snapped, still smarting over her husband's sarcasm. "And lipstick. Anne was wearing makeup."

Will mulled over further proof of his daughter's maturity. "Well, they didn't lollygag around, anyway."

"No. He *is* handsome, though, and very well mannered. I can see why she likes him. I just hope he wasn't bored."

Chapter 15

"Watch out, Dad, here she comes again!" Seth raced for the porch as Sophia turned the Maxwell's wheels sharply right, crushing the alfalfa stubble in the field that stretched between the driveway's east arc and the hog pen. Upstairs in the safety of her room, Sarah alternately cringed below and peeped over the top of the windowsill.

Will dodged behind the cottonwood's sturdy trunk seconds before the car swerved and came to a shuddering halt in the field. "Soph, I *told* you to ease your foot down on the clutch before you brake! That car's not much but by the time you get through with it it'll be nothing but the bucket of bolts Doc already thinks it is."

"Don't you swear at me, Will Macklin! This thing's got a mind of it's own. All I wanted to do was park it in the drive but *you* got in the way."

Will stepped over the stubble to the car and scratched his head. "Well, you have to slow it down before you park it. That's what the brake's for. Thing is, you have to remember to push the clutch in with your *left* foot and brake with your *right.*

"Never saw anyone so heavy-footed with a gas pedal. From here it looked like you were gonna take the hog fence with you when you did that last whirlygig." He scrutinized Sophia's determined face. "Okay, let's go over it again. Now, depress the clutch, put the gear in neutral and turn the key on."

A futile, grinding noise sounded from the ignition. "Oh, God, Will, what *is* that? Did I break it?"

"No, don't worry. The engine's just flooded. Might as well get out and let it rest a bit. I put a jug of that new batch of cider in the well bucket to cool." He opened the door and helped his trembling wife from the car. "Look, Soph, you don't have to do this, you know."

Sophia spoke through clenched teeth. "Yes, I do. I'm not going to let a machine get the best of me. Besides, if I don't learn to drive this…this…*demon* I'll have to *walk* into Macklin Corner every day next week to campaign for the fall election."

"Honey, it's just a machine. Once you learn to show it what to do, it'll behave like a lamb."

"A lamb? I've *seen* those spring lambs jumping all around the pastures. Can't you think of a better comparison?"

Will cupped his hand under Sophia's elbow and guided her toward the veranda swing. "Seth, you thirsty? Draw up that gallon of cider and bring it here. Get some cups, too. Bill should be home soon and Sarah will be down when she sees your mom's out of the car."

Late October lay lightly on the Macklin acres. Despite the abbreviated second planting, the corn harvest was good and the cribs stacked high. The scent of fresh-cut alfalfa perfumed the air. That Saturday morning, after the dew dried and before he left for Bridgeton, Bill hitched the team to the hay rake and piled the final cutting into neat rows. Will, Mike and Seth spent the remainder of the morning forking dried alfalfa onto the hayrick and transferring it to the barn.

As soon as noon dishes were done, Will had circled the driveway in the Maxwell, picked up Sophia, and driven into the newly shorn field. The lesson had begun.

"All right, Soph. The Maxwell shifts a little different from those modern cars. It's got what's called a reverse shift. It's still an H, though. Watch me now. Start in neutral. Clutch down. Shift all the way up right to low. Pick up speed. Clutch down. Shift down-*over*-down to second. Pick up speed. Clutch down. Shift straight up to high." Will drove slowly around the perimeter of the field. "Hear the way the engine picks up? It'll tell you when it's time to shift gears. Main things to remember are ease in the clutch *before* you shift or brake and take it easy on the foot feed." Will stopped the car, got out, and walked to the passenger side while Sophia slid behind the wheel. "Better practice shifting gears with the engine off."

"What's on the lower *right* leg of the H?"

"That's reverse. We'll get to that after you learn to go forward. Say, that's pretty good. Ready to try it with the motor going? Remember now, keep your right gas pedal foot light and steady."

Will had watched closely while she drove twice around the two-acre field and parked in the driveway by the back porch. He'd climbed out, walked to the driver's side, motioned for Sophia to roll the window down and kissed her lightly. "Good luck. You're on your own."

Now, in the swing, Will massaged Sophia's taut neck muscles. "It's my fault, Soph. You were doing so well with me in the car I thought you were ready to go it alone. And you were okay till you tried to park it."

"Do you think I'll ever learn, Will?"

"Sure you will." He sniffed the heady scent of fresh alfalfa. "Smell that? Good crop for the third cutting. Nice and dry, too. I'm always afraid a late cutting will mildew, but this was fine. Kind of a winter bonus for the livestock." He stroked Sophia's still-trembling hand. "Seth's doing real well with that pitchfork. Took him awhile to learn to criss-cross each forkful of hay on the rick so it didn't slide off, but once he learned how he worked right along with Mike and me."

"Maybe, but when he came in he was so exhausted he was white as a sheet."

"Didn't hurt him none. He needs to build up some muscle on that skinny body of his. Besides, don't see how I could ask Bill to pitch hay this morning when he had an out-of-town game this afternoon."

"Bill wouldn't even eat before he left."

"He had a good breakfast. If he *should* happen to get to play, it's best not to eat before a game. Somebody tackles you in the gut, you cough your cookies and he was sure hoping Coach Munson would put him in, at least a little. Looks like maybe we better try to see the next home varsity game."

"I don't think I can. You know how I am about violence and I couldn't stand seeing Bill get hurt. I don't hate many things, but I *do* hate football."

"You didn't say that when he brought home his six-week report card. First time that boy's gotten straight As in his life."

"What good will straight As do if he breaks his neck?"

"He won't. Probably get a few bruises, maybe a cracked rib or two, but he can live with that. Those uniforms are padded and the helmets protect their heads. Besides, Munson takes good care of his boys, shows 'em what to do and how to do it, then makes 'em practice till they know every move inside and out before he turns 'em loose. He says..."

"When did you talk to Munson?"

"Finished work early one day and drove by the practice field to pick Bill up. I watched the boys scrimmage awhile. You know, Bill's bigger than most of the seniors? Munson and I visited while the boys showered and he says Bill's a natural, the best freshman player he's ever seen, that if he proves out in high school he might even get an athletic scholarship. How about *that*? Our son going to college! Football's how Doc Campbell got to the University of Illinois, you know."

"Think of your *daughter* going to college. She's working for a scholarship, too, but it will be on *grades*." She sighed. "I know you're trying to make me feel better about Bill playing football. Believe me, I've gone over and over it in my mind. Of *course* there are good aspects to it. He's studying for the first time in his life. He seems so much happier, too, and Anne says he's very popular with his classmates. I can accept it, but I don't have to like it. Now hush, here comes Seth. How soon will the engine be unflooded?"

"We'll get back to it in a minute." Will poured three cups of cider and handed one to Seth, who took his into the yard with the dogs. Will settled back in the swing. "When'd you talk to Anne?"

"She called this morning while you were haying. I think she was lonely. This was supposed to be her weekend at home, but Ruth needs help with the boys."

"When's the baby due?"

"Mid-November. They're cleaning the house for Ruth's mother's arrival. She'll help with the baby and stay with Levi while Little Josh is in school. It sounds like they've gone over everything twice."

"Can't say I blame 'em. From what Ruth and the doctor said, she sounds pretty persnickety. Say, think we should dress up like Indians? War paint and all? Give her a real Illinois welcome? We could get Uncle Ed and…"

"That's not funny! You know perfectly well what Dr. Greenberg said the night the Klan tried to burn that cross. Anne may come home to stay while Mrs. Eisenfeld's there. You know they only have one extra bedroom and Anne's been using that. They're thinking of looking for a bigger house, too. They'll need another bedroom as soon as the baby gets old enough for a room of its own."

"Where'd Abe sleep when he was there?"

"On a cot in the boys' room, but Ruth says her mother needs her sleep and prefers a bed. And a room of her own."

"She may change her tune when she tries to handle those live-wire boys alone. Sure be nice to have Anne back home awhile, though." He called Seth from the yard. "Put this jug back in the well bucket. Bill won't want warm cider." The swing moved rhythmically. "Anne say anything about Abe?"

"She never mentions him. I'd feel a lot better if she did. You know how reserved and quiet Anne gets when she really cares about something. And it wasn't just a one-sided attraction. He liked her as much as she liked him. I'm sure they both realize that with their different backgrounds there's no future for them. Besides, Anne has other dreams. She really *does* want to be a teacher and women teachers can't be married. This is just something she'll have to work out herself."

"Poor kids. Young love can hurt like hell. Sure glad *we* found each other first time around. Say, you'll have to take a test for a driver's license. I'll look around the office for a book you can study."

"You mean I won't be able to drive into Macklin Corner next week?"

"Should be all right if you get the hang of it, and if you go the back way up the long hill and park by the school, but you can't drive on the slab or in town till you get that license. You'll have to take a behind-the-wheel test, too." He called his younger son, back at play with the dogs in the yard. "Seth, get up here on the veranda, show your mom the hand signals she has to learn."

Seth's deadpan look was relieved by the twinkle in his eye. "Well, *first* thing you have to learn is roll down the window on the driver's side." Sophia, intent on learning, missed the joke, but Will chuckled appreciatively. "Come on, do it with me, Mom. Left arm out the window. Bend your elbow and raise your arm *up* to signal a *right* turn. *Straight out* for a *left* turn. Point to the ground for *stop*."

Sophia stood behind Seth, following his directions. Sarah sidled onto the veranda. Seth in the lead demonstrating, the three formed a line, practicing signals in unison. Sarah began chanting "up-out-down la con*ga*" and the giggling, practicing conga line wove back and forth across the veranda. Will, content, leaned back in the swing and watched.

"Believe you've got it, Soph," he chuckled. "Finish your cider and we'll show your demon who's boss." He winked at Seth. "And be sure to leave your window down so I can kiss you *and* you can use your hand signals. Maybe this evening you can drive into

Macklin Corner. I still have to teach you how to shift gears on the long hill."

* * *

"Sarah! Seth! Let's go." Sophia turned the newscast off and collected her shopping bag filled with candidate literature, sample ballots and political buttons. She glanced down at the Democrat donkey and 'Kick out Depression with a Democratic Vote' pins on her coat lapel. "Do you have all your books?" she asked as the children clattered down the back stairs into the kitchen.

"Right here, Mom," Seth answered.

Sophia checked Sarah's meager collection. "Where's your reader? Sarah, what am I going to do with you? Look in my sewing chair, you were reading there last night. And hurry or you'll be late for school."

The final week before election had been busier than usual. In addition to her regular housework and cooking, each morning Sophia drove the two youngest children to her parking place near the school, walked from house to house campaigning, returned to collect the children after school, then drove home to another five hours of work. Instead of tired she was exhilarated.

On Friday morning, as she bent to retrieve her shopping bag, her coat button popped open. She muttered an oath under her breath and buttoned it again. With all the walking she'd done, she was sure she'd lost at least a little weight, but everywhere she went people insisted she have 'just a bite' before she continued her rounds. It was never much, they didn't have much, but it all added up. She was grateful this was the last day.

She'd wanted to spend Saturday in Macklin Corner as well, but Will insisted she see Bill's last home game of the season. "He won't play much," Will said, "but it'll mean a lot to him if you're there. Think we better ask Mike, too. He's been carrying part of

Bill's work load on the farm."

Seth picked up his sack of sandwiches and apples and looked for his mother's smaller sack. "Aren't you taking any lunch today, Mom?"

"Not today, Seth. Everywhere I go people feed me. I'm getting fat as a pig. Here's yours, Sarah." She locked the kitchen door, patted Blue on the head and admonished him to watch the house, and carefully steered the Maxwell out the oak-lined driveway and up the road.

Chapter 16

Sophia hummed as she put bowls and spoons on the table and arranged a box of shredded wheat, the sugar bowl and a pitcher of milk in the center. She pulled a kitchen chair to the pantry, climbed to retrieve hidden bananas from a high shelf and added them to the breakfast makings, along with a knife to slice them with.

No pancakes or biscuits today, but boxed cereal and bananas are a special treat.

She added an apple to each of the sack lunches and put them on the cabinet by three piles of books. Will's thermos, filled with hot coffee, sat on the table by his full lunch bucket. It was five a.m. Tuesday, November 8, 1932. John Hall, her driver, was to meet her in Macklin Corner in less than an hour. They were to pick up early voters and have them ready to cast their ballots when the polls opened at six.

Will shuffled into the kitchen rubbing his eyes. "Don't worry, Soph. I'll see to the kids this morning."

"Everything's done. Just see that they get to school. Did I wake you, Will? I tried to be as quiet as…"

"No, I've been awake since you got up at four. Just lying there, thinking. It's a big day for everyone. Looks like you're all ready to go. Got time for a cup of coffee?"

"I've already had two, but another one won't hurt. Oh, Will, I'm so *excited.* By this time tomorrow we'll know. I just don't see how Roosevelt can lose."

"Neither do I. John's got a dandy sign for the top of his car. 'ABOLISH BREAD LINES – VOTE FOR ROOSEVELT'. Wish I could go with you today. Office is closed for the election, but John doesn't think I should look like a campaigner, at least not yet. I'll spend the day at my desk."

"John's probably right. You've done such a wonderful job so far you don't want to hurt your chances in 1934. You know how people talk."

"Yeah, people like Harry Stone. Looks like folks would have enough sense not to listen to him, but some do. That man just loves to needle. I came close to calling him out last month at the feed store when he called me a turncoat in front of everyone."

"Harry doesn't concern us, Will. I don't know why you let him upset you. He won't admit it until the final results are in, maybe not even then, but he must realize Hoover's already beaten."

Will tried to contain his despondency. "Guess you're right. Just sour grapes on his part. Sure you want to stay at the courthouse after the polls close? It'll be awful late. Takes a long time to count all the votes."

"Yes, I'm sure. I've worked hard for this election and I want to see the results firsthand. There's soup and leftover roast beef for sandwiches in the cold box for the children and Mike's supper. And an apple pie. Mike will keep an eye on them and see they get to bed. And Bill will be here. I may rest for awhile at Ellen Campbell's this afternoon. I can't imagine getting tired today, though. I just wish I could be inside the polls while they're counting ballots, but I can't."

"Well, I'll pick you up at the polls when they close at six. Nice of Ellen to invite us for supper tonight." He fidgeted. "But I bet it was Doc's idea. Don't think Ellen cares much for me. Guess I was kinda short with her that night I had to ride in for Doc. She got pretty huffy." The old Seth Thomas clock struck the half hour. "You best be going, Soph. Don't want to keep John waiting. I'll wake the kids."

Sophia, blinded by anticipation, failed to see the signs of Will's growing dejection.

* * *

That evening, while John helped old Mrs. Turganyev to her

door, Sophia sat in John Hall's car checking her list. The two had spent the entire day carrying voters to and from the polls. With the exception of Tomas Lomaski, who had broken his leg the previous day, all her registered voters cast their ballots. For many, it was their first vote for a United States President. Turnout was heavy from the surrounding countryside as well. She flushed with anger as she remembered the veiled speculation on Harry Stone's face when he saw her riding with John. Lost in reflection about Harry's animosity toward the Macklins, she started as John opened the car door and slid into the driver's seat.

"Looks like that's it, Soph. Shall I take you to your car?"

"What time is it, John?"

"Quarter to six."

"Will's picking me up outside the polls after they lock the doors at six, then we're going to Campbell's for supper. I have to leave the car south of the school. Will doesn't want me driving in town or on the hard road until I get my license."

John nodded approvingly. "Good idea. Look, you're bound to be worn out. I know I am. No point in you standing out in the cold waiting. How about if I drop you by Campbell's, then swing by his office and tell Will where you are?"

"Would you mind, John? That would be wonderful." Sophia suddenly felt the long day's fatigue.

* * *

A tantalizing aroma of beef pot roast and garlic floated from the kitchen where Ellen was putting the finishing touches on supper. In Campbell's darkened parlor Sophia, feet propped on a disreputable leather hassock and looking forward to a meal she didn't cook, drowsed in the doctor's easy chair. Dr. Campbell was making his last house call of the day. She glanced at the clock on the wall and wondered about Will. It was already half-past six. Surely

John had given him the message.

Outside the front door, the doctor's voice raised in anger. Sophia sat up to listen.

"Dammit, Will. I don't know where you've been but you're sure in hell three sheets to the wind!"

Will's words were slurred. "Now Doc, I was just celebrating the election. Don't *you* start on me. Soph'll do that soon enough. Besides, I knew Soph wasn't standing around waiting. John found me out at Lizzie's and told me he'd dropped her off here."

"Lizzie's? Well that explains it. Spending time out there these days, are you? You oughta know by now there's men can drink whiskey and men that can't. I told you before, *you* can't. Beer's one thing, but whiskey…best thing you can do is stay completely away from it." The disgust in his voice would have wilted a sober Will. "Look, we can't stand out here on the porch all night. We might as well go in. Ellie will have supper ready. Food and black coffee's what you need now."

The door swung open and the doctor flipped the light switch. Sophia blinked in the sudden glare flooding the parlor and searched Will's face.

He returned her look with unfocused, glazed eyes. His mouth hung in a loose, twisted smile. "Well, Campaigner, you set the world on fire again today?"

"Oh, Will," Sophia moaned softly. The doctor went to the kitchen for coffee.

* * *

The meal was a nightmare. Under the doctor's stern gaze Will, hands folded in his lap, sat in a polite stupor. He ignored Ellen Campbell's carefully prepared food and angry face while Sophia picked at the pot roast and vegetables on her plate. When Ellen and the doctor cleared the table Sophia tried, unsuccessfully, not to hear the low voices in the kitchen.

"I don't care if he *is* your friend. You know how I feel about drunks! Just get him *out* of here. I worked all afternoon..."

"Will's not a drunk, Ellie. At least not yet. But he is one of those people whose system can't tolerate whiskey."

"He's certainly drunk now. And he's sitting at *our* table!"

"Shhh. They'll hear you."

Ellen's voice rose. "I don't care!"

Embarrassed, Sophia looked up as the doctor returned to the dining room. "I think we'd better leave, Dr. Tom."

The doctor glanced toward the kitchen. "Might be best, Soph. We'll talk about this later."

"I hate to ask another favor, but Will's got the office truck. He shouldn't drive it any more tonight and the shift is different so I don't think I can, but if you'll take us to the Maxwell I can get us home. We'll be back in the morning for the truck before Will goes to work."

"Wouldn't mind a bit, Soph. Say, I'll be at the courthouse. Want me to call you with the results? Probably be late."

"I'll be awake, don't worry. I really would appreciate that. Thank you, Dr. Tom. For everything."

* * *

Sophia drove in angry silence while Will mumbled apologies. She pulled around the driveway to the back porch in time to see Mike's lantern bobbing across the field toward the cabin, stopped the car and called, "Mike, are the children asleep? Good. Would you please come help me get Will into the house?"

* * *

The boys had forgotten to bank the furnace and the fire was

out. Wrapped in a heavy wool quilt, Sophia huddled next to the radio in the parlor. Returns were coming in from the eastern states. Roosevelt appeared to be winning there by a huge majority. She padded to the kitchen, poured herself a cup of muddy morning coffee, started to add cream and sugar, thought about her weight and resolutely picked up her cup, returned to the parlor, and gagged at the first sip of the thick, cold brew.

...no way to heat it...no one thought to bank the kitchen stove, either...too tired to build it up again...

She burrowed deeper into her quilt. The chill house creaked around her as she bent close to the radio to hear the latest returns.

Sophia brooded, wondering how Precinct Seven had done. Kickapoo County Courthouse would be bustling with activity. Precincts calling in results. Election judges carrying ballot boxes up the stairs. Reporters calling from Springfield, Chicago and St. Louis wanting the latest count. Watchers phoning results to candidate headquarters. And outside, crowds of excited people drifting from the courthouse to the bulletin boards mounted by the two Bridgeton papers, checking the latest information, then wandering back to the lights and activity of the courthouse. Tears of self-pity trickled down her cheeks.

A loud snore erupted from the bedroom. She stalked across the parlor, started to slam the door and thought of the children. She didn't want to wake them. She closed the squeaking door quietly and returned to the radio.

At four in the morning, twenty-four hours after Sophia's day started, the announcement came. Roosevelt was carrying forty-two of the forty-eight states. The telephone's jangle shattered the parlor's quiet. Sophia dropped her quilt and rushed to the phone.

The doctor's voice was jubilant. "Soph, Roosevelt took Illinois by a landslide. Precinct Seven just came in. You did it again!"

"Thanks, Dr. Tom," she whispered. Sophia replaced the receiver, turned the radio off, walked slowly toward the bedroom, and opened the door to be engulfed by nauseating, stale-whiskey fumes. She stood in the doorway and watched her husband sleep. Self-pity transmuted into pity and disgust for the stranger in the bed. Sophia stared at the tousled head on the pillow, picked up her own pillow, closed the door and once again retreated to the hard and lonely horsehair divan in the parlor.

Chapter 17

Will rolled over to snuggle against the warm body that had shared his bed for almost seventeen years. Empty space met his searching hand. He glanced at the Big Ben alarm clock, wondered why Soph was up so early, and groped for his missing wife's pillow to prop behind his throbbing head. It was gone, too. He groaned. Fuzzy images crept along the edge of consciousness.

Some kind of argument...must have had too much to drink again.

Had Lizzie switched him to rotgut? He never felt this bad when he drank local moonshine. Seemed like everyone wanted to buy him an election drink yesterday, though. He'd had to stand a couple of rounds, too.

Couldn't have 'em thinking I was a cheapskate.

He groaned again. Good Lord! He spent the money he'd saved for Soph's Christmas present—those knives, forks and spoons she was looking at in the Sears and Roebuck catalog.

His stomach churned, protesting the attempted fluid motion that normally propelled him out of bed. Head cradled in his hands, he sank to the edge of the mattress. More scenes from the night before invaded his brain. He quelled his nausea, struggled to his feet in the cold house, dressed, eased open the door between bedroom and parlor, and again reminded himself to oil the squeaking hinge. In the faint, predawn light he studied his sleeping wife's face.

She must be mad as a hornet to sleep on that cold leather. Can't say I blame her, either.

He tucked the blanket around her exposed left shoulder, made his way to the kitchen, lit the lamp, and inserted the handle to shake ashes through the stove grates. The harsh noise rocketed through his skull. He sneezed as a cloud of wood ash filtered into the kitchen. Checked the overflowing ash pan. Not only had Mike and the boys forgotten to bank the stove and furnace, they'd not emptied the ashes either. And a stack of unwashed dishes and pans filled the sink.

Looks like the house falls apart when Soph's not here to keep things running smooth.

Will carried the pan out to scatter ashes over the garden plot and collected kindling. He started fires in the furnace and stove, filled the teakettle from the half-empty water bucket, refilled the bucket, put coffee on to boil, ran his hand over his bristled face, and eyed the sink.

Can't very well shave with all those dirty dishes stacked in there.

He searched the pantry for aspirin, found a box of Fels Naptha and the dishpan, and went to work.

By the time he stropped his straightedge razor, the pain in his temples had eased. Self-disgust peered back at him from the steam-dimmed image in the mirror above the sink.

Maybe Doc was *right about whiskey.*

He poured boiling water in the wash basin, dipped his brush to work up lather in his shaving mug, and went to work on the offensive face. Better hurry if he wanted to wake Soph before the kids came down.

* * *

The tension that marred the Macklins' normally cheerful breakfast accompanied the family to the Maxwell. Even Sarah was quiet. Will dropped the younger children off at school before he drove to Campbell's. The minute Will parked, Bill bolted from the car to the truck, leaving his parents alone in the idling Maxwell.

"Soph, I've already told you how sorry I am. Please don't be mad."

"I'm not *mad*, Will. I'm embarrassed and ashamed and disgusted and disappointed. I've never felt this way about you before. You knew how much I wanted to be at the courthouse last night, but that's not as bad as what you did to the Campbells. And after all they've done for us. I guess you'll see Dr. Tom and make it up with him some way, but I doubt if Ellen ever speaks to you again." She stared out the window. "And I don't blame her," she added coldly.

"We'll talk about this later. Bill has to get to school and I have to head for the office." He got out of the car and Sophia slid to the driver's seat. "Soph, I am truly sorry."

Sophia pulled the door shut, shifted into low, and left Will standing in the street watching the retreating car, wondering why he'd taught his wife to drive.

* * *

She didn't want to go home, but where could she go? For almost seventeen years her life had centered on Will and the children. She considered talking to Father Riley, remembered that without her license she couldn't drive to the manse. Dr. Tom? Not yet. She shifted into second, circled the block and guided the car down the long hill. When she stopped at the box to pick up the previous day's mail, Mary Sullivan was sweeping her front porch and paused to wave.

"I just can't get used to seeing you behind the wheel of that big car, Sophia," Mary called. "Come have a cup of coffee and tell me about the election. Looked like quite a turnout when Les and I voted yesterday."

"It was, Mary, and thanks for the invitation but I can't today. I got behind on housework and have to catch up. And thanks again for taking Sarah while I was campaigning last March. I couldn't have done it without you."

Sophia vented her frustration on accumulated dirt. By evening the house was clean and Sophia exhausted. The cold lump in the pit of her stomach, however, remained.

* * *

Friday evening, after dinner, Sophia suggested a taffy pull. "Your dad's got a book to read," she said, dismissing Will from the kitchen.

Will's eyebrows raised. "Say now, I like taffy as much as the next person."

"Sarah will bring you some when it's finished."

Will, relegated to the parlor, sat down to read, but the conversation and Sarah's giggles from the kitchen blocked his concentration. Disgusted, he gave up and switched on the radio to drown out Seth's and Sarah's animated voices. Bill wandered in.

"Taffy done?"

"Nah. That's kid stuff anyway. Guess Mom's still mad at you though."

"Well, Bill, I made a jackass out of myself."

"Figured that. Not much fun around here when Mom's mad." Bill started up the front stairs.

"How about a game of checkers?"

"Have to study."

Will stared thoughtfully after his escaping son.

* * *

He waited until the children were in bed, then strode into the kitchen. Sophia, busily scouring the sticky taffy pan, ignored him. Moment by moment, Will's irritation increased. "How much longer is this going on, Soph?"

"I don't want to talk about it."

"Well I *do.* It's not just what you're doing to me, it's what you're doing to the kids. You may fool Seth and Sarah for awhile, but Bill knows exactly what's going on."

"Did it ever occur to you what *you've* done? Besides, I didn't tell him."

"Nobody had to tell him with you looking like a storm cloud all the time. Now let's get things cleared up before Anne comes home. Looks like your back would be broke, sleeping on that hard divan every night. And then folding up the blankets before the kids get up so they don't know. It's ridiculous, that's what it is." He touched her shoulder. "What do you want me to do, Soph?"

Sophia jerked away. Her eyes blazed. "Don't touch me!"

Will's hand dropped. His eyes narrowed. "Never again?"

"Not until I work things out with myself. Will, I didn't even want to *know* you the other night. You've had too much to drink before, but this time you shamed us. I heard what Dr. Tom said to you on the porch, too, but you were probably too drunk to remember."

"You mean about whiskey?"

"Then you *do* remember."

"Yes, I do. And I talked to him yesterday about it. Apologized, too."

"And?"

"I think you're both making a mountain out of a mole hill. Look, Soph, I know what I did was wrong, but you've been doing your best to take over for the last year and a half. First you steamrolled Anne into the Greenbergs. Then Fairwell showed up out here with John. I didn't want to get into this Democrat job tangle and you knew it, but I went along with it because I didn't know what else to do. And I'll admit it's made the mortgage payments with enough left over so we don't have to scrimp so much any more, but the guff I've had to take from people already is just a taste of what's coming."

"I don't know why you care what those people say. Is it more important than what happens to us? To the farm? Don't *listen* to them, Will. And if you're talking about Harry Stone, he's nothing."

"He may be nothing to you, but he's got the ears of a lot of country folks. My friends, or people I used to *think* were my friends. And my family, too." His voice rose. "Dammit, what do you think it's going to do to Ma when I run on a Democrat ticket?"

"Keep your voice down. It carries right through that register into Sarah's room."

"Then let's go to the dining room. I want this settled. Tonight!"

Sophia was white with anger. "Don't you think I'd like it settled, too? But you're trying to make *your* drunkenness *my* fault, and I don't see what else we could have done. Staying with Greenbergs was the only way Anne could go to high school. You know how much that meant to her. And that job was like manna from heaven. We were poor, Will, *dirt* poor! I told you I wasn't happy about the political side of it, either…"

"Maybe that's what you *said,* but you *loved* getting around town, being important, showing people what to do, how to vote. I think you're more mad about what Ellie and Doc think and missing the excitement at the courthouse than because I got drunk!"

Sophia smarted under Will's barb of truth. "Not more, maybe, but as much. I *do* care what Campbells think. And I worked hard for that election. For *us*! And I *did* want to be in on the victory celebration." Her chin lifted in defiance. "Didn't it ever occur to you that I might get tired of staying by myself all day, never seeing any adults but Mike and the bums? And in the winter even the bums aren't here. Since Sarah's gone to school I'm alone all day. And you're right, I *did* like feeling important, because around here I'm beginning to feel like nothing but a drudge for you and the children!"

Truths, half-truths and accusations flew back and forth. Buried resentments—minor when encountered but assuming monumental proportions in the heat of argument—were disinterred from shallow graves. By the time the clock struck midnight, both were emotionally drained with no resolution in sight.

"So what are we gonna do, Soph? Toss almost seventeen years of marriage in the toilet and sprinkle it with lime? Divorce is out of the question…you can't get one because you're Catholic and I don't want one. We can't afford that anyhow."

Shock widened Sophia's eyes. "Divorce? I don't want a divorce! I want a home with you and the children, but I don't ever again want to see you the way you were at Campbells. You shamed us both."

"And *I'm* saying I'm through letting you push me around!"

"Oh, God, Will." Sophia's whisper was a prayer of anguish. "We used to have something wonderful together. Do we have to be poor to be happy?"

* * *

Curled defensively on her side of the double bed, Sophia returned to the bedroom. In the pervading atmosphere of strained civility, even the children's conversations were stilted. Anne's temporary return brought a veneer of normalcy, but Will's and Sophia's mutual resentment smoldered just below the surface.

Anne questioned Bill the first morning the two walked from their father's office to school.

"It's been like this since election night, Anne. I don't know everything that happened, but I think Dad got roaring drunk."

"But he's been drunk before and it's never caused anything like *this*. Remember his trips to Macklin Corner with the wagon? And he always found a bottle in the bushes at the Moonlight Picnic. I used to wonder if Daddy hid it there himself. None of the *other* men ever looked tiddly. Well…maybe Mr. Stone."

"Yeah, but that's not the first time it happened." He told her about the night he and Seth put their father to bed. "And something worse must have happened election night. Mom and Dad were supposed to have supper with Doc and Mrs. Campbell before they went to the courthouse. I was almost asleep when they came home that night."

Anne listened quietly while Bill explained what happened, the argument that followed on Friday night and the unrest in the house since. "Now they're talking again and that's even worse. They act like strangers that hate each other. All polite and everything."

Anne frowned. "Mamma looks awful. She must have lost ten pounds. Seth stays in his room all the time and talks to that squirrel."

"Why do you think I study in Grampa's room?"

"Did you know Sarah cries herself to sleep and wakes up with nightmares? And she wet the bed last night. She hasn't done that in ages. Even Blue looks like someone just kicked him. Oh, Bill, I was so excited about being home. Now I can't wait to *leave*."

* * *

Sarah's high spirits returned briefly when she learned the Greenberg baby, a girl, was named Sarah.

"I'll have to start calling you Yahbut again so I can tell you two apart," Anne teased.

Anne spent Thanksgiving at home and returned to Bridgeton the following Sunday when Mrs. Eisenfeld left. Although Will and Sophia remained civil and cool, the Macklin household returned to normal routine. Will, always home shortly after five, assumed his share of the evening chores. Sweet holiday smells filled Sophia's kitchen. Yet—despite the temptation of her homemade butter cookies, caramels, fudge and divinity—Sophia continued to lose weight.

Christmas approached. Mysterious Sears and Roebuck packages, delivered by the mailman at Sullivan's and spirited home by Sophia, disappeared into secret hiding places. Determined to make Christmas as happy as possible for the children, she spent a large portion of her campaign money on gifts. She sewed Bill's big orange 'B' on his new black letter sweater before she wrapped it. Seth's guitar came with a 'Teach Yourself to Play' manual. Anne's soft wool dress was the exact shade of her eyes. And everyone could share the games. Sophia sat at the kitchen table surrounded by ribbon and paper, alternately raising and lowering Sarah's curly-haired big doll, watching its eyes open and close, remembering the newspaper-wrapped doll she'd made two Christmases before.

She thought of the gift she'd planned for Will and retrieved her purse from its hiding place in the buffet. The pawn ticket for Phineas' gold watch and chain was still in the secret compartment with the money she'd put aside. She'd found the ticket the previous summer at the back of Will's underwear drawer and stopped by the Bridgeton pawnshop to ask the owner to save the watch for her. Now, she wasn't sure.

* * *

"Mom's getting skinny," Sarah announced one morning at breakfast.

Will, who for the past six weeks had carefully ignored his wife, stared. Sophia's normally snug housedress hung shapelessly from her shoulders. "You on a diet or something, Soph?"

Sophia busied herself at the stove. "Not really. I've just not been hungry."

"Maybe you better see Doc."

"There's nothing wrong with me, Will." She sipped her coffee.

"You drink it black now?"

Bill looked up from his bacon and eggs. "All she does any

more is drink black coffee. You'd think she'd starve."

"Looks like that's what she's *doing*, Bill. Soph, I'll be back after I take the kids to school. You're going to see Doc. Today!"

"Thank you, but that's not necessary. I'd planned to see him anyway. My license should be here any day and I'll drive myself in." She turned back to the stove. "I may do some shopping, too, and I'd rather do it alone if you don't mind."

She didn't see the defeat that settled over Will's features. "Fine, Soph, if that's what you want." Bill's eyes flickered from his father's averted face to his mother. He threw his napkin on the table and left the room.

* * *

"Doesn't look like there's anything major wrong, Soph. Heart's going a mile a minute, though. You ought to know you can't live on caffeine."

"My appetite's gone. Coffee's the only way I can get enough energy to handle everything that has to be done, Dr. Tom."

"I don't have to tell you that you needed to lose weight. Not the way you went about it, though. Everything all right at home?"

Sophia raised her head and looked directly into the doctor's eyes. "How can you ask that after what you saw election night?"

The doctor chuckled uncomfortably. "Yeah, Will really went on a bender, didn't he? Ellie was about ready to kill him, but she's okay now. He been drinking since?"

"Not that I know of. At least he's been home every evening about five. And weekends."

"Then what's the problem?"

"I guess I'm afraid. Every time it's happened before and I've forgiven him he just does it again."

"So you've decided to *really* punish him this time? Only thing is, Soph, you're punishing yourself as much, maybe more, than you are him. Bet you've been using the headache excuse, too." Sophia avoided his probing eyes. "Uh-*huh*. Thought so. You *trying* to drive him away? If you don't know by now how much pride that man's got you're fooling yourself. Never before thought you were a fool!"

"Dr. Tom, I wasn't eavesdropping, but I couldn't help overhearing what you said on the porch. And Will told me he talked to you later."

The doctor ran his hand along his jaw. "I see. So now you're worried about him being an alcoholic? You've always known he likes his liquor, haven't you? And you know what it does to him?"

Sophia nodded.

"Soph, do you still love Will?"

She tugged at the handkerchief balled up in her hand. "I...I don't know. I feel like something died that night. He looked so pathetic and weak."

"Like a human being with a problem? Soph, that pedestal you put him on when you got married has cracks. *You* know that. Election night made a big one, maybe opened your eyes all the way for the first time. Sure, he's strong and handsome and kind. Good sense of humor. Good friend, too. And he's a working fool. But he's got weaknesses just like the rest of us.

"And *he* wants to wear the pants in the family. Most men don't like strong women. He needs to feel like he's taking care of you, but *you're* beginning to act like you don't need caretaking. Manhood's a fragile thing, gets bruised easy. Men fight to hold onto it." He whistled tunelessly while he thought. "I'd sure hate to have to fill the shoes you picked out for him. Might be part of his problem, you know."

Sophia raised angry eyes from the shredding handkerchief. "Are *you* saying his drinking is my fault?"

"Noooo, not exactly. But maybe the fact that he's trying to be something more than he *is* has a lot to do with it."

Her voice shook. "And what am *I* supposed to do? Just wash and cook and clean and stay at home all the time while he goes…goes…gallivanting around? I get so lonely! Now that Sarah's in school I've even thought about another baby but I'm afraid…"

"You've got good reason. With the damage that was done I don't think you could carry to term, and even if you could I'll tell you right out it might kill you. Well, *I* don't know what the answer is. You and Will have to figure it out yourselves. Not that I think he's an alcoholic, at least not yet, but maybe I can get some information for you. Might help you understand a little better.

"I've got a diet sheet here for you. Now that you've lost all that weight there's no sense putting it back on again. Main thing is to eat three healthy meals a day. Cut back on the coffee and lay off the butter and cream and sweets. I know how you like 'em. And see me if you don't feel better. Oh, thanks for the candy Seth brought by the house. Ellie says she loves your divinity better than me!"

Shaking with indignation, Sophia left the office.

* * *

Sophia parked the car in front of the church and walked to the manse next door. The housekeeper answered her knock.

"Come in, Mrs. Macklin. Father Riley's working in his study. I don't know if he can see you now."

Sophia's hands shook while she waited in the hallway. She struggled for control as she followed the housekeeper to the study.

The old priest rose and ushered her to the chair facing his desk. "Good to see you, Mrs. Macklin. We miss you and the children at Church. I was planning to drive out, but you saved me the trip." He returned to his chair. "How can I help you today?"

"Several things, really." She handed him an envelope. "I've

not been able to contribute for some time, but I worked in the last election and put this aside. I wish it were more."

"Thank you. In these times anything helps."

"And I wanted to ask when the new catechism classes start. Seth missed confirmation last year because... Well, because we just couldn't get him here for instructions. And Sarah is almost ready for her first communion. I'm driving now so I can get them to classes. We should be in Church more regularly, too."

The priest searched her strained face, watched her hands work the almost shredded handkerchief in her lap. Every Catholic in the parish knew the nuns arrived for June catechism classes the week after school ended. "And is that all?" he asked gently.

"No," she whispered. "I have to talk to someone."

"That's why I'm here, Mrs. Macklin."

Once started, Sophia's frustration poured out in a torrent. The priest listened, nodded, and waited between pauses for her to regain her composure before continuing. He meditated over praying hands for a time after she finished.

"How old is your husband?"

"Almost forty."

"And you?"

"Thirty-five last October."

"And how long have you two been married?"

"Seventeen years, Father. You weren't here yet when..."

"So you were both quite young. Is this the first time you've had any serious problems?"

"You mean between the two of us?" The priest nodded. "Yes, I guess so."

"Well, you made it longer than most. Trouble usually starts after ten years or so—sometimes only three years. The original attraction wanes and people have to settle down to the serious side of marriage."

"We were *always* serious. And so busy. We had four children in nine years. We bought the farm from Will's folks and almost everything we make goes to pay off the mortgage. Times are so hard now, too…not just for us but for everybody. And we're luckier than most. At least we have food."

"Everyone knows about the extra vegetables your husband grew and brought into Macklin Corner. I don't know him, but he must be a generous and compassionate man."

"He is, Father. That's why I don't understand this drinking."

The priest sighed. "Unfortunately, each of us has some cross to bear. It sounds as though the drinking is an escape from something. You wouldn't want him perfect, would you?" He templed his hands in thought.

"You said you and your husband had always worked together? And now he's away a great deal? And your youngest child has started to school, so for the first time you're alone on the farm?"

"That's right."

"Do you see what I'm getting at? Now you have at least a *little* time to think and you're sure you're the only one with marital problems. But my dear, everyone has them. You may have more than your share because your husband isn't Catholic and doesn't understand what your religion means to you, but you knew that when you married him."

Sophia, schooled to accept her priest as the ultimate authority, bit her lip and listened intently as the pontificating voice continued.

"Now, I'm afraid the Church remains very strict about birth control. The rhythm method is acceptable in cases like yours, however. Your conscience should be clear in that respect. As for marital relations they're considered a responsibility, one you accepted when you took the vows of matrimony. It's wrong, you know, to use love as a weapon—to withhold love as punishment."

"But I've always been attracted to Will before, and now…"

"It's your duty. It makes no difference that he's non-Catholic.

You were married by a priest. I suggest you respect your husband, forgive him and try to put your marriage in order. You may, in fact, find that your love will help him control his problem with alcohol."

His trite words, couched in condescending male wisdom, continued.

"You seem an intelligent woman, Mrs. Macklin. Think about everything you've told me and pray for understanding. You'll see. Prayer really *does* help." The priest checked his watch and ended the consultation. "Your marriage will be even stronger when you overcome these problems, you know."

Sophia's busy hands were stilled. "Can you hear my confession while I'm here, Father? I'd like to attend communion Christmas morning with the children."

"Of course, Mrs. Macklin, I'll be in the confessional in a few moments. You can go over to the church now."

* * *

"Bless me Father, for I have sinned…"

The familiar words and the confession that followed cleansed her mind. Sophia received absolution, left the curtained confessional and knelt to say penance. The quiet church, the jewel tones of the beautiful stained glass windows, the majestic altar brought a measure of serenity she'd almost forgotten. When she finished the rosary, she folded the kneeler in place and sat back to study the sacrificing, sorrowful face of the Virgin Mary gracing the altar.

Still dissatisfied, but more at peace than in weeks, Sophia left the church. She paused on the steps, checked her purse for the pawn ticket and money and drove straight to the shop in Bridgeton. She'd give Will the watch Christmas Eve, after the children were asleep.

Chapter 18

Sophia escaped into the vicarious world of fiction.

As a girl, her reading was limited to what the parochial school nuns considered proper. As a busy young wife, and within a year a mother, she was confined to daily papers and the outdated magazines Seth still picked up from Dr. Tom's office. But on a snowy, early January afternoon—housework done, Christmas tree dismantled and removed and decorations stowed away for another year—Sophia leafed through one of Anne's forgotten literature books, put her mending basket aside and settled into her sewing chair and Victor Hugo's epic LES MISERABLES.

Because Bridgeton Public Library issued cards only to residents and students, Sophia relied on Anne to quench her developing literary thirst. After Sophia finished the three books Anne was allowed to check out every two weeks, Bill delivered them to Anne, who returned them and checked out three more for Bill to take home. The shuttle established, Anne varied authors and content to stimulate her mother's interest, and hid a smile when the librarian complimented her for being an avid reader on such a *wide* range of subjects.

When the first of de la Roche's JALNA series arrived, Sophia fell in love with the turmoil-ridden Whiteoak family. In many ways Renny reminded her of Will, the remote Canadian Jalna setting of the isolated Macklin farm. Dreary February, spent with the Whiteoaks of Jalna, sped by in a blur of fantasy.

* * *

In South Central Illinois, March 1933 entered like the proverbial lion. On a blustery March 4, Sophia put aside her book to hear Franklin Delano Roosevelt, the newly inaugurated thirty-second President of the United States, declare "...the only thing we have to fear is fear itself." Roosevelt's 'Hundred Days' began with the Bank Holiday.

On the evening of March 12 Sophia popped corn, sent Sarah to the root cellar for a jug of cider, and invited Mike to join the Macklins grouped around the radio to hear the first fireside chat from the White House. Sarah drowsed on her father's lap while the president outlined his measures to firm up America's unsettled banking system. At the end of the broadcast, Will set Sarah firmly on her feet. "Just in time to save the Macklin Corner Bank! Heard there'd been a big run on withdrawals before the Bank Holiday and that the federal bank examiner was on his way." He stood and stretched. "You kids get on to bed. Six o'clock comes early."

"Past my bedtime, too, Will," Mike said as he rose from the divan. "Many thanks, Missus, for letting me join you. That was a mighty stirring talk."

Will saw Mike to the back door while Sophia turned the radio off, shooed the children upstairs, and collected glasses and stray popcorn kernels. She and Will met in the kitchen.

The negative electricity of November and December had gradually lessened. Politeness and elaborate concern masked remaining traces of antagonism. Mindful of the priest's advice, Sophia accepted her handmaid role, honored Will as head of the house, and tried to forget her brief taste of elevated self-esteem.

Will, in turn, controlled his whisky thirst and waited for his wife to forgive him as she had in the past. But unaware of her conversation with the doctor and her visit to Father Riley, he puzzled over the change in Sophia. His discomfort with her constant compliance was tempered with relief that she no longer bristled each time he walked into the same room. He had no way of knowing that Sophia was sacrificing her spontaneity on the altar of family stability. What he *did* know was the spark that ignited the Sophia he loved was missing.

The former intimacy and empathy—the strength of their marriage—was gone.

"You too tired to talk awhile, Soph?"

"I guess not, but *you* certainly look tired, Will."

"A mite. I've been trying to get everything in order so we can start work on the roads when the weather turns. At least it won't be as bad as last year now that I know what I'm doing."

Sophia lifted a pitcher of skimmed milk from the icebox Will had bought at one of the many farm auctions throughout the county. "Hot milk and honey, Will? It might relax you, help you sleep. It does me."

"Shoot, I don't need help to sleep. You go ahead, though." He watched Sophia pour milk in a pan and carry it to the stove. "You look lots better, you know."

Her laugh was guarded. "Better than what?"

"Well, your face isn't so gant. You're still skinny, though."

"Maybe a pound or so heavier now than when we were married. Besides, Dr. Tom had been after me to lose weight anyway and said I shouldn't put it back on."

"Guess he's right. Trouble is I got used to a nice soft bundle. You look more like a girl now than a woman." He grinned half-heartedly. "But yeah, I guess I sort of like it. Takes some getting used to, though."

Sophia poured hot milk into her mug, stirred in a spoonful of wild honey, and looked expectantly at her husband. "Well?"

"John Hall stopped by the office today. He said you told him you didn't want to be Precinct Committeeman."

Sophia, leaning against the sink cabinet, sipped her nightly brew, and studied the mug. "That's right."

"Why don't you sit down and tell me why?"

"Will, when that came up it was understood you'd be Precinct Committeeman when John resigned. I was only to step in when you became Road Commissioner. No one knew Rufus' health would fail so fast." She paused, remembering the funeral she and

Will attended in mid-January. "I'd counted on learning from you. I don't think I can do it by myself."

"You've been to every meeting with me and know as much about it as I do, Soph, maybe more. If you do run into any problems I'll help you. The thing is, John's counting on you. He's got that state job starting in April, says no one else can take over the precinct as well as you."

"The job's not elective. Why can't he do both?"

"He'll be working in Springfield and he's not sure he can make it back for the meetings. Between you and me and the gatepost, looks like he'll be spending most of his time toadying Fairwell. But that's John's choice." He studied Sophia's face. His question broke the uncomfortable silence. "Soph, are you turning it down because of me?"

Sophia considered her answer as she moved to the table and sat across from Will. "Maybe. Partly, anyway. We've been getting along so well I don't want anything to spoil it. And we'll be planting the garden before long. And there's always so much to do here."

"Sound like lame excuses to me. Didn't make any difference last year. You managed everything here and still got all those voters to the polls. And I don't think there'll be that much politicking to do. There's no election coming up until next spring's primary. Only thing you'll have to do is chair the meetings and see that any new people get registered. With the mine still down, I don't exactly see a bevy of folks rushing to live in Macklin Corner."

"There'd be the meetings. I 'm afraid to drive in alone at night."

"I can drive you in and go to the meetings with you. Wouldn't want you there alone, anyway. Someone might steal you."

Sophia lifted her head to search Will's perplexed face. "Are you saying you *want* me to be Precinct Committeeman?" He nodded. "Are you sure? You said you didn't want to feel you were riding on my coat tails and…"

"Forget what I said! You did a bang-up job in that election. If I hadn't been such a jackass I'd have seen it then instead of acting like a fool. I'm *proud* of you, Soph and don't you forget it."

Sophia's automatic smile didn't reach her downcast eyes. "Thank you, Will. Maybe I can manage it after all." She raised her eyes to meet Will's. "But only if you're sure! And *if* you're sure, you can tell John I've changed my mind. Under pressure."

"I'll make it a point to see him."

Quiet settled over the room. Will watched Sophia sip her warm milk. In the kitchen of the once love-filled house on the bluff, a husband's evocative silence went unanswered by a studiedly oblivious wife. Finally he stirred, rose, and moved around the table. Ran his finger down the soft curve of her cheek. Lifted her chin. His eyes questioned. The same automatic smile masked her reluctance. "I thought you were tired, Will."

"Never too tired to love you, Soph. Looks like maybe it's bed-time…"

Sophia abandoned her comforting mug of milk and followed her husband to bed. Later, when he drowsed, she slipped away and returned to finish the milk and honey that had become a substitute for passion. Will felt her go. She was unaware that his frustration matched her own. She had been a dutiful wife.

* * *

Tragedy struck in early April. The telephone rang on Wednesday morning shortly after Will and the children left. The flu that invaded William P's aging body in late March had developed into pneumonia.

Clothilde's voice was hostile. "…and I'm sorry to bother you, Sophia, but I don't have the office number and he's asking for Will..." Her convulsive swallow was audible over the phone.

"...and you, too, Sophia. He keeps saying he wants to go home to die, but the doctor says we can't move him."

"We'll be there as soon as I locate Will."

Sophia found him still at the office. "I'll pick you up in about fifteen minutes," he said.

Sophia buried memories of Lysol alongside her resentment against Clothilde, packed a small suitcase, and prepared to help care for William P as long as she was needed.

Clothilde met them at the door. "He's been out of his head most of the morning. The doctor was here again just after I called you. He doesn't think it will be long now."

Involved with their own problems, neither Sophia nor Will had seen William P since the January beef butchering. Both were shocked by his ravaged body. The rusty tobacco stains on his white beard and mustache accentuated his colorless lips and pale skin. Sophia laid a cool hand on his forehead then left Will alone with his mother and father.

Will found her kneeling at prayer in the living room. She made the sign of the cross and rose to face him.

"I think maybe he knew me, Soph, but I'm not sure. I've got to check on one of the crews. I'll be back in a little while." Will shielded his tears as he fumbled for the door knob.

* * *

"Ma'am? Is that you, Ma'am?" William P's voice threaded through a weak smile as Sophia approached his bed. "I'd know your step anywhere. And your smell, like those flowers along the edge of the garden at home. It's nice."

"Thank you, Pa. I came to stay as long as you want me to."

"I knew you'd come, Ma'am." He groped for her hand and squeezed it. "I wanted to be home to die but that damned doctor won't let me go. Sorry, Ma'am, didn't mean to swear."

"We'll take you home when it's time, Pa. Is there anything I can do for you now?"

"Think you could make me some biscuits and gravy? You make the best biscuits I ever…" His voice faded. He dozed again.

Clothilde stood by the door listening. "Hmph! Never heard him apologize to anyone *before* for swearing. Why does he call you Ma'am?"

Sophia, as always, carefully avoided any term of address. She couldn't bring herself to call her mother-in-law 'Ma' like Jim's wife, Sadie. She was uncomfortable with 'Clothilde'. And she refused to say 'Mrs. Macklin'.

"I don't know. Maybe because of the children." She knew, however, even though William P never put it into words, that it was respectful love. She reminded herself again that she was there to help Pa, not hurt Clothilde.

* * *

Will returned in time to feed his father a few bites of biscuits and gravy. William P smiled and drifted into a deep sleep.

"Think I ought to stick around awhile, Soph?"

"I don't know. I don't suppose anyone does. The doctor should be here soon, though, if you want to wait. And your brothers and sisters should be here by then, too."

"Maybe I better get home, let the kids know what's happening. I'll be back soon as I can. Will you be okay with Ma?"

"I'll be fine, but your mother's worn out. I'll sit up with Pa tonight so she can rest. There should be enough food in the icebox for a day or so. You'll ask Mike to see that the children get off to school?"

* * *

That night, his hand clasped in Sophia's, William P quietly slipped away. When the family met to discuss funeral arrangements, Clothilde was cautious. "Will, I know it's a busy time on the farm now, but do you think Pa could come home for his wake? That's what he wanted and with his eyes like they were he never made many friends here in Walnut Hills."

"Soph and I already talked about it, Ma. We hoped that's what you'd want. Pa's friends are there, the few that are left. Guess he'll be buried in the family plot at the country church?"

"Yes, there's still room for both of us. I reckon we'll be the last two Macklins there." Her eyes scathed Sophia.

Sophia ignored both the remark and the scathing look. "We'll be proud to have Pa with us a little longer, won't we Will?"

* * *

On an unseasonably warm, sunny April day William Phineas Macklin, dignified in his dark Sunday suit, his snowy beard and mustache impeccably groomed, lay in state in the parlor of the house on the bluff.

Relatives, old friends and former neighbors, all bringing food, came in droves to mourn his passing and pay their respects. Beef roasts, hams, casseroles and mounds of fried chicken crammed the icebox, while the overflow hung in the well bucket and covered the cool, winter-emptied root cellar shelves. Pots of vegetables simmered on the stove. Cakes and pies lined the cabinet top and pantry shelves. Trestle tables assembled from saw horses and boards, normally used for harvest crews, were scrubbed and set up in the front yard for serving and eating.

"Will," Sophia called, "you'll have to make a trip to town for more ice. All this food's going to spoil in the heat." Sophia moved things around, trying to make more room. "Thank heaven it's too early for flies."

One of Will's brothers-in-law followed him into the kitchen. "I'll go, Will. You oughta stay with Pa and the family. Besides, your brother Jim should've been here with Ma an hour ago and you need to be here when she comes. She was *supposed* to be here before all these people arrived." He escaped up the road.

The entire family dreaded Clothilde's return. Having rescinded her declaration to 'never set foot on the place again', everyone wondered what the deposed chatelaine would do and say next. People arrived, paid their respects in the hushed parlor, then waited in curious clusters on the veranda and in the oak shade of the freshly-scythed lawn.

Seth rushed into the kitchen. "Uncle Jim and Aunt Sadie are coming with Gramma, Mom. They just turned the corner."

Will's and Sophia's eyes met. Sophia slipped off her apron, hung it on its customary peg behind the kitchen door, smoothed her new black dress and joined her husband. One on either side, they escorted the widow from the car.

Clothilde's expressionless eyes stared straight ahead as the three passed through the parting throng, up the veranda steps and into the parlor. Inside, she approached the casket, studied the peaceful face of William P, patted his hand and assumed her seat of honor by his side. Sophia suppressed a smile. Her comfortable sewing chair had many uses.

The minister arrived to begin the service. "Is the family all here?"

Will's eyes skimmed the assembling relatives. "Where's Sarah?"

Seth spoke up. "Upstairs Dad, hiding under her bed crying. I can't get her to come out. She says she just can't tell Grampa goodbye."

At her father's nod, Anne slipped out of the parlor and up the back stairs to return with a tearful Sarah. Sophia, stoic until that moment, felt her own eyes fill. She moved to Will's side, behind his seated mother. Bill and Seth, ramrod-straight but sniffling, stood with the other grandsons who would serve as pallbearers. Will's brothers and sisters filed into the parlor with their families. Uncle Ed, uncomfortable and hot in his good wool suit, wiped his eyes, blew his nose and joined Mike at the back of the room. The Macklins were gathered to say farewell.

On the veranda and in the yard, neighbors and friends accompanied the inside family in song as Uncle Ben's fiddle led them into the closing hymn. Strains of *The Old Rugged Cross* resounded across the Macklin acres.

In the shadow below the bluff, a small cluster of ragged and travel-weary but respectful men who, from outside their encampment under the trestle had watched the mourners gather, removed their hats. Their voices blended into the concluding chorus.

"...I will cling to the old rugged cross and exchange it someday for a crown."

The minister intoned the last 'Amen'. William P's final journey began.

* * *

The mountain of food was depleted. At Will's behest, Mike filled a box with leftovers to carry to the trestle camp. Empty platters littered the tables. Children, already stuffed with sweets but taking advantage of their parents' preoccupation, snitched desserts and disappeared into the orchard. One of the more enterprising cousins hid an entire cherry pie under his shirt. Younger children played a wild game of hide-and-seek around the barns and outbuildings. Will moved from group to group accepting condolences.

Uncle Ed tapped him on the shoulder. "Thought I'd never get you by yourself, Will. I hid a quart of 'shine in the barn on the way in. If you're 'bout ready, thought we might have a snort together to send William P on his way."

Will looked into Uncle Ed's red-rimmed eyes, saw his grief, hesitated, then "Better not, Uncle Ed. Too much here to see to."

"Might be your last chance with Roosevelt fixin' to repeal Prohibition. When whisky gets legal we won't have the good stuff from the country stills no more."

"Maybe later, Uncle Ed. You go ahead, though." He watched Ed, bowed with sorrow over the loss of his younger half-brother, move toward the barn alone. Will looked to the veranda, saw his mother surrounded by his brothers and brothers-in-law and headed in that direction. "Where's Soph, Ma?"

Clothilde sniffed. "In the kitchen, acting like hired help. You'd think she...."

Will cut her off. "That's enough, Ma. Soph's the reason you're here today and don't you forget it. Besides, all the *other* women are out there helping, too." Ignoring his mother's shocked face, he turned away. "Jim, what's the news about Sadie's brother? He happy about going into the Civilian Conservation Corps?"

"Charlie's pretty excited. Looks like he'll be going to that Kentucky forest fire reclamation area when they get things set up. Did you know they're gonna run those CCC camps with army reserve men? Set it up like an army? Commanders and adjutants and sergeants. Tents, field kitchens, mess kits, the whole kit 'n kaboodle—all left over from The Great War. Maybe he'll finally learn to take orders. About all he does now is lay around the house. Ask him to take out the trash and he's too tired. Why, Will, that guy's eating us out of house and home. Don't know *why* I ever said he could stay with us. Never thought I'd feel so good about having a Democrat president!"

Both brothers ignored Clothilde's loud "hmph". "Sounds like a pretty fine program," Will said. "Good outdoor work for him, too. Might make a man of him yet."

Clothilde's second "hmph" was louder, followed by, "Well! I

certainly thought *I'd* lose what little money I've got left when Roosevelt declared that Bank Holiday!"

Will patted her hand. "Aw come on, Ma. If he hadn't stepped in, you probably wouldn't have *any* money now and you'd be just like the rest of us. Give the man a chance. Hoover sure wasn't doing anything. All Roosevelt wants is to get this country back on its feet. You want Communism like Russia? Or Socialism like Germany?" He looked appraisingly at his mother. "Bet you *like* that funny-looking little German, Austrian I guess, with the cookie-duster mustache who started that new Nazi party."

"Well, *you* worked hard enough to see a *Democrat* elected!"

"Now that's not true, but I wish I could have. I couldn't do all that much because of the road commissioner job. Soph's the one did all the work. She's the new Committeeman for Precinct Seven, too."

"She trading in her apron for britches these days?"

"Ma! I said that's *enough.*" He stared his mother down. "You better believe I voted for Roosevelt, too. And if he keeps on like he's going, I'll do it again. He's the reason I've got a job so I can make mortgage payments. Hadn't been for the Democrats I'd have lost the farm."

Jack, Clothilde's reclusive bachelor second son, a Great War veteran with lungs damaged by mustard gas in France, spoke up. "You bet your bottom dollar *I* voted for Roosevelt, Ma. What Hoover did to the Bonus Army in Washington last summer made my blood boil!"

Violent coughing interrupted Jack's vehemence. His attentive audience, unused to such an outburst from reticent Jack, waited while he fished a cloth from his pocket and spat loosened phlegm into it. "Ma," he wheezed, "if I'd been able, *I'd* have been living in those cardboard shanties and vacant government buildings alongside the rest of the veterans. Marching with 'em, too. Maybe been *killed* with 'em when MacArthur gave the order to fire. Wish

I had been. Be better off dead than the way I am now." He stopped to catch his breath. "Who ever heard of having to wait for your army bonus twenty-seven years? Why, most of us will be dead by 1945!"

"Don't you think that's what the Washington crowd had in mind, Jack?" Jim asked. Clothilde's favored child cast an abashed glance at his mother. "Have to admit it, Ma. I voted for Roosevelt, too." Clothilde's face froze. "Hell, Ma, at least folks are beginning to hope. And he's sure gonna get us rid of Charlie!"

Clothilde retreated to indignant silence.

* * *

With the exception of the family, everyone had finally gone home to do evening chores. Seth and Bill, along with their father and the other remaining men, dismantled the trestle tables and stacked the sawhorses and boards back in the barn. The children searched the yard and orchard for misplaced dishes, knives and forks while the women washed stacks of plates, pans and utensils.

Leaving the kitchen, Anne surprised Clothilde wandering through the house. "Does it look any different, Gramma?"

"Some, Anne. Pretty bare, too."

"Mamma and Daddy don't have any money for furniture. Mamma has some beautiful pieces from her Great Aunt Clarilla, though. The dining room set and the bedroom furniture in Sarah's and my room. And the big cedar chest in their bedroom."

"I saw that. It's certainly filled with fine linens."

Gramma had been snooping through Mamma's things!

Anne averted her face to hide her shock. "Those were from Aunt Clarilla, too. We've had to use them though. They're mostly worn out now."

"I've been thinking…" Clothilde stopped, studied the parlor and continued. "Old Phineas' walnut secretary-desk used to stand right there, where your grandfather was laid out this morning. We took it with us when we moved away, but it's really too big for my little cottage. Maybe I'll talk to Will about bringing it back here, where it belongs."

Sophia, stunned, stood in the doorway staring at Clothilde's back. She caught Anne's eye, put her finger to her lips in a shushing motion and quietly withdrew. Anne accompanied her prying grandmother through the rest of the house, ending in the kitchen with the women.

Friendly conversation between daughters and daughters-in-law died when Clothilde entered. Sadie glanced at Sophia, then at her mother-in-law. "We were just having a quiet visit and a cup of coffee, Ma. Won't you join us?"

Clothilde lifted her chin and glared at each of her daughters before her clipped reply. "I think not, Sadie, it's getting late. Find Jim and the children so we can be on our way." She assumed a haughty, aloof stance and turned to the woman who had appropriated what she still considered *her* kitchen. "Thank you for everything."

Sophia's fingers tightened around a Spode serving dish. She set it carefully on the table and faced Clothilde. "Please don't go. There's still so much food left there's no room to store it. We'll have supper as soon as Will and the boys get the milking done and the stock taken care of. Just family." She looked directly into Clothilde's eyes. "I think Pa would like that, don't you?"

The gathered women watched as the combatants locked eyes. Clothilde blinked. "Hmph. Well, I guess we have to eat somewhere."

Chapter 19

With the exception of Clara Stone's cake plate, all the food dishes had been returned. Neither Clara, a spinster, nor her brother Harry's family with whom she lived, had attended the wake. Sophia wondered why Clara sent the cake. Well, they were Will's cousins and *she* wasn't going to drive all the way down there over those back roads. Will could just take it back himself when he was going that way. She stored the plate safely out of the way on a high pantry shelf, then stood at the window watching the gentle shower. The spring rains that started the day after the funeral continued to fall.

The sky began to clear late the following week. On Friday evening, Will paused in the barn doorway and sniffed the warm, drizzly April air. "I can smell 'em boys! Well," he amended, "I can *almost* smell 'em." He snapped his fingers three times. "Pop! Pop! Pop!"

"*Please* can we go tonight after we finish the chores, Dad?" Seth pleaded.

"No, I already told you it'll be too dark to spot 'em. Best if we go early tomorrow morning, when the sun slants into that southeast hillside. Besides, it'll be better if we let 'em grow overnight. They'll be bigger, easier to find. We'll go before we milk, beat those folks from Macklin Corner. Won't hurt the cows a bit to wait. Bill, Mike, you coming with us?"

"You bet!" the other two milkers chorused in unison. "Never in all my born days seen better mushroom weather," Mike added. He smacked his lips. "You think the Missus will fry up a mess for me if I find 'em?"

"When it comes to mushrooms it's share and share alike, Mike. You *hunt* with us, you *eat* with us, too. Let's finish up the chores so we can have dinner and get to bed early."

* * *

South Central Illinois boasts no finer culinary treasure than the tender Morel mushroom, a fungus whose spores lie dormant in rich woodland humus until an ideal combination of spring growing conditions comes together. For only a few weeks in the spring, and only when the soil is warm and moist and the humidity high, Morels seem to burst through the soft ground overnight, setting off a madness known in Kickapoo County as 'Mushroom Mania'.

During the limited 1931 and 1932 growing seasons, the weather had been either wet and cold or warm and dry. A bumper yield of spongy Morels was expected in the spring of 1933. The Macklin clan, along with almost everyone else in the area, would be in the woods early the following morning.

* * *

That evening at dinner, when Sarah heard about the planned expedition, she settled into her usual pout. "Yah but why can't *I* go, Daddy? I never get to do anything."

"For one thing, Sarah, we're leaving at the crack of dawn. You'd never make it. And for another, you have to watch where you go. Mushrooms grow in the woods and they're hard to see because they're almost the same color as the dead leaves around them. Scatter-brained as you are, you'd step on 'em before you saw 'em."

Sophia shared a secret smile with her daughter. "Never mind, Sarah. You and I will just go later, by ourselves. I don't think you want to get up at five, anyway. We'll wait until the dew dries."

Mollified, Sarah smiled back and picked up her fork.

Bill was skeptical. "May be too late when the dew dries. You know how people flock down here in droves, even if it is our land. Dad, why do you let them trespass like that?"

"Why, Bill, I guess I never thought of it as trespassing. I figure mushrooms are kind of like wildflowers. They're a gift from nature and *everyone* has a right to enjoy 'em. Besides, we've let folks from Macklin Corner go mushrooming on our land as long as I can remember. Goes all the way back to Phineas. I reckon the Kickapoos taught *him* about Morels." He thought a moment, then grinned. "Probably didn't call 'em Morels, though. Anyway, weather like this, there'll be enough for everyone."

"But there didn't used to be so many people. I suppose they've got a right to hunt along the railroad, but…"

"That's enough, Bill. You know how I hate selfishness. Besides, I don't think anyone loves mushrooms more than me and I say they can hunt. We'll just play the game with 'em, be up earlier and beat 'em to the draw. Where'd you put those onion sacks, Soph?"

"They're right by your rubber boots, Will, behind the door. As wet as it's going to be, you'd all better wear boots tomorrow. You might leave one of the sacks for Sarah and me, though. Maybe two."

Bill hooted. "*Two*, Mom? Maybe we better leave *three* sacks. Or even *four*! Or how about a bushel basket?"

* * *

Only a sliver of light showed above the eastern horizon when Will led the way along the path through the orchard and down the bluff to the tracks.

"I found one already, Dad," Seth called, scrambling up the coal-strewn bank.

"By God, Seth, you've got eyes like a cat. I can hardly see my hands in front of my face yet." He inspected the mushroom Seth handed him and threw it away. "There'll be a lot along here, but they're all gritty. That fine coal dust and slack those train engines spit out sticks in the folds when they push through the ground and it's harder than heck to soak out. Don't even bother with those. We'll go on to the hill where it's clean. Nice lot of elm trees there. Mushrooms like to grow around elms. Especially dying elms."

The small band of hunters walked north along the tracks for a half-mile before making their way down the incline and cutting west on Phineas' long-deserted, overgrown logging road. Heavy dew clung to blackberry briars and budding sumac, soaking overalls above knee-high rubber boots. They arrived at the mushroom hill just as the sun rose.

"All right, boys. Fan out and start picking. We'll work our way up the hill. Figure this whole side oughta be covered with 'em."

Bill stared at the hillside. The sun's rays, coming in on a low angle, highlighted scores of ecru stubs dotting the leaf-strewn woods. The tender stems and darker sponge-coned mushroom tops were gone. He swore and threw his sack to the ground. "I told you, Dad! I *told* you!" He mimicked his father. "Now, Bill, don't be selfish. Everyone's got a right to enjoy the gifts of nature."

Will was as angry as his son. "You just hush your mouth, Bill." He bent to examine a ragged stub. "What the hell? Those are fresh tears. Sun's just now up. I don't know how they could see where they were going, let alone find mushrooms."

"Looky here, Will." Mike pointed to a round indentation in the decaying leaf cover. "From the looks of that, they used lanterns. See? There's another mark, over there by Seth. And there's more up the hill. And look at all those places the leaves are kicked up. Must have been a regular crew here, prob'ly picking most of the night." He shook his head in sorrow. "Never seen so many bare stubs. Why, there must have been maybe fifteen gallons of mushrooms here, that many gone they're selling 'em. Bring a quarter a pound."

Seth was almost in tears. "But they couldn't get them *all.* Let's look under the leaves. Maybe they missed some."

The disgruntled four scoured the hillside. Seth and Bill each found several just pushing through the leaves, but left them to mature and scatter spores for future springs. Will found nothing. Mike met them back at the bottom of the hill.

"You have any luck, Mike?" Bill called.

"Nope. Whoever was here got all the good ones and left the peckerheads for us. There's a patch of those up at the top of the hill. Guess we could eat 'em if we were hungry enough, but I never cared much for those long, skinny stems and little bitty caps. I like big fat spongy tops on *my* mushrooms." He brightened. "Say, we could head home, maybe pick the ones we saw on the railroad banks."

Will's face was glum. "Guess gritty mushrooms are better than none at all. Let's go."

* * *

Sophia was up and busy in the kitchen by the time the men and boys returned. "You mean you didn't get *any*?"

"Nary a one, Soph. At least I didn't. The boys found a few but left those to go to seed. When we found out the hill had been stripped, we figured we'd pick the ones along the tracks on the way back, but while we were checking the hill guess those varmints circled around and got those, too. Why, that hillside was *covered* with mushroom stubs. Whoever got 'em will sure have a feast."

"You're all welcome to come with Sarah and me. We're going out after breakfast."

"No thanks, Soph. I've had about all the disappointment I can enjoy for one morning. You boys can go if you want."

Bill and Seth, on their way to the barn in dry overalls, also declined. Bill snorted. "If they got the ones on our hill, they got the rest, too."

"Don't say we didn't ask," Sophia called after them.

* * *

Sophia halved another mushroom lengthwise, checked to make sure no snails or slugs or other unwelcome guests were curled up in the hollow interior, and added it to the ones soaking in salt water.

Will was dumbfounded. "And you mean there are *more*?"

"Well, another onion sack full, at least. Probably about two gallons more. Sarah and I filled both sacks and I tied my apron up and carried a lot home in it. We stopped picking when that black-snake slithered out of the leaves." She held up a four-inch spongy cone. "Look at the size of *this* one, Will."

"Okay, Soph. You just keep right on rubbing it in. You say they're up there at the corner of the hog lot?"

Sophia nodded. "On this side of the fence, around the big old elm that was struck by lightning last fall. We didn't look in the lot. The hogs will have grubbed those out, anyway." Will sulked. "Well, you always *said* the best place to find them was around a dying elm. I took a walk one day several weeks ago and only a few of those branches had leaf buds. The tree certainly *looked* like it was dying."

"Why didn't you tell me?"

"You didn't ask! Anyway, that tree was there for everyone to see, and you knew as well as I did that it had been hit. Remember? You were so worried about the hogs? And you're up at the hog lot at least once or twice a day. So are Mike and the boys."

Her satisfied smile bordered on malice. "Besides, you and Bill were so cocky about your big mushroom hunt I didn't want to spoil your fun." She glanced sidewise at Will. "You know, you wouldn't take Sarah and no one even *thought* to ask me." She cast mournful eyes at Will. Mock pity flavored her voice. "All I'm good for is to clean them and fry them, I guess."

She finally relented. "I wasn't really sure they were there, anyway. But, as it turned out, they were." A smug smile settled on her face.

Will watched her drain dirty salt water, mottled with floating bugs and dead leaves, from another mushroom-filled dishpan. She checked them again before adding fresh water for the final soak.

Sarah, watching and listening from her seat at the table, finished her bread and jelly. "And they're not even hard to find, Daddy. Mamma and I just walked along and pinched them off. It was like picking Dutchman's Britches, only better."

Will's irritation mounted. "Drink your milk," he snapped. He stomped to the doorway and shouted, "Get your sacks, boys. I'll get Mike." He picked up the two empty sacks lying by the sink.

Impish innocence cloaked Sophia's voice. "Where are you going, Will?"

"Mushroom hunting, by God." His face was grim. "And this time you better believe I'll bring home more than bacon!"

Chapter 20

On a hot, arid June morning, Sophia drove Seth and Sarah to catechism. By the time they returned, the blazing sun kept them from the garden. Sophia and Sarah waited until evening to harvest the first green beans, and were still picking their way up the row when Will came home from work.

"I picked up the mail," he called on his way to the house to change. "There's a letter from your mother."

"Oh, good. Leave it on the table." Despite the lack of warmth between mother and daughter, Sophia looked forward to Hattie's infrequent letters. "I'll be in as soon as we pick the rest of the beans. It's gotten so hot so soon we may not have many more. These almost cooked in the garden."

"Mike and the boys up from the field yet?"

"No, they should be here soon, though. It's almost half-past five, isn't it?"

"Nearer six. Sorry I'm late again. Had to clean up some stuff at the office after the men knocked off. Boys must've stopped to wash the dust off in the creek. I'll change and start chores. Fresh green beans for dinner? Sounds good." The screen door slammed behind him.

Sophia pulled onions to cook with the beans, then stopped by the well and rinsed them on her way to the kitchen. "Sarah, get the garden fork and dig a hill of new potatoes. I'll put them in the pot with the beans, too. And be sure you wash all the dirt off before you bring them into the kitchen."

She glanced at the letter on the table. If the beans were to be done in time, she'd have to get them on now. She admired the used oil stove Will had bought to cook on during hot weather, lit a burner with a kitchen match, and put water on to heat. Sarah snapped beans while Sophia scraped thin skin off the new potatoes.

Mamma's letter will have to wait.

* * *

Will, Mike and the boys finished evening chores and washed up outside. Will left the boys having a water fight at the well while Mike sat on the back porch watching and laughing and waiting to eat. When Will walked into the kitchen, he found Sarah dodging sizzling steam and struggling to adjust the flame under the pot of beans boiling over on the stove.

"Where's your mamma?"

The little girl's eyes were wide with fright. "In the bedroom," she quavered. "She's been in there a long time, too, Daddy."

Will lowered the flame and added more water to the pot. "Is she sick?"

"I don't know. She was reading Gramma Hattie's letter, then she looked funny and started to cry and ran in the bedroom and shut the door."

"Hmm. Well, Mike and the boys will be in to eat right away. You be a good girl and set the table. I'll go see what's wrong."

* * *

Will knocked softly before opening the finally oiled, no-longer-squeaking bedroom door. Sophia, still crying, lay facedown on the bed. "Soph? You okay?"

"It's not me, Will," she wailed. "It's *Mamma.*"

"Is she sick?"

"No, not sick, it's worse than that. She's getting m…m…*married.*" Sophia buried her head in the pillow and sobbed.

Relieved, Will sat on the edge of the bed and patted his wife's shoulder. "Nothing wrong with that, Soph. Unless of course she has to…"

Sophia sat up and glared through her tears. "At *her* age?" Will grinned. "It's not something to joke about, Will. Read this." She threw the crumpled letter on the bed and dried her eyes on her apron.

Will smoothed the pages and quickly leafed through them. "I don't see what you're so upset about. The way you're carrying on, I thought maybe she was marrying some young gigolo after her money. Says here he's a widower, an oilman she's known for years."

"Yes, known for years and never *mentioned* before. How could she do this to me? She's not been back for thirteen years. Right after Bill was born she ran off to Tulsa and opened that dress shop. She's never even *seen* Seth and Sarah. Months go by without a letter, and now she wants to come see us on her *honeymoon.*" Sophia pounded her pillow.

"Now Soph, pull yourself together. You've got Sarah scared to death. Besides, near as I can tell there's no reason at all she shouldn't get married if she wants. She's what? Middle fifties? You know the age of consent is eighteen, maybe fourteen in Oklahoma. And she says he's sixty. If he's an old oilman, you better believe he's not some poor tramp she'll have to take care of. I still don't see why you're so upset."

She sniffled. "I guess it's because she hated being married to Papa and she was so mean to him all the time. To both of us. Oh, she didn't beat me or anything like that. Sometimes I used to wish she would so she'd at least know I was there. She was…maybe she just didn't like me. She said there was something so…so unpredictable in Papa and me. Mamma called it a wild streak. Papa said it was the Russian soul and nothing could tame it. I didn't think she could love anyone, and now she says she loves *him*. Oh, Will," she wailed, "she calls him my new papa. How can we let him come here?"

Will cradled her head on his shoulder, averting his face so she wouldn't smell the beer on his breath. "She says she'd like us to come to the wedding if we can. You want to go?" Sophia shook her head violently. "Well, it's not until October. We've got plenty of time to think about it." He gave her shoulder a final pat and moved away. "Don't make yourself sick carrying on like this. I'll get a cold washrag for your eyes. They're all puffy. The kids and I will finish cooking. We'll talk later when you feel better. There any ham I can fry to go with that mess of green beans and new potatoes?"

* * *

Welcome rain and moderating temperatures had brought on a bumper vegetable crop. Anne and Sophia washed and scalded canning jars for the bushel basket of green beans Mike and the boys had picked early that morning before going to the field.

"I wasn't sure I'd get to come home this summer, Mamma. Mrs. Greenberg almost didn't go to New York. She didn't think she could manage *three* children on the train by herself. I'm glad Dr. Greenberg was able to go with her."

"Is he staying all six weeks?"

"Just a week. Five days, I guess, with a day going and a day back, but if Mrs. Eisenfeld isn't able to come home with her and help with the baby he may have to go again in August. They're not moving until September."

"Can't Abe help her again?"

"I don't think so. He's decided to study law, so he's working in his father's office this summer."

"Do you hear from him often?"

"Not really. We write once in awhile. He's worried about how Hitler hates Jews. His father still has family in Germany. He mentions the farm a lot, too. He told Mrs. Greenberg all about it and she said it's a shame they can't have an August hospital-fund dinner out here sometime."

"Here?" Sophia glanced at the well-dotted fly ribbon hanging over the table. "With all these flies?"

"I went with the Greenbergs last August and there were just as many at the school. Flies are everywhere, Mamma. Besides, that gym's so hot. She said it wouldn't be any more trouble to carry everything out here than it is to take stuff to the high school since they have to load the cars anyway. She thinks it would be a lot nicer. And cooler, too."

Sophia was dumbfounded. "Was she *serious*, Anne?"

"She sounded like it. I was going to say something last fall, see if maybe you and Daddy would let the hospital ladies have it here this summer, but you were so busy with the election and...and everything."

"No, it wouldn't have been a good time. Maybe next summer, though. No, not then either. Your dad will be running for Road Commissioner."

Anne, unsure of her mother's reaction to Ruth Greenberg's suggestion, pounced on Sophia's wavering thoughts.

"But Mamma, wouldn't that be even better? I mean, a lot of those people in town don't know Daddy and if they knew him they'd vote for him."

"I don't think it would be wise, Anne. We can't bring politics into the hospital. It might cause hard feelings, and they're having enough trouble equipping it now."

"But you wouldn't have to talk about the election. Just *having* it here would be enough. I'll bet everybody in town would like to eat in our front yard and look out over the fields and the creek. They'd sell lots more tickets, and might even make enough to buy the rest of the beds."

"Now just a minute, Anne. You're talking four or five hundred people."

"I know, Mamma, but they only serve a hundred an hour because that's what the gym holds. They print the time to eat on the tickets and could do the same thing here,"

"But think of the work. And all those dishes to wash…"

"There wouldn't be that much work, just clean it up like you did for Abe last summer. The ladies fix all the food. They even use their own tablecloths and utensils and serving dishes and people eat off paper plates and the men fry the chickens. Heck, Dr. Greenberg helped fry last year, even if the Greenbergs couldn't eat any chicken because it was cooked in lard. Dr. Tom kidded Dr. Greenberg a lot about that."

She paused, thinking. "We always have lots of tomatoes then. Maybe we can plant some extras and slice those. Everyone likes tomatoes. We don't have enough trestle tables or benches, but they could borrow tables and chairs from the school. And park in the alfalfa field. Daddy will have it cut by then so it'll be bare if he doesn't let another crop grow."

Anne's excitement was contagious. Sophia rolled the possibility around in her mind while she scalded another tray of jars. Anne held her breath. "Well, it might work. *You'll* have to talk to your father, though. And don't mention politics or the election. If he thinks he's helping the hospital he might agree, but campaigning? He wouldn't even consider it."

"Mum's the word, Mum," Anne giggled. "When are Gramma Hattie and her new husband coming?"

"Not until October. Your father's able to pay Mike now, and he wants him to scrape and paint the house and sheds after the last crop layby, before they get here. Not that it doesn't need it, but…"

"Good. It will look extra nice for next year's chicken dinner. I'll find Sarah to help snap beans."

* * *

"Wonderful spread you've got here, Will." After morning chores, Will found Dan, a bowlegged, wiry man who came only to

Will's shoulder, standing on the veranda enjoying October's dying beauty. "Got a few dusty Oklahoma acres myself I tried to farm before I started wildcatting. Nothing like this, though."

The new Mr. and Mrs. Daniel Murphy had arrived the previous evening in a new, dust-covered black Duesenberg. Sophia's mother kissed her and the children, embraced Will, pleaded exhaustion, and went straight to bed.

"How's Hattie feeling this morning?'

"Some better. Told her she might as well go back to sleep though. Guess I shouldn't have pushed so hard to get here, but she told you we'd be here on Friday and Hattie was afraid you'd worry. I wanted to stay over in St. Louis, rest up a bit, then drive out today. They got some *fine* hotels there. I told Hattie we could call you from Missouri, but you know women. Once they get an idea in their heads you can't shake it loose.

"We'd a' been okay, hadn't been for that *dee*-tour in Missouri. I've seen some rough roads in my time, but that one topped 'em all. Five miles an hour and still almost shook Hattie's teeth loose, even with that heavy car. She's a game one, though. Be okay once she gets rested up. Poor little thing, guess she never was very strong. Needs lots of care-takin'."

Will thought of the iron-willed woman who had supervised his and Sophia's courtship. He wondered if they were thinking about the same person but, "You're probably right, Dan. Of course, we haven't seen her for over thirteen years."

"That's what she said. Well, she was in that shop of hers every day, even Sunday. Started it on a shoestring, you know. At least she had the good years to get it going, before the Depression hit. Always carries quality stuff, too. That makes a big difference in oil country. It's a money maker, even now. My first wife used to buy clothes there. That's how I *met* Hattie. Always helped her as much as I could, too." He stopped abruptly and glanced sidewise at Will.

Will broke the awkward silence. "What did you grow on your

farm?"

"Mostly dust and tumbleweeds. Oh, we grew enough potatoes to go with the jackrabbits for the stew pot, keep the kids fed. Thing is, I was never cut out to be a farmer. Luckiest thing I ever did was sign on with that oilrig crew before the Great War and learn my way around the fields. No, I take that back. That was the *second* luckiest thing. The first was hanging on to the farm deed. Almost let it go for taxes, but decided to pay 'em at the last minute. I got a couple of wells on it now that just won't quit.

"Bad out there now, though. Dust's turrible. It's like that real fine face powder Hattie uses. Red Cross folks are even putting facemasks on the kids. Oil workers use those, too. And if they can get 'em, gas masks left over from the war.

"Not as bad this year, '31 was worst. See, there's no trees to hold the soil and the wind blows right across that flatland—Eastern Colorado, Oklahoma, Western Kansas…all alike. You prob'ly heard, folks call it the Dust Bowl.

"Indians tried to tell the early settlers not to break the sod so deep, but oh no, they wouldn't listen. Today them tractors dig even deeper. Somebody figured out it took a thousand years for nature to make one inch of topsoil out there and minutes to blow it away. Now there's drought. And whirlwinds. Indians say they've always had those, but for the past three years they've blowed red dust so thick you can't see your hand in front of your face."

"Red? I thought it was black, that's what *we* see in the clouds going over here."

"No, the black's from Kansas. Oklahoma dust's red. And the gray's from Texas and New Mexico. Color's how you tell where it's coming from."

"How come you know so much about soil, Dan?"

"Hell, I was a farmer before I was a oilman. Only difference is now I dig deeper. Anyway, folks out there got troubles. Them as can just pull up stakes and leave, but the ones that stay ain't got a lick of sense. They just keep on aplowin' and the wind keeps on ablowin'. Even the jackrabbits are dying 'cause there's no grass left to eat. Makes a body appreciate land like this." He gazed across the creek bottom. "It always this purty here, Will?"

"Mostly. Winters are cold, summers hot, but it's that way everywhere."

"Not in Florida and California. Now that Hattie's hired someone to manage her shop, I'd like us to settle in one or the other. California prob'ly, closer to the wells. And Hattie's shop, a'course. What I'd really like is for her to sell that damn place, but she's got this need to own something that belongs to just her. Been like that since I first met her, oh, ten years or so ago. Guess she had a rough life when she was young?"

Will wondered if Dan was fishing for information. Not knowing what Hattie had or hadn't told her new husband, he hedged. "Well, Soph was only five when her father was killed in the mine and Hattie had to work to support them both."

"That's what she said. Turrible cross to bear. *Turrible*! But she made it through and still hung on to her looks. Purty as a speckled pup, she is. Always did think so."

Sophia joined the two men, saving Will from further dissemblance. "I fed the children. They were too hungry to wait for Mamma. Do you two want breakfast now or later?"

Dan chuckled. "Well, now, Soph, if you're thinking of waiting for your mamma you might as well forget it. After that long ride yesterday, doubt if she's up much before noon. Will, I'm ready if you are. Say, we saw Roosevelt's 'blue eagle' National Recovery Act signs clean across the country. What do you folks around here think about the NRA?"

"To tell the truth, I haven't really made up my mind. Soph and I listened to his fireside chat about that. Roosevelt said it's going to help the economy, but he says that every time he thinks up a new program. Used lots of hi-falutin' words about stopping wasteful competition, encouraging better regulated pricing and selling policies, getting higher wages and shorter hours in the factories. Be interesting to see what workers and the unions think about collective bargaining."

The political discussion continued while Sophia fried bacon and eggs.

* * *

After breakfast, Will took Dan on a tour of the farm. Sophia washed the dishes, straightened the house, and prowled nervously waiting for her mother. Will was right, of course. Like it or not, she had to accept Mamma's marriage. She'd decided to like it, but now that her mother was here it was like having a stranger in the house. She didn't know what to say and wondered if that was why her mother had gone to bed immediately the night before and was still upstairs. Perhaps she didn't know what to say, either.

Sophia made a pot of the strong English tea her mother preferred over coffee, got out Clarilla's Spode and silver, sliced and buttered fresh-baked bread, arranged a tray and carried it up the back stairs. She found Hattie dressed and sitting by the window in William P's old room, vacated by Bill during the Murphy's visit.

"Oh, my, Sophia. You fixed a tray for me, like you used to. You didn't have to do that. I was just getting ready to come down."

"I wanted to, Mamma. It's been so long since I've seen you." She kissed her mother's cheek, noted her stylish dress, marcelled hair and...*makeup*? Sophia suddenly felt dowdy. "You hardly seem any older."

"Just tricks of the trade, Sophia. When you cater to women with rich husbands, you always have to look your best. *You* look well. I'm sorry we didn't get a chance to visit last night, but I was so tired..."

"That's what Dan said." She poured tea. "I didn't bring any

milk, you never used to take milk, but I'll get some if you like. Or lemon?"

"No, no. This is fine. Your home is lovely. I've never seen it, you know. You were still living in Macklin Corner when I left. I just can't believe that big strapping Billy. Well, Bill now… And Seth is almost as tall. I have the school pictures you sent, of course, but pictures are so flat. Sarah's beautiful. She's got Sergei's eyes and hair. Sergei was such a handsome man. She looks a lot like you did at that age. Did you say Anne will be home today?"

"I thought you might like to drive in with Sarah and me this afternoon to pick her up. She can only be here until Monday morning. The family she stays with has three children, one a baby, so they really need her. They outgrew their old house, too, and are just settling into a new one. Anne's very responsible, even if she is only sixteen. Well, seventeen in December. Remember? She came two days after Will's and my first anniversary."

Sophia poured more tea for her mother and a cup for herself. The two women, mother and daughter, began a cautious pilgrimage toward a new relationship.

* * *

Hattie and Dan spent a week at the house on the bluff. They left promising to return soon and stay longer. Will and Sophia stood on the veranda, waving and watching until the highly-polished Duesenberg rolled out of sight around the corner.

"Boys sure cleaned that car up, didn't they? Think they were more excited about the car than the visit." Will's hand clasped Sophia's. "That wasn't too bad, was it?"

"Not as bad as I was afraid it would be. And not at all what I expected. Once I stopped thinking of her as Mamma I began to like her. Do you know, Will, I don't think she likes children. She seemed so…so uncomfortable with Sarah. It was like watching her with me when I was that age. I wonder if that's why she left Macklin Corner? Maybe she just didn't want to be around her grandchildren."

"I noticed that, too. Seemed fine with the boys, though. And with Anne."

"Well, Anne looks so much like her. Except for age, they could be twins. It's funny. I never saw that much resemblance before."

"You two sure spent a lot of time jabbering. I think Dan explored every acre on the place twice and even took Sarah with him a couple of times just to let you two have time to yourselves. Seems like a nice guy. Wish I'd been able to be more company for him, but I had to use this good weather to get the roads in shape for winter."

"I understood that, Will. And I'm sure Dan and Mamma did, too. He followed Mike around a lot, though. I think they liked each other."

"Probably. From what I could pick up, bet Dan was something of a roustabout before he struck it rich."

"That could be. One noon he took a pan of food out to a bum for me. They visited over an hour. I tried to tell him later that we didn't encourage the bums to hang around after they ate. He *laughed* at me, Will! He said bums are some of the finest people in the world and that we're lucky to have them."

"Well, he's a talker all right. Funny, though. Nice enough fella, just not the kind of man you'd think Hattie would pick out. Common as an old shoe in spite of his money."

"I thought so, too. Papa was so refined, and Dan…well, he's awfully good to Mamma, though. You know, Will, I finally asked Mamma if she ever loved Papa."

Will whistled. "What did she say to *that*?"

"That she thought she did when she married him, but it was a mistake. Then I asked if she loved me or if *I* was a mistake, too.

Do you know what she said? 'Of course I loved you. I took care of you, didn't I?' Maybe she doesn't even know what love means."

A tiny spark of understanding began to glow deep in Will's mind. Understanding for the lonely, love-starved child Sophia had been.

Chapter 21

Routine preparations for the cold months ahead absorbed the excitement of the newlyweds' visit. By November, hay barns and corncribs overflowed with winter livestock feed. Carrots, turnips, potatoes, parsnips and apples filled the root cellar. Home-canned jars of tomatoes, green beans, peas, corn, beets, blackberries, peaches and pickles of every description lined basement shelves. Jewel-toned jellies waited to top hot biscuits and homemade bread. Hams, pork loins, sides of bacon and strings of sausages cured in the smokehouse, accepting the pungent flavor of slow-burning hickory. But in November 1933, lacking William P's ribald humor, butchering day had been just another hard day's work.

Bill, the only permanent sophomore on the varsity football squad, played in almost every game. Coach Munson told Will confidentially that Bill, popular with teammates and students alike and already a substitute quarterback, was almost certain to be chosen co-captain the following year, an unheard-of honor for a junior. Will's buttons almost popped off his shirt.

"When's your last home game?" he asked during a mid-November breakfast.

Bill opened his just-filled mouth to reply, saw his mother's stern frown, and hurriedly chewed and swallowed a bite of sausage. "This Saturday. Coach thought we might make it to the finals this year, but Oakville has a really good team and we're paired against them our first regional game. Now Coach says maybe next year. Why? You'll be there, won't you?"

"Wouldn't miss it for the world. We'll *all* be there, won't we Soph? Bring Mike, too, and Anne if she can get away. What I was wondering, you're coming up sixteen. Thought you might like to spend a Saturday learning to drive before we spread the cured manure on that alfalfa field."

Bill's grin was a mile wide. "Wondered when you'd get around to teaching me, Dad. I was about to ask Mom."

Sophia flipped another pancake for Seth and raised her eyebrows. "You'd let *me* teach you to drive, Bill? You're even braver than I thought."

"Heck, you're a good driver, Mom. The way you handle that old Maxwell's something. Could we do it Sunday, Dad?"

"Ground's too wet. We'll wait for a hard freeze. Besides, you've got church. And you can't drive legal anyway till you're sixteen."

"Aw, Dad, you know farm kids can get special licenses when they're only fourteen." He looked hopefully at his father. "So they can drive to school? And drop little kids off later so they don't have to wait outside? And their sister can come back home? And…"

"…and busy as your mom is these days she needs the car more than you?" Will laughed, enjoying his son's exuberance. "Good Lord, wish I'd never brought it up." He turned serious. "We have to nurse the Maxwell along, Bill. It's almost twenty years old. Afraid it's gonna fall apart on these rutty roads one of these days. Just hope it holds out till we get the mortgage paid off and can afford payments on a new car. Sure hate to see your mom stranded somewhere."

Sophia's second frown of the morning was worried. "What kind of car, Will?"

"Maybe a Dodge. Chrysler bought out Maxwell and Dodge still uses that reverse shift you're used to." He returned Sophia's relieved smile. "You kids get your books and lunches and let's go. We're late."

* * *

Sophia washed up the breakfast clutter, gave the house a lick-and-a-promise cleaning, and checked the calendar. Democrat meeting tonight, quilting at Mary's Wednesday afternoon, Friday's planning session at Ruth Greenberg's.

Will's enthusiasm for the fund-raising dinner matched Anne's. "Anything to help the hospital. Wish it'd been there when your mom needed it." When Anne was home the two spent hours talking and planning. *They* were the ones who should be on the Planning Committee.

What to wear?

Mamma would say 'First impressions are important, Sophia!' The black dress from Pa's funeral? Too severe. I'll add a white lace collar. Ruth says not to worry, it's just a get-acquainted tea and I can come with Ellen Campbell. Still...

She fretted.

And If Friday's meeting goes well, Ruth said they might want the next meeting here so they can see the farm.

She studied the old farmhouse rooms with critical eyes, trying to see them as the town women would.

Everything needs a good cleaning. The dining room's not too *bad. Maybe they won't notice where Sarah tore the wallpaper. Put a chair in front of it? And with all the leaves in we can sit around the table. I'll bake a devil's food cake. The Spode? I'll see what Ruth does Friday.*

She moved to the parlor.

Phineas' walnut secretary and armoire add a nice touch.

Will had quirked his eyebrow at her excitement over the armoire when he and the boys unloaded it along with the secretary. "You mean Phineas' old clothes press? Ma said Pa kept his things in it and she didn't need it any more. Just tell us where to put it."

But the kitchen was awful.

I'll move the slop bucket to the back porch and keep the kitchen door closed.

Sophia put aside her concern, set up the ironing board, checked the flatirons heating on the wood stove, and tackled the basket of clothes she'd sprinkled and rolled early that morning. She hated ironing. She always thought when she ironed, sometimes too much.

Will puzzled her. Since Mamma and Dan left, he was almost courting her again. And even before. Last spring's bouquet of the bluebells she loved…

Love.

She knew Will missed her once-ardent responses. She missed them, too.

Father Riley was wrong. Going through the motions *didn't* bring back the feeling, but at least she and Will were getting along better.

And Will didn't seem to be drinking. Well, just beer.

Where does he get it, though? He's late coming home so often, too, even with a lighter winter workload. He says *office work. With beer on his breath?*

She worried about Prohibition ending.

If whiskey is easier to get...

Friends in Macklin Corner talked about illegal taverns called 'blind pigs', ready to open legally when the Eighteenth Amendment was repealed. Election night…

Don't think about that!

Sophia's mind moved to the children.

I hope Will doesn't try to force Seth into Bill's football cleats. I am proud of Bill's report cards though. Maybe kicking a football kicked off his mind.

Seth was sensitive, like Anne. He lacked Bill's rough, competitive nature; wrote poems and stories left on his study table for her to read.

His way of sharing...

And his tender care of the baby squirrel, the way he helped when Belle's last calf was born. The vet said he couldn't have saved Belle without Seth, that Seth's strong, slender hands reached where his couldn't to turn the big bull calf into birth position.

Papa's hands...and Little Sergei's...

Seth, returning to the house covered with blood and mucous and reeking of antiseptic, had glowed with the miracle of birth. Now he occasionally helped the vet with livestock on other farms, and she cleaned around Seth's stack of Dr. Tom's old medical magazines.

She put the cooling flatiron back on the stove to reheat, folded the potholder around the handle of another, lifted it, spat on her finger and touched the bottom. The iron sizzled. She smoothed another of Will's shirts over the ironing board and thought about the new gas irons.

* * *

February, unseasonably warm when Bill grabbed his lightweight jacket for school, turned biting cold by dismissal. He loped by his father's office hoping for a ride the rest of the way home, but the truck was gone and the door locked. Veering off the slab, he cut through Macklin Corner to run down the railroad tracks.

Save a half-mile and running the ties is good footwork training. Season's over, but have to stay in shape.

Hands and ears freezing, he turned his collar up, jammed his bare hands in his pockets and wished he'd listened to his mother. She was always yelling at him, though.

Bill wear your warm coat. Bill don't forget your gloves. Bill where's your hat.

He jogged down Main Street, saw the county truck parked in front of the feed store and stopped.

"Nope, haven't seen your dad for an hour or so. He was in earlier, got some Bag Balm for the cows and visited with the other farmers. Might be down at Walt's Tap or the Wander In, though. Said something about having a beer."

"Thanks, Mr. Oliver."

Bill was undecided. Mom would kill him if he went in a tavern, but he was so cold. He'd try Walt's Tap, last year's Walt's Ice Cream Parlor, first. He didn't think his dad would go to the Wander In, a sleazy bar opened the fifth of December—the very day the Eighteenth Amendment was repealed—that already had a shady reputation for rowdiness and what his friends called 'goings-on'.

He cupped his hands around his eyes to peer through Walt's plate-glass window. Only three men at the bar, and his father wasn't one of them.

Shoving his hands deeper into his pockets, he headed toward the Wander In. As tall as Bill was, he had to stand on his toes to see over the heavy curtains that covered the lower part of the converted store's front window.

Quite a party going on in there! Jukebox playing, lots of people at the bar drinking. Women, too.

His eyes searched the length of the bar.

No Dad.

Despite the cold run ahead, he was relieved. Until he saw the tall man with auburn hair sitting in a booth, head tilted toward the inviting woman across the table.

He froze in place, watched the intimate scene in the booth and instinctively recognized lust. Icy pain cramped Bill's stomach. His heels dropped to the sidewalk. Shock and humiliation vied with shame. He *hadn't* meant to spy. Maybe he was wrong. He raised on his toes again, saw his father lead the woman to a small, secluded dance floor.

From the back she looks just like Mom before Mom got skinny.

He watched Will circle the woman's waist with a possessive arm and lead her into a slow, seductive dance. Saw his father's hand touch the long fall of dark hair hiding her face. Tears scalded Bill's freezing cheeks. Football training and biting cold disappeared into a slicing sense of betrayal. His choked animal moan was lost in the rising wind. Bill ran faster than he'd ever run before.

* * *

Sophia spread another wool blanket over her violently shivering son and slipped a hot, flannel-wrapped rock under the covers at his feet. Bill's chattering teeth kept both thermometer and hot broth at bay. When she leaned to feel his clammy forehead, he clasped her hand. Sophia, unschooled in the symptoms of shock, relied on common sense. She sat beside him and chafed his cold hands.

If only Will would get home. He's later than usual again tonight.

She sent Seth and Mike out to do chores, asked Sarah to set the table, and returned to her son's side. And tried to think.

Why is Bill so cold?

Even though the temperature had dropped, it was still only about twenty-five degrees and he'd run hard. That should have kept him warm, but he was shivering and gasping and panting when he burst into the kitchen.

"Bill, did something happen on the way home this evening?"

He shook his head, pulled his hands free and rolled away. Perplexed, Sophia remained by his side.

At last the combination of blankets, featherbed and hot rock stilled his vibrating body. She slipped the thermometer under his tongue, counted three minutes and checked the reading. "No fever, I guess you don't have pneumonia. But you have to get something warm in your stomach. Now drink this broth."

The authority in her voice brought Bill to a sitting position. He grasped the cup, drained it and burrowed back into the warm hollow of the featherbed. Mystified and worried, Sophia sat with him until he slept.

* * *

"Will, I don't know. He got home about half-past four, shivering and shaking with cold. He just wore a light jacket this morning, but that run home should have kept him warm. Instead, he almost collapsed on the kitchen floor. Seth helped me get him upstairs to bed and I warmed him as best I could. It's a good thing he moved into Pa's room for good after Mamma and Dan left. There was no fever so I don't suppose it's anything contagious, but I still don't think he should be around the other children."

Will's concern was as great as Sophia's. "Think we oughta call Doc?"

"Let's wait till after we eat. Mike and Seth will be in soon and they'll be hungry. Sleep's the best thing for him now, anyway. If he wakes up with a temperature, we'll call Dr. Tom then."

"Think I'll check on him."

"Don't wake him. I had a terrible time getting him to sleep!"

* * *

Will avoided the squeaky step on the back stairs, lowered the lamp flame, eased the door open, and tiptoed into the familiar room that had long ago been his. He studied the blanketed outline of the powerful body sprawled crosswise in the too-short bed; moved the dimmed light to Bill's taut, shadowed face. The rosy-cheeked, boyish look was gone. The emerging Macklin jaw line mirrored Will's. He listened to his son's deep, even breathing. Felt his forehead. Thanked God it was cool.

And thank God for such a son.

He swallowed choking guilt. Touched the auburn hair, smoothed the blankets, and quietly left the room.

Through slit lids, Bill watched his father leave. Disillusionment blotted the love in the eyes so like Will's own.

* * *

Bill withdrew from everyone, but continued to carry his share of the work and attend school. And each night he gulped his food before bolting for the solitude of his room.

"What's the matter with Bill, Mamma?" Sarah asked. "He doesn't even tease me and call me 'Brat' any more. Is he still sick?"

"No, Honey. I think he's just very sad about something. I'm sure he'll talk about it when he's ready and then he'll feel better." She tweaked one of Sarah's curls. "I'll bet he's teasing you and pulling your hair again before long."

Privately, Sophia suspected a girl. She questioned Anne during her late-February weekend at home. Anne knew nothing about any girl, but Bill avoided her at school much as he avoided the family at home. And his friends were beginning to ignore him. A sullen Bill wasn't much fun. Anne was as puzzled as the rest of the family.

Satisfied that Bill wasn't sick, unable to break through his barbed-wire defense, Sophia busied herself with campaign details. Everyone that knew Will said what a wonderful job he was doing, but not enough people knew him. With no opposition on the Democrat ticket, she was using the primary election to introduce the name Will Macklin to November voters.

She hoped the money spent on campaign pamphlets helped. The other Committeemen had promised to distribute them in their precincts, and Will's brothers and sisters—even Clothilde—were taking them door to door in Walnut Hills.

Sophia carefully checked each issue of the local papers for PTA meetings, weekend church socials, chili suppers and benefits where Will could meet voters and shake hands.

If only all the bums we've fed for the past three years could vote.

While Sophia assembled election packets, she wondered what the summer of 1934 would bring. Will said the bums went south for the winter and followed spring north. If so, they'd be coming soon. Like the robins.

Several times the previous summer Mike had taken his lunch to the field and she was alone when one appeared at the top of the bluff. She'd learned to trust Blue's judgement. After she quieted the dogs, Blue sniffed inspection. Not one had failed the test. The aging dog even allowed a few to scratch his ears. And the men were invariably polite. If one was lucky enough to own a hat, he tipped it.

There's something almost chivalrous about them. Maybe knights of the road isn't far from the truth after all.

She tucked the final packet into her bulging shopping bag.

* * *

"Got a minute, Will?" Coach Munson's massive frame almost filled the doorway of Will's office.

"Sure. I can even offer you a cup of coffee. Soph always keeps my thermos filled."

"No, thanks. I can't stay long, but I wanted to talk to you privately. About Bill."

Will carefully set his cup on the desk. "Bill? Is he in some kind of trouble?"

"No, not yet, but the way he's going he *will* be. His six-week grade point average has dropped from A to D. You'll see when report cards come out next week. I talked to his teachers. They say he just quit working. And his attitude's worse than his grades. I wondered if you had any idea what might be bothering him."

"No, Coach. I wish I did. Soph and I have both been worried about him." He explained Bill's sudden illness and subsequent withdrawal. "His mother and I finally decided it was a girl, something he'd have to handle himself. He say anything to you?"

The coach lowered his eyes. "Matter of fact, he did. Mind if I sit down?" Will waved him to the chair across the desk and waited. "Actually, I'm a little embarrassed about this but I like the kid. Hate to see him waste his potential. And *sure* don't want to lose him from the squad. If we can help him now, it might prevent a lot of trouble down the road."

He paused, cleared his throat. "You know, my boys all kind of come to me when they've got problems they're not comfortable talking about at home? Bill doesn't know I'm talking to you. If you have to tell him, you can, but I'd really rather you didn't. The boys trust me. I don't often break that trust, but this is serious."

Will tensed. "I'm glad you *are* talking to me. Want to tell me about it?"

"Sir, do you have a girlfriend?"

A telltale flush colored Will's face. "Does Bill *think* I do? Is that what this is all about?"

"I'm afraid so. That night Bill got sick, he was running home. He cut through Macklin Corner and saw your truck in front of the feed store. He was cold so he stopped to catch a ride. Mr. Oliver told him you might be at Walt's Tap or the Wander In."

"He saw me that night? At the Wander In?"

The coach nodded. "He knew his mom wouldn't want him in a tavern so he looked over the curtains to see if you were there. You know how idealistic boys that age are. And I'm sure you know your son looked on you as some sort of hero. *And* that he worships his mother. Catholic boys usually do, even though they don't always show it. What was probably nothing took on tremendous importance in his mind. He saw you talking to some woman, then dancing with her."

The weight of remembrance was heavy. Will buried his face in his hands. "Oh, God. How do you explain to a sixteen-year-old?"

"I don't know, but the way Bill's suffering I felt I had to tell you. Wish it hadn't been me, Will." His lumpy, homely face showed as much chagrin as Will's. He shifted uncomfortably and rose to go. "Well, I have to get back, get ready for basketball practice."

Will stood to shake the outstretched hand. "Thanks Coach. I really appreciate this. Don't know yet what I'll say to him, but I'll try to clear this up."

* * *

The following morning Will dropped the younger children off at school. As it had for the past weeks, Bill's surly quiet dominated the drive to the office. "It's still early," Will said when they climbed out of the truck. "Come on in the office a minute. Something I want to talk to you about."

Suspicion darkened Bill's face. "I've got a report to work on this morning."

Will's voice was soft but firm. "No, you don't. I think there's something you and I have to settle. *Your* misery is making the *rest* of the family miserable. You're mad as hell about something and you're going to tell me exactly *what* you're mad about. Right now!"

Rage surged through Bill's stiffened body. His face splotched, his clenched fists shook. "You and that goddamned woman!"

Will nodded slowly. "Um-*hmm*. Figured that's what it was. Took me awhile to put it all together. You saw me at the Wander In that evening? Had to be it, you getting sick just then and all. And acting like you hated everyone since, me most of all." He studied Bill's face. "You want to hit me? Go ahead. You think I wouldn't like to hit myself as hard as I could? Now come on in the office. No point airing our dirty laundry in public." Bill, unmoving, fists still clenched, watched his father unlock the door. "Come on. Please. I'm not ordering, I'm asking." Bill stomped inside and slammed the door.

"You're almost grown, so I think you may be able to understand, at least a little. If you try." He sat on the corner of the desk and watched his son's face while he spoke.

"First, it's important that you know I love your mother and you kids more than anything else in the world." Contempt twisted Bill's mouth, the anger in his eyes flared higher. Will thrust his palm out in a stemming gesture. "Hear me out. I know you might not believe it right now, but that's gospel.

"Now, you've got eyes in your head. You already know your mom and I have had a lot of trouble lately. It's true I made a jackass out of myself election night. But it's *just* as true that I've spent almost a year and a half trying to make it up to your mother. She's still skittish and I'm still trying. Think I'm making headway, too. What you saw at the Wander In was a damn fool of a lonely man trying to find the love I lost at home."

"But Mom *does* love you."

"Not all the way, not like she used to. I'm working on that, too, but she's holding back. I think right now she's afraid to love me like that again."

"Who'd blame her when you carry on like you do?"

"Bill, I've maybe had a beer or two after work once in awhile, but I've not been drunk since that night at Doc's. That's the God's truth. I can't prove it, so you'll just have to take my word for it. And I'm not going to see that woman any more, either."

Disbelief stained Bill's face. "That's what you tell Mom when she asks you not to drink any more. You say you'll never do it again and then you *do*. You think we didn't hear upstairs when you were drunk and yelled at her? When Anne was still home, we'd sit at the top of the stairs together and listen. Why do you think she'd rather stay at the Greenbergs' than come home?"

Will sickened. He clamped his teeth together, containing his angry shame. "I think that's called eavesdropping."

"Not when you're afraid someone might hurt your mother it's not."

"I'd *never* hurt your mother." The shock on his father's face penetrated Bill's rage.

"Well, *we* didn't know that."

"Now you do! Look, I won't ask you not to say anything about what you saw, because you don't want your mother upset any more than I do. Anyway, if you were going to talk about it, you'd have done it before now instead of holding your hurt inside. I won't ask you to forgive me, either, because I can't even forgive myself. What I *am* asking is that you try to understand. And I want you to know nobody, even you, could be madder at me than I already am at myself."

Will's foot swung back and forth like an overweight pendulum as he waited for Bill to sort out, perhaps understand, everything he'd said. Finally he stood, moved to touch his son's shoulder. Inches apart, hostile hazel eyes met earnest hazel eyes.

"Think we can ever be buddies again?"

Bill thrust his father's hand away, turned on his heel and ran out the door.

Will moved to the doorway. Stared after his treasured son fading into the distance.

Chapter 22

Primary returns from each Kickapoo County precinct littered the desktop of Phineas' walnut secretary. Sophia sorted, stacked, and wondered again how Will might have done without the huge Democrat turnout showing support for Roosevelt's programs.

*A*t least the returns showed where to concentrate the Macklins' fall campaign. In the west section of the county, where Walnut Hills was the big population center and where many Democrats left the circle by Will's name blank. Had word of Will's drinking leaked out? Was it a reaction to the unopposed Walnut Hills Republican candidate's slogan, 'Can a leopard change its spots'? Whatever the cause, his family's house-to-house campaign had failed. Still, support on the eastern side, where Will was known, was good despite Senator Fairwell's unfulfilled promise of support. The fall election was going to take a lot of work.

She smiled at the memory of March primary night and put down her pencil. When Will had picked her up at the polls at six, his teasing grin was a promise of the night ahead.

Suited, shaved and mysterious, he turned toward Campbells' instead of home. "You wait here," he said when her hand moved to the door handle. He returned with Ellen on his arm, settled her in the back seat, fingered the gold chain across his vest, and drew Phineas' watch from his fob pocket to check the time. "Ellen says Doc's running late again. We'll pick him up at the office."

She searched first Will's, then Ellen's, beaming faces. "What on earth is going on?"

"Us! Except we're going *out*. We haven't been to a nice restaurant since before Anne was born. Almost seventeen years." He winked at the doctor's wife. "Kind of figured I owed Doc and Ellie a dinner, too, so I made reservations at the Holly House for all of us. Then I thought we might go to the courthouse and wait for the returns." He laughed at the surprised pleasure flooding Sophia's face.

"But the children…"

"…aren't much children any more, Soph. Besides, they know all about it. Mike'll sleep on the divan till we get home." He laughed again. "Seems kinda funny, though, that little bitty fella taking care of those hulks of ours. Heck, our boys both tower over him and even Sarah's almost as tall as Mike now."

"But I didn't leave anything for them to eat."

"They'll manage. And they've got strict orders to clean up any mess they make. *And* to bank the fires and empty the ashes! Now you just let *me* handle things for once."

Remembering the pleasant, relaxed early part of that evening and the later excitement as each precinct reported, Sophia's smile widened.

They were overjoyed at the Bridgeton returns. She knew contacts made during the hospital fund-raiser planning sessions helped, but suspected the lion's share of credit went to Bill. Bridgeton supported its local football team and, it seemed, their fathers as well.

She was relieved that Bill seemed to be settling whatever was bothering him. He was still distant and avoided his father, but Anne said he was talking to her at school again. She shuddered at that last report card, hoped it didn't lower his final average too much. And he was working hard to repair the damage, studying every night and sometimes weekends. Will had started letting him take the Maxwell to Bridgeton on Saturday nights lately, too. It was hard to believe he'd turned sixteen in March, had a driver's license, and would be a junior in the fall when Seth started high school.

Time, you old gypsy man,

And Anne would graduate next year.

Will you not stay?

She considered the college scholarship her daughter was

almost sure to win. Once she went away to school, she'd be gone for good.

Put up your caravan just for one day?

It seemed impossible for anyone to carry all those subjects and still maintain a straight-A average. Anne might even be valedictorian.

Anne, always thinking ahead, was taking both college entrance and commercial courses. She said since she was going to work her way through college, she'd rather do it in an office than in a restaurant waiting tables. Sophia couldn't imagine *anyone* making sense out of those funny squiggles Anne called shorthand.

And Will couldn't understand Anne's determination to make her own way. When he offered to help with expenses at Eastern Illinois University, Anne said he needed the money for the mortgage and she was right, but Sophia wondered if Will's earlier offhand attitude about high school was at the root of her refusal.

Sometimes I think those children know more about what's going on around here than I do. They certainly know more than we think they do."

Whatever her reasons, Anne had planned everything. Even without the expected scholarship, she'd still attend Eastern. For room and board, she'd stay with and do housework for Dr. Tom's sister, a teacher at EIU. Because of Miss Campbell, she already had a part-time job promised in the university offices. During summers she'd remain with the Greenbergs, work daytimes for the doctor while his regular receptionist was home with her school age children, help Ruth at night. If the scholarship came through, she'd drop the campus job and carry a heavier course load, graduate sooner.

She wished the college were closer, that trains ran between Bridgeton and Charleston. She saw little enough of her older daughter now.

Sophia's eyes closed, watched Anne disappearing into a tunnel of time, drawing farther away from her family.

A delicate butterfly escaping its chrysalis. So small. So determined. So like Mamma.

With a shake of her head, Sophia dismissed her concern. Primary returns reclaimed her attention. She marked a big X by each precinct needing special work, stacked the reports, pigeonholed them in the secretary, and glanced out the window. The late-April weather was too glorious to waste indoors. She collected her trowel and the flower seeds saved from the previous summer and went outside to plant zinnias. The farm had passed approval. The yard must look its best for the upcoming August dinner.

* * *

Blue's sharp ears picked up the sound of the unfamiliar car before Sophia's. His bark brought the other dogs running. Sophia, digging in a flowerbed near the driveway, shaded her eyes against the noon sun to see who was coming, but didn't recognize the automobile.

A frenzy of protective barks shielded Sophia from the mud-spattered Ford that coughed to a halt in the oak-shade driveway. Harry Stone leaned through the open window. "Call off your dogs, Miz Macklin. I'm just here to get Clara's cake plate."

Damn! I forgot to send that plate back with Will and now here's that obnoxious Harry Stone...

Sophia scrambled to her feet. "I'm so sorry, Mr. Stone. I put it away in the pantry for Will to return and forgot about it." An edgy laugh accompanied her apology. "I guess I put it away *too* well. And after Clara was so thoughtful. Please tell her how much we all appreciated her kindness."

Harry's eyes appraised Sophia, noted her nervousness. "Well, it *has* been over a year, you know. Clara's been missing that plate of hers. It's kinda special, belonged to our mother. Will *shoulda* recognized it." He smirked. "Sure ate enough of Clara's cake off it, but then that was years ago, wasn't it? Been by here several times, always looked like nobody was to home, and I couldn't knock on the door. Those doggoned animals wouldn't let me out of the car."

Blue's tail was rigid. The hair on his neck bristled. Sophia belatedly calmed the dogs while Harry sidled out of the car and into the yard, one eye on Blue. "Planting flowers, huh?" His lips curled derisively. "Must have your spring cleaning already done, then? *My* wife was helping Clara scrub down the kitchen when I left this morning." He inspected the manure-enriched flowerbed. "That's good dirt! Guess Will did that for you? Oughta be planting today myself, but needed some things from town." Furtive eyes scanned the greening landscape. "Didn't see the horses in the pasture. Guess that hired hand of yours is in the bottom now?"

"Will's having him plow the fields farthest from the creek." She wished she hadn't packed Mike's lunch that day. Harry Stone upset her far more than any bum.

"Well, I still got time to get a good half-day's work done, just a mite after twelve now. Mind getting that plate so I can be on my way?"

"Of course." She wiped her hands on her apron and started toward the back porch. Stone followed her. "You can wait here," she called over her shoulder. "I'll be right out."

Blue, accepting Sophia's acceptance of the visitor, trotted behind his mistress. The other dogs, dismissed by Blue, wandered off. Sophia felt Stone's eyes on her retreating back. She fought the uneasy feeling that started at her toes and tingled its way up her spine.

Don't be ridiculous, Sophia Macklin! You have nothing to worry about.

She wondered if Harry had been drinking. His eyes certainly looked glassy.

...the eyes...familiar eyes...

Contemptuous, glittering eyes seen through holes in a Ku Klux Klan hood the night of the attempted cross burning on Greenberg's lawn.

...Harry Stone...the man who offered Sarah the flag...

Blue waited by the door. She suppressed the urge to take the dog into the kitchen and lock the screen behind her.

I can't let him know I'm afraid. I'm over-reacting. The man's harmless.

And she couldn't lock a farm neighbor out after he'd come for a plate that should have been returned a year ago.

Rattled, Sophia hurried to the pantry to begin a frantic search for the plate.

One of the children must have moved it.

Blue snarled. The screen door snapped open and shut. "Damned blue tick hound tried to bite me! I had a dog like that, I'd *shoot* him."

Stone was in the kitchen.

Fear became panic. Sophia fought to keep her voice even. "Blue's a watchdog, Mr. Stone. That's his job. He doesn't know you."

"Well, if he'd take the *trouble* to know me he'd find out I'm a pretty nice fella." His smile was ingratiating. "Find that plate yet? Maybe I can help." He was so close Sophia smelled the whiskey on his breath.

She moved aside and picked up a kitchen chair. "No, thank you. I just remembered it's on one of the top shelves. I put it there so it wouldn't get broken. I can get it."

Blue, scenting Sophia's acrid fear, growled outside the screen door. Sophia blocked the pantry doorway with the chair's high back and stood on the seat to search the top shelves for the plate. A hand brushed her bare leg.

"Mr. Stone! Take your hand off me!"

Stone withdrew his hand and touched it to his lips. "Just wanted to see what that fine white flesh felt like. I been watching you since Will brought you into the neighborhood. Just about burned a hole in my britches first time I saw you." Sly eyes skimmed her body, trailed upward to her face. "Bet you knew it, too. *I* knew why Clara wasn't good enough for Will once he saw *you*."

Sophia, jolted from fear to anger, stared down at the man below her. "What! Are! You! Talking! About!"

"O-*HO!* That got your attention didn't it? My, you are a looker when your eyes flash like that. Guess Will never told you we was supposed to be brothers-in-law? Nah…some things a husband don't tell his wife. Well, before Will saw you, him and Clara was promised, just hadn't set the date yet. 'Course I always *knew* Clara could never *hold* Will. He was randy from the start, but she'd a'been the kind of wife happy just to keep the home fires burning while he ran around doin' whatever he fancied. Funny, though, never figured *you* for being that-a-way." He smacked his lips. "That cool-as-a-cucumber look you wear don't fool me none."

Sophia clenched her teeth. "Mr. Stone, you seem to have had too much to drink. Will you please move away from the door so I can get your sister's plate?"

"Why sure, Ma'am. Didn't mean no harm. I'd say you're a mite tetchy."

He backed into the kitchen, chuckling like an old-time vaudeville villain. Sophia drew a ragged breath and continued her search while Harry Stone rambled on.

"Just had a snort or two with the boys up at the Wander In. No harm in that, is there? You know about the Wander In, do you? Lots of goings-on up there." He snickered. "But then, I reckon Will tells you all about that."

Sophia found the plate, climbed off the chair, drew herself tall and strode into the kitchen. "Here's your sister's plate, Mr. Stone. You'd better leave." Sophia's skin crawled under his lecherous up-

and-down assessment.

"Nope," he drawled. "Don't think so. Reckon maybe I'm gonna sample some of that ripe fruit Will's so careless with."

Sophia retreated, keeping the table between them. She edged toward Blue, trying to claw his way through the screen. Stone blocked her way.

"If you touch me again my husband will kill you."

"Oh? Well now, I'm not too sure about that. Took me a little while to figure out why you been lookin' neglected. Found out today, though." His lewd laugh matched his leering grin. "I got just what you been missin'."

He lunged at Sophia, grabbed her right arm. She pulled loose, dodged away. Blue hurled himself at the screen. His savage barks brought the other dogs. Blue drew back, gathered speed for another charge at the rusting wire mesh. Stone worked his way around the table. Sophia matched crab-like movements opposite his. Over the barricade, their eyes were level.

He's no taller than me. I'm afraid of that*?*

"Mr. Stone! If you don't leave this instant I will break your mother's plate over your drunken head!"

The man stopped short. "Now you wouldn't want to do somethin' like that. Clara'd *kill* me if anything happened to that plate."

"I will! Now get out!"

"Hmph. Always so damn high and mighty, ain't you? You can ride around with that John Hall, though, with your pretty nose stuck in the air. What *else* you been doin' with him, huh? Guess you think us plain country folk ain't good enough for the likes of you. Let me tell *you* something, *sister.* Now *you* ain't good enough for that husband of yours no more."

Choking rage coursed through Sophia. She threw the plate at Harry Stone just as Blue burst through the lower half of the screen, followed by the other dogs. Harry caught the plate, then dropped it trying to protect himself from the charging hound. He cowered in a corner by the stove. Shattered china littered the floor.

"Now look what you've gone and done!" he bellowed. "What am I gonna tell Clara?" He grabbed the poker from its hook to fend off the dogs. "You damned bitch! Just you ask Will what he was doin' hangin' around the Wander In! Just *ask* him!"

Blue's teeth fastened in the calf of his leg. Stone screamed and swung the poker blindly.

An urgent shout sounded above the chaos. "Ma'am? You having trouble Ma'am?"

The snarls and growls and roars reverberating through the kitchen had overridden the sound of running feet on the wooden back porch. Sophia whirled to see a ragged young giant filling the doorway.

"Yes!" she hissed. "This…this drunken maniac is trying to assault me. Get him out of here!"

"Be glad to, Ma'am, if you'll bring your dogs under control."

Sophia collared Blue and led him outside, followed by the growling pack. The young giant, Stone thrown over his shoulder like a wriggling sack of feed, brought up the rear. "What shall I do with him, Ma'am?"

"Throw him in that car in the driveway. Then wash your hands. And wash them *good.* That man's filthy!"

She threw a final venomous glare at Stone and knelt to inspect her hound's bleeding eye. A piece of rusty wire had penetrated the lid during one of his charges. Blue whimpered with pain as she removed the wire and poured peroxide in his wounds. Her soothing hands quieted the dog. Gravel scattered. Stone's car accelerated around the drive and sped up the road.

Sophia began to tremble violently.

* * *

"Think you'll be okay now, Ma'am?" Sophia's rescuer, not

much older than Bill, had brought her a cold drink from the well, unearthed a none-too-clean cloth from his hobo bundle, dampened it and placed it on her forehead, then moved to the far end of the porch to comfort Blue.

"I'll be fine, thank you." Sophia shakily inspected the darkening finger bruises on her arm and wrist. "Just let me pull myself together." She watched the troubled, honest face close to Blue's battered muzzle. "That horrible man! I don't know what I'd have done if you hadn't come along."

"Glad to help, Ma'am. You folks been awful kind to us wanderers the last couple of years. Besides, I'd like to think someone would'a been around to help *my* mamma if she'd a'needed it."

She smiled at the fleeting, tender look that crossed his face. "Well, your mamma would have been very proud of you today. Thank you."

The large, blonde head ducked in embarrassment. "Say, this here's some animal! I run up the path fast as I could when I heard all the ruckus, but he tore through that screen like a wolverine before I could get here." He chucked Blue under the chin and scratched his ears. "Never seen nothin' like it. Heard about this old dog before. Sure glad to make his acquaintance."

"Yes, he's wonderful." Sophia examined the demolished screen and splintered lath beading, wondering how Blue had found the strength to break through.

"Good thing that lath gave way when it did."

Sophia nodded. "But I was afraid that monster was going to kill him with the poker."

"Looks like he'll be all right. He's got some welts on him, though. Wouldn't hurt none to rub horse liniment on 'em. You got some, I'll do it for you." He explored Blue's side with gentle fingers. "Might have a broken rib here, too, but not much to do about that 'cept let it heal. I 'spect this old guy'll heal right quick, too."

"You must be hungry."

"A mite, but I'm used to it. No need to worry 'bout me after what you just been through. Say, I could fix that door if you got some extra screen wire around."

Sophia, slowly returning to normal, began to worry about what Will would say. And do.

If he sees that broken door...

The ruined door meant immediate explanation. She was afraid he *would* kill Harry Stone. "There should be a roll in that shed over there. Lath, too. But only if you'll let me fix you something to eat."

* * *

The young man tended Blue's welts, mended the screen, then ate on the porch while Sophia swept up broken china and put the kitchen to rights. Her mind swirled with the innuendoes and accusations spat out by Harry Stone. About Will! She had to talk to someone she could trust. After her last experience with Father Riley, she dismissed *that* idea. She hated to bother Mary, but…

As soon as the young man left, Sophia turned the hand crank two short rings and a long, let the phone ring Sullivans' party-line signal, and lifted the receiver. "Mary? I'm so glad you had a phone installed, too. Are you awfully busy? May I come up?"

* * *

For almost two hours, Mary Sullivan listened to Sophia. When she finished, Mary looked at her with sorrow. "But my dear, why did you wait so long to come to me? You know I think of you as a daughter."

Sophia, her face pale and drained, hands knotted in her lap, sat at Mary's kitchen table. "I know, Mary. Thank you. Maybe I just wasn't ready to open up yet, at least until today. I guess I thought I could work things out by myself." She looked up in alarm. "You won't say anything to Les?"

Mary's smile was sad. "Sophia, you must learn to trust. No, I won't, but I'll tell you we could both see there was trouble. We were worried, too. Les feels about Will like I feel about you. You two are the nearest thing to children we've ever had."

She sighed. "It's a good thing you didn't go to your priest this time. He'd put you at fault again. Never saw a man yet didn't think a good-looking woman was asking for it. What I *can't* see is why you went to Father Riley in the first place. I know you're Catholic, but how could you expect *any* man to ken what a woman feels? Especially a man with no firsthand knowledge of marriage."

"I know now, but at the time there didn't seem any other place to turn. And a lot of what he said seemed to make sense."

Mary snorted. "From a man's side, maybe. Does it make sense to turn off your feelings and become a zombie, like in that movie? Is that why you think Will married you? To take care of him like a Clara Stone? Sophia, he *rejected* Clara and married *you*."

"You already knew about Clara?"

Mary was exasperated. "Well, of course. The whole neighborhood knew. The Stones are shirttail kin of Will's through Clothilde. When they were growing up, Harry tried every way he knew to be like Will, but he just didn't have it in him. We used to laugh at the two of 'em, that little runt of a Harry trailing everywhere after big, tall, lanky Will. We called him Will's dog. When they got older, he'd tell everybody Will and Clara were kissing cousins, really cousins-twice-removed. And Clara *is* a good woman, but we all thought Harry was the one pushing that match.

"There's a mean streak that runs through the Stones, but Harry's double-mean. Maybe he got Clara's share, too. And he's a sneak, to boot. Clara does her best to keep a rein on him, but..." She glanced sharply at Sophia. "I hope you've not been judging all your neighbors by Harry!"

"No...maybe...I don't know. The only ones I really know are

Bert and Molly and they're family."

"Well, let me tell you my dear, except for the Stone family and Clothilde *everyone* approved Will's choice. We all thought you were just what Will needed. Someone to share his life and his fire with."

"Then why do they treat me like an outsider?"

"Why do you *act* like one? What they've been doing is respecting your privacy, waiting for you to come out of your shell."

"For *thirteen years!*"

"You know, Sophia, you're not the easiest person to get to know. At first, they were waiting for you to make the first move. Then it got to be habit, I guess. Will should have taken you around and introduced you when you first moved out here."

"There wasn't any time. The work. The babies. We only left the farm to shop and go to the Moonlight Picnic."

"That's another thing. While I'm at it, I might as well tell you they think you act uppity at the Picnic."

Sophia, unaware that her innate shyness and fear of rejection made her seem aloof, gasped.

"*I* know it's not true, that it's your way of protecting yourself, but it's truth time. And I'd have told you about Clara long ago if I'd thought it was important. Clara's not your problem with Will. *You're* the problem. You quit letting Will know how you feel, crawled into that shell of yours. Why even now, with me, you're peeping out like a turtle afraid of getting hurt again.

"Sophia, what you did after you talked to your priest was turn yourself into a cross between a Chinese concubine and one of those robot women in the Buck Rogers Saturday matinee serials. If there's any truth at all to what Harry said about Will, I can understand why he'd stray. *Any* red-blooded man would."

Sophia's tearstained eyes raised to Mary's. "Do *you* think it's true?"

"I don't know. From what you told me I'd say Will still loves you, but if it were *my* husband I'd damned sure find out. And I wouldn't waste any time doing it."

"Mary, you swore! Out loud!" Mary blinked at the realization of what she'd done. Her naughty-schoolgirl titter lightened the atmosphere. Sophia laughed at her friend's consternation, then sobered at a thought. "But if I ask Will about what Harry said, I'll have to tell him what Harry did today. You know Will's temper. He *might* kill him…"

Mary nodded. "And the snake deserves killing. I wondered what he'd been up to when he tore by here like a bat out of hell. He took our corner on two wheels, almost killed our best rooster. Well, he'll know he can't weasel out of this. He's been a thorn in Will's side since Will jilted Clara, and that's not counting what he did today. Could be he was trying to get even with Will through you. And him hiding behind that holier-than-thou attitude! Only reason he's an elder is because his daddy was and now the congregation doesn't know how to get rid of him.

"But you do have to tell Will. You've hidden too much for the past year-and-a-half. Maybe longer, but you'd know that better than me. If you're going to wipe the slate clean, do it all at once. There'll be a blow-up, but it'll clear the air. And if you can just keep Will away from Harry long enough for him to simmer down, he won't do anything foolish."

"And the drinking?"

Mary sighed. "That's an age-old problem, one it looks like Will's trying to lick. Les drinks, too. I don't like it, but I put up with it." She paused, thinking. "All the Macklin men liked the bottle. It's the Scotch-Irish blood in their veins I guess." She chuckled. "Did Will ever tell you what Clottie did to William P?"

"He never talks to me about his mother."

"Well, I guess maybe Will was just a tyke when it happened. He might not even know.

"William P always kept a bottle stashed outside. Every night, after he finished up chores, he'd have a nip before he went in for supper. Never enough to make him drunk, just enough to get him through Clottie's rambunctiousness. And he needed it. You know Clottie. The neighbor's used to say the best meal she served was hot tongue and cold shoulder.

"Anyway, she had a nose like a bloodhound, always smelled it on his breath. Raised Cain every night, too. Why, her own mother said Clottie would cut off her nose to spite her face. Today those psycho-somethings would probably say she was unhappy and wanted everyone around her unhappy, too.

"I tell you, Les and I worried about those kids. What they went through! And they all left home before they were ready. Will went west when he was only fourteen. Big, strapping boy who looked and worked like a man, but wasn't grown enough to be with those rough threshing crews. All they knew was work, drink and women. And Will's sap was rising. He was gone about five or six years and came back here looking like a whipped puppy. Les and I always figured something terrible happened out west…

"Oh, my, didn't mean to rattle on like that. Where were we? Oh, yes…Clottie and William P…

"Well, for two years Clottie searched high and low for that bottle. Almost took every building on the farm apart. Then, one summer, she spotted a setting hen in an old straw-filled wooden box in one of the empty corncribs, close to the stable. She checked on that hen every day so when the chicks hatched she could put them in the brooder and start the hen laying again." Her laugh was nasty. "Clottie never missed a chance for profit, wouldn't even let the biddie enjoy her babies a few weeks.

"Anyway, one day when she was checking, she caught her shoe on a nail sticking up out of a board. Had to take her shoe off to pry it loose. That board lifted right up with the shoe and there was the bottle, half full.

"William P's eyes were never very good and Clottie knew it.

She dumped most of the whiskey out in the field where he wouldn't smell it, hiked up her skirt, dropped her bloomers and filled that bottle right up to where it had been."

"Mary, she didn't! You mean she…"

Mary's slap on the table was emphatic. "Yes Ma'am, I'm telling you that's what she did."

Sophia's initial shock exploded into laughter. Months of accumulated stress melted under the tears rolling down her cheeks. Mary's purposely-droll expression slipped. Her chuckle dissolved into an answering belly laugh.

"And he *knew*, Mary?"

"Well of course he knew, child. How could he not know? Neither one of 'em ever said a word to each other about it. But William P never hid another bottle, either, at least where Clottie might find it. Naturally, Clottie couldn't stand to put one over on somebody and not tell about it so she spilled the beans to Harry's mother and pretty soon it was all over the neighborhood. The men took to cackling every time they saw William P, asking him what he was trying to hatch now. Or if he liked his eggs scrambled with moonshine. Or…"

"But what did Pa *do*?"

"He stood up and faced the music! He'd drilled that into his kids so much he didn't figure he had any other choice. Besides, he couldn't lick 'em all, so he laughed right back at 'em and offered 'em a drink."

Sophia wiped her eyes. "Oh, Mary, I've not laughed like that in years. It's true what they say. Laughter *is* good medicine."

Mary rose, patted Sophia's shoulder. "You bet it is, Honey, and don't you ever forget it. Now let's have a cup of coffee while you tell me what the kids have been up to. Then I want to show you my latest quilt squares."

"I can't waste the *rest* of the afternoon, Mary."

"Waste! You think these past hours that got rid at least *some* of that bane you've been carrying were a *waste*?" Kind eyes eased the sting of sharp words. "When are you going to learn? You keep on like you're going and you'll be no good to your children *or* Will, let alone yourself. Nobody loves a martyr, Sophia."

Sophia's eyes widened in shock. "Is that what I've been doing, Mary? Playing the martyr?"

Chapter 23

The two women visited while Sophia waited to give Seth and Sarah a ride the rest of the way from school. During the drive home, Sarah's chatter covered Sophia's introspection. Today's excitement was about the school's spring program, the song she was to sing, and the costume Sophia had to make. Seth sat quietly, his eyes riveted on his mother's face. When Sophia pulled into the garage and parked, Sarah hopped out of the car, raced to the porch, and rummaged through her lunch sack, salvaging sandwich scraps for the dogs.

Seth walked by his mother's side. "What's wrong, Mom?"

"Oh, Seth…something's always wrong somewhere in the world. If we could just go back and undo the mistakes we make."

"Gee, Mom, I…"

Sarah's shout interrupted. "Mamma, who put this new wire on the screen door? It wasn't here this morning."

"A friend, Honey. I had a little accident today. Go change your clothes now."

Seth followed his mother onto the porch and inspected the screen. Blue struggled to get up, failed, and settled for thumping his tail in greeting. "Blue's hurt, too! Mom, what happened?"

"Blue broke through the screen."

"He *what*? Did you have trouble with a bum?"

"No, Honey, a bum *helped* me. I'll tell you about it when I can, but I have to talk to your dad first. Blue should be all right, though. I pulled a piece of wire from his eyelid and cleaned it and the cuts on his muzzle with peroxide. The same young man who fixed the door put liniment on those welts." Seth knelt by the dog, checking his injuries. "Be careful. He may have a broken rib."

"He's pretty banged up. And his eyelid's swollen bad." Seth expertly parted the lids with thumb and forefinger. "Looks okay inside, though. Think we ought to take him to the vet?"

"We'll see what your dad says, but I think, except for his eye and that rib, his other injuries aren't serious. And the rib can't be set, anyway."

"Was the wire rusty? Can dogs get lockjaw?"

"Maybe you'd better call the vet and ask. You might rub more liniment on those welts after you change, too. I left it on the porch."

"Mom?"

"Oh, Seth, I…" She hesitated, denied herself the luxury of responding to the sympathy and love in her son's questioning eyes. "…I have to start dinner. Bill should be home any minute now. You and he can handle the chores. Your dad will probably be late again and Mike will be worn out when he gets up from the field."

* * *

Routine kitchen tasks masked the soul-searching thoughts spinning through Sophia's head. She sifted through Mary's homespun wisdom. Hoped Will would be late, that it would be dark enough when he got home so he wouldn't notice the screen. The new bottom section stood out like a beacon below the old, rust-tinged wire in the top frame.

I should have had the entire screen replaced.

She didn't want to talk to Will tonight. With all the spring roadwork, he'd be tired. She checked the spreading bruises on her lower arm and wrist, and hurried to the bedroom to change into a long-sleeved dress. And brought herself up short.

I'm doing exactly what Mary said. Trying to hide things from Will.

Tired or not, she'd talk to Will as soon as the children were asleep.

* * *

Will was late. Sophia put his meal in the warming oven and ate with Mike and the children.

From the boys subdued conversation, she knew Seth had reported to Bill in the barn. She was grateful for Sarah's blind exuberance about the school program. Mike, sensing tension, ate hurriedly and left the table with a muttered excuse about mending harness. She breathed a sigh of relief when the meal finally ended.

"I'll clean up the kitchen, Sarah. Get started on your homework. You boys, too."

Delighted over her escape from dirty dishes, Sarah skipped upstairs to her room. Bill glanced speculatively from Sophia to Seth and followed his sister.

Seth sat at the table, his inquisitive eyes following his mother around the kitchen.

Sophia stopped to touch his shoulder. "Seth, I know you're worried, but there's honestly nothing to worry about now. Things will work out. And I promise I'll tell you about it as soon as I can."

Seth hugged his mother, touched the bruises on her exposed wrist, and followed the others upstairs.

* * *

Will arrived at dusk. By the time a recalcitrant grader was repaired by amateur mechanics, parked off the road in a nearby field and the crew dismissed, he was exhausted. He ate, went to the parlor and fell asleep over the paper while Sophia finished the dishes and cleaned up the kitchen. She checked to make sure the children were sleeping before making her way to the parlor.

"Will? Will, are you asleep?"

"Mmmmm. Just resting my eyes. Think I'll go on to bed, though."

"I've made fresh coffee. Come have a cup with me. We have

to talk."

The urgency in his wife's voice brought Will to attention. "Something wrong?"

Long-practiced control covered Sophia's emotions. "That's what we need to find out. Sarah's asleep so she won't hear through the register. We can talk in the kitchen."

She avoided his eyes, poured coffee, and sat across from him, wondering how to begin. Finally, she straightened and squared her shoulders. "First, and most important, do you still love me?"

Will's skin prickled at the intensity in his wife's voice. He understood this was more than an idle question from a woman needing reassurance and chose his words carefully. "Yes I do, Soph. And I've done everything I know to prove it. If there's anything else I can do you'll have to tell me." His intensity matched hers. "Soph, I can't even imagine life without you."

She searched his face and nodded, satisfied. "I'm not going to jump all over you about this because I realize that, if it's true, it's partly my fault, but…Will, have you been seeing another woman?"

His guilty face answered Sophia's question. "Who told you?"

"I'll get to that. Right now, I need to know why. And if it's serious."

Will ran his fingers through his hair. "Oh God, Soph. No, it wasn't serious, at least on my part. And it's over. I was just so damned lonely.

"Maybe 'why' was because living with you the past year or so's been like living with an ice woman. Just like now. Most women would be screaming bloody murder. Or throwing things. Or at least *mad,* like *you'd* have been once. But you sit there like a talking statue, not showing a thing."

Tears seeped from Sophia's eyes, threatened her armored control. "Do you think because I'm not screaming I don't hurt, Will?"

"I don't know any more. You've shut me out, won't say anything except 'yes, Will…whatever you want, Will…I'll do that for you, Will…'. And when I make love to you it's even worse, like you're not even there. I've tried everything I know to get through to you, to find that fire you used to have. I didn't blame you for being so damned mad about that mess at Campbells, but you just won't let me forget it.

"When you gave me Phineas' watch I thought things would get better, but instead they got worse. I've even wondered if you hate me."

"I think maybe I did, Will, at least for awhile. You've never seen yourself drunk. You don't know what it does to you. That night, all I could see was the scarred shell of the man I married. It was…it was like you'd died and a stranger moved into your body. Something in me died that night, too." Her voice dropped. Will strained to catch her next words. "Or I thought it had. Until today."

Her eyes met Will's. "I talked to Dr. Tom over a year ago. Or *he* talked to *me*. He made me feel your drinking, even what happened that night, was my fault. I was so angry when I left his office I was shaking, so I went to Father Riley and *he* as much as told me my place as a wife was to take care of my husband's needs. In *all* ways. And I did, but I hated doing it. I guess I didn't hate you after all, but I certainly hated feeling owned."

"Soph! I never felt like I owned you! You're part of *me*. Anyway, you used to be. Maybe we just got so busy we lost touch with each other."

"That could be part of it, Will. Or it could be that our life changed. Do you still want to give up your job and just work the farm? Because if you do…"

"Maybe someday, but not right now. And for sure not until the mortgage is paid off and we start getting decent farm prices again. If I'd had any gumption, I'd have known you were right about needing the money. It might not buy happiness, but it sure is buying the farm.

"I *was* mad about the job at first. I'd look at that old equipment we have to keep patching up and all those rutted clay roads and think about Mike plowing up rich bottom ground. *Good* ground. With horses that don't need parts. And the creek…think I miss the creek most of all.

"Hell! Without the job we wouldn't *have* the farm. But yes, dumb as it was I was still mad.

"Look, Soph I've not had a… Well, at least I've not had whiskey for over a year and a half. I *am* trying, but it doesn't seem to make any difference. You still act like some kind of a stranger."

"I know. I've had my own problems to work out, too. I didn't know it then, but talking to Mamma helped a lot. And today I began to realize I was so busy feeling sorry for myself because I was doing what I thought I *had* to, I'd forgotten how to love."

Somber quiet mushroomed between them. Sophia broke the silence with an abrupt question. "When did you start seeing that woman?"

Will's eyes lowered to hide naked shame. "Last summer. And I didn't go after her, Soph. She came after me, but I guess I was ripe for the picking. Anyway, after Bill saw us together in February that was the end of it."

"Bill! He *saw* you?" Sophia blazed.

"You mean Bill wasn't the one who told you? Figured he let something slip."

"No, it wasn't Bill. Is *that* why he got sick, then mad at everyone? Will!"

Omitting nothing, Will told Sophia what had happened, adding, "And it doesn't look like Bill will ever forgive me." Sophia stared at his grief-stricken face.

"Oh God, Will, what hell we put ourselves and our children through. Maybe I can talk to Bill, help him understand. Are you sure it's over between you and...no, never mind, I don't want to know her name. But are you sure it's over?"

"It's over, Soph. She never was anything but a substitute for you anyway and, to be honest, I wouldn't have gone with her in the first place if I hadn't had too much beer."

She swallowed her hurt and reached to touch his hand. His fingers clasped hers.

"Everything leads back to drink, doesn't it? Since we've come this far, don't you think it's time you tell me what makes you want to escape into a bottle?"

Will's well-organized defense mechanism slipped into gear. He dropped Sophia's hand. "I told you, I like it. Uncle Ed…"

"No, you've never really told me. You go so far and stop and I know you too well. There's something more."

Elbows on the table, head cupped in his hands, Will sat deep in thought for what seemed an eternity to the anxious woman across the table. "You're sure you want to hear this? It's not pretty."

"I think I have to. We all have ghosts, some just hide better than others, but ghosts don't live in sunlight. I've brought my share out of the shadows, too. Papa. Little Sergei. Even Mamma." She acknowledged Will's startled look with a nod. "I know, she's not a ghost, but the way she was when I was growing up haunted me. And sometimes still does."

His eyes lifted to Sophia's, saw their clear October-blue understanding. His decision reached, he sat up and placed his hands palm down on the table.

"You know I worked out west in the wheat fields, harvesting?" Sophia nodded. "Ever wonder what I did when the season ended?"

"You never mentioned it, so I assumed you came back here. No, I guess I never thought of it before today."

"I went to Denver. The town was wide open then. Drinking, gambling, you name it, Denver had it. First year I was there, I spent all my money in a month. Had to take a job as a sort of bouncer getting rid of troublemakers. I got my room, board and a little spending money. After that, I worked there every winter and saved my harvest money. That's what I bought the Maxwell with when I came back…

"One night in January, fifth winter I was there, I had to throw a real troublemaker out the back door. About three that morning, after the place was locked up, I headed for an all night bar I knew. Snowing. About a foot on the ground already, with the wind whistling down the mountains from the Great Divide. Had my head down, walking into the wind. Next thing I knew, the guy I'd pitched earlier was blocking my way. Him and two of his buddies, laying for me.

"Those three came after me. The one I'd pitched had a knife. Guess the other two were supposed to hold me while he cut me, but they were all drunk and I'd learned a thing or two when I was with the crews, so I went after the guy with the knife first. And instead of me getting cut up it was him. He slipped in the snow and the knife got stuck in his side. The other two took off yelling for the police. I saw all that blood melting into the snow and thought about landing in the Denver jail at nineteen and the stories I'd heard about that place and I ran. Back to the house, grabbed my bedroll and gear and money stash, saddled my horse and took off east, scared to death, storm chasing me all the way out of town. Figured with the snow and wind covering my trail they'd never be able to track me down. And that's how I left Denver. As a murderer.

"I headed back here since nobody out west knew where I was from—kind of life I was leading I didn't *want* anybody to know. Guess Ma's church teaching kicked in after all, even if I did my best to fight it. And I reckoned Macklin Corner was the safest place to be. I got back early spring, rented a room, holed up in the mine job a couple of months and crawled in a bottle, trying to forget Denver. Then that constable job opened up and a year or so later I saw you.

"Knew you were what I wanted, but there was still Denver to

worry about and I couldn't saddle you with that. Since I was a lawman by then I could check with the Denver police, so I did. I knew the date it happened and the man's name. Couldn't forget either of those, even though John Barleycorn and I sure tried hard enough! At least till I met you…

"Telegram came back, the guy I'd thought I killed was in the Denver jail for knifing and killing a man and under suspicion for another murder. I hadn't killed him after all. Figured that trouble was over, I was free to go after you. But turned out it *wasn't* over."

"But I don't see the problem. Why you…"

"It wasn't just the idea of killing, though that was bad enough, but even if he'd been dead I'd learned about self-defense by then. And things were fine till the riot and all those bodies by the tracks brought it back, made it worse.

"The *problem* is *I ran away.* Scared as a rabbit." He slapped the table to accentuate each word. "*No* Macklin worth his salt *ever* ran away. Pa never had many rules, but he had one he lived by and he made us boys live by it, too. 'Stand up and face the music, you'll be a better man.' What I live with is I'm a coward. And I've spent my life since trying to live it down, but every time I think of Denver I know. And worries make it worse. I try to watch out for it, but sometimes it's like…you know that game in the carnivals that travel through here? People throw balls at a target to try to dunk the man on the trip seat? Well, I feel like that man, only people are throwing horse turds at me from all sides and I'm hanging over a manure pile. *That's* when I drink.

"Never told anyone about Denver before, not even Pa, and sure never thought I could tell you."

Sophia sat quietly, absorbing Will's confession and the guilt he carried. Finally, her voice a raspy whisper, "So that's the boil that's been oozing poison into your mind and our lives all these years? Thank God you've lanced it. I knew there was something you wouldn't, I guess couldn't tell me. What I don't understand is why."

"Didn't ever want you to know. You thought I was brave, called me your 'stalwart hero', at least when we were first married. Huh! Some hero! Figured you wouldn't like me, let alone *love* me, if you knew. You used to think I was special. *I* knew better, but I didn't want *you* to know it."

"But you were only nineteen, not much more than a boy. You weren't a coward then and you're not a coward now. Would a coward have stood up to the Klan like you did? Or beaten off that intruder? I thought you were something worse, a drunk that didn't care enough about us to stop being one. How could you have *thought* I wouldn't love you if I knew?"

"I don't know, guess maybe because I don't like *myself* much. I shamed me *and* the Macklin name."

Again, Sophia reached for Will's hand. They sat in the quiet house feeling the emptiness of the past months, the possible promise of the future. "What do we do now?"

"I've been doing better, Soph. You know I have."

"But how can we know it won't happen again?"

"Look, I'm through making promises I might not be able to keep. That thing with Bill taught me that. All I can say is I'll do my best. If that's not enough for you..."

"I don't know, Will. I've got to have time to think."

"You still have to tell me how you found out about...her."

"Not unless you promise me first you won't kill the person who told me."

"Kill? It's that serious?"

"It's that serious. And he's not worth killing. Promise?"

Will's face was alert, reluctant. Finally..."Promise," he grated.

Sophia clung to Will's hand, holding him with both her words and fingers as she related the day's events. Will grew angrier with every word, his body more and more tense. By the time she finished he was rigid, his temper at fever pitch.

"I'll tear that son-of-a-bitch apart!"

"No, Will, because there's one thing more, the most important of all. When Harry Stone told me I'd lost you, it was like a knife in my heart and I was ready to kill him myself. But later, when I thought about it, I had to be honest and admit it was really what *we* did to *each other* that caused all this. And I began to realize that maybe I *did* still love you." Her fingers tightened on his. He briefly returned the pressure then sprang up, pacing the floor. He stopped, carefully rolled up her sleeve and examined the bruises.

"He do this?"

"Yes, but you know how easily I bruise. And it doesn't hurt."

"I can't let him get away with this. Soph, I've got to do something."

"You promised, Will."

"Promised I wouldn't *kill* him. Didn't say I wouldn't teach him a lesson. What you don't understand is the way he twists the truth to suit himself. He could make it sound like you invited him and there'd always be someone who'd believe it. No. For your sake—for *our* sake—I've got to shut his mouth." He resumed pacing while he thought. "Where's that broken plate?"

"I swept it up, put it in a sack and threw it in the trash." Will rummaged through the basket behind the stove. "What are you going to do?"

"Return Clara's damned plate, that's what."

"It's almost midnight!"

"All the better. Harry knows about nightriders. I'll give him a taste of his own medicine, show him how it *feels* to be threatened in the dark." He found the sack and started for the door.

"Don't hurt him, Will."

"Didn't say I wouldn't hurt him, Soph. Said I wouldn't kill the son-of-a-bitch."

* * *

The Maxwell's headlights bounced over the washboard road leading to the slab. Will concentrated on keeping the car in the ungraded ruts and wished he'd not listed his road's grading last.

He thought of everything he and Soph had said to each other. She'd not asked him to quit drinking this time. With this new attitude of hers, he didn't figure she would. It was all on his shoulders now. He knew what would happen if he fell off the wagon again. He'd lost her once. And now he'd lost Bill, too, maybe for good.

Guess if it comes to a choice between Soph or a bottle, I'd a hell of a lot rather have Soph. And *the kids.*

Funny, he didn't miss whisky all that much now. Before it was legal, he took a drink every chance he got. He didn't count beer, wondered if Soph did.

Harry! That no-good son-of-a-bitch! Touching Soph like that. He's always been squirrely, didn't think he was dangerous, though...just a fool. Nothing worse than a dangerous fool.

He left the rutted road, headed south on the slab, saw the poorly marked Stone turnoff. More ruts and, finally, Harry's driveway. A lamp in the kitchen. Harry's face at the window.

Will restrained his impulse to break down the door and haul Harry into the yard by the scruff of his neck.

No point waking the Stone kids. The fewer that know about this the better.

The lamp went out. The kitchen door creaked open. Will picked up the sack, left the headlights on, the engine running, and got out of the car.

Harry's voice was reedy with fright. "Who's out there? I got a shotgun! Don't try nothin' fancy!"

"Put that damned gun down, Harry, before you shoot yourself in the foot. I brought Clara's plate back."

"Will? That you, Will?" Harry scuttled from the dark kitchen doorway to the edge of the porch, away from the headlight beams.

"Just you stay where you are. Don't come no closer, hear? We got nothin' to say to each other."

Will raised his voice so the shadowed listener at the window could hear. "I got plenty to say to you, you rotten bastard. For starters, you keep your filthy hands off my wife. You ever try to touch her again, I'll beat you within an inch of your life. Now put that shotgun down."

A match flared in the kitchen. Lamplight flickered, stabilized. A stocky woman in a faded flannel robe, her graying mousy hair in a single thin braid down her back, stepped onto the porch. The lamp in her hand highlighted dull brown eyes in a tired, earnest face.

Clara Stone approached her brother with deliberate steps, took the gun from his hands and faced Will. "Harry said your wife broke the plate. That she set your dogs on him and threw Mamma's plate at him. His leg's tore up so bad he could hardly drive home. That's why he got me up tonight, to make a new poultice and fix him another dose of laudanum."

"Well, Clara, that's about what happened but he left out a few things. Just like always. Harry, you want to tell Clara the truth of it or you want me to?"

Harry limped into the pool of light cast by the Maxwell's headlamps and leaned against a porch post. "Can't stand to put no weight on that leg a'tall," he whined. "Not enough to have your damned hound cripple me, is it? Now you got to turn Clara against me, too. What you want me to do, Will?"

"Just tell the whole, unvarnished truth for once in your life."

Headlight beams pinned Harry against the post like a mounted moth. Will watched cold sweat slick his forehead, his hands begin to work then clutch at nothing. Saw a flash of madness in his eyes. Suddenly, his face contorted with hate, Harry straightened against the supportive post.

"I'll tell her all right. I'll tell *you*, too, and you ain't gonna like it one little bit. What happened is all your fault. You been lordin' it over me my whole life, from the time we was kids when Aunt Clottie brought you to play with me and Clara. You couldn't even *play* fair. I was a year older but *you* had to show off. Run faster, throw straighter, jump higher. And *I* had to listen to Pappy say…" he pitched his voice gruff…'Why can't you be more like your cousin Will?'"

"Got worse when we started school. The teacher moved you a grade ahead of me, up with Bert, right after Christmas, said you was smarter but I knew better. It was because your name was Macklin. And girls always hangin' all over you and you makin' fun of my church-goin' and treatin' me like a piece of horse shit in front of 'em and them laughin' at me. And when I had to stay to help Pappy on the farm, *you* run away to kick up your heels out west.

"Thought we'd smoothed things over when you come back courtin' Clara in that big, fancy car." He stopped to squint at the Maxwell idling in the lane. "Same car. Hmph, don't look so fancy now.

"You was decent to me then, at least for awhile, but turned out Clara wasn't good enough for you so you kicked the traces again, dumped her for that damn high-and-mighty good-lookin' Catholic you married. Wasn't enough what you done to me, just look what you done to Clara! She grieved like she was dyin', then turned into a dried up old maid I've got to take care of the rest of her life."

Will stared in disbelief while Harry caught his breath and rubbed his injured leg. Clara, eyes trained on the outline of Will's tall, muscular body in the headlights' glare, listened in stoic silence as her brother spewed forth a lifetime of envious hate.

"Huh! You actin' like a Lord of the Manor when your granddaddy wasn't no more than a Mississippi gambler what got lucky. Didn't know I *knew* that, didja? Well my granny told me all about it. Hell, even your kids act high and mighty, too good to go to a country school like your neighbors. *They* gotta go to a *town* school. And *high* school. And now I'm hearin' *college.* And that oldest girl of yours livin' with a Jew family, nothin' but a maid and actin' like a princess. Wish we'd a'burned their house down that night with her and those kids in it!"

Will stepped forward to stop Harry's vitriol. "You're *admitting* you organized that Klan march?"

"You bet I did…still tryin' to help you in spite of what you done to me, scare that girl into goin' back home where she belonged. *I* knowed her bein' there couldn't a'been your idea, but look at the thanks I get. And I'll tell you somethin' else, too. You thought the bums killed that calf? It was me! Huh! You braggin' about your prize-winnin' new heifer calf at the feed store. But I was *still* tryin' to help you. Figured if you blamed the bums you'd keep 'em scared away before they killed all of you. That bluetick damn near got me that night, too, sneakin' up behind me at the tracks while the other dogs was still eatin' the meat I left at the far end of the pasture. And then the whole pack chased my car 'most all the way home on the bottomland road. Hell, I shoulda just poisoned 'em all. Got away then, but look at me now. *Your* fault…all your fault…"

Will stalked toward Harry. "I've always known you're a sneak and a hypocrite and a liar, but I didn't know you were sick in the head and that's the only reason I'm letting you live. But if you ever come around my place or me and my family again or cause us trouble, you'll *wish* you were dead. And if you ever mention the Macklin name again…I mean *mention* it…I'll shove every word down your throat and tell everyone what you did today. And you know they'll believe me, too. We'll see how your preacher likes *that.*" Will's unforgiving eyes stabbed the squirming, finally silent man. Sickened by the sight, he turned to Clara.

"I'm truly sorry about that plate, but your brother got in my house today and tried to assault my wife. I planned to whale the tar out of him, only looks like Blue marked him up better than I ever could." Disdainful eyes flicked toward Harry. "Just hope your blood didn't poison my wife's dog! You're damned lucky, Harry, and you can thank Soph for your life. She was right. You're just not…worth…killing."

Clara kept her eyes on Will. "That was the laudanum talking, Will, but I'm sure he did all those things. I know my brother, too. You can go now. I'll see he don't cause you no more trouble."

"Thank you, Clara." Will strode to the porch and handed her the sack. "Harry was attacking Soph in our kitchen. She threw the plate at him just as Blue broke through the screen. He caught it, then dropped it when Blue attacked. *That's* how it got broken. Wish this hadn't happened. If I could replace it, I would." He aimed a final malevolent glare at Harry and left.

Shards of her mother's plate clutched in her hand, Clara Stone watched the Maxwell's taillights disappear into darkness for the last time.

* * *

Sophia watched the clock. Worry over what might be happening at Stones jumbled her already disorganized thoughts and wrenching emotions even more. A familiar, protective, empty feeling began to blanket the jealousy and anger and hurt the afternoon and evening had uncovered; to smother the embers of love Harry Stone had exposed.

No. We've come so far. I can't go back to that.

The stabbing pain she'd felt in her heart when Stone made his accusations returned. Her own arguing voices bounced back and forth in the chaotic silence of her mind.

DO I EVEN KNOW WHAT LOVE **IS** *ANY MORE?*

Love isn't taking, it's giving. I gave.

(Who was she?)

But love is giving freely, not with conditions.

(You told Will you didn't want to know.)

MAYBE I HAVE FORGOTTEN HOW TO LOVE.

(Bill saw *them together!)*

Poor Bill. How he suffered!

(What does she look like?)

Bill's so much like Will. Combative, demanding.

DO I WANT MY CHILDREN TO GROW UP WITH THE SAME LOST FEELING I KNEW? BEFORE WILL?

Strong! Protective! Bill held everything in rather than see me hurt.

(Is she prettier than me?)

DO I LOVE WILL?

I think so, but…

ENOUGH TO ACCEPT HIM AS HE IS? TO FORGIVE AND FORGET?

I don't know.

THEN I'D BETTER FIND OUT.

(She doesn't matter. Will said so.)

Blue stirred restlessly on the porch. Sophia looked out the window. No returning headlights bounced over the rutted road. She stepped outside to comfort the injured hound. Devotion shone in the old dog's eyes. The discordant voices returned.

What do I want? A husband or dog-like devotion?

WILL'S TRYING SO HARD…

A husband. But I don't want to lose myself again…

TEACHING ME TO DRIVE, THE POLITICAL POST…

(What if he starts drinking again?)

AND NOW HELPING THE HOSPITAL BECAUSE I ALMOST DIED.

…and I want things the way they were between us.

(At least now I know why…)

They can't be. Ever again. Too much has happened.

AM I GOING TO STAY AN EMOTIONAL CRIPPLE OR CAN I BECOME THE PARTNER AND WIFE MY HUSBAND NEEDS?

He broke our marriage vows!

(Will I always wonder about her?)

Because I shut him out, denied the love we used to have.

(He said she didn't matter, but...)

I offered love.

(A substitute for me?)

No! I offered my body, not love. Remember what love was...remember...remember...

Sophia patted Blue's head. The lamp lit her way through the house to the old cedar chest in the bedroom. As she lifted the lid, the blended fragrance of sun-washed lavender and cool cedar forests filled the room. She searched the chest, fingered silk, drew out an ivory-tinged nightgown. And remembered...

AM I SURE THIS IS WHAT I WANT?

Yes. Oh, yes!

The voices stilled. Sophia could begin to love again.

* * *

"Let 'em sleep, Bill!" Seth's hoarse whisper woke Sophia and stopped his brother at the bedroom door.

Bill's voice dropped to an answering whisper. "But Dad'll be late for work. And Mom has to start breakfast and fix lunches and..."

Seth's voice cracked, dropped from treble to baritone. "We'll wake 'em when we finish the chores. They talked till all hours last night."

"Whatever you say, *Runt.*"

"Not Runt for much longer, big brother. And when I catch up, you better watch your step!"

Sophia stirred in Will's arms as the whispers faded. The

kitchen screen door slammed. “Will, are you awake?”

“Ummmm.” He nuzzled her neck while his fingers traced her silk-gowned body. Sophia banished thoughts of the day ahead and nestled close to the man she loved.

* * *

“Sarah, I’m not going to call you again. Now hurry, or you’ll have to *walk* to school.”

Hickory-cured bacon sizzled in the skillet. The smell of fresh coffee wafted through the house. Lunch sacks and schoolbooks stood in a prim row on the cabinet. Contentment softened Sophia’s lips. She hummed to herself as she moved about her kitchen.

“Soph”, Will called from the veranda. “You better come see this.”

She moved the skillet to the back of the stove, filled two mugs with coffee and carried both outside, expecting to see Will stretching and admiring the almost-his, dew-dark bottom land below the house on the bluff. Instead, she found him staring at a rusty can sprouting a bouquet of bluebells.

October-blue eyes sparkled. “Oh, Will! When did you pick the…”

“Wish I had, Honey, but they’re not from me.” He chuckled. “Reckon Blue knows who put ‘em there, though, since he didn’t raise a ruckus. This note was under the can.” He held out a soiled piece of wrinkled paper. Written in crude, penciled letters were the words

FOR THE LADY

Epilogue

The bluff still stands like a bastion, guarding the creek and what remains of a section of rich, South Central Illinois bottomland. Sophia and Will are gone, their blended essence of lavender and cedar vanished in a shroud of memory. The children, like the bums, are scattered on the winds of time.

* * *

Variant time: Constant when measured in days, years and centuries. Amorphous when yesterday advances to the infinity of tomorrow.